Promise Me Darkness

PAIGE WEAVER

Promise Me Darkness
Copyright © 2013 by Paige Weaver

All rights reserved. No part of this book may be reproduced, transmitted, downloaded, distributed, stored in or introduced into any information storage and retrieval system, in any form or by any means, whether electronic or mechanical, without written permission from the author, except by a reviewer who may quote brief passages for review purposes. If you are reading this book and you have not purchased it or won it in an author/publisher contest, this book has been pirated. Please delete and support the author by purchasing the eBook from one of its many distributors.

This book is a work of fiction and any resemblance to any person, living or dead, any place, events or occurrences, is purely coincidental. The characters and story lines are created from the author's imagination or are used fictitiously.

Published by Paige Weaver, P.O. Box 80016, Keller, Texas 76244

ISBN 978-1-4895158-2-7 (Distribution)
ISBN 978-0-9892698-0-3 (Kindle)
ISBN 978-0-9892698-1-0 (eBook)
ISBN 978-0-9892698-2-7 (Smashwords)
ISBN 978-0-9892698-3-4 (Print)

Cover design ©Sarah Hansen
okaycreations.com

Promise Me Darkness
A Novel

Chapter One

This is the story of the end of life as I knew it. We thought the world would continue as it always had. Society would stay the same. People would stay the same. We were wrong. In a heartbeat, the world changed. I changed.

"I can't believe you talked me into this!"

An Eminem song blared loudly from speakers as I followed my best friend through the smoky bar. Men covered in tattoos stood shoulder to shoulder with women in barely-there clothing. As for me, I stuck out like a sore thumb in my light pink sundress and matching sandals.

"Relax, Maddie. I just wanted to check the place out," Eva said, bopping her head to the music as we walked through the crowd. I wasn't sure if she noticed the nasty stares we were getting or was just oblivious to them. Knowing Eva, she just didn't care.

I stuck close behind her, afraid of being separated among these people. Eva and I had been to many of the bars near our college and seen some crazy things but this place was just plain scary. Talk about a hole in the wall. The smoke was thick and suffocating. The music was the kind your mama wouldn't want you listening to - loud and full of every damn cuss word that existed. Most of the bar patrons looked either like convicts or members of a local motorcycle gang. I bet a few even had switchblades hidden somewhere on them. Two college girls definitely didn't belong in here.

"TABLE!" Eva squealed when she saw two empty chairs. Pulling on my hand, she charged forward, bumping into a couple of leather-clad men who scowled at us.

At least the seats were in the corner. *Maybe no one will notice us here.* Eva could have her fun and then we could leave. Hopefully, in one piece.

"WOOO HOOO!" Eva shrieked as one of her favorite rap songs started blasting from the speakers. It earned us a few more dirty looks.

To my dismay, she started rapping along with the song. The girl couldn't sing worth a darn but I had to give her credit for trying. I hugged my purse closer to my body and glared at her. *She was so drawing attention to us!* I hushed her but this was Eva we were talking about; there was no hushing her.

Out of nowhere a waitress appeared next to our table. "You girls want anything?" she asked with a bored expression. Her blond hair was stringy, her tank top cut too low, and her tiny shorts didn't cover her butt. She had about an inch of makeup on and it was starting to cake in her wrinkles.

"Two shots of whiskey," Eva yelled over the music.

The waitress nodded and walked away, her shorts trying so hard to cover her behind.

"I don't drink, Eva, you know that!" I leaned over to shout.

Eva waved me off as she went back to singing. I cringed as she rapped about sex and someone getting shot.

We were so different. She was the exact opposite of me. Spontaneous and unpredictable, Eva was a true wild child who wasn't afraid of anything. Some people found it amazing that we were friends but I've known her since the first grade – fifteen long years now. We had been through thick and thin together. There was no separating us. That's why I had agreed to come to this dive in the first place. Needless to say, she owed me big time.

Out of the corner of my eye, I saw some men staring at us, practically drooling. "Those guys are gawking," I said.

"Wooo, baby, come to mama!" Eva growled dramatically as she studied them.

I rolled my eyes at her version of a sexy purr. She loved bad boys and these men fit the bill perfectly. They were cute if you liked the tattooed, muscular, badass type of man. I didn't. My type was more the khaki wearing, BMW driving, tattoo-free gentleman.

The men were forgotten as the waitress appeared and delivered our shots. She took our money and stalked off, not thanking us for the tip or looking our way again. *The customer service in here rocks.*

I picked up the small glass and studied it closely. It was dirty and whatever was in it smelled awful.

"I'm not drinking this," I said, sitting it back down with revulsion.

"You've got to. It's bad luck if you don't."

I eyed Eva with skepticism. "That's not true and you know it."

"Okay, well, just drink it for me. You need to relaaaax."

I picked up the dirty glass and sighed. *The things I did for a friend.*

"Okay, on three. One, two, THREE!" Eva said, smacking the table with each count.

I tossed back the drink quickly. Fire raced - no, scorched - down my throat. My eyes watered, making it hard to see. I squeezed them shut, feeling the burn as the whiskey traveled from my throat to my stomach. *Oh, shit! That was terrible!*

Eva started giggling as she watched me. "Another!" she laughed, pushing the second glass my way.

"What? No freakin' way! That was awful!" I shuddered in disgust.

"I bought it for you. Drink up. You need it."

I knew Eva would win this argument so I threw back the drink. My throat instantly felt as if someone dropped a lighted match down it.

"I love this song! Let's dance."

She grabbed my hand and pulled me out onto the dance floor before I could protest or recover from the drink.

There were only a couple of people dancing but Eva didn't care. She started moving to the bass, really getting into the music. By now, my muscles were starting to relax thanks to the alcohol. Moving my hips to the pounding beat, I began dancing.

By the second song, we were having a good time. Eva turned to shake her butt at me, sending me into fits of laughter. We started rubbing against each other, grinding to the music and acting silly.

After the song ended, I noticed we had gathered an audience. Many of the rough looking men were now standing on the sidelines, watching us. I nervously scanned the crowd, afraid we were over our heads here. These men looked at us like we were their dinner and they were starving.

I was about to tell Eva that we should leave when someone caught my attention. He was at a pool table in the back, lining up to take a shot with his cue stick. A voluptuous blonde was rubbing up against him like a bitch in heat. She wore a short black skirt, plunging neckline blouse, and five-inch stilettos. Her hands were all over him.

I watched as he took the shot and straightened up to survey the table. Turning to the woman, he grabbed her by the waist and pulled her closer.

I sucked in a breath when I saw his profile. His ball cap was pulled low and unruly brown hair peeked out from the edges. His broad shoulders were outlined beneath a black shirt and well-worn jeans fit his long, muscular legs perfectly.

I would recognize him anywhere.

"Who's that hottie?" Eva asked when she noticed me staring.

"It's Ry..."

She beat me to it. "Holy *shit!* It's Ryder!"

I felt my heart rate go spiraling out of control as I watched him laugh at something the blonde said. When he leaned over to whisper in her ear, I couldn't look away.

Ryder Delaney was a legend around here. The women couldn't keep their hands off him and the men were scared to death of him. He was good-looking and dangerous. A little bit bad and a whole lot sexy. And just like Eva, he was wild and liked to live life to the fullest (sometimes a little too much). He had no rules and did what or who he wanted. Apparently, he was working on his latest who - the blonde wrapped around him.

Believe it or not, besides Eva, Ryder was my best friend. We've known each other since we were little kids playing house in my daddy's barn. When I was six, my dad bought the small farm next to his parent's ranch, making us neighbors and eventually friends.

"Let's go talk to him," Eva said, dancing in place.

"No, he looks busy," I mumbled with a smidgen of jealousy. His hand still rested on the blonde's waist. The tattoos that started at his right wrist and circled around his arm captured my attention. I remembered when he got those tattoos. I had been there.

"Pleeeease! The guy can stop kissing on that slut long enough to talk to us," Eva said, looking the blonde up and down.

Without waiting for me, she headed their way.

Oh, crap! I rushed to catch up with her. Eva and Ryder didn't mix well together and that was putting it lightly.

"Hey, stranger!" Eva shouted over the music when we were within a few feet of him.

Ryder stopped sweet-talking the blonde to look our way. Under the brim of his hat, I saw his eyes widen in surprise.

Oh, wow. The color of his eyes would never cease to amaze me. They were a clear blue that put the color of the ocean to shame. Combined with his dark tan and sun-kissed brown hair, the blueness of his eyes was striking. Breathtaking. Gorgeous.

Seeing him again, I realized how much I had missed him since leaving for college. *Was I supposed to feel this way about a friend?*

My stomach did a weird flip. He was so much taller than me. The top of my head hit the middle of his chest. On a good day, I was five feet two inches; short by most people's standards but next to Ryder, I was tiny.

"What are you two doing here?" he asked, detangling himself from the blonde's arms. She pouted, which made me want to smile and do a fist pump.

"Clubbing!" Eva answered as she looked over at Blondie. "I would ask you the same but it's pretty obvious."

He ignored her sarcastic comment.

"When did you get into town, Maddie?" he asked, leaning toward me to be heard over the music.

"A few days ago," I answered. "I texted you but I never heard back."

Okay, I'll admit he was the first person I texted when I arrived in town. When he didn't immediately answer or show up on my doorstep like he usually did, I was slightly upset. *How sad was I?*

"Sorry. Damn phone is a piece of crap," he said, sticking his hands in his pockets.

"I've heard that before," Eva muttered, rolling her eyes.

Ryder shot her a look of annoyance. The blonde chose that moment to lean closer, pressing her ample breasts against him. *Yeah, we know you're still here, Blondie.*

He detangled himself from her grasp with ease. "I'll catch you later, Mandy," he said, dismissing her without a second thought.

The girl gave me a dirty look before sulking off, wobbling slightly on her high heels. A tiny bit of jealousy flared up again. She was tall and beautiful, just the way he preferred them.

"You shouldn't be in here dressed like that," Ryder said, pointing to my sundress. "You trying to get killed?"

"What's wrong with my dress?"

"Nothing except you look like a little girl trying to play with the big kids," he said, smirking.

"Well, it was Eva's idea to come here!" I blurted, feeling as if I had just got caught doing something wrong.

Ryder's blue eyes slung to Eva, turning cold and calculating. In return, she gave him her best 'I-dare-you-to-say-something' stare.

I saw an argument brewing between the two of them as usual. Before I could put a stop to it, Ryder grabbed my arm and pulled me toward him, out of the way of three large men walking by. The air was knocked out of my lungs as I lost my footing and landed hard against his chest. I had to admit, it wasn't such a bad place to be.

"Have you been drinking?" he asked, dropping his hand away from me.

"Two shots," I answered.

He didn't look too pleased.

"Eva made me do it," I explained, laying all the blame on her.

He looked over at Eva again, not happy in the least. She smirked at him boldly and danced around us, not afraid of him at all. I watched Ryder grind his teeth in frustration, something I did quite often around Eva.

He turned his attention back to me, trying to ignore her. "I'm going to the bar for a drink. Want anything? Maybe a water?" he asked.

I shook my head no and couldn't help but watch as he walked away. More than one woman stopped to admire him and a few tried to strike up a conversation but he simply smiled and moved on.

"He's so good-looking. Too bad I can't stand him," Eva said as she watched him with a dreamy expression.

Before I could tell her to behave, two men were standing in our line of vision. Both were covered in leather, piercings, and tattoos. Just Eva's type.

"We were watching you dance earlier. You were really good," one of them said to Eva.

She smiled at him with a sexy smile that made me want to gag.

"Thank you," she said, holding out a well-manicured hand. "I'm Eva, by the way."

Within seconds, she was out on the dance floor with the guy, leaving me alone with guy number two.

He smiled down at me, stretching his pierced lips wide. I tried not to stare at the numerous rings in his lips and ears. He had a shaved head and skeleton tattoos crawling up and around his neck. To say the guy was scary was an understatement. And apparently he was also drunk, swaying on his feet as he took another swig of beer. *Great.*

"My name's Jacob," he said, holding out a hand tattooed with numbers and letters.

I forced a smile on my face and placed my hand in his. "Maddie," I said. I didn't want to give him my name but what else could I do? My daddy raised me to be polite.

"You from around here?" he asked. I tried not to cringe at the bad pickup line or the way his eyes moved up and down my body with interest.

"Yes," I answered, looking around the club. Maybe if I looked uninterested, he would take the hint and leave.

"Nice dress," he said, staring down at my chest.

Okay, this was getting ridiculous. I attempted to walk around him but his hand slipped around my waist.

"Let's dance," he slurred.

I moved out from under his arm and started to walk away when he stepped in front of me.

"Just one dance," he pleaded, drunkenly.

"No, thanks." Polite me again.

He was about to say something else when there was a commotion at the bar. I heard yelling and glass breaking. Looking around 'Jacob the Drunk,' I was stunned. *What the hell?* I think my mouth even dropped open.

Ryder and a very large man were fighting, looking ready to kill each other. All I could see were fists and fury.

People started rushing over, scrambling to get a good view of the fight. I left Jacob behind to push through the crowd, just in time to see Ryder's head snap back and blood go flying. I shoved my way to the edge of, watching as Ryder recovered and swung an uppercut to the big man's jaw. When the guy's eyes rolled back in his head, I thought it was over. Instead, he shook his head to clear it and threw a hard jab. His fist connected with Ryder's stomach, shoving him backward.

Someone grabbed my arm and yanked. I swung around, prepared to do battle myself, but found only Eva.

"What the hell is going on?" she shouted. The crowd surged around us, everybody wanting to get closer to the action.

"Ryder's getting his ass kicked! We have to help him!"

"Are you crazy? We can't do anything!" Eva shouted as she struggled to stay on her feet against the jostling crowd.

The sound of beer bottles shattering had me turning back around. I watched as Ryder's fist connected with the man's face followed by his elbow whacking the man's jaw, all in one fluid movement. This time the stranger went down cold.

I rushed to Ryder's side as he flopped down onto a nearby barstool. His lip was cut and a nasty bruise was already forming on his cheekbone. He was wiping the blood from his nose when his eyes met mine.

"What the hell was that all about?" I shouted over the music.

"I told you that you shouldn't be in here!" Ryder said, loudly.

"What has that got to do with you fighting?" I asked, trying to ignore how close I was to him.

"The bastard was talking shit about you in that dress."

"What did he say?" I asked, watching as the man's friends tried to peel him off of the floor.

"Believe me, you don't want to know," Ryder growled. He stood up gingerly, wincing at the movement. When the pain passed, he grabbed hold of my arm.

"Time to leave, little girls."

With his fingers wrapped around my upper arm, he led me out of the bar. Eva followed, protesting the entire time. I wasn't going to say anything. I didn't want to be here anyway. He was saving me from a potentially bad night.

Outside the hot Texas air hit us like a blowtorch, wilting everything in its path. Gravel crunched under our feet as we maneuvered around motorcycles and muscle cars, finally finding Eva's pickup.

"Go straight home, Maddie," Ryder demanded as he opened the passenger door for me.

"You're not going back in there are you?" I asked.

He paused. I saw the indecision on his face. This wasn't an easy decision for him. Not when he never walked away from a party. Or a woman.

"No, I'll follow you home."

Secretly, I was glad he was leaving. It meant no more girls, no more fighting, and no more drinking for him tonight.

Eva waited for Ryder to pull behind us in his '66 Ford Bronco before she drove out of the parking lot. A few minutes later, we hit the empty, two-lane highway that would take us home.

The truck gave a violent shudder as Eva leaned over to turn the A/C on full blast. It was a beat up, hardly running, seen-better-days old Ford pickup from my daddy's generation of gas guzzling vehicles. The paint was chipping, the seats were torn, and on a bad day it smelled like cow manure but it got us where we needed to go. Sometimes.

"So…interesting night," Eva said, keeping her eyes on the road.

"Yeah, I told you the place was a hole but you never listen to me."

"If I listened to you, what fun would we have?" She floored the accelerator and the truck jerked forward. "I never thought we would see Ryder there."

"It's his kind of place," I said, peering in the side mirror.

I could see his headlights a short distance behind us. This late at night, we were the only two vehicles on the road. It was an eerie feeling being out here in the middle of nowhere. There were no lights and no people; only the stars and moon above.

"I have no idea why the two of you stay friends," Eva said. Out of the corner of my eye, I saw her gather her long blonde hair in one hand and hold it off her nape, letting the cool air reach her neck. "I mean, the two of you are so different. He's such a pain in the ass and you're so…I don't know…sweet? I don't get it."

I didn't get it either. Maybe it was because Ryder and I had known each other forever. Or maybe it was because we knew everything about each other. Whatever it was, we remained friends. When I moved six hours away to go to college, I worried our friendship would fade. It didn't but it changed. There was something there, lingering between us, leaving me nervous and confused.

I would never admit it to anyone, even Eva, but I always had a thing for Ryder. Maybe it was love or maybe it was just lust. In high school, I watched as he dated girl after girl. I spent many nights wishing it was me that he wanted. Me that he loved. When I left for college, I thought the feelings would disappear. I thought it was only a silly teenage crush that would fade over time. I was wrong. My feelings only grew stronger.

"On the topic of boys, what are you going to do about Ben? You gonna take things to the next level and sleep with him like he wants?"

I grabbed the door handle as she gunned the truck and took a curve too fast. Eva was hell on wheels. She drove as if she was competing in the Indy 500 (and winning). I took my life in my own hands every time I got in the car with her.

"No," I answered, trying to talk myself into being brave and letting go of the door handle. "He keeps pressuring me but I'm not ready."

Ben and I had been together for a few months now. We met at a party and instantly hit it off. When he asked me out, I didn't hesitate to say yes. Everything had been great between us until he started insisting we have sex. I told him no repeatedly but still he pushed and pushed. Figuratively not literally. I had made it to the ripe old age of twenty-one as a virgin and I planned to stay that way despite good looks and sweet words.

"Don't ruin your last year of college with him," Eva said. "He's a jerk."

"No one is going to ruin my last year, Eva. Especially a boy."

"Good. We're so close to getting our nursing degrees that nothing can mess it up now."

I was majoring in nursing. Eva was majoring in boys and parties with some nursing thrown in as well. The past three years had been interesting sharing an apartment with her. There was never a dull moment.

"Damn, A/C. You would think my dad would fix it since we live in frickin' Texas where it's frickin' hotter than hell!" Eva muttered, messing with the A/C knobs again.

Knowing the air conditioning worked for only a short amount of time, we both rolled down our windows to let in the night air. The wind immediately started wreaking havoc with our hair, probably tying it into knots.

"I don't know what you have against Ben," I said, pushing strands of hair out of my eyes only to have the wind whip it around my face again.

"He has too much ego, strutting around with his blonde hair and perfect tan. I mean, the guy is too perfect. Something's up with him, I just feel it," Eva said, whipping the truck around another corner.

I wasn't surprised by her words. She told me all the time that Ben was too possessive and controlling. I didn't see it but she had always been overcritical of the guys I dated anyway.

"You need to have sex for the first time with someone more…I don't know…badass." I saw the gears turning in her mind, hatching an idea. "And I know the perfect person! Ryder!"

I felt redness creep up my neck. "I don't think so, Eva. He's only a friend."

"A friend who is super hot! Ever heard of friends with benefits?" she asked with a wide smile.

"Never happening!"

"Why? Ever think about it? All those hard abs and sexy tattoos? The man is definitely fuck-worthy. Come on, Maddie, you can't tell me you haven't thought about it."

"Nope."

"Liar."

Maybe I was a liar but he was my friend. I wouldn't go there.

Soon we were pulling into Eva's driveway with Ryder behind us. Eva and her parents lived in town. Around here, they were considered city folks even though the town boasted only 4,000 residents. Silly, I know.

I started to jump out of the truck when Eva's voice stopped me. "Your dad's not home. Feel free to take my advice and sleep with Ryder," she said with a wink. "If you can't walk tomorrow, I'll know why."

I rolled my eyes and slammed the car door shut. Sex was always on her mind. I swear that she was as bad as Ryder.

His old Bronco rumbled loudly as I slid into the passenger seat. Since we lived right next door to each other, he was taking me the rest of the way home.

"Eva drives like a lunatic! You shouldn't get in the car with her," he said after I shut the truck door.

I glanced over at him. His cheekbone had one big nasty bruise and the cut on his lower lip looked painful. The ball cap shadowed his eyes but the intensity of his stare made me uneasy.

"She's never gotten a ticket so she must be doing something right," I said.

"Pure luck," he reasoned, backing out of the driveway. He pulled out onto the street and I felt him look over at me but I kept my eyes locked outside. *Why was I so nervous? Two shots of whiskey must really be messing with my head.*

"My phone really was acting up, Maddie. I didn't get your text," he said in a low voice.

"No big deal, Ryder. I was going to call but I've been busy."

"I noticed. Don't go to a place like that again. Stick to your little college kid bars."

"Yes, sir," I said, sarcastically under my breath. I snuck a peek at his tattooed arm, resting lazily on top of the steering wheel. Tribal tattoos in big, bold designs swirled around his wrist and traveled upward. Eva was right. They were sexy. *Too bad we were just friends.*

The silence stretched between us, becoming uncomfortable and awkward as we left the town behind. I clasped my hands tightly in my lap, wondering why I was so nervous. *It was only Ryder, for Pete's sake!*

For miles only the countryside surrounded us, dark and empty. Finally, we turned down a deserted dirt road. On either side of us were acres and acres of farmland and not much else. This is where I lived – in the middle of nowhere, Texas. Population - a few people, but plenty of cows and horses.

Within minutes, we were driving along my gravel driveway, leading to the only home in sight.

"Your dad's not home?" Ryder asked when he saw the dark house.

"No. He's in Dallas for business."

I opened up the car door and was surprised when Ryder turned off the ignition and climbed out of the truck.

"I'll walk you in."

I couldn't say why the butterflies took flight in my stomach or why my hands started to shake when I attempted to unlock the front door, but they did. I had been alone with Ryder plenty of times but tonight felt different.

In the kitchen, I flipped on the light and grimaced. His face looked awful, painful. To think those bruises were there because of me...hurt.

"Your face looks horrible. Have a seat. I'll get something to doctor it."

"Its fine. Don't worry about it," he said, taking a seat anyway. That put his eyes closer to my level, making my nervousness double and my heart pound.

"Doctoring you is the least I could do after you defended my honor," I said, teasingly.

A smile slowly spread across his face. Stretching out his long legs, he watched me closely, studying my every move.

Ryder's a friend. Only a friend. The words kept replaying in my mind as I headed to the bathroom for the first-aid. *What was wrong with me that I needed to remind myself of our friendship all the time?*

For some reason, I dropped the butterfly bandages twice before walking back to the kitchen.

When I rounded the corner and saw him, I almost stumbled. He had taken off his hat, leaving his hair messy and flattened. He looked innocent and sweet. Nothing like his true self. As I poured antiseptic on a cotton ball, he ran a hand through his hair, making it spike all over. Now he looked like the bad boy I knew him to be.

Taking a deep breath, I stepped toward him. He spread his knees so I could stand closer but I kept my distance. Even this close, I could smell his aftershave, something clean and manly, unlike the heavy cologne that Ben wore.

"You don't have to do this, Maddie."

"Sure, I do. Someone needs to be my guinea pig so I can practice my nursing skills. Might as well be you," I teased.

He grinned and put a hand on my hip. "What's your deal? I'm not going to bite," he said, pulling me forward to stand between his legs. His hand lingered on my hip a second before dropping away.

I blushed as the skin on my hip burned beneath my dress. His eyes were now level with my breasts and his legs were mere centimeters away from my thighs. One more small step and I would be in his lap. Where I wanted to be.

What was wrong with me?

I avoided his eyes as I put the cotton ball on his cheekbone.

"Shit!" he hissed.

"So you get tattooed but you can't handle a little burn. What's wrong with this picture?" I asked, unable to hold back a grin.

He laughed lightly. His eyes dropped down to my chest and quickly back up again. My blush returned, turning my face a bright red. I quickly placed the butterfly bandage on the cut, needing to hurry and get away from him before I made that straddling wish a reality.

Wetting another cotton ball with antiseptic, I leaned closer, planning to put it on his lip. Instead, he took it from me and placed it on the cut himself. Hissing, he closed his eyes at the pain.

I was still standing between his legs when his blue eyes opened and looked at me, searing me with heat. I took a step back, putting a safe distance between us.

"You and your boyfriend still an item?" he asked, putting the hat back on his head.

"Yes, Ben and I are still together."

"Is it serious?"

I shrugged indifferently. I was not going to tell Ryder that Ben had been pushing me to have sex. Ryder and I shared everything but our sex life (or in my case, lack of one) was not something we talked about. Thank goodness too. I hated his promiscuous behavior. Ryder was the ultimate player and seeing him with so many women hurt. A lot.

He stood up, towering over me. The kitchen suddenly felt small and crowded. Intimate, if kitchens could feel that way. Moving closer, he ran a finger underneath the spaghetti strap of my sundress. Shivers raced across my skin.

"This dress is dangerous," he whispered.

"It's just a dress, Ryder."

"It's more than just a dress, Maddie. It makes you look so innocent and sweet. Ripe for the taking. You don't know what that does to guys. Your boyfriend would kill you for wearing it to a bar."

"He doesn't tell me what to wear."

"If I was your boyfriend, I wouldn't want you to wear that unless it was to bed and then I would just rip it off of you. With pleasure."

My breath caught in my throat as his eyes burned into mine and his finger continued to run across my skin.

Seconds ticked by on the kitchen clock.

He finally removed his finger and broke the silence, ending the moment between us. Whatever it was.

"I'm teasing, Maddie." he said with a smile, the heat leaving his eyes. "I like to see you blush."

I frowned and felt a tiny bit of hurt. Teasing like that wasn't funny.

He stepped away from me, putting a safe distance between us.

"So I wanted to talk to you about something. Guess this is as good a time as any." He took a deep breath and let it out in a tumble of words. "I'm enlisting in the Army."

I stared at him in shock, not expecting those words. His strong jaw flexed as he waited for me to say something. Words escaped me. I lost my voice. *What do I say to that?*

"I wanted you to be the first to know. I can get in as an officer since I have a college degree." He leaned back against the table and crossed his arms over his chest. "I've got to get out of this town and decided the Army was the best way to do it."

Words stuck in my throat. *He wanted to leave?* I guess I took it for granted that Ryder would always be here. To me, he was a constant and I couldn't imagine my life without him.

"You can't enlist," I said.

One corner of his mouth lifted in a lopsided grin. "Leave it to you, Maddie, to tell me I can't do something." His eyes locked onto mine with intensity and his grin faded. "But before I sign up, there is one thing that I want to do."

My heart went crazy as my imagination went wild.

"I have an appointment in a week at the military entrance processing station. They'll do my medical evaluation and other tests to make sure I qualify. The place is right by your campus so I thought maybe I could go back with you. We could hang out for a few days, raise some hell just like old times."

Ryder in my apartment? For days? Sleeping and showering? I could handle it. Well, maybe.

"I never raised hell, Ryder. You did it enough for the both of us," I said with a nervous laugh. "But having you around sounds great. Who knows, maybe you will meet the love of your life and decide not to enlist."

Ryder shook his head and scoffed. "When hell freezes over, Maddie. You know I'll never marry. Too many women out there I haven't met yet."

I rolled my eyes. He thought it was all fun and games but I couldn't stand to see him with so many women. He deserved better.

I decided the comment wasn't worth fighting over.

Now him enlisting, that was worth fighting over. Maybe while he was with me, I could talk him out of it.

"We're leaving in two days," I warned.

"Works for me."

I followed him to the front door, trying not to notice the way his shirt outlined the muscles of his arms or the way his jeans hugged his butt. I wanted to smack myself for looking.

He was almost out the door when he turned around. I winced at the sight of his battered face under the porch light.

"Lock the door behind me and call if you need anything," he said, sternly.

I nodded. "Night, Ryder."

With one more glance at me, he jogged down the porch steps and across the dark yard. Closing the door, I looked around the hallway, not seeing the childhood pictures of me on the wall or noticing the quietness of the house. My mind was only on Ryder.

Chapter Two

"Ramen noodles?"

I looked over at my dad. He was holding up God's gift to the broke, starving college student.

"Yeah, we'll eat that," I answered, searching my purse for my always-disappearing phone charger.

Every time I left, my dad sent bags of groceries back with me. Secretly, I was glad he did because Eva and I usually survived on coffee and grilled cheese sandwiches.

"So Ryder is going with you?"

"Yep," I answered, searching under some farm and ranch magazines. "Do you know where I put my charger?"

When he didn't answer, I glanced at him and was surprised to see a worried expression on his face.

"Is he staying with you?"

The question caught me off guard. Never before had my dad questioned what I did with Ryder. He lectured me about Ben all the time. 'Don't get too serious,' 'Don't do anything you will regret later.' But the time I spent with Ryder never concerned him. *So why all the questions?*

"I'm sure he'll stay with us," I answered, finally finding my charger under an old phone book.

He still looked worried.

"You feeling okay?" I asked. Consistent worry for him was a way of life for me. My mother was diagnosed with ovarian cancer when I was eight and died the same year. Since then it had only been my dad and me. When he developed a heart problem last year, I pleaded with him to move closer to town so he could be near a hospital but he refused. No matter how much I argued with him, he insisted he was fine by himself.

"I'm feeling great, sweetie. I just worry but I know Ryder will keep you safe."

I wasn't sure what he meant by that but I didn't get a chance to ask.

"Hello!" Eva called out, slamming the front door shut behind her.

"I'm ready!" I shouted, walking out of the kitchen and into the hallway.

Eva met me halfway. "I'm so ready to get back to the apartment. My parents are driving me nuts with all the questions! 'Where are you going?' 'When will you be home?' It's so frustrating!" She flung an arm around my shoulders as we headed into my bedroom. "Tomorrow night we're going out and dancing our asses off!"

I couldn't help but smile. Eva's answer for everything was a good club and a lot of dancing. For once, I agreed with her. With Ryder around, I could use the distraction.

~~~~

It was a hot, blistering summer day, typical for Texas. Merely walking outside was torturous. Eva and I slipped on our sunglasses and crossed our fingers that the truck's air conditioning worked today.

Our first stop was to pick up Ryder.

He lived on a thousand-acre ranch belonging to his parents. A few miles separated his property from my dad's but the land was adjacent to each other. South of his parent's house was a small home that Ryder built for himself after graduating from college. He once told me he needed the privacy for his late night visitors. I didn't think it was very funny.

Besides Ryder, his parents also had another son, Gavin, who was three years older and worked in Dallas as an EMT. Ryder and his brother were like night and day but Ryder had always been my favorite Delaney son.

We took the gravel road leading to the old white ranch house a little too fast. A few feet from the porch, Eva slammed on the brakes, bringing the pickup to a sudden stop in a cloud of dust and gravel. I jumped out, glad to be out of that deathtrap.

Ryder's mom, Janice, met me at the front door. She was tall and lithe with brown hair and blue eyes just like Ryder. A kind and caring woman, Janice was the mother I never had and always wanted, giving motherly advice when I needed it most.

"Maddie!" she squealed, throwing her arms around me. "We've missed you around here! How is school?"

"Great! Keeping me busy," I answered. My decision to go to nursing school was thanks to her. She was an ER nurse at the local county hospital and had more experience than most of the doctors there, combined.

Just then Ryder caught my eye. Standing behind his mom, he looked good in his jeans and faded t-shirt. Too good. More like gorgeous. By his side, he held a large green duffle bag, ready to go.

"Mom, we've got to go. It's a long drive," he said, setting the bag down to give her a quick hug.

"Be good, Ryder," she whispered, hugging him tightly.

After letting go of her, he picked up his bag and stepped around me, heading for the truck. I watched as he threw his duffle bag into the back, making his biceps flex with the movement.

"Keep him in line, Maddie," Janice said.

"I'm not sure that's possible."

"If anyone can make him behave, it's you," she said with a gentle smile.

That was true. For some reason, Ryder seemed to listen to me more than anyone. I liked to think it was because he appreciated my opinion, but I knew it was just because I would bug the snot out of him until he did what I wanted. It worked when I was a little kid and it still worked today.

Promising to do my best, I gave Janice a hug goodbye and headed to the truck.

Somehow, Ryder had talked Eva into letting him drive her precious piece of crap. She could deny it all she wanted; like most women, she couldn't resist him either.

I moved to the middle of the bench seat, wedged between both of them. *Six long hours with them. Should be interesting.*

"You promise to show me a good time, Maddie?" Ryder asked with a wicked grin as he shifted the truck into drive.

"Yes," I answered, hoarsely. A vivid picture of a good time with Ryder popped into my mind and it wasn't PG-rated. It was more the unrated version, involving a sundress and a certain ripping of it.

~~~~

We finally arrived at our apartment late that night. The place wasn't that impressive. It contained one living room, a tiny kitchen, two bedrooms, and a single bathroom. We filled it with cheap furniture from Ikea and some hand-me-downs.

"I'm heading to bed. My parents had me up at the ass crack of dawn this morning and I need my beauty sleep," Eva announced as she headed for the bathroom. "Nightie night, y'all."

"So which room is yours?" Ryder asked as he picked up my suitcase, making those biceps flex again.

"You don't have to do that, Ryder."

"I'm trying to be a gentleman," he said with a smirk.

"You a gentleman? When did that happen?" I teased, leading him to my bedroom.

"Only for you," his deep voice rumbled behind me.

I turned on the light, my nerves going haywire with him in my room. My tiny bedroom suddenly felt minuscule with him in it.

He sat down on the edge of my bed and stretched his long legs out on either side of me, trapping me in front of him. Bouncing up and down, he smiled at me with mischief.

"Nice bed."

I couldn't help but laugh. "That seductive tone doesn't work on me, Ryder."

A deep chuckle vibrated from his chest. Lying back, he folded his hands under his head. "Works on most girls. Why not you, Maddie?"

"I'm not most girls."

"That is the truth." He closed his eyes then patted the bed. "Sit down," he said, so quietly that I almost didn't hear him.

I sat beside him and studied his face while his eyes were closed. His unshaven jaw made him look rugged and unapproachable. The bruises and cuts from the fight added to his bad boy persona. Remembering he was only here because he was joining the military, I felt fear at the thought of losing him.

"Don't enlist, Ryder."

He sighed heavily. Without opening his eyes, he laid his work-roughened hand on the bare skin below my shorts.

"Let's go to sleep, Maddie."

The warm touch on my bare thigh had me leaping off of the bed.

"I'm going to change. Don't fall asleep in my bed, Ryder," I warned, grabbing pajamas and racing out of the room.

In the bathroom, I leaned against the counter, feeling breathless. *Why was I so jumpy?* If there was one man that I could trust in my bed, it was Ryder. He had lounged on my bed plenty of times growing up so why was this any different?

Feeling a little bit naughty, I let myself wonder what it would be like to be desired by him. To lie in bed with him as more than friends. To be one of those girls he took home for a night.

I stopped brushing my teeth to study myself in the mirror. A blush had chased away the light color of my skin. Straight hair framed my oval face. Full pink lips and finely arched eyebrows couldn't compensate for my too-large dark brown eyes. I sighed with resignation. *I could never compete with the beautiful women Ryder chose. They were models while I was the girl-next-door.*

Chastising myself for such silly thoughts, I changed quickly into pajamas. *We were friends, nothing else.* If I was feeling awkward around him, it had to be because I hadn't seen him in weeks. *Yeah, that sounded about right.*

Returning to my room, I found him sitting on the edge of the bed, looking sexy and oh, so tempting.

"The couch is all yours," I said.

He looked over my university t-shirt and cheeky boyshorts. I tugged the shirt's hem down lower, suddenly feeling self-conscious. Under his scrutiny, I wondered if maybe I should have picked something less revealing.

"I'm going." He didn't move. The corner of his mouth

turned up in a smirk. "Sure I can't share this bed with you? Just two friends having a sleep over?"

Did he just ask to sleep with me? The fast beat of my heart was impossible to ignore.

"Go to bed, Ryder," I said, really needing him out of my room before I did something unpredictable.

"Goodnight, Maddie," his deep voice rasped before standing up and leaving.

I laid down after he left and listened to him moving around the apartment. *When had Ryder become such a flirt with me?* We've always teased each other but this was different. Underneath the flirting lurked something real. Something dangerous.

And I wasn't sure I could resist it.

Chapter Three

The ear-splitting music blasted us as soon as we opened the door to the club. The place was packed. The DJ had the crowd on its feet, filling the dance floor with moving, grinding bodies. The bartenders kept everyone in drinks. From longnecks to the hard stuff, the alcohol was flowing.

I followed Eva as she pushed her way through the club. I almost stepped on her heels more times than I could count. Ryder stayed close behind me, bumping into me every few seconds.

At the bar, Eva and I waited as Ryder ordered a drink. I couldn't help but watch him. Tonight he wore a crisp white dress shirt tucked into jeans that fit him just right. His hair looked like he had run his fingers through it as an afterthought, giving him a sexy, just-out-of-bed look.

"You look hot, Maddie," Eva whispered in my ear, grabbing my attention. She had talked me into wearing my new five-inch, knee high boots over skinny jeans along with an off-the-shoulder black shirt. Not my usual attire but I was feeling pretty sexy.

"You look great too," I said. If Eva was wearing a paper sack, she would still look beautiful.

"Maddie!" Ryder called out, motioning me over. I maneuvered my way to him as he waited by the bar. When I was a foot from him, someone bumped into me. I lost my footing but he grabbed my elbow quickly to keep me steady. Either I was a klutz or invisible. People just didn't seem to see me.

After making sure I was okay, he asked if I wanted something to drink. I said no and tried to ignore his warm hand on my elbow. When the bartender handed him his beer, he dropped his hand away to pay. I felt silly. *How pathetic was I that a simple touch could excite me so much? Must be the virgin in me.*

As we moved away from the bar, he took a long drink of ice-cold beer, somehow managing to make drinking look sexy. I tried not to stare. Instead, I focused on following Eva through the crowd. Stopping near the dance floor, we stood close together as people pressed around us. I was practically squashed against Ryder's chest. His arm rubbed against me every time he raised his arm to take another long drink of beer. It was then I decided that a crowded club wasn't a bad thing.

I tried to focus on the music and the scene around me. Flashing blue, red, and yellow lights illuminated the dance floor, moving in perfect rhythm to the music. The DJ was up on stage, keeping an eye on the sound system controls and moving to the bass also.

Eva grabbed my arm and started to pull me out onto the dance floor. I glanced back and found Ryder watching me. His eyes never left mine as he took another long drink of beer. Slowly, his gaze moved down to my boots, caressing me from across the room. When his eyes traveled just as slowly back up my body to meet my eyes again, I sucked in a breath. Pure unadulterated desire flared back at me. In that moment, he wasn't a friend. He was a man wanting what he saw. Me.

Suddenly, I couldn't see him anymore. The crowd was closing in around Eva and I, blocking my view of him. Eva tugged on my arm and pulled me further onto the dance floor, further from him.

As we started dancing, I wondered if maybe I had been wrong. Maybe I was reading more into it. Ryder and I had never crossed that line from friends to…well…more but what would happen if we did?

I craned my neck, hoping to find Ryder. I caught a brief glimpse of him before Eva stepped in front of me, giving me an inquisitive look.

"What?" I asked.

"Nothing." She shot me another curious look. "I'm just wondering if something's going on between you and Ryder."

"Don't know what you mean," I said, dancing.

A man moved between us, separating Eva and I. He started doing some sort of pelvic thrusting thing as he stared at me blatantly.

Eva ignored him and danced back over to me. "I'm just picking up on something between the two of you," she said.

Were my feelings that obvious? I wouldn't admit out loud that I had always found Ryder amazingly handsome. Each time I saw him, my wayward feelings seemed to intensify, no matter how much I fought it. But I needed to set the record straight.

"There's nothing between us, Eva. Ryder sleeps with anything that has boobs so I'm not going there." It was the truth. He did sleep with any woman and despite what I felt, I wasn't going to be one of his groupies.

"Whatever you say, Maddie. I'm just making an observation. He looks at you like he wants in your pants."

I opened my mouth to argue when the guy wedged himself between Eva and I again. *Unbelievable!* I looked up into his sweaty face as he gyrated his hips toward me.

Looking to Eva for help, I realized that the crowd had swallowed her up and I could no longer see her. I attempted to dance around the guy but he intentionally blocked my way, stubbornly refusing to move. Taking a step closer, he reached out and touched my arm.

I moved back to escape his roving hands and bumped into another man behind me. This guy was much more aggressive. He put his hands on my waist and pulled me back against him. A hard body rubbed against mine as strong fingers squeezed my waist.

This was outrageous! I swung around, ready to give this guy a piece of my mind, when my heart stopped.

Ryder's striking blue eyes met my stunned stare.

"Come here," he rasped low.

I held my breath when he grasped my hips and pulled me closer. Giving the guy behind me a deadly look, Ryder tightened his hold on me and started moving to the music. The man took the hint and faded into the crowd, forgotten.

"Shit, I forgot what a good dancer you are!" Ryder whispered in my ear. Warmth raced along my neck as his breath brushed against my ear.

Something happened then. A rebellious streak ran through me. The good girl in me disappeared. Ignoring my pounding heart, I started dancing within the circle of his arms.

He wrapped an arm around my waist, drawing me closer. His hips started moving against mine. We were touching everywhere, moving intimately to the deep bass of the music.

His movements mimicked sex. Words that were normally foreign to me were now rattling around in my head - desire, need, passion.

I could do this. I could play too. I moved down his body, my hips swaying to the music. As I traveled back up, our eyes locked. Eva's words came back to haunt me. 'He wants in your pants.' But she was wrong. He didn't see me that way. We were just having fun. Purely innocent.

I was rethinking that when one of his hands spanned my bottom to bring me closer. Leaning down, he whispered in my ear, "That was fucking hot!"

I swallowed hard as his fingers remained on my butt, burning me through my jeans. He started moving slowly, his crotch intimately nudging against me.

We were playing with fire.

The song was almost over when Eva appeared beside us. Ryder released me and moved away, leaving me disappointed when I should have been relieved. Evading Eva's stare, I continued to dance. This time alone.

When the song ended, Ryder placed a hand back on my waist.

"Want a drink?"

"Water, please."

His hand lingered longer than was necessary before leaving for the bar. I watched him walk away. I swear the crowd parted to let him through.

"What the hell was that all about?" Eva asked.

I shrugged and avoided her eyes. "We were dancing, that's all."

"Bullshit! I've never seen you dance like that with anyone."

She was right.

"Maddie, be careful. He might be your friend but he's also a womanizer. If you're looking for a bad boy fix then he's your guy but don't get in over your head. It would be like playing with fire. You'll get burned."

"I'm not going to do anything crazy," I said and meant it. Some teasing and close dancing didn't mean Ryder and I were going to fall in bed together.

The latest song from Muse started blaring and people flocked to the dance floor like an angry mob. Eva grabbed my hand and led me away, pushing and shoving to get through the crowd.

Ryder met us halfway.

"Sorry it took so long," he said, handing both of us plastic cups of cold water.

"Thanks," Eva and I said in unison.

Leaning closer to me, Ryder voice rose over the music. "So there's this blonde by the bar...I'm going to go talk to her."

Heat left my body in a whoosh. Reality hit me like a cold bucket of water. I watched as he turned and disappeared into the crowd, to his newest conquest.

"Like I said, he's a player," Eva said, taking my hand and pulling me back toward the dance floor. "Forget him. Let's dance."

I forced a smile on my face and tried to force Ryder from my mind. An impossible feat.

~~~~

I only saw Ryder once after he went in pursuit of the woman. I had caught a glimpse of him draped around a gorgeous platinum blonde but that had been hours ago.

At closing time, we found him in a dark corner of the club. The blonde was all over him. Her hands roamed his body boldly as she pressed up against him. I wanted to roll my eyes. I wanted to tell her to back off. What I didn't want was to see his hand on the blonde's thigh.

"Douchebag," Eva muttered, walking next to me.

Not bothering to argue with her, I stopped in front of them. "We're ready to go, Ryder," I said over the music.

He looked away from the girl and a smile spread across his face. *Oh, no, I knew that grin!* Ryder was drunk.

"Maddie, baby!" he said, weaving unsteadily on his feet as he pushed away from the blonde and threw an arm around me.

He was so wasted.

"I can't live without this woman," he drunkenly told the blonde. She didn't look too pleased as her heavily mascaraed eyes ran over me hatefully.

Ryder hugged me to his chest, making me bury my nose into his shirt. His hands ran down my back slowly as he nuzzled my hair.

"God, Maddie, you smell good," his deep voice rumbled.

Tingles raced along my nerve endings. *This was too much.*

"Let's go, Ryder," I said, detangling myself from his arms but still helping him stay upright. *Lord, he was solid muscle!*

He mumbled a goodbye to the blonde as we turned to leave. Getting through the club with him was no easy task. His arm stayed around my shoulders as he leaned on me heavily. He probably outweighed me by a good ninety pounds but somehow I got him outside.

"That girl offered to do things to me you wouldn't believe," he said, slurring his words.

"Gross, Ryder. Did you even know her name?" Eva asked, wrinkling her nose.

Ryder laughed and shrugged his shoulders. "Who friggin' cares what her name was! She was willing to do anything with me." His bloodshot eyes watched me. "But you wouldn't know anything about that would you, Maddie?" He grinned a lopsided grin, full of mischief. "I could always teach you. Would be my pleasure."

I blushed a deep red. I knew it was the alcohol talking

but the idea of doing things with him made my face burn with embarrassment.

Eva laughed loudly. "They say people speak the truth when they are drunk."

I looked at her in disbelief. She wasn't helping. Ryder didn't need any encouragement.

In the truck, he scooted closer to me, brushing his leg against mine. I jumped, earning me another lopsided grin from him. Reaching past him, I turned down the truck's A/C. Texas was fiercely hot even in the middle of the night. At least, that was my excuse for the heat burning through me.

~~~~

Back at the apartment, I dumped Ryder on the couch with annoyance. Seeing him with another woman completely ruined my night. I just wanted to crawl into bed and forget.

After a hot shower, I felt more like myself. But that was about to change. I was in my room, wrapped in a towel and searching for underwear, when he walked in.

"Sorry about tonight, Maddie," he said, slurring his words. My tiny nightlight cast shadows on his face as he stood in the doorway.

"Sorry about what?" I asked, holding the towel tighter around me.

"Getting shit-faced. I know it bothers you. You've still never been drunk, have you?"

"No, still haven't done that," I answered. "Can't say I want to either," I added, watching him weave on his feet.

He smiled and staggered into my room. "Still a virgin in more ways than one, I guess."

Redness flooded my cheeks. *Now wasn't the time to discuss this.* I was naked. He was drunk. We were alone. I needed him out of my room. Pronto.

"Go to bed and sleep it off, Ryder."

He ignored me and took a step closer. Leaning over, he kissed the corner of my mouth gently.

"Night, Maddie."

Before I could react, he turned and walked away.

I stood in shock, trying to comprehend what had just happened. Ryder had never kissed me before. Ever. Yeah, it was a simple kiss but it seemed to mean so much more.

Crawling into bed, I discovered the urge to sleep had deserted me. I now had a different urge.

I now had desire.

~~~~

In the middle of the night, I woke up to movement in the bed. Drowsily, I turned over and found Ryder crawling beneath the covers next to me.

"What are you doing?" I squealed with alarm, suddenly wide wake.

"I can't take another night on that couch. Go back to sleep," he grumbled, lying on his side, facing away from me.

My body went on high alert when his leg moved against mine. I eased to the edge, putting as much space as possible between the two of us.

It was going to be a long night.

Chapter Four

I woke up alone. Glancing at the time, I groaned. *It was too early.*

After Ryder crawled in bed with me last night, I couldn't sleep. I told myself that sharing a bed with him was harmless. He had been so drunk last night, he probably wouldn't remember sleeping with me anyway. Or remember that kiss.

Loud, angry voices came from somewhere in the apartment, interrupting the visions of Ryder in my bed. *What was going on?* Jumping out of bed, I sprinted into the living room.

What I found was not what I expected. A half-dressed Ryder faced off with one very angry boyfriend. Ben.

I tried not to stare. I really did. But it was difficult. Ryder's bare chest was tanned and ripped. There was not an ounce of fat on him, just a six-pack of muscles. Intricate tattoos started at his right wrist and covered one side of his body. Well-worn jeans sat teasingly low on his hips, leaving the rest to imagination.

I tore my eyes away from Ryder to look at Ben. No one had the right to look that perfect this early. He was wearing a blue polo shirt and starched khakis, looking well rested and *GQ* ready. I felt inadequate next to him. My ratty hair and wrinkled pajamas just didn't compare.

"Who's this, Maddie?" Ben asked, glowering at me from across the room.

"Ryder. The friend from home I told you about."

"Yeah, her friend who was fucking asleep," Ryder snapped.

"Calm down, Ryder, you're hungover," I said, stepping

in front of him. He looked down at me with animosity, making me understand why no one messed with him.

Knowing I had to calm both of them down before the situation turned volatile, I grabbed Ben's hand and pulled him into the kitchen. As soon as we were alone, Ben pulled me against him.

"I've missed you," he said, lowering his head and kissing me. It felt forced. Cold. Not at all like the simple kiss from Ryder.

"Aw, hell!"

Ryder's voice jolted me, breaking me away from Ben. He stood in the kitchen doorway, fully clothed and glaring spitefully at us. Shame made the blood drain from my face. Kissing Ben in front of Ryder felt...wrong.

"What the hell is going on? I'm trying to sleep," Eva yawned, walking in around Ryder. She came to a standstill when she saw the three of us squaring off. "Oh, shit!"

I couldn't have put it better.

"Ryder's staying here for a few days," I told Ben.

"He's staying here? In your apartment?" Ben asked, growing louder with each word.

"You got a problem with that?" Ryder growled, taking a threatening step closer.

They stared at each other with hostility, leaving me standing in the middle.

"This is shit, Maddie! You have some guy living with you? Are you fucking him too?" Ben lashed out at me.

Eva gasped.

I was shocked. Ben had never talked to me like that before. Never.

Hearing Ben's words, Ryder exploded. He pushed me out of the way and threw a punch, landing a blow to Ben's face. Ben's head snapped back and he fell against a chair, toppling it over. He recovered quickly and went after Ryder, hell bent on taking him down.

Eva screamed and I scrambled to get between the two of them. Before I could, Ben swung at Ryder's side, pummeling his ribs. I winced at the sound of a fist connecting with solid muscle. Ryder didn't seem to notice. He raised his arm for another shot to Ben.

I saw my opportunity. I had to stop this madness. Without thinking of the danger, I pushed myself between them.

"Listen to me, Ben!" I shouted, smacking his chest to get his attention. His expression was so full of hate that I wondered briefly who it was directed at; Ryder or me?

"You need to calm down! Ryder's just a friend!"

"Don't play games with me, Maddie," he hissed, grabbing my arm and jerking me toward him.

"Get your damn hands off of her!" Ryder roared, wrenching me away from Ben and purposely stepping in front of me.

Eva pulled me safely to her side. "You okay?"

I nodded, refusing to take my eyes off of Ryder and Ben.

"She's my girlfriend, asshole! I'll put my hands on her if I damn well want to!" Ben yelled, getting in Ryder's face.

Deciding I had enough, I shook off Eva's hand and tried to push my way between the two of them again.

Ryder was having none of it. His hand snapped out, stopping me with his palm flat on my sternum.

"Touch her like that again and you're a dead man," he told Ben with a coldness that made me shudder.

Ben scowled at me. I wanted to cringe from the loathing I saw in his eyes but I refused to back down.

"Why don't you go and we'll talk about this later?" I asked him in a shaky voice.

Ben nodded and started to walk out of the kitchen when he stopped abruptly in front of me.

"Love you," he said with a smirk. Without waiting for a response, he threw Ryder a cocky, go-to-hell look and left. We stood motionless in the kitchen until we heard the front door slam shut.

"Oh my God, Maddie!" Eva exploded. "What got into him?"

"That's your boyfriend?" Ryder frowned at me. "Great guy."

"Not now." I moved past them and headed to my room, shutting the door behind me.

My mind raced as I got undressed. Never before had I seen Ben so possessive. I shuttered, remembering the way he grabbed my arm. Ryder was prone to fighting and had a bad attitude but he never scared me. Ben did.

Feeling a little agitated, I flung my clothes across the room. When my door banged open, hitting the wall, I yelped and quickly grabbed a shirt to cover myself.

"Knock much, Ryder?"

He froze in the doorway. His eyes moved over my panties and barely covered breasts. I watched as he swallowed nervously.

"Sorry."

When he looked away, I hurried to put a bra on and pull a shirt over my head. Keeping my eyes on him, I slipped on a pair of shorts.

"Okay, you can look now," I said, pulling my hair up into a messy ponytail. I watched as he gingerly walked further into my room, one hand on his ribs. "You okay?"

"Yeah, the asshole got lucky," he said. "I'll be fine."

"I don't know what got into him."

Ryder scoffed sarcastically. "He just walked right in this morning. Does he have a goddamn key?"

"Actually, yeah, he does."

"Really? Because he shouldn't. He's a shithead."

"He's not a shithead," I said, pausing a second, the wheels turning in my mind. "Did you say something to him?" I asked, cocking my head to one side. Ryder was a master at causing trouble.

He leaned against my dresser and crossed his arms over his chest, defiant.

"I said I slept with you."

"You WHAT?"

"I told him the truth. I did sleep with you. He had such a cocky attitude when he walked in the door that I had to put him in his place."

My mouth fell open in disbelief. "He doesn't have an attitude, Ryder, that's you."

Ryder scoffed. "Whatever. The guy's a jerk. How many times has he grabbed you like that?" he asked. "Let me see your arm," he demanded, pushing off the dresser and reaching for my arm.

I moved out of his reach, not wanting him to touch me, not wanting to feel the heat his hand would cause.

"He's never hurt me before. He was just angry."

"I don't care if he was pissed, he better not touch you like that again." He clenched his jaw hard. "I don't think you should see him anymore. He's dangerous."

I stopped searching for my running shoes to look at him. *Did he not know how dangerous he was?* Ryder could break a girl's heart within minutes of meeting her. He could make a girl believe she was his world then walk away without a second thought. *And he was lecturing me on danger?*

"I don't think I need your opinion on who I date."

"Oh, I'm sorry! I forgot, you can give your opinion on the girls I date, but I can't do the same?"

"You don't date girls, Ryder, you sleep with them. There's a difference," I said, irritated. I really didn't want to have this conversation. Sitting down on the edge of the bed, I pulled on my running shoes. Glancing up, I caught Ryder rubbing a hand over his face in frustration.

"I don't want to fight, Maddie. I just don't want you hurt by some jackass."

I finished tying my shoes and stood up. "I won't let anyone hurt me, Ryder. You know I'm tougher than I look."

"I just hope you can handle that jerk."

"If I can handle you, Ben will be a breeze."

Before the last word was out of my mouth, Ryder closed the distance between us and grabbed my long ponytail in one hand. Pulling me gently by the hair, he tugged me closer.

"I would rather you handle me. I won't hurt you," he rasped, looking deep into my eyes. His hand moved from my long hair to the back of my head.

"Stop it, Ryder," I whispered, breathlessly.

"Stop what, Maddie?" His voice was so husky it made my heart skip a beat.

I ignored the humming in my body and rolled my eyes at his question. He knew what he was doing. He knew all the moves, all the right things to say and do. He probably used them on every girl he met. And I wasn't going to be another sucker for a hot body and smooth words.

"I'm going for a run," I mumbled, leaving him standing in my bedroom. I needed to put some distance between us. If I didn't, I might say screw it and do something rash, like kiss my best friend.

~~~~

I ran. As my legs covered the miles, the fresh air cleared my mind. By the time I returned to the apartment, I decided the whole thing was silly. Ryder and I were friends. That was all. A little attraction and some innocent flirting wasn't going to change that.

By the time I returned to the apartment, everyone was gone. Eva was at work and Ryder was nowhere to be found. I should have been relieved to have a few hours alone but instead I found myself wondering where Ryder was and when he would be back.

While I was running, Ben texted me numerous times, apologizing and begging to have lunch with me. I wasn't ready to face him yet but knew we needed to talk. So I agreed to meet at a little sushi place by campus.

He was, as always, a perfect gentleman. He apologized profusely for fighting with Ryder and believed me when I said we were only friends. When he asked about Ryder sleeping in my bed, I assured him that nothing happened. I was able to convince him that there was nothing between Ryder and me. Now, if I could only convince myself of that maybe things would return to normal.

I was enjoying my California roll and trying to act normal around Ben when my phone beeped. My heart raced when I saw who the text message was from - Ryder.

Where r u?

I started typing, peeking up at Ben once.

Me: **w/Ben**

Ryder: **Asshole. Ur not alone w/him r u?**

Me: **No**

Ryder: **Good. U deserve better.**

Hmmm. Should I? I started typing again.

Have someone in mind?

Staring at my phone, I waited. There was no response. *What had I been thinking?* I wanted to kick myself for sending that text. Then my phone beeped.

Me

I was still staring at the text when Ben reached out to take my hand. Forcing a weak smile, I slipped the phone back into my purse.

"You okay? You're shaking," Ben said, covering my hand with his.

"I'm fine."

"So about the frat party? Will you be there tonight?"

"Sure," I answered. I smiled at Ben again but my mind was on the text.

Me. One simple word that had my heart racing and my stomach doing flips.

~~~~

After lunch, I returned home and found Ryder on the couch watching television. Empty beer bottles were scattered on the coffee table and he was working on another.

"Why are you drinking this early?" I asked, taking a seat beside him.

His bloodshot eyes glanced over at me. "I'm bored without you here," he answered, taking a swig of beer.

I wanted to ask about the text but couldn't get the words out. I was being a chicken shit (Eva's words not mine).

Not sure what to say to him, I glanced at the TV. He was watching the national news. Scenes of soldiers boarding planes played out while a frazzled anchorman reported from a foreign location. In big, bold letters, the words "USA AT WAR" flashed across the bottom of the screen.

The images reminded me of why Ryder was here - to enlist. The thought made me ill. If the United States was going to war, he would leave faster than I thought. *What would I do without him?* I took a deep breath, not wanting to think about it anymore.

"So Ben invited us to a frat party tonight but it looks like you started early," I said, pointing to all the beer bottles.

"I can't be around that shithead."

"Well, I'm not going to leave you alone," I said. "You're going."

He stood up, towering over me. "I don't know if that's a good idea, Maddie. When I'm around you..." He took a deep breath and started over. "Things are getting weird between us. It's probably best that I stay here." Without elaborating, he walked away, heading for the bathroom.

Apparently, I wasn't the only one confused on what was going on between us. My dad always said that if something was bothering you, don't ignore it. Deal with it. And that's what I was going to do. I jumped up and rushed to the closed bathroom door before I could change my mind.

Water was running in the shower and Ryder was in the process of taking off his shirt when I walked in.

I swallowed hard. His abs flexed as he dropped his shirt on the floor. The ink on his body was beautiful, there was no other way to describe it. The black designs swirled and disappeared below his wickedly, low-riding jeans. I wanted to reach out and touch them, find out how far down they went. I crossed my arms over my chest instead.

He put his hands on his hips, unaware of the effect his bare chest had on me.

"What?" he asked, impatiently.

I took a step into the small bathroom and leaned my hip against the counter. Steam filled the room, fogging the mirror and swirling around us.

"What do you mean 'things are getting weird'?"

He sighed. "Just forget I said anything."

"No. We need to talk about it."

"We are NOT going to talk about this now. I've had too much to drink."

"We ARE talking about it!" I argued, putting my hands on my hips. "We're friends, Ryder, we need to get whatever this is out in the open and deal with it."

He rubbed a hand over his face in frustration. "I can't. There are some things even friends shouldn't talk about."

"Like what?" I asked, annoyed. "Maybe your wonderful attitude?"

"Don't push me, Maddie," he warned in a low voice.

"Then talk to me!" I shouted, livid.

He stepped closer, crowding me. "You want to talk? Fine, we'll talk!"

I saw the fire burning in his eyes. I saw the tension in his body. What I didn't see were his next words coming.

"I want you, Maddie. I want to fuck you. I want you beneath me in bed."

What?

"You happy now? Got the information you wanted?" He scoffed, disgusted. "Hell, you're not even my type! And you're a goddamn virgin!" His voice dropped, the anger disappearing. "I know it's wrong but I want you, Maddie."

I was speechless. *Say something*, my inner voice shouted. *Tell him you want him too!*

Placing his hands on either side of me, he trapped me against the bathroom counter. "Years, Maddie," he said, huskily. "I've wanted you for years."

His lips slammed down on mine.

Shock had me frozen for a second before his mouth demanded a response. When he forced my lips open, I relented. His tongue ran lightly over my lower lip before delving into my mouth, tasting me. His hands grabbed my hips, gripping me with need. Heat traveled down my body to pool somewhere private, somewhere intimate.

My hands had a mind of their own as they lightly touched his stomach, finding rigid muscles beneath my fingertips.

Without breaking the kiss, he lifted me to sit on the bathroom counter. Nudging my legs apart, he moved between them. His hands left my hips to tangle in my hair, holding my head steady as his teeth gently nipped at my bottom lip. His kiss matched his personality - wild with no holds barred, demanding and taking what he wanted.

His lips moved over to graze my ear. "I want to be inside of you, Maddie," he said in a whisper. "Let me be the first."

I closed my eyes at the tingle his words sent through me. The softness of his jeans against my bare thighs made thinking impossible.

"Forget the party. Forget Ben. Stay with me."

His mouth took control of mine again, his tongue teasing and tormenting.

In the back of my mind, I knew this wasn't right. I loved Ryder. I really did. I couldn't live without him. He made me feel things I've never felt before. But this was wrong even if it did feel so right.

It was impossible to think with his lips hot and full on mine. But when his hands slipped beneath my shirt to glide over my bare stomach, I knew I couldn't do this.

Using both hands, I pushed him away, breaking our kiss and separating us by inches. We were both breathing hard, staring at each other with hunger.

"This is wrong," I whispered.

"Does it feel wrong?" he asked huskily, moving between my legs again. His hand eased under my hair, caressing the back of my neck.

"No, but we can't do this," I said, breathlessly. It would be so easy to give into my feelings and pull him to my bedroom. To give him what he wanted.

"One time, that's all I'm asking for," he said in a raspy voice, brushing his lips against mine. "No one has to know. It will be between us. Our secret." He trailed his lips down to my jawline while his hands cradled my head gently.

I closed my eyes, his lips hot against me, his frank words ringing in my ears. *One time? Was I just another girl he was trying to score with?* I couldn't be that kind of woman even if I wanted him.

I needed more.

I put more strength behind my push this time, shoving him far away from me. He hit the bathroom wall with force, stunning him. Before he could touch me again, I jumped off the bathroom counter and ran to my room. Slamming the door behind me, I slumped against the wall.

My heart was pounding wildly. The air was rushing in and out of my lungs quickly. I felt exhilaration and worry at the same time.

Ryder. Kissed. Me.

The scary thing was I wanted him. I wanted him in my bedroom. I wanted him to be my first. *This couldn't be happening.* I couldn't want my best friend this much.

"Open the door, Maddie," his deep voice said sternly from the other side.

I stared at the door, afraid he would open it. Afraid of what I would do if he did.

"Go away, Ryder!"

"I want to talk to you. Open up," he said, low and calm. "Now."

"No!"

It grew quiet. Thinking he left, I lay down on the bed and stared at the ceiling. I needed to get my head on straight. Eva was right. Ryder was a player, the worst kind. I refused to be added to his collection of women, no matter what my body wanted.

I suddenly grew angry. *How dare he treat me like another one of his floozies! Me, the girl who knew him better than anyone else!* The girl that was always there for him no matter what stupid things he did or said. *He couldn't scare me away or ruin our friendship, damn it!* Determined not to hide from him, I pushed off the bed and yanked open the bedroom door.

He was leaning against the wall, staring at me solemnly. I started to walk around him when he reached out to grab my arm.

"Wait, Maddie."

I moved out of his reach and walked quickly to the kitchen. Jerking open a cabinet door, I took down a coffee mug and slammed it on the counter. I heard him walk in but I refused to look up.

"Talk to me," he demanded in a low voice.

I filled up the coffee pot and measured out a heaping portion of coffee. After pushing the on button harder than was necessary, I finally turned to face him. I tried not to let my eyes stray down to his bare chest or the jeans slung suggestively low on his hips. It was bad enough staring into his heated blue eyes. The thought just made me angry.

"You're going to drink this pot of coffee and sober up. I'm going to the frat party. Alone." I turned to leave when he grasped my upper arm, stopping me.

"Don't touch me, Ryder. Don't you dare touch me ever again."

When he let go of my arm, I walked away. It was the hardest thing I've ever done.

Chapter Five

For hours, I remained at a local coffee shop. I couldn't be in the same house with him. I was too afraid of what I wanted. So I caught up on emails and cruised the Internet. I was tempted to call Eva at work and cry on her shoulder but instead, I checked in with my dad and tried to keep my mind off of Ryder.

It was early evening when I finally headed home. Rain fell softly, making the streets slippery and the heat all that much more oppressive. I should have been paying more attention to driving in the rain but there was only one thing on my mind – who waited for me at home.

My nervousness shot up a notch at the thought of facing Ryder. I knew if he touched me, I would be lost. And despite the fact that I loved him, one night in his bed would never work. I just wasn't that type of girl.

I wasn't sure how I was going to face Ben either but I had to if I wanted our relationship to work. *But did I want it to work?* I wasn't sure anymore.

By the time I made it home, I decided to be truthful with both of them. We were all adults. We could handle it. Taking a deep breath, I opened the apartment door.

Ryder was sitting on the couch, holding a cup of coffee. He didn't try to talk to me. In fact, he didn't even look at me. It kind of hurt.

I somehow managed to walk past him without falling apart. In my room, I changed into a short black skirt and a dark red blouse with matching heels.

Back in the living room, I tossed my keys on the couch beside him. He gave me a questioning look.

"Just in case you need to go somewhere you can use my car. I've got a ride to the party. Just make sure you're sober if you drive," I said.

"Maddie, listen to me...."

I turned to leave. I couldn't talk to him right now. I didn't trust myself around him. I shut the front door quietly behind me, not wanting to go. Each step I took away from him caused an ache in my chest, a yearning to stay.

Through the rain, I spotted Elizabeth's car parked next to my small Honda. The rain made walking in heels a challenge but I was intent on leaving.

"Hey, Maddie," Elizabeth said as I climbed into her BMW. She was a fellow student and a friend of mine, thanks to a semester of tutoring her in chemistry.

"Thanks for the ride. I didn't want to leave my friend without a car tonight," I said.

"No problem. I saw Ben earlier today at the campus gym."

"Oh, really?" I murmured.

"Yeah. He said he felt really bad not driving you tonight but he said that you understood, with his responsibilities and all."

I nodded but didn't feel the need to respond. Ben took his fraternity very seriously. He was working on his master's degree in finance, had a summer internship at a large accounting firm, and was president of his fraternity. He had so much going for him. He was successful. He wanted a family. He wanted me, only me.

But he wasn't Ryder.

I watched the windshield wipers try to keep up with the falling rain. The radio played some latest, greatest pop song. Every few minutes, Elizabeth would try to strike up a conversation but she gave up when I only responded with one-word answers.

Through the windshield, I watched the houses and businesses fly by and tried not to think about Ryder. My body still burned from his lips and hands. His words still rang in my ears; 'I want you, Maddie. I want to fuck you.' *How would I ever be able to forget them?* But I had to. There was no other option.

Soon we were pulling into a crowded parking lot. The frat house sat in front of us, white with enormous pillars. Huge, imposing Greek letters were proudly displayed above the door. Loud, bass-filled music echoed from inside, hitting me like a force when we walked through the front door.

People were crammed inside, making the once regal home come alive with energy. Laughter and yelling competed with the mind-numbing sounds of techno music. Everyone who was anyone seemed to be here.

I pushed my way through the frat boys and sorority girls to a large room complete with a pool table, old-school video games, and a foosball table. Right away, I spotted Ben playing pool with some other frat brothers. When he saw me standing in the doorway, he motioned me over.

"Hi, sweetheart. Wow, you look good," he said, leaning over to kiss me.

It was a light kiss. Simple. Nothing like Ryder's scorching one. *Dammit, why did I have to think of him all the time?*

"Come on, Ben, get in the game," one of the other players said, annoyed.

"I'm out, boys," Ben answered, laying his cue stick on the table. He put his hand on the small of my back and guided me out of the room.

"Do you want a drink?" he asked as we maneuvered our way through the crowd.

"Sure," I answered. Maybe a little alcohol would help me relax and not think of Ryder every single second of the every single day.

Ben led me to the kitchen where tequila, vodka, and other various bottles crowded the countertop. Empty pizza boxes and half empty potato chip bags competed for space with the makeshift bar. The room was packed with people but Ben pushed his way in.

"What would you like? We have beer, margaritas, the hard stuff, or I can make you a mixed drink."

I wasn't exactly an expert on drinks so I went with something girlie. "How about something fruity?"

He grinned. "Coming right up!"

I watched him pour juice into a red plastic cup. Next, he added a shot of something clear.

"Here you go, sweetheart."

A silly grin was on his face, making me wonder how much he already had to drink. Being drunk went against Ben's golden boy façade so seeing him toasted was something new for me.

Unlike Ben, Ryder was notorious for his drinking. Before I left for college, I woke up many nights with him outside my bedroom window, hammered. He spent most of those nights passed out on our couch, sleeping it off until the next day. Ben was opposite. He was always in control, never deviating from his stellar reputation. I was definitely seeing a new side to him tonight but for some reason, I felt uncomfortable with it.

I forced the unease out of my mind and followed Ben, now with a fruity drink in my hand.

In the main room, the furniture had been pushed back against the wall, leaving more room for dancing. The chairs and sofas were still full of couples and wannabe couples, clinging to each other and trying to take things to the next level.

Ben led me into the middle of the crowd and swung me into his arms. "I'm glad you're here," he said, holding me close.

I forced a smile. He looked really nice in his dark jeans and gray fraternity shirt. All the girls liked him and the boys admired him. *So why couldn't I be head-over-heels in love with him? Why couldn't he make me feel like Ryder did?*

~~~~

I lost count of the number of drinks I had. Ben kept refilling my cup, never leaving it empty. The alcohol didn't help me forget about Ryder but I was having a good time anyway.

I was dancing with Ben to the pounding bass when Eva finally arrived.

"I've missed you!" I said, throwing my arms around her and almost toppling her over.

She pulled away, scrutinizing me and frowning. "Have you been drinking, Maddie?"

A giggle burst from me. She didn't look too happy, which was ironic because she was always telling me to loosen up.

"Just a little tipsy," I answered, sweetly.

She rolled her eyes and faced Ben. "What the hell are you doing, Ben? She's drunk."

"Relax, Eva. She's fine. I'm not letting her out of my sight," he said, irritated.

I giggled again as Ben and Eva stared each other down. They looked made for each other. Blonde, tall, tan, and picture-perfect. They were like two Greek gods. And here I was – short, skinny, with dark hair and pale skin. A mortal among Gods.

In a show of ownership, Ben wrapped his arms around me and pulled me close. I wanted to resist but my legs felt like rubber.

"You never drink, Maddie. Take it easy on those things," Eva said, pointing to the drink in my hand. I tried to focus on her face but the room tilted around me.

Ben leaned down to whisper something in my ear but I edged away. He smirked and pulled me close again, this time leaning over for a kiss. I turned my face away just in time, avoiding his lips.

Ben might be beside me but I was still thinking of Ryder. The alcohol wasn't erasing the memory of him standing between my legs or pushed up against me in the bathroom. I wanted to be with him now, not Ben.

Eva grabbed my hand, rescuing me from my terrible thoughts. "Let's go to the bathroom, Maddie." That was her code for 'we needed to talk.' I followed her obediently, stumbling along the way and bumping into a few people.

"No more drinking," she said, shutting the bathroom door behind us.

Maybe that was a good idea. The room was spinning so quickly that I had to sit down on the closed toilet lid before I fell down.

"I'm okay, Eva. I don't need a babysitter," I said around a loud hiccup.

Eva raised one eyebrow. "You sure about that?"

"Don't start!" I hiccupped again. "I've had an awful day so I decided to have a few drinks. No big deal."

"Yeah? Well, Ryder looked like he had a shitty day too. You know anything about that?"

I debated whether I should tell her or not. The alcohol seemed to make it hard to keep quiet.

"He told me he wanted to sleep with me."

Eva's mouth dropped open in shock. "He said that?"

"Well, those weren't his exact words, but yeah, that's what he said," I answered, covering my eyes against the spinning bathroom.

"And what happened? What did you say?"

"Nothing happened, Eva! He's my friend. We can't do stuff like that!"

"What about the friends-with-benefits thing?"

"Isn't happening! I'm waiting on the right person to fall into bed with," I said, trying to focus on her face.

She kneeled down in front of me. "Maybe he is the right person, Maddie. You two are very close and you've known him forever." She thought for a second. "Plus, he's smoking hot."

She had a point. He was extremely dreamy.

"I knew it!" she squealed when she saw my face. "You do like him! So what are you going to do?"

I frowned as I tried to stay upright. Losing my virginity to Ryder wouldn't be such a bad thing. It had lots of appeal. He obviously knew what he was doing and if that kiss was any indication, sex with him would be...amazing. Then there was the fact that he knew me like no one else did. He knew all my secrets. I knew all his. When I was around him, I was happy, complete. But to him, I was only his friend. That's what I'd always be.

"I'm going to do nothing."

Before she could question me again, I made it to my feet and escaped. I couldn't talk about Ryder. I couldn't think about him. If I did, I might race back home to pick up where we left off.

~~~~

The party lasted long into the night. At some point, Ben pressed a shot glass into my hand. I wasn't sure how many of those I tossed back but I was starting to feel numb. It wasn't long before I could no longer think clearly. Eva tried to keep a close eye on me but a few times I managed to disappear without her knowing.

One of those times, I was stumbling out of the bathroom, hanging onto the wall for dear life, when my phone beeped.

Ryder's name weaved in and out on the screen. *Why was he calling me?* My mind was so fuzzy, I couldn't think straight.

"Hello?" I slurred.

"Maddie?" I heard him let out a relieved breath. "I'm sorry. I really fucked things up. I want to talk when you get home."

I couldn't hold back the giggle. He sounded so polite, not like himself at all.

"Have you been drinking?" he asked, sternly.

"Maybe," I said with another giggle.

There was only silence.

"Hello?" I asked, confused.

"Where is Eva?" He sounded so angry that my giggles vanished.

"I don't know."

"Are you there by yourself?"

"No, silly, I'm here with Ben," I answered as if he was clueless.

"Shit! Go find Eva and stay with her. I'm on my way."

I heard a click then silence. Looking at my phone, I was confused. *Did he just hang up on me? Why would he do that?*

My head was spinning. I tried to remember what he wanted me to do. *Find someone? Or was it something?*

Giving up, I managed to make it down the hallway when I saw Ben heading my way.

~~~~

I had no idea how much time elapsed after talking to Ryder on the phone. A few minutes? An hour? All I know was that I was sick.

"I don't feel so good, Ben."

We were standing in the kitchen watching some freshmen play quarters with shots of vodka. Yells of victory and cries of defeat muddled my mind, overwhelming me with noise. Watching them throw back shot after shot made me want to empty my stomach right there on the floor.

"Follow me," Ben said, taking hold of my hand.

The next thing I knew, we were in a dark and quiet bedroom. I crawled onto the bed, not caring whose room I was in. I just needed to lie down.

"You okay?" Ben asked, leaning over me. He brushed strands of hair away from my flushed face, letting his fingers linger on me.

I was so sick. My stomach was hurting so much that I just knew I was dying. I kept my eyes squeezed shut, trying to block out the spinning room. *Why had I drank so much?*

Suddenly, Ben was kissing my throat and moving his hand to my waist. The smell of alcohol on him was revolting. It seemed to surround me, choking me.

"Ben.... I can't do this," I said, trying to push him off me. My alcohol-soaked mind still thought of Ryder and how it should be him touching me, kissing me.

But Ben ignored me. His hand moved down to my bare thigh. His thumb made slow circles on my skin as his lips moved to cover my mouth.

I turned my head away, nauseated, wanting him off of me.

"Ben..."

"Relax, Maddie. I'll do it fast," he said, pushing my skirt up higher. His short fingernails scrapped my thigh, waking me up to what was happening.

"Ben, NO!" I screeched. I tried to move out from under him but my muscles were weak and wouldn't obey.

"I've waited so long for this." He threw a leg over me, holding me down as his hand ran along my inner thighs.

I pushed him hard, my subconscious screaming at me to run. His heavy body pressed me further down into the mattress, holding me secure. I struggled, trying to kick and hit him.

"STOP!" I shouted. The fog in my mind cleared when his hands started to tug at my underwear. I made another feeble attempt to push his big frame off of me. He didn't budge.

Oh, God! I couldn't stop him!

I tried to crawl out from under him but he just held me down tighter. His hands roamed and squeezed me cruelly, no longer trying to be gentle.

THIS. WAS. NOT. HAPPENING.

I hit him hard with my fist, catching his lower jaw. His grasp loosened for a second and I scrambled away. *Run! Run!* My head was spinning but I was desperate to escape.

I was almost off the bed when he grabbed me around the waist and hauled me back.

"You're not going anywhere, Maddie," he hissed.

I let out a sob as he threw me back under him brutally. When his fingers dug into my hipbone, I yelped with pain.

Before he could grab my arm, I slapped him hard across the face. The sound of flesh hitting flesh rang loudly in my ears. I wanted to do it again and again.

Rage transformed his perfect face into the vision of a monster. Terror raced through me when he grabbed both of my wrists and pushed them above my head, smashing them into the mattress. His fingers squeezed the delicate bones, making me wince.

"BEN, NO!" I screamed, as his free hand reached beneath my skirt again.

"Shut up!" he snarled.

Sobs shook my body. *He was going to rape me, my own boyfriend.* I cried out when he roughly shoved his hand between my legs.

Accepting my fate wasn't an option. I had to fight until I couldn't fight anymore. I was gathering strength to struggle again when suddenly he was no longer on top of me. He just...disappeared.

Shaking badly, I pushed my skirt down and sat up in time to see a fist fly. Ryder's fist. It connected with Ben's face, smacking him to the ground.

"I'm going to rip you apart!" Ryder roared.

Within seconds, Ben had recovered and jumped to his feet. He wrapped his arm around Ryder's neck in a chokehold, cutting off his air supply.

Ryder fought against him, but Ben had a strong hold on him. I scrambled off the bed, wobbling on my feet unsteadily. Grabbing Ben's arm, I tried pulling him off Ryder but he was too strong.

I yanked again, using all my strength. Ben let go of Ryder long enough to reach out and shove me hard. I fell to the floor painfully. My head snapped back and the jolt sobered me up quickly.

Ryder's fist shot out to pound Ben mercilessly on the side of the head. He didn't stop there. He landed a solid punch into Ben's stomach, doubling Ben over in pain. An uppercut to Ben's face had blood spurting out his nose in rivers.

Suddenly, the room was full of people, itching to get a front row seat.

Ryder was back on Ben within a second, pummeling him into a bloody mess. I thought he would never stop but two guys jumped in to grab Ryder, hauling him off the blood-soaked Ben.

"You piece of shit!" Ryder shouted. "You're fucking dead!"

Ben staggered to his feet and got in Ryder's face. "Let's finish this shit," he spit. Before anyone could stop him, Ben nailed Ryder in the stomach using every ounce of power he had.

Ryder grunted with pain but didn't flinch when Ben pulled his fist back for another punch. Before he swung, two more guys raced forward to hold him back.

It was all too much; the fighting, the yelling, the spinning room. My stomach protested and I started gagging.

"Let me go!" I heard Ryder yell. A second later, he was beside me.

"God, Maddie, you look terrible," he said, picking me up off the floor.

His body felt warm and safe as he cradled me against him, carrying me through the house. The next thing I knew, we were outside in the heavy rain. Ryder moved quickly across the muddy yard, protecting me from the rain with his body but my stomach churned with each step he took.

"Put me down. I'm going to be sick," I groaned.

Ryder eased me to the ground, where I crumbled to my knees like a rag doll and lost everything in my stomach. I felt him behind me, holding my long hair, angling his body over mine protectively.

After the dry heaves passed, he silently picked me back up. I was in and out of consciousness, hardly aware of what was happening.

Unlocking the car door, he put me in the passenger seat, reclining it as far back as it would go. His arm reached across my lap to buckle my seatbelt securely. I was soaking wet from the rain and shivering. With the absence of his arms around me, I grew cold.

Ryder started the engine then looked over at me in the beam of the streetlights.

I thought he looked stunning despite the bruises already darkening his face. I wanted to reach out and touch his strong jaw. I wanted to pull him toward me to repeat our kiss.

But blackness took over.

Chapter Six

I slowly woke to a pounding headache. The screeching of a cell phone radiated pain through my skull. I was afraid if I reached over and answered it, my head would explode and every muscle in my body would scream in protest.

Someone moved beside me, rustling the sheets, making the bed dip. My heart rate quickened when Ryder sat up to lean over me. His arm stretched across my chest, turning off the cell phone. After it was silenced, he loomed above me, looking down and studying me closely. His face was lined with exhaustion and worry. I felt responsible for putting them there.

"Maddie, thank God you're awake," he said, lying back down beside me. His arm brushed against mine as he scrubbed a hand over his face.

I attempted to sit up but my head throbbed, sending shooting pain everywhere. I peeked over to find Ryder staring at the ceiling. *What was he doing in my bed?*

"What happened?" I asked. My voice sounded hoarse, my throat raw from vomiting.

Ryder looked over at me. His jaw was covered in black stubble and his lips were set in a firm, hard line.

"You were blindass drunk. Threw up about a hundred times. I was scared to death you had alcohol poisoning." His eyes dropped down to my lips. "Don't do that to me again, Maddie."

"Why were you at the party?" I whispered, grimacing from my sore throat.

He turned to lie on his side, facing me. "I needed to make sure you were okay." His eyes ran over my face slowly, studying each feature. "I found you barely conscious with that shithead holding you down. You spent half the night in the bathroom, throwing up, before I finally carried you in here."

I felt ill as all the memories rushed back. Ben's hands on me, holding me down. His unwillingness to stop. The feeling of helplessness. I felt abused, vulnerable. When the tears splashed down my face, I didn't try to stop them.

"Shit!" Ryder swore. Reaching over, he pulled me toward him. I went willing. His arms wrapped around me, holding me close. One hand stayed on my waist while the other cradled the back of my head.

"You're safe," he said so quietly that I almost didn't hear him.

"Thank you for taking care of me." I said, sniffling.

"I'll always take care of you, Maddie."

~~~~

I woke up later to an empty bed. I felt colder, lonelier lying here without him. A forbidden thought raced through my mind - *What would it be like to sleep next to him every night?* I chastised myself. Thinking that way was wrong on so many levels. I forced the thought from my pounding head and crawled out of bed. Throwing on a faded tank top and shorts, I headed for the bathroom.

The girl staring back at me in the mirror was a fright. Smeared mascara, a bad case of bed-head, and pale, greenish skin made me look like the walking dead. I quickly stripped and took a fast shower, scrubbing last night away. But no amount of soap could replace the loss of my dignity.

As the remains of last night washed down the drain, I thought of Ben. I needed to call him. After last night, it was definitely over between us and the sooner he knew, the better. That relationship died the minute he refused to take 'no' for an answer.

But first I needed coffee.

The apartment was eerily quiet. I found Eva sitting at our small kitchen table with her eyes glued to a laptop.

"Maddie! Oh my gosh, are you okay?" she asked when she saw me.

I almost started crying again as I nodded and took a seat beside her.

"Ryder told me what happened. I'm glad he beat the crap out of Ben."

"Ben was drunk," I said, cringing when I heard my own words. It sounded like a lame excuse for what he tried to do.

"No man should behave that way, drunk or otherwise." She narrowed her eyes at me. "You sure you're okay? He didn't…do anything did he?"

"No, but if Ryder hadn't got there when he did…" I didn't finish the sentence, the thought too terrible.

She offered me her Starbucks coffee, which I gladly took. The hot liquid felt wonderful going down my parched throat, warming my insides.

"Stay away from him, Maddie. The man is psycho."

"I know. I'm ending it. I just have to tell him," I mumbled, resting my head in the palm of my hand.

"Don't confront the bastard by yourself. Wait until Ryder's around. He won't let the asshole touch you again."

"Okay," I agreed, wanting to end this conversation. I didn't want to talk about Ben anymore. The less I thought of what he tried to do, the better grasp I could keep on my sanity.

"I feel awful. Remind me never to drink again," I said, rubbing my forehead. One night of hitting the bottle was enough to last me a lifetime.

"So…" Eva leaned toward me with a mischievous gleam in her eyes. "When I got home last night, the two of you were sitting on the bathroom floor and you were draped all over Ryder."

I felt embarrassed, knowing I probably looked pathetic.

"I've never seen him look so scared. He wouldn't leave your side. It was romantic in a grotesque kind of way since you were puking your guts out."

"Eva, it was..."

She interrupted me. "I also know he slept in your room. And this morning, he came strolling out, looking all sexy and giving me strict orders to take care of you." She rolled her eyes. "Like I wouldn't anyway."

Her eyes narrowed when she saw the blush on my face. "I want details."

I took a deep breath and let it out slowly. "There are no details. He just wanted to make sure I was okay so he stayed in my room." I shrugged my shoulders indifferently. "You know how he is." Ryder was always saving the day. Even my childhood was filled with him rescuing me. My own personal superhero.

Eva sighed, probably hoping for a juicer answer. "The guy is such a badass but when it comes to you, he's a big baby."

"Where is Ryder anyway?"

"No idea but he took your car," she said, taking the coffee from my hand to take a sip.

I jumped when my cell phone vibrated, emitting a low hum on the table. Before I could grab it, Eva picked it up and glanced at the screen. When she saw who it was, her back stiffened.

"Ryder doesn't want you to have it. But here." She held the phone out to me like it was a ticking time bomb. "He's been calling nonstop. Answer the damn thing and tell him to go screw himself."

I took the phone from her, knowing instantly who it was. Ben. Seeing his name sent a tingle of fear down my spine. I tried to ignore the feeling, knowing I would have to face him eventually. For now, I let the call go to voicemail. Scanning through the phone, I found numerous missed calls and text messages from him.

U ok? I'm SRY.
Acted like a fool.
SORRY
Call me. Plz.

My voicemail was full of messages from him but I couldn't bear to hear his voice. I deleted them all, wanting to erase all traces of him from my life.

"So I guess you're not going to tell me what happened between you and Ryder?" Eva asked.

"No, because nothing happened."

She sighed with disappointment. "Fine, but if something happens, you better tell me."

I nodded, which was a good enough answer for her. Turning back to the laptop, her fingers started typing furiously.

"So my dad's having a major meltdown about this war. Have you seen all the shit going on?"

"I watched some of the news yesterday. Why? What's happening?" I asked, half listening since my head was pounding.

"Well, the terrorists are now threatening us with a nuclear weapon, saying they can drop it on us at any time.

The Pakistanis, Afghanis, Iranians, North Koreans, and Syrians are all gathering forces so the U.S. is sending more and more troops overseas. It doesn't look good. This war might go global," she said, clicking between pages.

I thought again of Ryder enlisting. *How could I let him go, knowing he was going into a war that he may not return from?* I knew, without a shadow of a doubt, that I wouldn't survive if something happened to him. *How could I when he meant so much to me?*

Eva shut the laptop, jerking me out of the terrible thoughts. "On a happier note…last night Brody called and asked me on a date."

I sat up straighter, my headache forgotten momentarily. "That's great, Eva!" I said, truly happy for her.

Brody was Eva's on-again, off-again boyfriend. They were inseparable in high school but broke up the first semester of college. Since then, they had broken up and gotten back together too many times to count. One minute they were in love, the next they hated each other but I knew she secretly missed him.

"I invited him to go out with us tomorrow night."

I shook my head firmly. "I can't. The way I feel, I'll still have a hangover tomorrow."

"Please, Maddie? I need you with me so I don't do something crazy like go home with him."

I chewed the corner of my lip in indecision. I was Eva's wingman. She always had my back and I always had hers. I could drag myself out again. *I was such a pushover.*

"You owe me," I said.

"Thank you!" she cried, jumping up and grabbing her laptop. "I've got to hurry or I'll be late for work. Again."

She turned around and walked backward, facing me. "And remember, Maddie, no Ben without Ryder."

I nodded and waved her away. After she left, I dragged myself to the living room and plopped down on the couch. My eyes wandered over to Ryder's duffle bag. A dark blue shirt was neatly folded on top and a pair of scuffed boots sat next to the bag, looking right at home in my apartment. I thought of him in those boots - dancing close to me on the dance floor, fighting for me last night, and saying he wanted me. *Ryder wanted me. Would I ever get used to that idea?*

My phone chirped, reminding me of the one man I didn't want to think about.

"Hello?"

"Hi, Maddie. Why haven't you returned my calls?"

"Sorry, Ben. I've not been feeling well thanks to all those drinks," I said, sarcastically.

"I'm sorry. Can I see you?"

I didn't want to answer.

"Please? I need to see you," he said with a whiny voice. *Why was I just now noticing how annoying that was?*

I dreaded facing him after last night but knew I had to end this. "You can stop by for a minute. We need to talk."

"Great! I'll come by after work."

The happiness in his voice was irritating. *Did he not remember trying to force himself on me?* What happened to the man I first met? He had become Dr. Jekyll and Mr. Hyde. Perfect one minute, a monster the next.

After hanging up, I laid down. I just needed to close my eyes and lose the searing headache. I needed to escape Ben and thoughts of Ryder.

~~~~

The closing of the front door jerked me awake. For a second, I was terrified that it was Ben, using his spare key but I was relieved to see Ryder walking in.

Butterflies took flight in my stomach. His light brown hair was perfectly disheveled and the stubble on his chin made him look amazing. His jeans hung on his hips, teasingly. The simple t-shirt couldn't hide his perfect physique or the badass tattoos on his arm. For a man who spent the last twenty-four hours drunk, fighting, and taking care of me, he looked very good.

Glancing at me briefly, he sat a paper sack and a Starbucks cup on the coffee table in front of me.

"Still sick?" he asked, sitting down at the end of the couch.

I sat up slowly, still feeling woozy. "I'm okay," I said. *Never again would I drink.*

"I bought you coffee and donuts."

"Thank you." I picked up the cup and took a sip. My eyes closed in bliss. *My favorite!* Mocha Frappuccino with whip. Opening up the paper bag, I let out an audible sigh. Two chocolate glazed Boston Cream donuts stared back at me, full of wonderful sweetness.

I looked over at Ryder. In that moment, holding the coffee he remembered I loved and my absolute favorite donut, I knew that I was hopelessly in love.

"I thought something sugary might help you feel better," he said, watching as I pulled a donut from the bag.

I licked the chocolate off of my fingers and smiled at him. My grin quickly disappeared when I saw desire flaring in his eyes.

"Want one?" I asked, holding the donut out to him.

"Nope. They're all yours."

I watched as his jaw clenched hard and his fingers rubbed down his thighs, making me remember them stroking me. *I had to stop thinking this way. It would only get me in trouble.*

I started eating the donuts slowly, afraid my stomach would revolt if I ate too fast. By the time I was finished, my headache was back with a massive force. I lay back down on the couch, leaving my feet to dangle off the edge.

A comfortable silence stretched between us as we watched the news. Again, war and terrorist threats were the main headlines.

I was starting to drift off when Ryder threw a blanket over me. Reaching down, he lifted my legs into his lap. I tensed when his hand rested on my calf, warm and rough against my skin.

"Relax, Maddie. I'm not going anywhere," he said, quietly. "I'll still be here when you wake up. Trust me."

And I did.

~~~~

Ryder and I spent the rest of the day lounging in front of the television. I was too sick to move and Ryder refused to leave my side. At some point, I must have slept because I woke up to a dark room and Ryder asleep beside me. His hands were warm on the bare skin of my legs, keeping me immobile. In his sleep, he didn't appear very dangerous but I knew better. The bruises on his face, the ink racing up and down his arm, and the always-present five o'clock shadow on his jaw told a different story. This man was nothing but danger.

I didn't care. I wanted to crawl into his lap and wake him. Tell him to love me. But I did neither. Instead, I picked up my phone and tried not to groan when I saw the time. *Ben would be here soon.*

After easing away from Ryder, I went into my bedroom to change. A simple tank top didn't give me enough protection against Ben. I needed to be covered, every inch of my skin hidden.

I was digging through my closet when I heard Ryder walk in. His eyes moved casually over my unmade bed, making my imagination run wild with what we could possibly do in it.

"Feeling better?" he asked, stopping close by me.

With shaky hands, I hurried to button a shirt over my tank top.

"Yeah." I paused a second, knowing this wasn't going to be pretty. "Ben is coming over in a few minutes."

Before my eyes, Ryder went from relaxed to someone cutthroat, ready to battle. He flexed his fingers and tightened them into fists. The blueness of his eyes turned cold and harsh.

"Shit, Maddie! I don't want you around him! He almost raped you last night!"

"Ryder…"

He started pacing, furious. With a roll of his shoulders, he clenched his fists, reminding me of a fighter about to enter the ring.

"I don't want you near him."

"Ryder, I'll be okay."

"Just like you were okay last night?" he asked, disgusted. "If I hadn't shown up, what would have happened? Could you have fought him off?"

When I didn't answer, he scoffed. "I didn't think so. Since I saved your pretty little ass last night, you owe me," he demanded. "Stay away from him."

Did he just call my bottom pretty? I shook the thought from my head. That wasn't important right now.

"I don't need someone to save me! I'm not a little girl anymore!"

"Believe me, I know…" he grumbled as he ran a hand through his hair, frustrated.

"And what about you? I pushed you away but you didn't stop kissing me. That's okay?" I asked, growing angry.

He backed me further into the room, advancing on me boldly. "I would never, NEVER hurt you, Maddie!" he shouted.

"That's what Ben would probably say too!" I yelled back, standing my ground and refusing to cower.

"The difference is I mean it! You mean everything to me! You always have!" he shouted, inches from me.

I blinked in confusion. *I meant everything to him?*

A strange look crossed his face. He seemed surprised to hear his own words. Backing away from me, he rubbed a hand through his hair, looking everywhere but at me.

Finally, his eyes met mine. Desire, raw and powerful, stared back at me. My heart started beating double time and my breath quickened when I saw the craving on his face.

This was it. The moment when I decided what to do. Kiss him or walk away? Give him what he wanted or keep my innocence? I took a step toward him, knowing what I wanted. But fate had other plans.

The doorbell chimed loudly.

"Shit!" Ryder muttered.

All desire fled my body. I instantly went cold. Ben was here.

"Stay in here. Let me handle this," I told Ryder, silently pleading with him not to lose control.

"If he touches you, he's not walking out of here in one piece," he promised. "One finger on you and he's dead." His eyes turned hard, making me believe the threat.

I gave him one last pleading look before walking out of the room, hoping he wouldn't do anything stupid. Trying to control my overheated body, I crossed the apartment. With each step, I reminded myself that Ryder was off-limits. My feelings and screaming nerve endings could go to hell.

Opening the door, the one person I didn't want to see stood there, looking cool and classy as always.

Ben.

He moved past me into the apartment, striding with cockiness. When he brushed against me, the shaking started in my hands and spread to my other extremities. Fear of him was making me ill. I couldn't get the image of him holding me down out of my head.

He turned to face me with a pained expression on his face. "I'm so sorry, Maddie. I was drunk last night and got out of hand. Please forgive me?"

Watching Ben warily, I came to the realization that I had never loved him. I had only been fooling myself for the last couple of months. There was always something missing between us that I could never figure out. Now I knew. He didn't know me. He never did. Maybe the 'perfect' man wasn't right for me. Maybe I needed someone else.

"We need to talk, Ben," I said, keeping a safe distance from him.

He took a step closer. "Don't say anything, Maddie, hear me out first. I never should have given you so many drinks or taken you to that bedroom. I'm sorry. I was drunk and you felt so good in my arms…but I would've stopped, I promise."

He seemed so sincere and trustworthy, hiding behind a perfect gentleman mask. If I had been any other girl, I might have believed him but I wasn't any other girl. And I would never trust him again. I knew where my heart lay and where it always would.

"It's over, Ben."

"WHAT?"

"We're finished." *How much simpler could I say it?*

"Why?"

"I don't want to be with you anymore," I answered.

"You can't do this, Maddie!"

A shiver of fear ran down my spine when he advanced on me, backing me up against the wall. He spread his legs on either side of mine, boxing me in and leaving no way of escape.

I opened my mouth to cry out for Ryder when Ben's face filled with rage.

"You'll regret this, Maddie! I'm not giving up that damn easily!"

In two strides, he was out the door, slamming it shut behind him.

I closed my eyes. *He was gone. I was okay.* With trembling hands, I pushed away from the wall.

A great weight had been lifted off of my shoulders. Ben wasn't what I wanted or needed. I wanted someone who knew me, the real me. I needed the person who knew all my secrets and fears. I wanted a person who fought passionately and lived passionately.

I wanted my best friend.

Chapter Seven

Taking a deep breath, I walked down the hallway to my room. With each step, my heart pounded harder.

I found Ryder standing in the shadows, looking menacing and dangerous next to my rumbled bed. He waited for me to speak, watching me with blazing eyes.

"I broke up with him," I said.

With two strides, he was in front of me. My breath caught at the hungry look in his eyes. I opened my mouth to speak but never got the chance. His lips stopped me.

He kissed me hard, causing fire to explode within me. An involuntary moan escaped at the feel of his lips against mine. There was nothing simple or gentle about it. He possessed me.

"What are you doing to me, Maddie?" he rasped against my mouth.

I didn't answer him. I couldn't.

His lips covered mine again as his hands pulled me further into the room. The back of my legs hit the edge of the bed as his lips ravaged me. His tongue was hot as it swept into my mouth. My tongue met his, earning a deep moan from him.

Long fingers tangled in my hair, bringing me closer to his body. The space between us disappeared. My hands had a mind of their own as they ran up his arms, feeling the bunching of muscles beneath my fingers. I let out a weak sound of pleasure as his mouth moved down my neck, searing me with heat.

He grabbed a fist-full of my hair and gently yanked my head back, giving him more access to my throat, leaving me at his mercy.

"I want you so much," he murmured before his tongue darted out to touch my burning flesh. "I've never wanted something so damn much before."

This was all new for me. Him. Us. The warmth spreading down my body. The hunger I felt for him. For his touch. For his lips.

For him.

I threaded my fingers through his silky hair and pulled him to my mouth again. He obliged me, hungrily possessing my lips, hard and urgent.

Within seconds, he had me on the bed, never breaking our kiss. My hands moved on him. His hair. His shoulders. Lower. I wanted to explore all of him.

Suddenly, he sat up, pulling me along with him. With impatience, he ripped my shirt off. With another yank, my tank top followed. I saw him swallow hard as his eyes dropped down to my lacy bra. Ever so slowly, he ran a finger down between my breasts. His eyes followed the path, taking in the view in front of him. I should have been embarrassed. I should have been worried. I wasn't. This was Ryder. This was meant to be. I wanted him to be the first.

"You okay with this?" he asked, his voice thick with desire.

I could only nod. My brain was in overdrive right now.

He eased me down to the bed. Leaning over me, he kissed the swell of one breast. His hand moved to my back, caressing my skin along the way. With a smoothness born of experience, he unhooked the clasp on my bra. Ever so slowly, he slid it off of my shoulders, leaving me bare. His eyes drank in the sight of me lying beneath him, his for the taking.

Then, *oh, sweet Jesus*, he touched me. His hand cupped my breast, fitting me into the palm of his hand as if I was made for him. One of his fingers flicked lightly over my nipple and I couldn't help but arch my body at the sensation.

He chuckled low at my reaction.

"You're beautiful," he whispered, glancing up my body to meet my eyes. "I'm almost afraid to touch you. But I have to. God forgive me, I have to."

He dipped his head and his warm breath moved over my exposed breasts. My flesh seemed to come alive as his lips hovered above me. With something that sounded like a growl, his head descended, taking my nipple into his mouth. I couldn't hold back a gasp. The feeling was new and unlike anything I could have imagined.

I grabbed a fist full of his hair and urged him closer. His tongue swirled around and teased. Sucked and nipped. He moved to give the other nipple just as much attention. Hands cupped both my breasts as his mouth worked to drive me crazy.

I thought I would come unhinged.

As his mouth tortured my breasts, one of his hands traveled down to rest at the top of my shorts. I wanted his hands everywhere on me. Touching me. Exploring me. Inside me.

"I need to hear you say it, Maddie. Tell me you want this," he demanded as his fingers teased me, running an inch below my waistband.

"I need you," I said, hoarsely.

He moved back up to possess my mouth again. *Please, more!* I opened my mouth slightly and he deepened the kiss, his tongue meeting mine. His hands pushed my shorts down, achingly slow. As soon as they were out of the way, he ran his fingers under the elastic of my panties, touching me.

I sucked in a breath.

"Do you want me to stop?" he asked as his mouth moved to my neck.

I tried to think but it was impossible with his fingers...*Oh, God! There! Where my heat was, where my need was.* They were just giving me a taste of what was to come and I wanted more.

"No stopping," I managed to say as my breath hitched from what he was doing to me.

"Say it again," he demanded, taking my nipple into his mouth.

His tongue was going to kill me.

"Don't stop."

His fingers started moving, slipping inside me. A shudder worked its way from my toes to the top of my head. I grasped at his arms, needing to hold onto something solid as his fingers teased me without mercy.

I was going to fall to pieces beneath him. I didn't know how it could get better than this.

His mouth left my breast to slash across my lips. At the same time, he pushed the silk panties down my legs with a frenzied need. I kicked them off quickly, not caring where they landed. His hands moved to his jeans and I heard a zipper lower.

In a flash, his jeans and shirt were gone and he was lying on top of me. His fingers tightened in my hair, holding my head still as his tongue explored my mouth again.

When his knees nudged my legs apart, I obeyed, moving so he could settle between them. His erection bumped against me, searching for entry.

"Tell me no," he whispered as his body rocked against mine. "Tell me to stop. Because I need you now. I can't wait any longer."

I didn't want him to stop. I needed him like I've never needed anything before in my life. I craved him. I had to have him.

"Then don't wait, Ryder. Make love to me."

At my words, he took my mouth roughly. His tongue thrust inside, branding me as his, owning me.

Suddenly, he moved away from me. I moaned with disappointment, feeling empty.

"Just a second," he said, leaning over the bed.

I heard him searching the floor for his jeans and then he returned to me. His lips covered mine again, making up for that second of lost time. While his mouth tormented me, the sound of a foil package being open resounded throughout the room.

His hands drifted down my ribcage, leaving my nerve endings screaming for more. Stopping at my hips, he grasped me with both hands as he settled between my legs again.

That's where I needed him.

As his strong lips dominated mine, he pushed against me. I tensed as I felt him enter. As if it was the most natural thing in the world, I wrapped my legs around his waist, needing to get closer to him. One of his hands grabbed a fistful of my hair while the other hand intertwined with mine. His fingers tightened, both in my hair and on my hand, as he plunged his entire length into me.

I gasped at the pain. My body stiffened at the intrusion.

"God, you're so tight," he rasped as he held still inside of me, letting me get used to him.

Breathing hard, his body tensed as he pulled halfway out and plunged back into me again, harder this time. I threw my head back and cried out as his fullness filled me.

His lips found my neck, brushing against my skin.

"You feel incredible, Maddie. So damn tight," he said, his breath hot against my throat. "Does it hurt?"

"No," I answered. *It felt amazing.*

"Good."

His hips rocked against me, pulling away then plunging ahead, picking up speed. The friction caused my back to arch, thrusting my breasts closer to his waiting mouth.

As his skillful tongue teased one of my nipples, he started moving faster. His hand let go of mine to hold my bottom. His fingers dug into my flesh while the other hand stayed tangled in my hair.

A new sensation, unlike anything I've ever experienced, rolled through me. I felt every nerve ending come alive. Incredible intensity washed over me. I felt as if I was on the verge of falling into an abyss. An abyss full of nothing but pleasure.

I moved beneath him, wiggling, wanting, and begging. The orgasm rippled over me, flooding my body with an ecstasy I didn't think I could handle. Wave after wave hit me, almost making me weep. I wanted to scream with pleasure. His lips ravaged mine when I did.

I was slowly spiraling down, returning to earth, when he increased the rhythm of his thrusts.

"Fuck, Maddie!" he moaned against my mouth as he drove into me. Faster. Harder. Deeper.

When I grabbed his hair, he groaned deep in his throat and his hips started pumping frantically, reaching for his own release. With one last powerful thrust, he stiffened above me. A long tremor vibrated through his body.

"Hell," he whispered, breathing hard.

I kissed the corner of his mouth, uncurling my hands from his hair. He caught my chin in one hand and claimed my lips, giving me a deep kiss.

My skin felt alive and flushed. Every nerve ending screamed AGAIN, AGAIN! I took a deep breath, trying to control my racing heart.

"Are you okay?" he rasped.

I nodded, my body still humming. He lowered his head and kissed me again, tenderly this time. Taking me with him, he rolled onto his side. His hands ran over my spine, pulling me against him. Squeezing my hip possessively, his lips brushed against mine.

The amazing heat coming from his body relaxed me but one thought raced through my mind - *I just lost my virginity to my best friend.*

Chapter Eight

Somewhere outside a car horn beeped. I peeled my eyes open and shut them quickly when bright sunlight blinded me through the bedroom window.

Stretching carefully, I glanced over at Ryder. He was sleeping peacefully on his stomach, one arm draped over my waist. The sheet was wrapped around his hips, barely covering him. Thick eyelashes rested below his eyes, hiding the cool blue irises from the early morning light. He took up most of my bed, leaving me to either hug the edge or sleep next to him. I had chosen him all night.

Everything replayed in my mind. Each touch, each kiss was branded in my head and on my body forever. *Sex with Ryder.* I bite my lip and glanced over at him again. *Holy shit, I slept with Ryder!* The bad boy, the ladies' man, the boy I grew up with. It had seemed so right to lose my virginity to him, to do something I swore I wouldn't do until I was in love. I had no regrets. *How could I, when I loved him?* Had always loved him.

I suddenly felt shy. He had touched me in places I had never been touched. His body had claimed mine like no one else's. But I didn't know what to expect in the light of day.

I slowly started to ease out of bed when my cell phone rang loudly, the sound ear-piercing. Reaching over, I quickly grabbed it before it could wake Ryder.

"Hello, sweetheart!"

It was my dad, sounding unbelievable too chipper this early in the morning.

I sat up in bed and pulled the sheet tighter around me. Sheer embarrassment had me panicking. My dad was calling, I was without a stitch of clothing on, and Ryder was naked in my bed. *Was there a worse time for a daughter to talk to her dad?*

"Good morning, Dad" I whispered, glancing over when Ryder started to stir beside me.

"I just wanted to call and check up on you. Did I wake you?"

"I was awake. You doing okay?"

"I'm fine, honey. Trying to stay out of this heat." He cleared his throat and I knew the small talk was over.

"Is Ryder still staying with you?"

"Yes," I blushed. *If he only knew…*

His voice turned serious. "Listen to me, Maddie. If something happens, I want you to go with Ryder. Stay with him. Do as he says. Understand?"

The lingering glow from last night fled, replaced by a chill at his words. He sounded distressed, worried. *Was he feeling bad? Was it his heart again?*

"Dad, what's going on?"

"Things are unraveling with this war and if anything were to happen…well, just promise you'll stay with Ryder."

"Okay," I said, frightened.

I felt Ryder sit up behind me. Glancing over at him, my mouth went dry. The sunlight hit his body, showcasing each muscle to perfection. The tattoos marking his arm and back flexed as he threw the covers off of him. He stood up, naked as the day he was born. A blush colored my cheeks as his perfectly formed buttocks filled my vision. I couldn't tear my eyes away.

"He'll keep you safe," my dad said, reminding me he was still on the phone. "Ryder won't let anything happen to you."

"Don't worry about me. Just take care of yourself," I said, trying to control the rapid beating of my heart as Ryder tugged on his jeans.

My dad sighed. "Okay, sweetheart, I'll let you go."

I clicked my phone off and watched as Ryder put on his shirt and avoided looking my direction.

I have to talk to him. I needed his reassurance that everything was okay. That we were okay.

"Ryder?" I asked, hesitantly. I clutched the sheet tighter around me, suddenly feeling the need for extra protection.

He looked down at me coldly. His icy blue eyes ran over my body quickly, without any emotion.

I didn't know what to expect but I was surprised to see coldness staring back at me. My stomach plummeted and my hands started shaking. I immediately had a bad feeling.

"What?" he asked, flatly. His frosty eyes stayed on me as he buckled his belt buckle.

"We need to talk." *Was my voice shaking as bad as my hands?*

"What's there to talk about?"

"Us. What we did last night."

"We had sex. I acted insane, which is not surprising around you," he smirked, sarcastically. "It was a mistake. It shouldn't have happened."

A mistake? I swallowed past the sudden lump in my throat. *Last night meant nothing to him? Had I been stupid to think otherwise?*

"What do we do now? I think this changes things between us," I said, trying to hide the hurt.

He cursed under his breath and ran a hand through his hair. "Shit, Maddie. What do you want me to do? Marry you? Put a ring on your finger? It was only sex."

I flinched. He said it so callously as if what we did meant nothing to him.

"But, Ryder…."

Motioning between the two of us, he laid on more hurt. "We're just friends, Maddie. That won't change. But I told you before, I don't do relationships and I don't have girlfriends. You knew that before you crawled into bed with me."

My heart felt like it was breaking into a million pieces. Pieces that rested in the palm of his hand, easily crushed and easily forgotten.

"So I'm just another notch in your damn belt?"

"You know that's not true," he said with harshness, becoming angry.

"How do I know it's not true? I just became another one of your one-night stands!" I screeched with more hurt than rage.

"Listen to me, Maddie," he said, crawling next to me. His hand went to my thigh, resting there and bringing back memories of last night. Regardless of his cold words, I wanted him again. *Damn my treacherous body!*

"Look at me," he said, softly.

I looked at him with hurt, dying a little from his words.

"Being with you was…hell, it was beyond anything I could imagine but if we took this further, if we tried to make this work, I would just screw it up like I do everything else. Everything I touch turns to crap, Maddie. I can't let that happen to us. No matter how much I want you, I'm not willing to lose you."

I tried to process his words but the ache wouldn't go away. He wouldn't lose me after fifteen years of friendship, no matter what he did. *Didn't he trust me more than that?*

"You're not going to lose me but I think this…"

His fingers wove through my hair, pulling me into his lap. His lips slashed across mine, quieting me. I felt my insides melt as his tongue ran lightly along my lower lip.

"Maddie, for once just shut up," he whispered against my lips. He kissed me gently again before setting me aside and rising from the bed. Without a backward glance, he walked out of the room.

I sat stunned. I tried to make sense of what had just occurred. One minute he wanted me, the next he swore it was a mistake. One minute he was telling me the sex meant nothing, the next he was kissing me with unleashed passion. Confusion was playing havoc with me. *How could I pretend that nothing happened or that I didn't have feelings for him?* He wanted me to believe he was cold and uncaring. But I didn't. Not for one moment.

Making up my mind not to lie around and cry, I crawled out of bed onto wobbling legs. After running a hand through my hair and throwing on a shirt and shorts, I opened up the bedroom door to the smell of freshly brewed coffee.

Across the hallway, the closed bathroom door mocked me, symbolic of Ryder slamming the door on our newfound relationship. But the sound of the shower teased me, luring me to Ryder and his body again.

I ignored the yearning and went in search of that coffee.

~~~~

In the kitchen, I found Eva eating a burnt piece of toast. She looked up when I walked in and raised her eyebrows.

"You look like you had a rough night. What happened?"

I sat down across from her and gathered my knees to my chest, hugging them tightly.

"We had sex," I said, studying my pink toenails.

She almost choked on a mouthful of bread. "What? With Ryder?"

I nodded, waiting on the preverbal shit to hit the fan.

"I knew it!"

I cringed. It wasn't worth a celebration. At least, not anymore.

Eva's wide smile disappeared when she saw the forlorn expression on my face. "Are you okay, Maddie? He didn't hurt you, did he? Because if he did, I'll kick his ass out the door."

"No, of course he didn't hurt me." I sighed. "It's just that this morning he said we could only be friends. He said it was nothing but a mistake." I hurt beyond words. The urge to cry was strong but I refused to shed a tear. I was stronger than this.

"The dumb shit. He loves you, you know."

I looked at her like she was crazy. Ryder didn't believe in love. Everyone knew that.

"It's obvious the way he looks at you. He'll come around, Maddie, just give him time. And if he doesn't, well…screw him! Oh wait, you already did," she said, smirking.

I couldn't hold back a smile at her lame attempt at humor.

"I've got a date with Brody and you just lost your virginity." She leaned closer and whispered dramatically, "and I never thought you would, by the way. Thought you would be a hundred year old virgin. I think this calls for breakfast at IHOP. It'll make you feel better."

I wasn't sure food would cure me of Ryder but before I could argue, he walked into the kitchen.

All the air was sucked from my lungs. His hair was wet from his shower and his chiseled jaw was clean-shaven, leaving his face baby-smooth and begging for my fingertips to caress it. He smelled like soap and aftershave, intoxicating scents. The sight of him had me feeling weak all over again. I tried to ignore the fluttering in my stomach but the memories of last night had the butterflies going crazy.

He eyed Eva and me warily, waiting for us to pounce.

Eva cleared her throat and stood up to throw away her half-eaten piece of toast. Walking past Ryder, she gave him a look that threatened bodily harm if he didn't behave.

"You told her, didn't you?" he asked, taking a seat across from me and watching me closely.

"Yes, she's my best friend so I tell her everything. Is that a problem?" I asked, daring him to argue.

"No, but she's going to make my life a living hell."

"Good. You deserve it," I snapped.

Lowering my feet to the floor, I stood up to leave the kitchen. I needed a shower and some space. If he wanted to act as if nothing happened, that's what I would do.

"We're going to breakfast as soon as I get out of the shower. You coming?" I asked, walking away. I hoped I sounded like I didn't care what he did, but my voice was shaking too bad to sound convincing.

Reaching out, he wrapped his long fingers around my wrist, stopping me.

"You should have told me no, Maddie. I would've stopped. I would've ended it before we went too far. I know you want it all. Love, a relationship. But I can't give that to you. I won't because I'll just end up hurting you."

"I guess we'll never know, will we?" I snapped, yanking my wrist from him. I narrowed my eyes at him, wanting to know the truth. "Tell me, Ryder, was it worth it? Did you get what you wanted?"

He shot to his feet, shoving his chair back to tower over me.

"Don't talk like that, Maddie." His voice was low, threatening. Not scary at all.

I closed my eyes, hiding the desire that flared again. When I felt under control again, I opened them.

"I've got to go," I whispered.

I made myself walk away. If I remained, I would have kissed him. Or done something silly like told him I loved him.

Chapter Nine

I scooted into a booth and was surprised when Ryder slid in next to me. Any other day, I wouldn't think much of it, but now, I was so confused by his actions and words that I just wanted to scream in frustration.

Feeling nervous, I tried to look anywhere but at him. My eyes landed on the flat screen TV on the opposite wall. Multiple scenes played out, leaving me stunned. A newscaster looked frazzled as he read the news. A clip of soldiers moving through a desert played on a loop along with a shot of fighter jets taking off for parts unknown. And in big red letters, the words "Threat Risk Rising" blinked across the bottom of the screen.

For a moment, my relationship with Ryder was forgotten. Not only did I feel as if I was falling apart, but it seemed the world was falling apart too.

Eva noticed me watching TV and turned to look at it over her shoulder. She let out a loud sigh. "I hope this doesn't put us in another world war."

"Chemical warheads, nuclear bombs, death threats – its war," Ryder mumbled, looking over the menu.

I peeked at him out of the corner of my eye. Strands of hair fell over his forehead and curled around his ears. I couldn't hold back the blush that traveled up my neck when I remembered grabbing his hair while he was deep inside of me, taking my innocence.

I took a deep, cleansing breath, determined to act normal and ignore my raging hormones.

"Is your dad worried?" I asked him.

Ryder's dad was ex-military. Special Forces to be exact. He kept up on all current affairs, both military and political. When he wasn't running a ranch, he was a survival expert. For as long as I could remember, Robert Delaney believed in stockpiling supplies in preparation for a national catastrophe. Most people thought he was crazy. I just thought that the things he saw while serving in the military made him realize how vulnerable we were in an emergency.

Ryder's father also insisted that everyone in his family learn how to survive. Ryder never took his dad too seriously. He had always been more interested in girls and parties than in worrying about the end of the world.

His ice blue eyes turned to look at me. "My dad is always worried." He glanced at the TV and shrugged. "I'm sure he's watching the news around the clock and driving my mom crazy with all his end-of-the-world talk. They're going to shit a brick when I tell them I'm enlisting."

I chewed on my lower lip, worried. I knew that sex with me wouldn't stop him from enlisting. It might make him more in a hurry to leave. There was nothing holding him here, including me, but I had to try.

"You can't enlist, Ryder," I said. The words came tumbling out faster. "You just can't. You would be sent overseas immediately. I don't want you to go. Stay, please."

He looked over at me, hiding his emotions. "Maddie, you don't understand. I can't be here. I have to go."

"No, you don't," I said with conviction. "I'll forget everything if it means you won't enlist."

Ryder's eyes slowly moved to my mouth. Leaning toward me, his voice dropped, sending vibrations through me. "Could you really forget last night, Maddie? Because I won't."

A now familiar flush ran over me. I couldn't help but wiggle in my seat, feeling need flood my body. I wanted to crawl into his lap and kiss him, beg him to stay. His eyes alone were setting me on fire. A blush warmed my face as pictures flashed in my mind – him touching me, nudging my legs apart, and taking me hard. No, I would never forget.

"What you kids want?"

The Texas drawl of the waitress snapped our attention away from each other, bringing us back to reality. She waited impatiently for us to place our orders, the pen in her hand tapping on her pad of paper.

Ryder turned to her with a friendly smile. The woman seemed to melt under his gaze. I understood the feeling.

After she took our orders and left, Eva started talking nonstop about her date with Brody. I tried to listen. I nodded when I was supposed to and I commented when she expected me to but it was hard to focus on the conversation while trying not to focus on Ryder.

What was I going to do? How did you stay friends with someone you had sex with? He was right - I couldn't forget last night. The memory would always be lingering between us, waiting to bring me to my knees without warning. *How were we going to get past that?*

Maybe he was right. Maybe it had been a mistake. I loved him and that frightened me. But not having him as a friend frightened me more.

~~~~

Back at the apartment, I walked out of my bedroom ready to go for a run. I needed a few miles of mindless running to clear my mind. Looking down at my Ipod, searching for the perfect song to run to, I almost bumped into Ryder. He was standing in the hallway, talking on his phone. His expression was grave as he held the phone to his ear and glanced down at me.

I skirted around him, putting my earplugs in and heading for the front door. Halfway there, my phone chirped in my hand.

Ben's face lit up the screen. I really didn't want to answer but I knew he would call over and over until I did.

"Hello, sweetheart," his voice said, sounding genuine and happy.

"Hey, Ben."

Why was he calling me sweetheart? It seemed so endearing before but now it graded on my nerves. *And why was he calling me anyway?*

When he heard Ben's name, Ryder's head whipped around, looking at me sharply. Eva also glanced up from her magazine to watch me warily from the couch. I was uncomfortable with the stares but I refused to be intimidated. Ryder had no right to be jealous. He made that very clear when he said there was nothing between us.

"So I know we broke up but I wanted to see you tonight," Ben said.

"I don't think that's a good idea, Ben. We're over," I said, glancing at Ryder. His eyes never left mine as he said goodbye to whoever he was on the phone with and walked further into the living room.

"At least tell me where you will be tonight," Ben said.

Before I could give him a vague answer, the call dropped, leaving only silence. I hung up, thankful for the bad reception. It saved me from trying to explain again that it was over between us.

Ryder's eyes were cold as they watched me. I could practically see the rage rolling off of him in waves. He didn't say anything but turned and walked to the kitchen, slapping the door open a little too hard.

"Someone's jealous," Eva said as she went back to flipping through her magazine. "Interesting."

This time, I didn't disagree with her.

Chapter Ten

I leaned closer to the mirror and applied some "Pink Afterglow" lip-gloss. The name was appropriate for the way I felt but I tried not to dwell on it as I smoothed down the hem of my dress. Hitting me mid-thigh, the material felt like silk next to my skin. The back dipped low, leaving my spine bare while the front covered me completely. After slipping on a pair of strappy high heels, I took one more glance in the mirror before leaving my bedroom.

When I walked into the living room, Ryder's eyes slowly ran over me, from my heels to my perfectly straight hair. The heat in his eyes disappeared, replaced by anger.

"You can't wear that," he said, rising from the couch slowly.

"She can wear whatever she wants, Ryder. Leave her alone," Eva said, walking into the room and looking great in a short skirt and a pale pink blouse that enhanced her tanned skin and blonde hair.

"Go change, Maddie," he demanded.

"She's not going to change! You aren't her boyfriend, so back off!" Eva lashed out.

It was obvious that Eva was trying to get him to own up to his feelings but I knew Ryder better than she did – he wouldn't break that easily.

"I'll have to fight guys off of you all night," Ryder said hoarsely as his gaze dropped down to my legs.

My heart rate took off for the millionth time in less than a day. As always, he took my breath away. The well-worn jeans looked impeccable on him, sexy despite the frayed edges and faded color. A black shirt clearly defined his well-muscled torso and couldn't hide the ink on his arm. The way he looked, I would be the one fighting women off of him all night.

"Who says I want you to fight guys off me?" I retorted, feeling like a child sticking my tongue out at him.

Ryder took a step closer and opened his mouth to argue but I stood my ground, one eyebrow raised, daring him to continue.

We held each other's gaze for a moment, neither of us willing to back down. Finally, Eva had enough.

"Let's go! We're late and Brody will be waiting."

~~~~

The late evening heat was torturous and I could feel it sucking all the evening's excitement out of me. We stood impatiently in front of the club, sweating and hot as we waited for the bouncers to check everyone's ID.

Ryder kept close behind me. I could feel him inches away as I listened to Eva. I tried to focus on what she was saying but it was impossible with Ryder standing guard over me. By the time we made our way to the front of the line, I was hot and irritated. I handed the bouncer my ID and tried to ignore Ryder.

The big, beefy guy glanced at the card quickly before looking me up and down.

"You're too pretty to be hanging out in this club," he said with a grin.

The guy seemed harmless so I smiled back. A little flirting never hurt anyone. But Ryder had a different theory on that.

I sucked in a breath as his warm fingers slid onto the bare skin of my back. Fire raced along my nerve endings, making my body betray the promise I made to ignore him.

The bouncer's smile disappeared when he saw Ryder's death-dealing stare. Handing my ID back, he motioned us into the club. No one messed with Ryder when he was mad, even a big bouncer. It irked me. But what really got me fired up was when Ryder guided me away, keeping his hand on my back. *Possessively.*

"What are you doing?" I hissed, giving him my best 'how-dare-you' glare. He had no right to be possessive. Men that only wanted one thing didn't get that luxury with me.

"Jerk was flirting with you."

"Why do you care? We're just friends remember?" I said, sarcastically.

Before he could answer, I hurried to catch up with Eva. I needed some distance between us before I screamed at him in frustration.

The music grew louder as I followed Eva deeper into the club. The place was dark and packed. Half of the people were on the dance floor, bodies pulsing and grinding to the thumping music.

Eva spotted Brody by the bar. They were hugging when I walked up.

"Hey, stranger!" I said with a smile.

Brody was tall and cute. He had cropped off brown hair, light green eyes, and a face that every girl loved. He had the trim body of an athlete and the personality of a good ol' boy.

"Hey, Maddie! Wow, you look good!" Brody exclaimed, letting go of Eva to hug me tightly. "I've missed seeing your gorgeous face." His smile slipped then disappeared when he glanced behind me.

I turned around and found Ryder behind me, looking furious. His cold eyes glowered at Brody and his stance spoke volumes – he was ready to pounce and kill.

"Ryder, this is Brody, Eva's ex," I said, stressing the word ex. I wasn't sure I could defuse the hostility rolling off of him but I wasn't afraid to try.

Looking a little nervous, Brody stuck out his hand for Ryder to shake. "Hey, man."

Ryder still looked ready to injure someone but he leaned around me to take Brody's outstretched hand and shake it.

"Wait a minute! Are you 'the Ryder'? As in Maddie's Ryder?" Brody asked with awe.

Redness rose in my cheeks.

"The one and only," Ryder said deeply.

"Well hell, dude! I've heard all about you! You're a legend at home. There are rumors…Is it true you beat the living daylights out of Peter Jacobson in an underground fight ring when you were a senior? You won five hundred big ones in less than five minutes."

"Yeah, that's true," Ryder answered.

"And is it true that you nailed Miss Roland after class one day? On a desk?" Brody asked.

"Disgusting," Eva muttered.

I couldn't help but stare at Ryder with disbelief. Miss Roland had been my high school chemistry teacher. She had been nice and sweet. Also, blonde and young. Just his type.

"That one's not true."

I let out a relieved breath.

"You going to school here?" Brody asked, taking a drink of his beer.

"No. I'm here with Maddie."

Wow. He made that sound so intimate.

"Cool. So are y'all...?" Brody asked, motioning between the two of us.

"Let's dance!" Eva cut in, grabbing Brody's hand and tugging him to the dance floor, saving us from answering his question.

Ryder and I stood in awkward silence. A few inches separated us but it might as well have been a mile.

"I'm going to get a drink. Want anything?" he asked, looking down at me coolly.

I shook my head and watched as he walked away. In a moment of self-pity, I felt out of place. Alone. I was here for Eva but I didn't belong here, pretending Ryder and I were just friends, trying to mask what I really wanted.

I glanced over at the bar. Ryder was leaning casually against the glossy wooden counter, looking right at home as he waited for his drink. A smile was spread across his face, lighting up his eyes and making him appear mischievous. But his smile wasn't for me. It was for the redhead standing near him. She was tall and gorgeous. And looked perfect next to him.

Tears stung my eyes as he laughed at something she said, his eyes crinkling in the corners. It was now more than obvious that last night meant nothing to him. Nothing except a good time.

I brushed away the tears, refusing to cry. *I was such a fool!* I should have known better. He played me just like he did every other girl.

I had to let him go.

"There you are! Let's dance!" Eva shouted, grabbing my hand and dragging me to the dance floor.

The crowd surrounded us as we pushed our way to the middle of the oak floor. People danced and laughed around me. Happy. Carefree. Not stupid for giving their hearts away.

Hurt squeezed my insides until I thought I would cry. I had given up my virginity – the one thing that I could never get back – for what? A best friend who thought it was all a mistake. A man incapable of loving. *What had I been thinking?*

"What's wrong?" Eva asked.

"Ryder is standing at the bar flirting with someone. Proving I was just an easy lay."

"Forget him!" she yelled over the booming music.

If only I could.

~~~~

Eva coaxed me to start dancing and threatened me if I didn't. I moved to the music but thought of Ryder. I scolded myself each time I scanned the crowd for him, hoping to see him heading my way. Praying to see him smile at me like he smiled at the redhead.

One song rolled into another. I never saw him. I cursed him silently. I raged at him for staying at that bar, flirting, smiling, maybe touching someone else.

I was just beginning to enjoy myself when a hand inched around my waist.

Damn, him! I will not be his plaything! I whipped around, planning on giving him a piece of my mind.

"Hello, Maddie."

A thread of fear slithered through my veins. My stomach dropped and my voice left me.

Ben stood next to me, a smirk on his face and his fingers tight on me. The smell of alcohol on him was overwhelming.

My limbs started shaking, making me feel weak. When I looked at him, I felt as if I was suffocating, gasping for my last breath. A cold chill raced along my skin despite the heat of the club.

He took a step closer. His clammy hands rested on my waist, feeling like weights against me. I managed to wrangle out of his hold and take a hasty step back. My heartbeat pounded loudly in my ears, making thoughts impossible.

"What the hell are you doing here?" Eva asked, pushing me behind her.

"I came to talk to her. Back off, bitch!" he snapped, snarling down at her with unleashed hate.

Eva's eyes rounded with shock and her anger disappeared, replaced by fright. She was speechless as he pushed her out of the way to get to me.

"Ben, you need to understand that it is over between us," I said firmly despite the trembling of my body.

"And you need to understand that I love you. I can't let you go. I won't." Snatching both of my hands, he yanked me toward him. I tried to pull away but he held tight. His fingers bit into my wrists painfully, cutting off the circulation.

Panic flooded me. *Oh, God! Not again!* I struggled to break his hold but he just pulled me tighter against him.

"LET HER GO!" Eva shouted as she tried to pry his hands off me. He transferred my wrists to one hand and shoved her away again. This time she stumbled backward and almost fell.

Tears swam in my eyes from the excruciating hold he had on me.

"Ben, please let me go," I begged.

"I can't, Maddie!" he cried hoarsely, jerking me to him hard. "I can't tear you out of my mind!"

I looked to Eva. I tried to send her a silent message to go for help. I had no idea where Ryder or Brody were but I needed someone. I couldn't fight Ben on my own. Eva gave me a helpless look but I felt a glimmer of hope when she pulled out her cell phone and start texting quickly. I knew then that Brody or Ryder would be on their way soon.

Ben turned around and started to drag me off the dance floor. I dug in my heels, refusing to go easily, but he just tightened his hold on my wrists and yanked. My bones felt as if they were breaking under his strong hold.

"Ben, you can't do this!" I cried loudly, frantically looking around for help. That's when I saw Ryder and Brody.

The murderous look on Ryder's face scared me as much as Ben's crazed one.

"Get your fucking hands off of her!" Ryder roared, pushing people out of the way to reach us. His fierce eyes darted down to the bruising hold Ben had on me. If possible, Ryder's expression became even more deadly.

Ben let go of me and threw his hands up in a nonthreatening gesture. But I doubted he was giving up that easily.

Ryder stepped between us, pushing me behind him with one hand pressed to my hip. He didn't remove his hand but kept it on me, keeping me behind him.

As much as I hated to admit it, I felt safe now that Ryder was here. We might have messed things up between us but I knew he would protect me at any cost.

"I love her, man! Don't keep her from me!" Ben sobbed, incoherently. "I love you, Maddie," he wailed in grief, swaying on his feet.

"You need to get it into your shitty head that it's over between you two!" Ryder said, taking a threatening step toward Ben but still standing rigidly in front of me, hiding me from any danger.

"Man, she doesn't...."

"She's mine now, asshole," Ryder growled.

The sorrow suddenly disappeared from Ben's face. In its place, I saw hatred so terrible that I reached out to pull Ryder back. He didn't budge an inch.

"So she's finally letting someone between those tight legs?" Ben asked, an evil grin splitting across his perfect GQ face.

"Shut the fuck up," Ryder snarled between clinched teeth. I could feel the flexing of Ryder's biceps under his shirt, wanting to throw a punch.

"You may have been the first but I'll be the last," Ben sneered. "The very last." Without a backward glance, he turned and disappeared in the crowd like an apparition.

Ryder's fist clinched, ready to explode. When he started to push through the crowd, I knew he was going after Ben. What would follow would be bloody and leave some nasty bruises. Or worse.

Reaching out, I grabbed a handful of his shirt, stopping him.

"Ryder!"

Turning around, his cold eyes peered into my brown ones.

"Forget Ben. Stay with me," I said softly, repeating his earlier words to me. The words I would never forget from that day in the bathroom. "Dance with me."

He threw one last glare into the crowd. I watched as the tension slowly ebbed out of him. The savage look on his face disappeared, replaced by a mask of cool indifference. Taking my hand, he led me to the middle of the dance floor.

Putting his arms around my waist, he pulled me close. I wasn't sure what to do with my hands. *Should I rest them impersonally on his shoulders or wrap them around his neck like I wanted to?* I decided to rest them on his shoulders. This was the same man who said we could only be friends.

"Did he hurt you?" he asked, moving slowly to the music.

"No. I'm…I'm okay," I answered. But I was still shaky with fear.

"I should have been with you. I'm sorry," he said huskily, his eyes burning down into mine.

I remembered the redhead he was flirting with. "You were busy."

He looked at me sharply. "Hell, Maddie. You saw that girl talking to me, didn't you? It was nothing. Trust me."

"It's okay, Ryder. You can do whatever you want."

"Shit!" he said, frustrated.

I flinched at his harshness.

"Maddie, I'm doing what I want. I'm here next to you." His hands moved to the small of my back and pulled me closer.

My heart raced as he looked down at me. Desire was evident in his eyes. I wondered if mine reflected the same.

We moved slowly to the song, swaying back and forth on the crowded dance floor. Ryder's hands ran up my back, lightly caressing the skin exposed by the low back of my dress. Delightful shivers followed the direction of his hands.

"You said I was yours," I said, remembering his words.

He leaned down to whisper in my ear. "You're off limits." His lips touched my ear, feather light against my skin. "I feel guilty as hell for sleeping with you but I want you again, Maddie. I've been fighting it all day."

My body heated with those words.

"I keep telling myself to leave you alone, that once was enough but I don't think it will ever be enough. I need you. I need you under me. On top of me. In front of me. I just fucking need you."

One of his hands moved to hold the back of my head. My lips parted as his mouth descended on mine, hot and urgent.

Flashing lights swirled above us. Couples moved around us. But no one existed but him and me.

We stood on the dance floor, our lips hungrily tasting each other. One of his hands reached down to cup my bottom. He pressed me against him, searing me with heat, proving to me how much he wanted me.

"Scream at me. Tell me not to touch you again," he rasped against my lips.

"I don't want to," I whispered.

Without another word, he took my hand and led me off of the dance floor. Pushing through the crowd, he led me to Brody and Eva.

"Can you take Eva home?" Ryder asked Brody, straight to the point.

Brody nodded, confused.

Ryder didn't say anything else. He just led me toward the exit with my hand still in his.

"Wait, Ryder!" I said, pulling him to a stop when I realized we were heading for the door. "Where are we going?"

"I want you home. In bed. Now. I'll be lucky if I can wait until we get there," he growled, hungrily.

I was surprised my skin didn't catch on fire as his scorching gaze slowly looked me up and down. I now knew what it felt like to be undressed with his eyes.

He grabbed my waist and yanked me closer. I landed hard against his chest.

"You look so damn sexy in that dress. I want to yank it up right now and have my way with you," his voice said low. His hand moved down to squeeze the back of my thigh, pushing the hem of my dress up a little at the same time. Teasing me, taunting me to let him do his worst. Or best.

"And those legs..." His thumb ran lightly over the skin of my thigh as his voice rasped in my ear. "They are begging to be wrapped around my waist while I'm deep inside of you."

I was new to this whole sex thing but *oh, my!* I could have had an orgasm right then and there. Instead, I blushed at the idea of him taking me again.

But reality rudely pushed its way into my mind, like a royal bitch that had to get her way. *What about us? Was I turning into his bed buddy? Here at his beck and call when he was ready?* I wanted to go back to the apartment with him and have a repeat of last night but I also wanted so much more.

I bit my lip with indecision. I couldn't live with myself if I went willingly, ignoring what my heart said. Even if he didn't want more, I did.

"What about us, Ryder?" He looked pained for an instant but I continued. "I need more than sex, you know that. I mean, I want you more than anything but how do we do this?" I asked, motioning between the two of us.

He blew out a frustrated breath. "Shit, Maddie, you're killing me," he mumbled, rubbing a hand over his face. "I…I just don't know."

Those three words – 'I don't know' – broke my heart and a small part of my spirit.

"Okay, I get it," I whispered, looking away. I couldn't let him see how much this hurt.

He took my face in his hands, making my eyes meet his.

"No, listen to me, Maddie…."

I interrupted, putting a hand up to stop him. "I need a minute, Ryder. Just a minute."

Before he could stop me, I turned and hurried away. To the ladies' room. To safety. I needed to get away from him before I agreed to whatever he wanted.

Inside the crowded bathroom, I wet a paper towel and dabbed my forehead and neck. Brushing the hair away from my face, I leaned closer to the mirror. My face was flushed and I didn't recognize the strange look in my eyes. *Was it desire or love?*

I took a shaky breath and pinched the bridge of my nose. *How was I going to resist him at every turn and with every heated look or touch he threw my way? Was I that pitiful?*

No. I was stronger than this.

Pulling myself together, I headed out of the bathroom. I could deal with him. I just needed to say no. N.O. Such a simple word but so hard to say to Ryder.

I scanned the crowd. People were packed together like sardines, making it impossible to discern one person from another. I had only gotten a few feet from the bathroom when someone tugged at my arm.

I turned around, expecting Ryder. My heart froze to find Ben.

"Ben! What are you doing?" I shouted over the music, trying to untangle myself from his arms.

"Maddie, why can't we work this out?" he whined, jerking me closer.

Panic wiped all other thoughts from my mind. I went rigid with fear. Frantically, I looked around for help. *If I screamed would anyone come to my aid?*

His fingers tightened. I tried to yank my arm free but he had a death grip on it. Bruises were already forming where his fingers dug into me.

"I love you so much. Please…"

"Ben! LET ME GO!"

He grabbed both my wrists and hauled me closer. I was now completely immobilized against him. Chills raised the hairs on my nape as his hand roamed over my back.

"I should have been the first," he snarled, his fingers crushing my wrists.

I opened my mouth to scream for help when everything changed.

The club shook violently.

The building moaned in protest. Lights flickered. The crowd stood frozen in confusion. Music continued to blare loudly but all talking and laughing had ceased.

An earthquake? An explosion? Oh, God! A bomb? My mind went crazy with possibilities, dismissing each one as ridiculous.

My hands were still encased in Ben's strong hold but I didn't care. I was still trying to comprehend what was happening.

Suddenly, people started yelling. A few screamed.

The club groaned and the floor vibrated.

Then the place went pitch black.

Chapter Eleven

Screaming. Pushing. Shoving. Blackness. Chaos surrounded me.

I was blind. The blackness all-consuming.

I shook in fright. Bile rose in my throat, making me nauseous.

People rushed by me in the darkness, desperate to escape. Someone bumped into me. Ben's tight hold on my hand kept me upright. When he yanked me toward him, I yelped with pain. It felt as if every one of my fingers were being pulled out of the socket. But I stood my ground as Ben tried to pull me again.

"COME ON!" he yelled when I wouldn't budge.

I couldn't leave. I had to find Ryder. And Eva. I couldn't leave without them. Using all my strength, I wrenched my hand away. Severe pain, unlike anything I've felt before, shot through my fingers.

Suddenly, Ben wasn't beside me anymore. The crowd had swept him along, heading toward the exit.

Pandemonium reined around me as I turned around, confused. The paralyzing fear and the pain in my fingers was making it impossible to think straight.

I knew I needed to find Ryder and Eva. I couldn't leave until I found them. *Stay together! Stay together!* I started to push my way against the mass of panicked people shoving and pushing to get to the exit.

The darkness made me blind to my surroundings. The screams and cries echoed around me, making the scene horrific. Nightmarish.

I tried to concentrate on where I was going and ignore the pounding of my heart. I had made it a few steps when someone shoved me backwards. Somehow, I stayed on my feet despite the jostling of the crowd.

My lungs worked harder. It seemed the terror was sucking all the oxygen out of the room. Without air conditioning, the club was becoming hot quickly. With the press of so many bodies trying to get out, the heat was suddenly unbearable.

I pushed forward but was propelled backward almost immediately. A new kind of panic began to bubble up inside of me. I was too short to fight this crowd, most of who towered over me, but I had to get back to Ryder and Eva.

Someone hit my shoulder roughly. Another person bumped my side painfully. I wobbled on my feet, trying to maintain my balance against the surge of people running by me.

"Ryder!" I screamed, struggling to fight the crowd. The only answer was screams and the sound of running feet.

I cried out when someone shoved me hard. The force sent me down. I put my hands out to stop my fall but it was no use. My head smacked against a chair with a sickening thud. Pain exploded behind my eyes, making me feel as if I was hit with a brick. I fell flat to the floor as stars twinkled across my vision.

Get up! Get up! The pain in my head didn't matter right now. Later. I would deal with it later. For now, I had to get up.

Suddenly, a heavy boot slammed down on my hand. When I felt bones crunch underneath the weight, I screamed a blood-curdling scream that could wake the dead.

Before I could recover, a sharp high-heel stepped on my back, right on top of my ribs. The pain was excruciating but only one thought raced through my head; *oh, God! I was going to be trampled to death!*

NO! NO! Dammit, I wasn't dying today! Despite the agony, I forced myself to my feet. When I was standing upright, the first thing I did was kick off my heels. They would get me killed. My life was more important than a pair of shoes.

My ribs were on fire and my head throbbed with the smallest movement. Instinctually, I clutched my injured hand to my chest. If someone brushed against it, I was afraid I might pass out from the pain.

Hysteria bubbled up but I pushed it back down. I had to think rationally. It was the only way I could make it out of this alive.

I took a few steps forward when someone slammed against me. My ribs screamed in pain but I was determined to get out of the stampede of people. They would kill me if I didn't.

A woman not much bigger than myself fell against my back, propelling me toward the bathroom doors. It was just the momentum I needed.

I cowered in the doorway of the women's restroom, safe for the moment. By now, my eyes had adjusted to the darkness but I could barely discern one person from the next as they rushed past me.

It had now been, what, five minutes? It felt like an hour. I prayed that Ryder and Eva were okay, that they had gotten out.

Now that I was safe, I stifled a cry. *What was happening?* The shouting and wailing continued around the club. *Why was it still dark? Don't they have generators in this place or at least some emergency lights?*

If it had been an earthquake, I knew I needed to get out of the building but I was terrified of being trampled. I wasn't strong enough to fight my way out and I was injured. My hand was possibly broken and I was having trouble breathing, either from a cracked rib or because of utter terror, I didn't know. All I knew was that I had to leave. *Okay, I could do this! Suck it up and get out of here!*

I was just about to take a step into the madness when I heard my name called.

"MADDIE!"

A sob broke from me. *Ryder!* The uncontrollable shaking started. First my hands, then my whole body.

"MADDIE!"

He couldn't see me yet.

"RYDER!" Yelling for him took all my energy and hurt like hell.

"RYDER!" I screamed again, growing scared that he would walk right past me. Tears raced down my face, blurring my vision. *Oh, Jesus, what if he couldn't find me!*

A sob caught in my throat when a hand touched my face and I felt him beside me.

"Maddie! Thank God!" His thumb lightly wiped the tears from my cheeks as he shielded my body from the danger.

"I thought I lost you," he said hoarsely as his hands threaded through my hair. Leaning down, he kissed me with desperation.

With my good hand, I reached up to grip his shirt as his lips turned gentle on mine. I thought I would never see him again. I thought my last words to him would be in frustration.

He broke the kiss off to shout loudly over the screaming. "I'm not going to let go of you, okay?"

"Okay…Okay," I stammered with fright.

He grabbed my good hand and tucked me in close to him. We moved into the crowd with only one purpose. Escape.

When we finally cleared the heavy front doors, a blast of summer heat hit us with vengefulness. But the scene outside the club didn't hit me; it smacked me hard, making my legs lose all power of motion and my feet become lead.

Groups of people stood together, huddled in shock. People were crying and wailing all around us. A few were lying in nearby patches of grass while people bent over them, tending to injuries. The worse was the sound of screaming from inside.

Ryder tugged on my hand, reminding me to move and make my legs work again. We quickly weaved between the cars, heading for Eva's truck.

The pavement was hot on my bare feet but I ran anyway. My breathing was forced and ragged, each breath causing pain. Something was wrong but I didn't notice. All I noticed was the darkness.

A cloud passed across the full moon, obscuring all moonlight. The streetlights above us and the storefront windows around us were dark, dead.

There was no light anywhere.

We were yards from the truck when a loud screeching filled the sky. The sound was so ear-piercing and high-pitched that it threatened to bust my ear drums. I let go of Ryder's hand to cover my ears, cringing at the noise. Looking up, I gasped in alarm.

An airplane was flying very low above our heads. So low, I could see each individual window. The 747 had its nose down and was soaring toward the ground rapidly. *No, it wasn't flying. It was falling.*

Silence descended around me. There were no more cries from the crowd. Everyone was watching the plane.

The large buildings around us blocked the view as the plane flew out of sight. Seconds later, there was a loud boom that shook the ground. The earth vibrated underneath me. Ryder grabbed my arm to keep me from falling.

"Oh, shit!" he said, looking up at the sky.

A huge bloom of smoke rose in the distance, grey against the dark sky. *Did…did that plane just crash?* I felt all the blood drain from my body. *What was happening?*

Ryder tugged on my arm, urging me to run.

I tore my gaze away from the horror to follow him through the parking lot. We were feet away from the truck when I saw Eva and Brody. My tears started falling faster as I let go of Ryder's hand and ran to them.

Eva grabbed me tightly, throwing her arms around me as tears fell down her face.

"We didn't know where you were! Oh my God, Maddie, I thought you were dead!"

Despite the pain in my side and hand, I squeezed her hard, never wanting to let go.

"We need to go! NOW!" Ryder said, glancing around us. The urgency behind his words was frightening.

"I'm going with y'all!" Brody yelled, grabbing Eva's hand and running with her over to the passenger side.

"Fine! Just get in!" Ryder shouted.

He pushed me into the truck as Eva and Brody climbed in. I tried to hold back a wince when I scooted across the seat. My ribs were on fire, my head was pounding, and it was impossible to use my injured hand but I moved as quickly as I could.

Eva started crying hysterically from beside me, reminding me that I wasn't the only one scared.

"What the hell is happening? Was that a freakin' plane that crashed?" Brody shouted.

No one answered. We couldn't.

Ryder's crisp black shirt rubbed up against my quivering arm. The shaking was worse now and I couldn't control it. It was as if I had no control of my muscles. I just wanted to curl up in a little ball and close my eyes to the absolute terror but my instincts were telling me to run and run fast.

Ryder took a deep breath and turned the key in the ignition. The truck roared to life. He floored it and the wheels screeched in protest before taking off.

He drove through the parking lot at breakneck speed. We passed people sitting in vehicles, not going anywhere. A few had their hoods popped up, as if their cars weren't working.

I didn't ask what was happening. The fear threatened to choke me. Pain and shock made words impossible.

The truck jumped over a curb to hit the main road. Ryder was driving so fast that the buildings we passed were nothing but a dark blur in the night.

I expected to hear fire trucks or police sirens but there was only silence. *If an earthquake large enough to shake buildings and blow all the electricity just occurred, shouldn't emergency vehicles be on their way? Shouldn't the area be ablaze with red and blue police lights?*

Something wasn't right. I started to feel woozy. Tired. Lifeless. My eyes started to lose focus, turning everything into a blur.

A sharp curve appeared in the road ahead. Ryder didn't slow down but instead hit the gas. As the truck took the corner too fast, I was thrown against him. I tried not to cry out but the pain was too much.

Ryder looked down at me sharply. "What's wrong? Are you hurt?" he asked with panic.

I felt something wet run down my face. Reaching a hand up, I smeared the wetness away from my cheek. *What was that?*

"Answer me, Maddie!" Ryder shouted.

I winced, his loud voice hurting my head.

"I fell in the club. Was trampled," I said, drowsily.

I suddenly felt the need to lay my head down. *Must be from the adrenaline rush leaving my system.* I leaned against Ryder. *I needed to rest my head for just a second. That is all I needed. A second.* My eyes drooped heavily.

"Maddie! Maddie!" He nudged me with his arm, forcing me to lift my head.

I just want to rest, I thought with annoyance. I closed my eyes, hoping to sleep.

"SHIT! SHIT!" Ryder shouted as he watched the road. "EVA!" he shouted, glancing over at Eva who continued to cry hysterically.

I jerked my head back up when I heard the panic in his voice.

"EVA! Snap out of it. Maddie's hurt!" Ryder yelled as both his hands gripped the steering wheel tightly.

"What?" Eva asked in a daze.

"Maddie's hurt," he said, sounding upset. He glanced over at me quickly before his eyes darted back to the road. "Fuck! She's covered in blood!"

He yanked the wheel hard to the right, swinging the pickup over to the side of the road. Throwing it into park, he turned to face me. His hands started roaming over me with urgency, making me wince.

Eva had stopped crying by that point and I could hear her rummaging in the glove compartment. A second later, a small beam of light bounced around me.

"Shit! Where is all this goddamn blood coming from?" Ryder shouted as his hands cupped my head and his eyes searched my face.

"Shut the hell up, Ryder!" Eva yelled as she pushed his hands away from me. "Calm down and let me look at her."

"Where are you hurt, Maddie?" she asked.

"Jesus Christ, she's blacking out," Ryder said, sounding far away.

"MADDIE!" Eva shook me and I opened my eyes, not realizing I had shut them again. *How long were they closed?*

"Where are you hurt?" she repeated frantically, shining the penlight over me.

I thought for a moment. *Where was I hurt? All over, pretty much.*

"I hit my head," I weakly said, reaching up to touch my forehead. My fingertips came away sticky and wet.

"I'm bleeding," I said, numbly. I heard Ryder swear as Eva shined the light on my forehead.

"Look at me, Maddie," she said, the nurse in her taking over. She aimed the flashlight at my pupils, leaving me blind for a few seconds.

"You've got a nasty gash on your head," she whispered.

"How bad?" Ryder asked, gravely.

"It looks like a minor head wound. They can bleed a lot. It probably needs stitches but I don't think she has a concussion. Her pupils dilate just fine."

"Shit," Ryder muttered softly.

"Brody, in the glove compartment are some napkins. Can you get them for me?" she asked as her fingertips pushed around gently on my head. I could feel the blood start to trickle down my face and with it, pain.

She took the fast food napkins from Brody and pressed them to my forehead.

"Hold the napkins there to staunch the blood. It should stop soon, I hope."

"YOU HOPE? Do you even know what you're doing?" Ryder snapped, all patience gone.

"Hey! Back off man!" Brody shouted.

My eyelids started to close again, wanting the peacefulness that sleep would bring.

"Both of you stop it!" Eva hissed. She shined the light over my body. "Where else, Maddie?" she asked in a quieter voice.

"Someone stepped on my hand and right ribcage. I probably have some broken fingers. And Eva, I'm having trouble breathing." Three years of nursing school taught me that something wasn't right.

"Fuck! I can't deal with this," Ryder said. He climbed out of the truck and started pacing back and forth outside, leaving the door wide open and the truck idling loudly.

"He's just upset because you're hurt," Eva whispered as she looked at my fingers. "But that's nothing. You should have seen him when we lost you in the club. I thought the man was going to tear the place down with his bare hands to get to you."

"He would try," I said, my voice sounding raw.

"Yeah, I know. Asshole is in love with you."

I didn't have the strength to argue. *What was the point?* She was sticking to her guns on this.

The penlight cast a small amount of light on my hand. I grimaced when I saw my fingers. They were already turning black and blue. One was very swollen, almost twice its normal size.

Eva gently started to move each of my fingers. The pain was excruciating. When she touched the swollen finger, I jerked my hand away with a cry. Ryder quickly reappeared, looking concerned.

"Her fingers are a mess, Ryder. Possibly broken but I'm not sure. They may only be dislocated," Eva said, glancing over at him.

I sucked in a breath as she started to poke around on my ribs. Blackness loomed at the corners of my vision.

"Ryder." His name slipped out between my ragged breathing. The pain was so great that I didn't know if I could handle it. I needed him beside me.

"I'm right here," he said. His arms wrapped around me in the darkness, pulling me toward him. One of his hands took over holding the napkin against my bleeding forehead.

"I'm guessing she has a cracked rib, Ryder," Eva said.

"Does she need a hospital?" his deep voice rumbled.

"Yes, she could use stitches and x-rays," She answered, turning off the penlight. The truck went black again.

Ryder held me for another minute. We sat in silence, unsure what to do.

I was starting to lose consciousness when he slowly unwrapped his arms from around me and let Eva hold the napkin to my bleeding head. Looking out the side mirror, Ryder threw the truck into drive. Turning the wheel sharply, he floored it, whipping the truck around.

"What the hell are you doing, Ryder?" Brody asked, holding onto the door handle as the truck fish-tailed all over the road.

"Going to the hospital," he answered, bringing the truck back under control.

We took a corner at top speed, not slowing down. I slammed against him, unable to keep myself upright anymore.

"Maddie?" he asked, glancing down at me, gauging my condition. "You staying with me?"

I heard the worry in his voice but the grayness at the edge of my vision grew. My eyes closed again.

"Eva, keep her alert, damn it," he snapped, glancing down at me.

"Wake up, Maddie," Eva said, nudging me. "You need to stay awake. If you have a concussion, you can't sleep. You know that."

I nodded weakly and lifted my head. *Open your eyes! Focus!*

For the next few miles, I was in and out of awareness. Each time my eyelids closed, either Eva or Ryder would prod me awake, keeping me alert for short periods of time. The blackness was taking over, capturing me and pulling me under, when a shout brought me back.

"Holy shit!"

I was pulled back into consciousness by the voice. I slowly raised my eyelids, grimacing at the pain in my head.

"Sweet Mother of God! What is happening?" Eva whispered, staring outside the windshield.

Wincing, I sat up straighter to see what was going on. We were at the ER and it looked like a battlefield.

There were people everywhere. Nurses, doctors, patients – too many people to count. Gurneys were being hurried away. Patients in hospital gowns were standing outside, looking lost and frightened. Police officers were barking commands, pointing this way and that, trying to keep order.

It looked like ground zero.

Ryder threw the truck into park in the middle of the road. Next to us sat two abandoned cars and an ambulance, each one with its doors opened, empty.

Turning off the ignition, Ryder tossed the keys to Brody. "Stay with the truck."

Throwing his door open, Ryder got out and reached for me. Putting an arm under my knees, he swept me out the door. I tried not to cry out when his hand wrapped around my ribcage but I couldn't hold back a whimper.

"I'm sorry, Maddie," he said, upset. "God, I'm so sorry."

"Ryder, I can walk," I said, weakly.

"Like hell," he said, looking into the truck. "You coming, Eva?"

I watched Eva scoot over to the driver's side and climb out, looking ready to take on the devil himself.

"Of course," she said.

Ryder turned and started walking, holding me close. The nighttime air had turned humid, making everything wet and sticky. I felt sweat start along my hairline, mixing in with the blood already there and making the gash burn.

The closer we got, the more chaotic the scene. We passed an elderly person clutching her chest painfully. A doctor screamed for help. Someone else yelled, asking if anyone had seen his pregnant wife.

Mayhem reigned.

Ryder made his way through the crowd, carrying me like I weighed nothing. When we passed a doctor performing chest compressions on an older gentleman, I buried my face in his shirt, not wanting to see the devastation around me.

The once sliding doors of the ER were now popped open, allowing people to rush in and out uninhibited. Eva pushed ahead of us, leading the way. Ryder followed, trying not to bump into men and women as he carried me through the doorway. What I saw on the other side had me sliding out of Ryder's arms, appalled.

The ER waiting room was dark and jammed full of people. Screaming, crying, shouts of despair – I could hear it all.

Numerous flashlight beams bounced around the room, shining on one person before moving onto the next. Doctors and nurses ran from room to room, from person to person, their flashlights the only thing lighting their way.

"Come on," Eva said, motioning for us to follow.

Ryder picked me up again, despite my assistance that I could walk.

"I'm carrying you, Maddie. Don't argue with me. I said you were mine and I take care of what's mine," he said in a deep baritone voice that left no room for argument.

Well, when he put it that way, how could I refuse?

We followed Eva into the madness. She led us down a narrow hallway, packed with patients and gurneys. If it wasn't for the small flashlight beams racing around we would have been left blind in the darkness.

"Excuse me, can you help us?" Eva asked, stopping a woman in scrubs.

"I'm sorry, you'll have to wait," the woman said over her shoulder, rushing by without pausing.

Eva looked around, searching for something or someone. Spotting an empty gurney, she pulled us over to it.

"Keep her here, Ryder. I'll see if I can find help."

Ryder placed me on the gurney carefully. The crisp cotton felt warm beneath me, sleep worthy. I just wanted to lie down and rest but knew that wasn't an option, at least not with Eva and Ryder around.

"Find someone soon, Eva, or I'm going postal on this place," Ryder threatened, keeping a hand on me.

"Okay, Ryder. Damn, you're pushy," Eva mumbled.

"For Maddie, anything," he growled.

"DOCTOR RUSSELL!" I heard Eva shout a second later. In the darkness, I could see a flashlight beam bouncing our way.

"Miss Andrews?" a deep voice asked, shining the flashlight on Eva.

"Yes, it's me!"

"What are you doing here?"

I could see the man now. He was older, possibly in his sixties, with grey hair and a small mustache. He looked worn-out and stressed, pushed to his limit.

Seeing his white doctor's coat, I suddenly remembered where we were – Texas Health General, the hospital where Eva completed her ER rotation. This place was her second home.

"My friend is hurt, can you take a look at her?" she asked.

In the dim light, I saw him glance down the hallway with uncertainty. *Surely, he had more important patients to tend to than one with a gash on her head and a few broken bones.*

Looking back at me, he sighed deeply, deflated. "Fine. What's the problem?" he asked, pulling his stethoscope from around his neck.

"Gash on head. Possible concussion. Fingers discolored and swollen. Possible cracked rib," Eva said.

The doctor shined the flashlight on my forehead. I winced when he started to prod and poke at the gash. Next, he took a penlight out of his coat pocket and aimed it into my eyes. Moving the light back and forth, he studied my reaction.

"Gash is deep. Probably needs stitches but not necessarily. Her pupils dilate just fine. No concussion."

He picked up my right hand, holding the flashlight above it. "Fingers are a mess." He gently rested my hand back in my lap. "Lay down, please."

I carefully laid down on the gurney, gasping at the pain that ran all over me. The doctor's hands went to my ribcage, tracing each rib individually. When his fingers pressed against the broken rib, I cried out and tried to curl into a fetal position. Ryder's hand was there instantly; touching me, somehow giving me his strength.

"Yep, one broken rib," the doctor said, matter-of-factly. "Wrap the rib, bandage the hand, and I'll get you some pain meds."

"Wait!" Eva said, reaching out to grab his arm when he started to walk away. "She needs x-rays."

I saw the doctor study Eva quietly, looking indecisive. Finally, he spoke, sounding weary and defeated. "We're without power and the back-up generators aren't working. I'm sorry but there's nothing I can do except give her some meds."

He started to walk away but stopped and turned back around.

"Go home, kids. Lock your doors and don't leave. Something's happening and it's not good. Not good at all."

Chapter Twelve

"There's some major shit going down, isn't there?" Brody asked when we climbed back into the truck, now with pain pills tucked into Ryder's pocket.

"Yeah, we're in it deep," Ryder answered.

The dash lights cast a small amount of light on Ryder's face. I could see his uneasiness. He was always so confident and cocky that to see him like this shook me like nothing else could.

"You going to be okay, Maddie?" Brody asked.

"I'll be fine," I told him. If all that was wrong with me was some injured fingers and a cracked rib, I was pretty lucky. I could have died in that club.

I looked back at Ryder and caught him clenching his teeth. With more force than was necessary, he threw the truck into drive and pulled away. Within minutes, we left the hospital district behind, heading home.

"So what's happening? What was all that back there?" Eva asked, fear making her voice higher-pitched.

Instead of answering, Ryder simply asked, "Anyone's cell phone work?"

Both Eva and Brody tried their phones. "No," they both said in unison.

Ryder reached over and turned the radio on but there was only silence. He switched stations. Nothing. Not even the emergency broadcast could be heard.

Ryder's next words were calm despite what he said. "We're packing and leaving."

My head was still pounding painfully. *Did I hear him correctly?*

"Pack? Where are we going?" Eva asked, confused.

"Where do you live, Brody?" Ryder asked, ignoring Eva's question.

"A mile from the girls' place but I'm not leaving Eva."

"Fine, we'll stop at your place first. Grab what you need and only what will fit in a backpack or duffle bag. Then we'll head to the girls' apartment and pack," Ryder said, gripping the steering wheel tightly. "We need to leave the city immediately."

I cradled my injured hand against my chest and glanced out the windshield, trying to process his words. I began to notice something. There was an emptiness that seemed wrong, unusual. The businesses around us were dark. The streetlights above us were unlit. There were no cars. No people. No lights. This was not normal.

"Why do we need to leave?" I asked, feeling fear.

"When the club first started shaking, I thought it was an earthquake. But when the place went dark, I knew it was something else," Ryder said. He paused as he turned a corner to a residential street. "When I saw that plane go down…I started to think maybe…"

He stopped, the memory of that plane crashing too awful to go on. Finally he spoke again. "Iran, Russia, some of the Asian countries…they all have the power to take out our power grids and they've been threatening to do it. With this war…I think the U.S. just got attacked."

In the beam of the dash lights, I saw his fingers tighten on the steering wheel, turning his knuckles white.

"I think it was an EMP," he said, clenching his jaw. "There are only three power grids in the United States and one of them is in Texas."

"No, that can't be right. It has to be something else," I said, feeling rattled. I had spent a better part of my life listening to Ryder's dad talk about end of the world scenarios. I knew about EMPs, nuclear bombs, and so much more (more than I wanted to know). *Ryder had to be wrong. There had to be another explanation.*

"My dad warned about the possibility of it happening. An electromagnetic pulse. A nuclear bomb detonated high above us. The pulse from the bomb would destroy our electrical grid, frying everything in its path. An enemy could shut down the entire United States and send us back to the dark ages with just a few strategically placed explosions," Ryder said, looking down at me to gauge my reaction. Scared and shocked would describe it.

"If an EMP hit, all electronics would be fried. That means no television, no internet, and no phones," he added.

I watched the truck's lights pierce the darkness around us. A shiver raced up my spine at the nothingness.

"Is that why no one at the club could start their cars?" Brody asked.

"Most car engines have computers so when the EMP hit, they stopped running. We're lucky Eva has this old truck or we would be walking right now," Ryder answered, glancing out his rearview mirror. "Most vehicles before '75 don't rely on a computer to run them."

"So why do we need to leave?" Eva asked.

"Because chaos is going to break out. I don't want to be here when that happens," Ryder said.

My mind went numb. This seemed too surreal, like something out of a sci-fi movie. I thought of my friends, so far away from home, and of my dad, alone in the country. I prayed each of them was safe but especially my dad.

"Are you sure we have to go? Maybe we should wait it out," I said.

"No, we go home. We hunker down and we wait this out," Ryder said, firmly.

"But, Ryder…"

He shook his head, glancing down at me. "I'm taking you home, Maddie, if I have to drag you kicking and screaming."

That had me silent for a moment.

"What if the government can have the power up and running in a day or two?" I asked, obstinately. I was starting to feel like myself for the first time that night, thanks to the pain medication working quickly in my system. But Ryder could always get me riled up and he was doing a good job of it now.

"It might take weeks or months to get the power grid back up and running. I'm not waiting around for the government to fix it. They'll have food rations and curfews set up in days. I'm getting you out of Dodge, Maddie," Ryder said, sternly.

"I'm not surprised this shit happened. These guys have been threatening us with nuclear weapons and bombs for weeks," Brody said, furious at the unknown enemy. "This weakens us. Just what they want. Next thing you know, they'll try landing on our soil."

We were just jumping to conclusions, I reassured myself. *Everything will be okay.*

Minutes later we were pulling into Brody's apartment complex. It was quiet. Too quiet. *Yeah, something was definitely wrong.*

The beams of the truck cut a narrow path through the parking lot, highlighting the cars and trucks that were now just big pieces of scrap metal.

Ryder pulled to a stop near Brody's apartment. "Remember, pack what you can carry and make it quick – ten minutes top."

Brody and Eva started to climb out of the truck when Ryder spoke again. "And Brody, you got any weapons, get them."

His words sent a shiver up my spine.

As Eva and Brody ran to his apartment, Ryder kept watch out the window, ignoring me for the most part. As we waited, I expected to see a raging mob storming us, demanding to have the truck. Obviously, I had watched too many movies.

Sitting up straighter, I tried to take some pressure off of my cracked rib and at the same time force myself to stay awake. The need to close my eyes and sleep was overwhelming me, thanks to the pain pill.

"You doing okay?" Ryder asked as he watched the parking lot.

"I'll survive," I said, touching my fingers. The pain that shot up my arm was excruciating. It wasn't the first time I broke a bone. When I was ten, I had been climbing a tree, trying to go as high as possible, when it happened. Ryder had been standing at the bottom, yelling at me to get down before I broke my neck. I broke my arm in two places instead. But the pain this time was different, made worse by my other injuries.

I felt the gash on my forehead. It was about an inch and a half long and not very deep. A scab seemed to be already forming. Yes, I would survive but maybe with a new scar.

A few tense moments of silence stretched between us. Despite my pain, I remembered what happened between us before the blackout and what he had said since.

"Ryder, I know this is not the time but we still need to talk about us."

"There's nothing to talk about."

A tiny bit of hurt wove around my heart.

"So are we just going to play like nothing happened?"

Ryder sighed deeply with resignation then turned to look down at me. His eyes were bleak.

"Your dad made me promise to bring you home if something happened. He told me to take care of you and that's what I'm going to do."

"He called you?"

The light from the dashboard made shadows play across his features.

"Yeah, you were in the shower. Hard talking to him after having mind-blowing sex with you."

My pain was forgotten. *He thought it was mind-blowing?* I didn't know how to respond.

"And my father threatened me within an inch of my life if I didn't get home in one piece with you," he said with a gruff laugh that held no humor.

"I hope my dad's safe," I said, troubled to think otherwise.

Ryder scanned the parking lot carefully. "He knows my parents are prepared for disasters. When he realizes what happened, he'll head to their place. I'm sure he's more worried about you right now, anyway," he said, distracted. Leaning forward, he stared across the parking lot. "Oh, crap!"

"What?" Terror spread through me quickly.

"Two guys walking toward us. Shit!"

My heart threatened to jump out of my chest. I remembered Ryder's father saying that if society fell, it would be man against man. Survival of the fittest. Were these two the beginning of that struggle?

Ryder laid his arm across my lap, urging me closer to him. His hand rested on my bare knee, reminding me of how short my skirt was.

"Just relax, Maddie. I've got you," Ryder whispered as the men passed in front of the truck and over to the driver's side window. One of the men rapped on the glass with large, meaty knuckles.

Ryder cranked down the window but never removed his hand from me.

"Help you?" he asked in a friendly, Texas drawl.

"You know what's going on around here?" the guy asked. He was beefy with flat brown eyes void of life. He leaned his large arm against the door as the guy behind him sniffed loudly and stared at me with a glassy, faraway look.

"No clue, man. My girlfriend and I were driving home when the electricity kicked off. Must be a problem with the transformer or something," Ryder said, casually.

The leader turned those empty eyes on me. He glanced at Ryder's hand in my lap then slowly ran his eyes up my body. Ryder gripped my knee tighter, warning me to stay silent.

"She okay?" the man asked, motioning to the blood on my dress.

"Yeah. She had too much to drink and tripped over her own feet. She's a clumsy drunk," Ryder smirked, like it was funny.

"Hell, dude, can't complain about a drunk girlfriend," the guy said with a chuckle. "They don't put up a fight, if you get my meaning."

Ryder's body tensed with animosity.

"She may not but I do," he snarled.

A minute ticked by while Ryder and the man stared at each other, both unwilling to back down.

My heart pounded. My hands were shaking. Any second, I expected the man to jerk the truck door open and haul us out.

The guy must have recognized the deathly threat on Ryder's face because he finally backed down.

"So...my damn car ain't running either," the man said suspiciously as he glanced around the cab of the truck.

"Bad luck, man," Ryder said with a cutting edge in his voice. "Hope nothing else shitty happens to you tonight."

The threat was there, just beneath the surface of Ryder's words, challenging the man to push him further. The stranger heard it too. I thought I saw a tiny flicker of fear in his eyes.

"Hey, let's go," the second guy said nervously, yanking on his friend's arm.

With one more hostile look, they walked away, dismissing us without a backward glance.

Ryder watched them until they disappeared in an apartment.

I let out a breath that I didn't know I had been holding. I knew then that we were sitting ducks in this truck. People would figure out soon that cars were useless. A running truck would be a great commodity when the only other form of transportation was walking. Since we had no way to defend ourselves, fighting off would-be carjackers might be a problem. *And without the truck, how would we get home?*

Ryder removed his arm from my lap to grip the steering wheel tightly. I didn't want to admit it, even to myself, but I wanted to pull his arm back to me. It gave me a sense of security. Always had. I just needed it now more than ever.

"Come on. Come on," he muttered, scanning the darkness for any other threats.

A few more tension filled minutes passed. I held my breath. *What if something had happened to Eva and Brody?*

Suddenly the passenger door flew open, making me jump in fright. Eva and Brody climbed inside quickly, hauling a backpack with them.

Before Brody could close the truck door, we were driving away. The tires squealed in the silence of the night as the truck took off.

"I got all the food and water that I could carry and some clothes. I also have this. A hunting knife," Brody said. A large steel knife gleamed in his hand. It was around seven inches in length, black, and looked razor sharp.

"Keep it handy," Ryder said, keeping his eyes on the road.

The streets were still quiet when we pulled into our apartment complex ten minutes later. The parking lot was dark but there were a few people lingering outside. They looked at us briefly before turning away, rejoining their conversations.

I wondered how long it would take before the reality of the situation set in with the public. I had to agree with Ryder. I didn't want to be in a large city when that occurred.

We pulled into an empty parking spot and Ryder turned off the ignition. Eva and Brody immediately jumped out and ran up the cement steps to our third floor apartment.

Ryder studied me under the moonlight. "Can you walk?"

"I'm fine. Let's do this," I answered with more strength in my voice than I really felt.

I placed my good hand in his and tried to hold back a wince as he helped me out of the truck. My hand throbbed and my ribs ached. Each step sent pain radiating through my skull and body but I had to do it on my own.

Brody handed Ryder a small flashlight as soon as we walked into the dark apartment. Thank goodness our fathers had insisted we have flashlights when we moved to college. At the time, Eva and I rolled our eyes at their overprotectiveness. Now I was thankful.

Seeing my home in utter darkness was upsetting. A few hours without electricity was not a foreign concept for me. In the country, electricity was spotty during storms but this was different. If Ryder was correct, this was an evil set upon us by an enemy.

"Let's get you bandaged up, Maddie," Eva said as she walked out of the kitchen carrying a flickering candle.

"I'll start gathering supplies," Ryder said from behind me.

I followed Eva to her room, the candlelight guiding our way. I gingerly sat on the edge of her unmade bed and watched as she rummaged around in her closet.

The heat was already unbearable in the apartment. After a few hours in here without air conditioning, I think we would all be ready to leave.

I picked the sticky fabric of my dress away from my chest and watched as Eva retrieved a large container from the top of her closet. She placed it on the bed beside me with a grunt.

"Practice equipment," she said, explaining the wide assortment of bandages, ointments, and antiseptic wipes.

"If someone had told us we would be using them for the end of the world, we would have laughed," I said, sadly.

Now that I was in my home, surrounded by my things, my tears started. They flowed down my face, unchecked, running from my eyes like a faucet turned on. The horror of the night was pressing down on me. I felt helpless, afraid, and desperate to forget it all.

"Oh, Maddie, it will be okay! We're safe," Eva said when she saw me crying. Sitting beside me on the bed, she threw an arm around my shoulders and hugged me against her side. "We'll get home."

"And what about school?" I sniffed. "We only have one year left of nursing school! How do we walk away from that?"

"I don't know. Let's take it one day at a time," she said, letting go of me to wrap my injured hand in a bandage.

I brushed the tears away but they kept coming. Things were not going as planned. I was supposed to graduate in one year, not be on the run. Ben and I were supposed to stay together. And Ryder. *God, Ryder.* I loved him but we were supposed to remain friends, never to go into that forbidden zone of love and lust.

"I'll check your fingers later when we have more light but for now, keep them wrapped," Eva said, laying my bandaged hand gently down. "Your head wound will have to wait too."

She eyed me under the candlelight. "Take off your dress, Maddie. It's covered in blood. Then I'll wrap your ribs."

I unbuttoned my dress with one hand and slipped it off. Eva started to feel along my ribcage, gently pushing each rib and running her fingers along the bones. Tears rolled down my cheeks from the pain.

"You're going to be sore and have tons of bruises," Eva said, searching the container for another roll of gauze. "Now where is that bandage? I know I have a large one," Eva muttered to herself as she searched her container.

Sitting on her bed, wearing only my bra and panties, I felt the darkness descend on me, suffocating me in its grasp. I felt as if I was falling and unable to grab something to hold on to.

"I can't do this, Eva," I cried.

"Yes, you can, Maddie. You're the bravest person I know. Don't prove me wrong now," she said.

But I couldn't hold back the tears.

As if he knew I needed him, Ryder was suddenly standing in the doorway, his tall frame outlined in the candlelight. With two strides, he was kneeling on the floor in front of me.

"I can't do this, Ryder," I hiccupped.

His blue eyes studied my face before skimming over my bra and panties. Through my tears, I saw him swallow hard.

"Maddie, listen to me. I thought I had lost you in that club. When I couldn't find you, I went berserk. Then to find out you were hurt…" He stopped and glanced away as pain crossed his face. "Hell, I can't handle it."

Moving closer, he pushed my legs apart to kneel between them, bringing him closer. His large hands cupped my face.

"Look at me, Maddie."

When I did, I saw the blue warmth in his eyes, the candlelight reflected off of them.

"After sleeping with you, I vowed not to touch you again but when I thought I lost you tonight...my world collapsed," he said, his voice husky. "All I wanted was to be able to kiss you one more time. And I did but I'm greedy. I want more."

He slowly lowered his mouth to mine and kissed me with a tenderness that made me ache.

My tears dried up as he leaned into me. I was almost naked and he was between my legs. There was nowhere better I wanted to be.

Eva cleared her throat from behind Ryder, reminding us that we were not alone. I blushed from my head to the tips of my bare toes as Ryder broke off our kiss.

"Her ribs need to be wrapped," Eva said, handing the bandage to Ryder. After he took it from her, she left, leaving the flickering candle behind.

Without a word, Ryder started to wrap my ribs. His hand followed the bandage around me, below my bra, across my bare skin.

"I need you with me, Maddie," he whispered, making another sweep around me with the bandage. This time his hand moved even slower.

"I need the girl who isn't afraid of anything. The one that will put me in my place when I need it. You're the only one that can do that to me. Just you."

With one touch, he took away my fear and left desire in its place. My tears were now completely gone. The pain from my injuries was still there but somehow seemed more bearable. He did that to me. He just made everything better.

"We're doing this together," he said, standing up and gently pulling me to my feet. "I'm not leaving without you."

Leading me to my room, he pulled a pair of shorts and a t-shirt from my closet. I tried to protest when he started to help me put the shorts on but he insisted despite my embarrassment. Next came the shirt. His fingers seemed to linger a bit too long on me but I didn't complain.

"Where's your backpack?" he asked after sternly telling me to sit on the bed.

I pointed to the corner of the room.

He emptied all the paper and pens from the bag. In my closet, he took clothes off of hangers and stuffed them in the backpack. I had no doubt that Ryder would know what I needed.

"What if we can't come back?" I asked.

Ryder stopped to look down at me. Despite the events of the evening, he still looked good in his jeans and shirt. Very unruffled and sexy.

"You can't think that way, Maddie. We won't get through this unless we stay focused and believe things will be fine. If we give up, the terrorists win."

Walking over to my dresser, he yanked open drawers and started pulling out underwear and bras, stuffing them into the backpack.

"You stay here. I'm going to get stuff from the bathroom," he said, his eyes moving over me once before leaving.

After struggling to pull on a pair of socks and running shoes with only one hand, I sat in silence and looked around my room. I was leaving stuff here, pictures and history. Things that couldn't be replaced.

I carefully walked over to my dresser and picked up a picture of my dad. I prayed that he was safe at home, untouched by this nightmare.

I sat the picture back down when Ryder walked in with my backpack slung over his shoulder. He glanced at the bed before looking at me. I blushed, remembering what we did under those twisted, wrinkled sheets. I wondered if he was thinking the same thing.

"Let's go home, Maddie," he said, his voice sounding rough in the darkness of the room.

It was time to leave. I couldn't look back as we shut and locked the door. I didn't want to say goodbye.

Chapter Thirteen

We remained silent as we left the city behind. Each of us was lost in our own thoughts, trying to come to terms with what was happening. Our worlds had just changed. We were confused and scared. Frightened.

As I watched out the windshield, a sense of foreboding filled me. I knew I would never return here. I was now going home for good.

Looking over at Eva, I was glad that she was with me. She had fallen asleep almost immediately. I envied her for that. Now that the medicine was making my pain tolerable, I was too terrified to close my eyes. Too haunted by the situation to sleep.

We were now on the four-lane highway that would lead us further from the city. Cars sat abandoned on the road but no people lingered. If the EMP had hit during the day, chances were slim that we would have been able to leave town so easily. The roads would have been blocked with stalled cars. Panicked people would have been gathering everywhere, making traversing the city a problem if not impossible.

For miles, Ryder kept his eyes on the road and both hands on the wheel. I felt his urgency to get home. We had food and water but not enough to last for days. If, for some reason, we couldn't make it home, we would have a problem. Thirst and hunger would make traveling almost impossible if not deadly.

Ryder looked down at me with worry etched around his eyes. "You okay? Are you in pain?"

"I'm better. The medicine is helping," I said. I felt the gash on my head and winced. It was a good-sized cut that would scar.

"I should have been waiting for you outside the bathroom," Ryder said with self-loathing.

"You had no idea something was going to happen."

He put a hand on my bare leg and stroked his fingers over my skin in a gesture that spoke of more than just friendship.

I studied his profile in the darkness. His eyes remained on the road while his hand stayed on me. Feeling a tiny bit brave, I ran my hand down to his. Without a word, his fingers intertwined through mine, holding my hand.

The wind whipped through the open windows, chasing away the nighttime heat. I saw nothing but darkness outside the windshield. Homes were dark, businesses were dark, even the sky was void of stars tonight. It felt as if we were the only four people left in the world.

Brody broke the silence, asking a question that never occurred to me. "What are we going to do about gasoline? The gas pumps are powered by electricity and since this old truck is a gas guzzler, we'll have to refuel soon."

Ryder let go of my hand to grip the steering wheel.

"We'll have to find a hose and suction gas out of an abandoned car," he said. "It's either that or walk home so I would rather steal the gas."

The thought of walking home made me shudder. We would either fry in this heat or die of dehydration. No, walking wasn't an option.

My stomach growled with hunger as we past a stalled eighteen-wheeler. The picture of a huge hamburger and fries stared back at me along with the world famous McDonald's logo. I thought of all the food inside that would rot in a few days, causing an awful smell. If power wasn't restored quickly, all food would become a commodity, a bargaining chip, a new form of money. And we were passing a truckload of it.

Ryder's deep voice rumbled beside me, dragging my attention away from the hunger. "Why don't you try to get some sleep, Maddie?"

I doubted that I would be able to sleep but it would help me escape reality for a short period of time. With sleep, the pain and fear of the unknown would disappear and when I woke up, we would be all that much closer to home. So I leaned my head back against the seat and closed my eyes, praying for a respite from this hell.

~~~~

The next thing I knew, Ryder was shaking me awake gently.

Sitting up, I winced with pain. My body felt battered and bruised. My broken rib was killing me, my head was pounding, and my finger throbbed with each beat of my heart.

The early morning sun glared through the windshield, making the pavement in front of us shine and shimmer as if it was a liquid river. The lonely stretch of highway loomed ahead, vast and unending. Only pastures and farmland surrounded us. Not a house or person could be seen for miles. We were alone.

Ryder handed me a pain pill and a warm bottle of water. I couldn't help but notice the stubble on his jaw and the exhaustion around his eyes.

"We're taking a break. You want to get out?" he asked, his mouth set in a grim line.

"Sure," I said, with a scratchy voice. "What time is it?" I asked, slowly following him out of the truck.

"Seven maybe? We're trying to avoid towns but it's adding onto our time," he said, rubbing a hand across his face.

In the bright sunlight, I stretched carefully, mindful of my aching body. Ryder leaned against the truck near me, making me acutely aware that he wasn't leaving my side. Crossing his arms over his chest, he stared off into the distance. He seemed relaxed but I knew he would be ready to pounce if danger appeared.

I pushed away from the hot metal of the truck and walked further onto the road, needing to stretch my legs. The blacktop beneath my tennis shoes was hot despite the early morning hour. A slight breeze lifted strands of my hair but it wasn't enough to cool me down. I knew that in a few short hours, the heat would be almost unbearable, making Texas feel like hell on earth.

Ryder was watching me, staring at me with his blue eyes.

"Get out of the street, Maddie," he said in a deep, commanding voice.

Earlier he had been gentle and caring but now he seemed hard and dangerous. This was his don't-fuck-with-me attitude, the one he presented to most people. The one that annoyed me.

"Why should I move? There's no one around," I said, spreading my arms wide and looking around me. "No one's going to drive by and run me over."

"Maddie."

He said my name as a warning, an ultimatum. I heard it. I believed the unspoken threat. I took a few steps closer to the truck and was instantly angry. *Since when did I obey him?*

"Happy?" I snapped, crossing my arms over my chest.

"Always with you, baby."

I sucked in a breath and felt my body leap to attention.

Ryder's gaze lingered on me a moment longer before he turned to Eva, dismissing me.

"You have a map in this thing?" he asked her.

"Yep, in the glove box. Another thing my old-fashioned dad insisted I have. Thank God for over-protective parents," Eva said.

Ryder sauntered over to the passenger side of the truck, his hips rolling with ease. Opening up the glove box, he pulled out a neatly folded map of Texas. Walking to the back of the truck, he lowered the tailgate and spread the map out. Brody joined him, both of them studying the map for the safest way home.

"Let's look at your fingers, Maddie," Eva said when she noticed me holding my injured hand against my chest.

Reluctantly, I climbed into the driver's seat, glancing back at Ryder one more time. Eva slowly began to remove the bandage from my hand. I held back a cry, wondering how much pain one person could take.

She gasped when the bandage was completely off. My fingers looked terrible. No longer were they a healthy skin-toned color. Instead, each finger was covered in black and blue bruises. The worst was my ring finger. It was swollen and at an odd angle. It didn't resemble my finger at all.

"Lord, Maddie, this is not good," Eva said, clearly worried. She took a deep breath. "Okay. I'm going to touch them."

I nodded, understanding this needed to be done. Sweat broke out on my upper lip and my stomach roiled with pain.

"Try not to move."

I tensed as she felt along my black and blue fingers. When she touched the broken one, I cried out and yanked my hand away.

Immediately, Ryder was standing outside the truck door.

"What's wrong?" he asked.

Eva sighed heavily. "Her fingers are a mess."

When Ryder looked down at my fingers, all the blood drained from his face. "Oh, hell, Maddie."

"Let's just leave them alone," I pleaded. The pain was too awful. I couldn't handle Eva touching them again.

"That's not an option. You know that broken one won't heal correctly if it's not fixed," Eva said.

I saw her mind working as she studied my fingers.

"I'm going to have to do this the old fashioned way," she muttered to herself.

"No, Eva," I whispered in fright.

"What's the old way?" Ryder asked, looking back and forth between us.

"Brody! Find me a stick that is around three inches long. And straight!" Eva yelled, not answering Ryder.

I felt queasy, knowing what was about to happen. In seconds, Brody handed her a small stick about the length of my finger.

"Ryder, sit behind her in the truck," Eva instructed.

He climbed into the truck, scooting across the bench seat to sit behind me.

"Put your arms around her and hold her tight. Don't let her move, no matter how much she pulls away," Eva said.

I knew that this was for my own good but I shook my head in denial anyway. Ryder put his arms around me, making me feel like a child being held down for a shot.

Eva started applying light pressure on each finger. A whimper escaped me when severe pain hit. Instinctively, I tried pulling away but Ryder held me firmly.

"It will be okay," he said. "Just breathe."

Eva continued to poke around on my fingers, feeling along the bone for any breaks or dislocated joints. The pain was awful. I bit my lip to keep from crying out until the coppery taste of blood filled my mouth.

"You almost done?" Ryder snapped.

"No. Hold her tight," Eva answered.

After pushing around on my wrist, she gently laid my hand down.

"It looks like three of your fingers are out of socket, Maddie. One is broken." She gave me a questioning look. "How did three of your fingers get pulled out of socket? I thought you said you were trampled."

I froze, remembering what happened before the lights went out.

"Maddie? Someone stepping on your fingers couldn't have pulled them out of the socket. What happened?" Eva asked again, suspiciously.

When I answered, my voice cracked with fear. "Ben was waiting for me outside the bathroom. We struggled. That's when I felt them pop out of the socket."

"Asshole!" Ryder growled, tightening his arms around me. "If I see him again, I'm putting him in the ground."

"Not if I get to him first," Eva spit, angry. "The guy deserves to be beaten within an inch of his life for hurting her." She took a deep breath and closed her eyes. When she opened them, the anger was gone. "For now, let's take care of her."

"Just do your thing. I've got her."

I should have been mad that they were talking about me like I wasn't there but I just wanted to get this over with.

"I'm going to pop them back in place and it's gonna hurt like a sonofabitch," Eva said, glancing up at me. "You can handle this, Maddie."

I smiled weakly at her. She was always joking with me that I could handle whatever Fate threw at me. I wasn't so sure anymore.

I hissed with pain when Eva picked up one of my fingers. She looked at Ryder.

"Hold her tight."

I felt him nod and tighten his arms around me. Eva took a deep breath and yanked.

I screamed. Then there was only blackness.

~~~~

I woke up slowly, feeling groggy and sore. The bumpy road jarred my cheek against a firm muscle. Opening my eyes, I saw a jean-covered leg beneath me. I blushed, realizing that my head was in Ryder's lap and his large hand was on my hip.

He was asleep, his head resting on the worn headrest. When we hit another bump in the road, his hand tightened on my hip, holding me securely against him.

I sat up slowly, brushing the hair out of my eyes. The sun was now high in the sky, bringing with it the sweltering heat that made the inside of the truck feel like an oven despite the open windows.

Looking around, I recognized the area immediately. I had traveled on this particular road many times before. A few miles back, we would have passed a beer joint and a strip club, sitting unsuspectingly on an old country road.

Also near here was a prison, set miles off of the road, hiding it from most people.

I glanced over when Eva whimpered softly in her sleep. She had her head in Brody's lap while he kept both hands on the wheel.

For one blissful moment, I forgot about my injured hand. Forgot about the electricity going off, the plane going down, or the scene at the hospital. Then the pain hit me again, reminding me why we were traveling down this lonely road, desperate to get home.

A stick now protruded from my bandaged fingers. The makeshift splint would help stabilize the broken finger but without proper medical care, the broken bone may never heal correctly. I pushed the thought out of my mind when Ryder stirred beside me.

"Maddie, you okay?" he asked, groggy.

When I nodded yes, he sat up straighter and removed his hand from my hip.

"You scared the crap out of me passing out like that," he said, rubbing the growing stubble on his jaw.

"Sorry," I said, peevishly. "Setting a broken bone will do that to a person."

His eyes ran over me, making me aware of every brush of his leg against mine.

"Shit, Maddie. I'm sorry. I should have been standing outside that bathroom. Waiting on you."

"You can't be with me 24/7, Ryder. Don't beat yourself up about it," I said with annoyance. I was sore and hungry. It was not the best time to have this discussion.

"I shouldn't have let you out of my sight. You would've been safe if I had been thinking straight instead of thinking with my dick."

"True, but I made the choice to walk away because your dick is the only thing that wants me," I snapped in anger.

Grinding his teeth in frustration, he glared at me. "Damn it, Maddie! You really want to go there now?"

I opened my mouth, planning to tell him what I wanted, when Brody interrupted.

"Shit, guys. We've got a problem."

Chapter Fourteen

About three hundred feet in front of us were two stalled vehicles blocking the lanes of Business 265.

Squinting against the sun, I tried to see what had made Brody and Ryder suddenly uneasy. *We had passed numerous stalled cars, so why were these a problem?*

Then I saw him.

Heat waves rose around the unconscious man. He was lying between an old Chevy truck and a dusty minivan.

Apprehension made my heart thump harder. Something about this scene bothered me. Something was off.

"Brody, take the ditch around them." Ryder said, never taking his eyes off the man.

"Someone's hurt," Eva said, now wide-awake. "We need to stop."

"No, we need to keep driving," Ryder said, each word clipped.

"We can't just drive past if someone is hurt!" Eva countered. "We have to help."

Ryder shot Eva a frustrated look. "The world changed when that EMP went off, Eva. It's every man for himself…"

"And screw everyone else? Is that your answer for everything, Ryder?" Eva asked, annoyed. "And what if it was Maddie lying there hurt? Wouldn't you want someone to stop and help her?"

We were almost to the vehicles now. Someone needed to make a decision. Quick.

"You can't save the world, Eva," Ryder said, trying to reason with her.

"But at least I'm willing to try," she muttered, her meaning obvious. She turned to Brody and laid a hand on his arm. "Brody, please."

When I heard the seductive tone in her voice, I knew we were stopping.

"Your girlfriend is going to get us killed, Brody," Ryder mumbled in anger as he put the hunting knife into the back of his jeans and pulled his shirt over it.

"Just keep your eyes open, Ryder," Brody said, stopping the truck a few feet from the stalled vehicles.

"You two stay in the truck while we check it out," Ryder said, looking at Eva and me.

The man on the ground appeared to be in his early thirties. He was big and muscular, wearing black jeans and a blue shirt with heavy combat boots. From where we were, he didn't appear injured. There was no blood, no sign of struggle, and nothing that could explain why he was unconscious. All the more reason why I felt uneasy.

"Leave the keys," Ryder told Brody, watching the van closely. He looked at me, his eyes hard. "If something happens, Maddie, take off. Don't do anything stupid like get out of the truck."

I nodded in agreement but knew I would never leave him behind.

Brody handed the keys to Eva before both him and Ryder jumped out of the truck. As they walked away, I wanted to cover my eyes, afraid to look but afraid not to. I waited for the inevitable to happen.

My heart felt like it would leap out of my chest. *Something wasn't right!* I couldn't take my eyes off Ryder as he crept closer to the unconscious man. He kept an eye on the truck and minivan as he bent down to check the man's pulse.

Suddenly, all hell broke loose.

The doors of the minivan swung open and three large men jumped out, shouting and surrounding Brody and Ryder. The man on the ground was no longer unconscious. He was now on his feet in a fighting stance. But what frightened me the most was the sight of the guns.

The now conscious man had a semi-automatic pistol aimed at Ryder's chest. The other men carried various weapons; a shotgun, a hunting rifle, and a revolver. We were no match for the deadly power.

"Holy shit!" Eva screeched with terror.

Everything seemed to move in slow motion. Eva scrambled into the driver's seat and attempted to insert the key in the ignition but her hands were shaking too badly. She tried again, cursing when the keys dropped to the floorboard.

As she bent down to find them, I watched, frozen in fear, as Ryder and Brody raised their hands above their heads. Four guns were now aimed at their chests and heads, waiting on them to make one wrong move.

Oh, God! I quickly scooted over to the passenger door and pushed the door open, planning to jump out of the truck and run to Ryder. I had no idea what I was going to do once I reached him. I just knew I had to be next to him.

But my plan was short-lived.

Two men approached the truck with menace. Both had guns. The barrels were pointed directly at Eva and me despite the windshield.

My eyes quickly snapped to Ryder. He was watching the men with murderous rage but then his eyes moved to me. Making the smallest movement, he shook his head. That was my cue to sit still and not make any sudden moves.

The biggest man walked over to the driver's side while the other headed for the passenger door, blocking my escape route.

"Out!" the bigger man yelled with authority. He yanked opened the heavy metal door easily, still keeping his gun aimed at us.

The guy was scary. He was large with ruthlessness written all over him. His sweaty face was covered in old knife scars and pockmarks. There were tattoos on the entire lower half of his jaw, making him appear nonhuman. His hair was shaved off, revealing a dented and imperfectly shaped skull.

And he had on prison garb.

"I said get the fuck out of the car!" he roared.

I looked down the barrel of the gun and felt my stomach drop. These were prison inmates. We were as good as dead.

Eva scrambled out of the truck, edging away from the gun pointed at her face. I could tell she was barely holding it together.

I winced as I climbed out after her. My ribs ached from sitting for so long but that wasn't my biggest problem right now.

The second, smaller man walked around the truck to join his partner. They were both aiming at our heads like they were going to use us for target practice.

"Move away from the door, girlies," the small man said with a high-pitched and overly excited voice. This was obviously a game for him.

Eva and I moved to the back of the truck. Coming to a stop at the tailgate, I glanced back over my shoulder when someone shouted, "MOVE IT!"

Ryder and Brody were slowly walking toward us with their hands above their heads and guns aimed inches away from their spines.

As soon as I was within his reach, Ryder yanked me behind him, shielding me from danger. I peeked around his tall frame at the weasel-like man in front of us. He was greasy and unkempt. I could actually smell him from a few feet away. His beady eyes peered at me but his weapon of choice, a pistol, was pointed steadily at Ryder's stomach.

"Open the fucking tailgate!" the leader yelled as he kept his gun trained on us.

I looked around frantically, terrified. All four men were now aiming at us with itchy trigger fingers. We were overpowered and unarmed. There was nothing we could do.

Ryder lowered the tailgate but continued to stand in front of me, practically stepping on my toes. He wasn't going to leave me exposed to these men.

The leader motioned behind Ryder to me. "You there, crawl in the back and throw everything on the ground. NOW."

My hands shook and my rib screamed with pain but I managed to throw one leg up onto the tailgate.

Ryder stopped me with a hand on my waist. "She's hurt, I'll do it."

"Don't fucking move, boy, unless you have a death wish," the leader snarled, taking a step closer. "Back away from the truck before I fill you full of lead!"

Ryder took a step away, reaching out to grab my hand and pull me along with him. I tried to follow, wanting to stay as close as possible to him.

"Oh, no, sweetheart, don't you move a pretty little muscle. I want only your boyfriend to move away," the leader said, cocking the gun pointed at Ryder. He thrust his chin at Brody. "You too, pretty boy. Move over next to him."

The leader studied the two of them for a second. "That ain't gonna to do it. I don't trust you two fuckers. Move over there on the grass," he said, motioning with his head toward the side of the road.

Ryder glared at the leader before slowly following Brody to the ditch. Two homicidal looking inmates followed them with guns pointed. Greasy (my new name for the smaller man) snickered. The sound made the hair on the back of my neck stand up.

The leader and Greasy moved closer, now fixated on Eva and me. The hot metal of the tailgate was pushing painfully against my spine but there was nowhere else to go. The temperature was climbing and the sun was burning high in the sky. Another hour and this heat would be deadly to anyone standing outside. *Maybe these guys would keel over from heat stroke.*

I managed to hide my fright when Greasy stepped in front of me and grinned. His body odor was revolting. The whites of his eyes were yellow and a drop of drool hovered in the corner of his mouth. His breath reeked of decay and the teeth he had left were yellow and rotten. I tried not to gag with disgust.

"I ain't never seen such a pretty girl before, Elrod," Greasy said, leaning closer to sniff my hair. "Ain't she a tiny little thing? And look at all that dark hair! I always had me a thing for girls with black hair!"

I turned my face away, repulsed. My eyes instantly found Ryder's. He looked ready to kill with nothing but his bare hands. I prayed he would keep his hot temper in check and not do something stupid.

"Can I touch, Elrod? I've always wanted me a college girl. And look at all this perfect skin," Greasy said, reaching out a finger and running it up my arm.

A shiver ran through me. As he leaned closer, I felt bile rise in my throat. I had to do something before Ryder exploded and all hell broke loose.

Somewhere deep within me, the strength rose to stand up to this slime ball. My survival instincts kicked in.

"Back off," I said in my best kick-ass voice, glaring at him with hate.

Greasy started giggling like a little girl. The sound was terrifying.

I thought I had put him in his place when the laugh suddenly died on his lips, replaced with an evil look that could've killed. He raised the pistol and aimed it within inches of my forehead. The sound him cocking the gun made my blood run cold.

Terror had me frozen in place. The kick-ass girl in me was long gone.

"Leave them alone!" Brody yelled.

He got a gun butt to the stomach for his outcry. Eva and I watched with horror as he doubled over in pain. She reached out to grasp my hand tightly, panic behind her grip.

"She has some spunk, don't she, Robbie?" the leader chuckled, looking me up and down. "I ain't saying I ain't interested but we just want their shit for now."

He motioned to Eva with his gun. "You don't look hurt, sweetie. Crawl up in there and get that stuff out. Now."

Eva dropped my hand and hurried to crawl into the bed of the truck. Maybe the faster we handed over our supplies, the faster we could leave.

I took a chance and glanced at Ryder. His hands were balled into fists as he stared at Greasy with pure rage. His eyes flickered over to me once before moving back to Greasy.

One by one our bags were dropped to the dusty ground at my feet. Eva climbed out of the truck bed as Greasy bent down to open the bags and backpacks.

"Clothes." He pushed one backpack out of the way and moved on to a duffle bag. "Shitload of food and bottled water in this one," he said, tossing the hefty bag to the leader. He went through the other backpacks, finding only our clothes.

The leader chuckled as he bent down to search through everything. "You kids are prepared, I'll give you that!"

He squinted at us against the sun. "No weapons?"

Eva and I both shook our heads, afraid if we spoke, we might get the same treatment Brody did.

"I can pat them down, Elrod. Be my pleasure," Greasy said with excitement, keeping his eyes and gun trained on me.

"Another time, Robbie," the leader mumbled, motioning Ryder and Brody back over.

They walked toward us slowly with the other inmates following. Ryder's eyes never left Greasy. If looks could kill, Greasy would be long dead by now.

The leader held up a hand, stopping Brody and Ryder a few feet away.

"Tell you what boys, you let me have the food and water and I'll let you go with the clothes. On foot," he said, cradling the shotgun in the crook of his arms and standing with his legs spread apart.

"We'll die! You can't take our food and water!" Brody exploded in outrage.

The leader seemed to take offense at Brody's outburst. "Let me tell you a story, boy. These men," he motioned to each inmate, "have been locked up for years. You know what that means? Hmmm? It means they ain't had a girl for a long, long time."

He waited for that to sink in with us. "So I'll take all your supplies and the truck and you get the clothes." He paused and swept his eyes over Eva and me. "If you have a problem with that, well, let's just say that my men will have a fine time with these young things."

The evil expression disappeared from Greasy's face as his eyes ran over me. "Please. Please. Please," he pleaded, giddy.

"Take it all," Ryder growled.

"Good decision, kid," the leader said with an evil smile.

With panic, I watched him pick up two of the bags and turn to leave.

"Wait!" I shouted.

Ryder glared at me, silently telling me to shut up as the leader turned back around. I swallowed hard past my fear as I tried to ignore Greasy and the gun in my face.

"We..." I was too afraid to talk. Taking a deep breath, I tried again. "Can we have some water? Please?"

It had to be over a hundred degrees. Without the water, we wouldn't last very long in this heat.

The leader regarded me with indecision before reaching into a bag and tossing four cans of vegetables and four water bottles at my feet.

"Good luck, sweetheart. You'll need it," he said, walking off.

Greasy hadn't moved away from me yet. His pistol was still pointed at my head. I realized that with one little slip of his finger, I would be dead.

"Maybe next time, babe," he said with a giggle. "You and me will have a little party and get to know each other better. When this shit blows over, I'll look you up."

Instantly, Ryder was there. In front of me, protecting me, standing in front of a gun for me.

"Don't look at her, asshole," he said, fiercely. He towered over Greasy by at least a foot and could easily break him in two with one powerful hand.

But Greasy had the gun.

Greasy's laugh disappeared as his gun moved slowly from my head to aim at Ryder's forehead. Now that Ryder was the target, I started to shake with terror. It was one thing to have a gun pointed at my head, it was another to see it pointed at someone I loved.

A full minute passed as Ryder and Greasy stared each other down. Ryder stood his ground, not flinching and not scared of the gun in his face. I knew him too well to know that he was probably bloodthirsty by this point.

"Start walking, kids!" the leader yelled from a few yards away.

Eva and Brody picked up the backpacks, stuffing the bottled waters and cans of food inside. Greasy kept his gun on Ryder, refusing to back down. Ryder stood deathly still, protecting me with his body.

Greasy finally took a step away and motioned off in the distance with his gun.

"Git!" he barked.

Ryder grabbed my hand and took two backpacks from Brody. Pulling me with him, we followed Eva and Brody at a quick pace.

We hurried past the vehicles, trying to ignore the convicts. I avoided looking in their direction but I could feel them, watching us, waiting to open fire if we made the slightest wrong move.

I couldn't help but glance over at Eva's truck. She had driven that thing since she was 17 years old. It was her pride and joy. I hated to see it left behind with a bunch of criminals but more than that, I hated to see our only form of transportation disappear.

She started to cry silent tears. I let go of Ryder's hand to wrap an arm around her as we walked down the road.

"What are we going to do now, Maddie?" she asked, tearfully.

"I guess we walk. What choice do we have?"

"Walk? It's summer in Texas! We won't make it with only four bottles of water!" she cried, hysterically. Brody hushed her, afraid we would draw the men's attention.

Without breaking his stride, Ryder looked over his shoulder, giving Eva and I a warning look.

I glanced back at the men. We were a safe distance away from them now but they still watched us closely with their guns ready.

As we walked, the heat pressed down on us from the merciless sun. I could feel the sweat rolling down my back as the afternoon temperature rose to dangerous levels. Up ahead some trees formed a canopy over the road, providing some shade. I tried to focus on that one spot and not think of the long walk ahead of us.

Ryder walked ten feet in front of us, moving at a faster pace. His long legs covered more ground than mine despite the backpacks on his shoulders.

I hurried to catch up with him, ignoring the hitch in my side.

"I'll carry my backpack now, Ryder," I said, holding out my good hand to take it.

Ryder scowled at me. "You're hurt. I've got it."

Not only was my skin beginning to blister from the heat but also it had my blood boiling. I stopped in the middle of the road, causing dust to swirl around my feet.

Eva and Brody stopped when I did but Ryder ignored me and continued walking.

"What is your problem, Ryder?" I asked in frustration.

He stopped and turned to face me. The expression on his face said it all; he was fuming mad. With a few steps, he was towering over me angrily, invading my personal space.

"What's my problem? My problem, Maddie, is that you're hurt, we have no car, it's freakin' hotter than hell, we have very little water, hardly any food, and we still have miles until we get home!"

I stared into his ice blue eyes, unafraid.

With frustration, he threw the backpacks down on the ground, covering our shoes in dust.

"And I'm mad as shit that you took it upon yourself to stand up to those assholes! What the hell were you thinking?"

"I was thinking we needed water!"

"Well, I had to stand there and watch that jackass eyeing you and touching you! So what the hell do you think my problem is?" he yelled.

"I'm okay! He didn't hurt me so calm down!" I snapped, growing angry too.

Ryder put his hands on his hips and glared down at me. "I'll calm down when your ass is safe at home!"

My patience snapped.

"I'm not your responsibility! How many times do I have to say that? Not. Your. Responsibility!" I yelled, poking my finger into his chest with each word. "Just because we had sex doesn't mean you have to take care of me!"

I saw Brody turn away in embarrassment. I didn't care. *This was too much. I couldn't handle this anymore.* I was barely holding it together as it was.

"I've been taking care of you for fifteen years! I'm not about to stop now just because we screwed!" Ryder yelled, taking a threatening step closer.

I flinched at his choice of words. *That's all I was to him – someone he screwed?*

Brody swore softly. "Hey, man, back off. We're all freaked out here. Don't take it out on her," he said, grabbing Ryder's arm.

Ryder shrugged him off. "Don't touch me," he said coldly, glaring down at me. He picked up his backpack and left mine on the ground at my feet.

"Take care of yourself, Maddie. I'm done."

Then he walked away.

Chapter Fifteen

I watched him walk away. His shoulders were rigid and tension made his back even straighter.

Tears threatened to fall. My throat felt clogged. I suddenly had trouble swallowing. *Screw him! I didn't need him anyway!* So why did the sight of him walking away hurt so much?

Eva put her arms around me. "We're all scared here, Maddie. What happened with those men just shook him up. He didn't mean it."

"You're supposed to be on my side, Eva," I said as tears fell silently down my cheeks. I wiped them away and felt grime on my fingertips.

"Well, he's an ass but I don't blame him for being pissed. You took a big chance standing up to those men." She leaned closer and whispered, "He may be an ass but he loves you so, damn it, I have to tolerate him."

I cringed at her words. Ryder wasn't capable of feeling love, not even for me. That was apparent when he walked away.

"Now let's get the hell home," Eva said.

I took a deep breath, trying to build the courage to face what was in front of us. We had to walk. It didn't matter if it was hot, I was sore, or Ryder was furious; we had no choice - we were walking home.

Shading my eyes against the sun, I watched as Ryder continued down the road, walking further and further away from me.

I swung the backpack onto my shoulders. The pain in my hand and ribs was agonizing but I was determined to carry my own stuff. I didn't need Ryder taking care of me anymore than he needed me.

~~~~

Two hours later, I was wishing for some suntan lotion. And a pair of sunglasses. And a meal. The dry dirt under my feet swirled with each step. The sun was like a giant fireball, blazing unmerciful. Empty farmland surrounded us while the sounds of grasshoppers and locusts echoed around us.

No one talked as we walked. Like me, Eva and Brody were suffering from the heat. It was better just to focus on putting one foot in front of the other than on the sweat rolling off of us.

The hot weather kept my mind off Ryder, now far ahead of us. Not once did he slow down or look back. It hurt but I was too miserable to dwell on it.

I wasn't sure how much longer I could go on. The heat was taking a toll on my injuries. My cracked rib was screaming in agony. I took shallow breaths, afraid if I breathed any deeper it might cause excruciating pain. Even my broken finger throbbed with each beat of my heart and each step I took.

We hadn't eaten anything, afraid of consuming what little amount of food we had until it was absolutely necessary. It was now almost twenty-four hours since I ate. With nothing in my system, my energy level was dwindling fast.

I had to stop.

I almost toppled over from the weight of my backpack but caught myself in enough time. When I wiped the sweat out of my eyes, the motion made me dizzy and I almost fell again.

"Maddie?" Eva asked, stopping beside me.

"I have to stop, Eva," I said, weakly.

"You don't look so good."

"I'm okay, just too hot."

I didn't tell her it was more than the heat bothering me. The pain was intolerable. I had to sit. My legs couldn't hold me anymore. I let the backpack fall to the ground. That simple movement caused pain to radiate through my body.

I collapsed next to the bag, not caring that there was only hot, dusty blacktop beneath me.

"I run three miles every day. Walking should be a breeze," I muttered, more to myself than anyone else.

Eva kneeled down in front of me. "You have a cracked rib, Maddie. Give yourself a break." She started rummaging in my backpack. "Where's your water?"

"Front pocket."

Pulling it out, she looked at the half empty bottle of water. "You need to drink more."

I had been taking small sips for the last hour, just enough to keep my mouth moist. If this bottle was all I had, I needed to conserve as much as possible. But I knew she was right. I needed more water.

"Guys! Hold up!" Eva yelled. Brody stopped but Ryder continued walking as if he hadn't heard.

"Ass," Eva said under her breath.

I weakly laughed and then winced with pain. Eva wasn't afraid to speak her mind on a normal day and this was far from a normal day. But I was surprised that's the best she could come up with.

"What's wrong?" Brody asked, closing the distance between us. He looked hot and exhausted, just like Eva and me.

"Maddie's having trouble," she said, squinting at him in the sunlight.

"Do we need to walk slower?" Brody asked before taking a drink of his own water.

We were already walking slow enough. Any slower and we would be crawling. I peeked around Brody. Ryder was still walking down the center of the road, his long legs eating up the miles. It hurt to see him walk away with no regard for us.

"I'll try to wrap her ribs again and see if that helps," Eva told Brody. "Turn around."

Brody turned, giving us some privacy. The small breeze felt good on my bare skin as I held my t-shirt up. She rewrapped the binding. Stars appeared before my eyes when she touched my broken rib.

After she was finished, Brody picked up my backpack and slung it over his shoulder. Eva took my hand and tugged me along with her, giving me the strength I needed to carry on.

But another hour later, I was struggling to put one foot in front of the other. Eva must have noticed because she started talking about random subjects. School, boys, TV. She tried everything. I commented when she expected me to comment but wasn't really listening. My head was throbbing and I was dehydrated. But soon her words got my attention.

"Ryder's being a jerk but I'm holding back on kicking his ass. I think he's just worried about you and all you've been through the last twenty-four hours."

"But we never fight like this, Eva," I said, stepping around a huge pothole in the road.

"I think he's fighting his feelings, Maddie. I didn't think the man was capable of feelings but obviously he is." Eva laughed lightly. "The all-mighty Ryder has been brought to his knees by love. Never thought I would see the day. It has to hurt."

"I don't know, Eva."

"I have more experience with men than you do, Maddie, so believe me when I say he's gaga over you." She paused and looked around. "Where the hell are we going?" she muttered under her breath. "Does anyone know where we are?" she yelled louder so Brody or Ryder would hear.

No one answered. Brody was yards away and Ryder was just a speck on the road now. I wondered how much longer before I wouldn't be able to see him at all.

I made the mistake of looking down at my shoes. The world tilted at a weird angle, leaving me lightheaded. I leaned on Eva. If she hadn't been beside me, I might have landed on the ground, face first.

"Whoa, Maddie! You gonna pass out on me?" she asked, studying me closely as we stopped in the middle of the road.

Her face wavered in and out of focus. The dizziness made my empty stomach churn. I couldn't answer her as I tried to keep what little water I drank from coming back up. Vomiting would just make dehydration worse.

"Okay, let's sit a minute." Eva dropped her backpack and helped me sit down in the middle of the empty road. I really wanted to lie down but not on the heat and grime of the pavement. No, I wanted a nice comfortable bed, crisp cotton sheets, somewhere in an air-conditioned room.

"Look," she said, tipping her head in the direction of Brody and Ryder. "They didn't even notice that we stopped. What great boyfriends we have."

"Ryder is not my boyfriend," I insisted.

"Pleeeease! You two are a couple. He just doesn't know it yet."

"Why don't you try to convince him of that?"

Eva scoffed. "Are you kidding? I like to see him suffer. It makes me happy."

"You are a very bad person, Eva," I told her, attempting to lighten the mood.

"I never said I was an angel. That's your job," she said with a grin.

My smile turned into a grimace when the gash on my head pulled taut. Lying down, I rested my head on her backpack. I really didn't care if we were in the middle of the road. *Wasn't like we would see a car anyway.*

"Maybe we should eat," I said when my stomach growled loudly.

"Yeah, you need the energy." Eva put her fingers to her lips and let out a shrill whistle.

Brody turned and started walking back to us, his stride slower than before. "You doing okay, Maddie?" he asked, breathing hard and red-faced.

"Not really," I answered. "Can we eat something and rest for a while?" I struggled to keep my eyes focused on him. *Maybe I was worse off than I thought.*

He looked back over his shoulder at the empty road. "Ryder has the food."

And he was nowhere to be seen.

"Shit!" Eva swore as she rose to her feet. Shielding her eyes, she peered down the road. "Where the hell is he?"

I struggled back to my feet. "Let's go. Maybe we'll catch up with him." I didn't want to slow everyone down.

Eva picked up her backpack and the three of us started down the road again. We hadn't gotten very far when Eva glanced over at me and stopped. "That's it! We aren't moving another inch! You're white as a ghost!"

I stopped, more than happy to oblige her.

"Brody!" Eva yelled as her hand gripped my arm, holding me up.

He walked back to us, this time exasperated. "What the hell is it now?"

I wasn't the only one suffering in this heat. One hundred and five degree temperatures could turn a sweet, caring person into the devil reincarnated. Add that to our hunger and we were ready to declare war on each other.

"Don't 'what the hell' me, Brody! Maddie's about to pass out! We're not moving until it's cooled down. Not one more step," Eva snapped.

Brody looked down the road for Ryder, shielding his eyes against the sun. I had gotten a brief glimpse of him a few minutes ago but now he was nowhere in sight.

"Forget Ryder. He'll come back when he figures out we're not following," Eva said, putting her hands on her hips.

"Fine. Let's sit under some shade," Brody said, pointing to some large trees a few yards ahead.

I followed both of them to the grassy shoulder of the road, beneath the thick branches of the trees. The brown weeds were brittle beneath my shoes but they would provide a more comfortable place to rest than the hot asphalt. The temperature in the shade was cooler and the absence of the burning sun felt wonderful. I sank down to the ground, using my pack as a backrest.

Eva dug my water bottle out again and handed it to me. I took a sip, trying not to think of how little was left. In another hour, we would be out of water and in serious trouble.

"Ryder will realize we aren't following and double back," Brody said, taking a seat beside me and pulling out the last of his water.

Eva scoffed. "When I see him again, I plan on giving him a piece of my mind and maybe a piece of my fist."

"Cool it, Eva! He's just scouting ahead so we don't walk into a trap again!" Brody snapped.

Eva rolled her eyes at his lame excuse. "When he gets back, first I'm going to kick his ass than I'm going to eat."

I sighed, knowing Eva wouldn't touch him but the words she said to him wouldn't be pretty.

Lying on my back, I stared up through the tree branches. The sun peeked through the leaves every once in a while, making me squint against the brightness. My head throbbed with each blink of my eyes and each breath had me seeing stars.

Miles lingered ahead of us. My dad was days away. I wasn't sure I had any energy left to go on. But I still had hope.

Chapter Sixteen

I must have fallen asleep because the next thing I knew, my eyes opened to see Ryder walking toward us, staring at me intently.

I sat up slowly, wondering how long I had been asleep. Eva and Brody still sat a few feet away. The sun was still high in the sky and the heat was still hellish despite the thunder that rumbled loudly overhead. A storm seemed to be brewing. I hoped for rain but knew that summer storms in Texas sometimes produced nothing more than high humidity. All talk and no action.

I watched as Ryder drew closer. His face was sunburned, making his eyes appear bluer and the angles of his face sharper. His trim, muscular body moved effortlessly, full of purpose. At some point, he had changed from jeans to shorts that hung loose on his hips. Exhausted and sweaty, he was still the best thing I had ever seen. But I wasn't sure what to expect from him after his earlier words.

"What's wrong?" he asked curtly when he was near me. His eyebrows were drawn together, the frown on his face directed at me.

Eva jumped to her feet, beating me to the answer. "What's wrong? You're what's wrong, Ryder! You're going to get us killed! Where did you go? You had the damn food!"

Ryder ran a hand over his face in aggravation.

"Maddie was on the verge of passing out and you were off having a little hissy fit. Grow up!" Eva screeched.

His gaze swung back to me, searching my body for more injuries. The concern in his eyes was blatant and surprising after his earlier words.

"Don't look at her, asshole! You don't deserve her!" Eva yelled, getting in his face. Brody grabbed her around the waist and held her back as she went on attack mode.

Any other time, I would have thought the idea of Eva beating up Ryder hilarious but we couldn't waste precious energy fighting like this.

I got to my feet and planted myself between the two of them. "Calm down, Eva," I said.

She ignored me and so did Ryder.

"You're right, Eva! I don't deserve her! But I would never leave her behind!" he shouted back from behind me.

"Maybe you should! Maybe she's better off without you messing with her mind!" Eva yelled, scrambling to get out of Brody's hold.

"Both of you shut up!" I shouted and instantly regretted it. All the blood left my head, leaving me woozy, when my rib screamed in pain.

Ryder's hand snapped out to grab hold of my arm. "Easy, Maddie," he said gently, helping me to sit back down.

"Maddie?" Eva whispered, taking a step closer. "I'm sorry."

I waved her off as I put my head in my hands, trying to stop the dizziness. Pain shot through my forehead when I accidentally touched the gash.

"You okay?" Ryder asked, sitting beside me on the ground.

"Sure," I said with as much sarcasm as I could gather.

He watched me closely before digging around in his backpack and pulling out a can of peas. Using the knife, he cut an opening in the lid.

"Here. You need to eat," he said, waiting on me to take the can.

I gladly took it. I was starving, my stomach feeling emptier than ever. I popped some warm peas in my mouth. They tasted amazing.

Moments ticked by in silence. Ryder's eyes stayed on me, making me conscious of how close we were sitting. One little move of his hand and he would be touching me, running his fingers over my leg.

"I would never leave you, Maddie, you know that, right?"

I nodded. His eyes drilled into me, marking me with heat. I looked away, needing to avoid his scrutiny.

"How far away from home are we?" I asked, popping a few more peas in my mouth.

"Walking? Five or six days."

I held back a groan. *Five or six days in this heat?* We would have to find more food and water. But what choice did we have? Sitting around waiting for someone to rescue us seemed silly.

I ate a few more peas and handed the can back to him. We needed to conserve our food if we had days ahead of us. I finished all the water in my bottle and looked at the empty container with despair.

"You can have some of mine," Ryder said, his blue eyes so piercing. His hair was curling slightly around his ears from the heat. The silky strands begged to have someone's fingers tangled in it, grabbing fistfuls in the height of passion.

What was I thinking? We were in the middle of nowhere, the U.S. was collapsing, and we were on the verge of dehydration. Sex shouldn't be on my mind.

I cleared my throat and brought my thoughts back on track. "You need the water," I said to him, indicating his bottle. "You're bigger than I am and require more."

He sighed in frustration. "One of these days, Maddie, maybe you will do as I say."

"Probably not," I muttered.

With another frustrated look at me, he stuffed the water bottle back in his bag and pulled out a baseball hat. He set it on my head and pulled my ponytail through the back. His hand felt intimate in my hair, sending a spark of want through me.

"You're getting sunburned," he explained so low that I hardly heard him. His eyes lingered on my face while his hand held my ponytail longer than was necessary. Clearing his throat, he tore his eyes from me and dropped my ponytail. Pulling another hat out of his bag, he put it on his head.

"Thank you," I whispered as I watched him pull the hat low to hide his eyes.

He looked up at me then. Our eyes locked and I could feel the desire grow between us.

The desire changed to surprise when thunder cracked loudly above us. I jumped when a few fat raindrops hit the top of my head.

"Is that rain?" I asked in a hushed tone, afraid if I spoke louder it would scare away the storm.

The wind picked up, whipping the tree branches above us into a frenzy. Ryder grabbed my hand and helped me to my feet.

"This might be a bad storm," he said, looking up at the sky.

We didn't have long to find out. Within seconds, the sky opened up. Rain came down in sheets, drenching us.

"Get your water bottles!" Ryder shouted over the sound of thunder.

As Eva and Brody fumbled to get their water bottles out and opened, I struggled to stay on my feet against the force of the wind. It battered me, slinging strands of hair into my eyes and trying to knock me down. Against the rain, I watched as Brody quickly tossed the bottles to Ryder. He ran to prop them against a small outcropping of rocks, leaving them open to the elements. It suddenly occurred to me what he was doing - collecting rainwater for us to drink.

"Come on, Maddie!"

Eva grabbed my hand and pulled me next to a large tree. I leaned as close as possible to the rough bark, desperately seeking cover. In a matter of minutes, I was soaking wet. My t-shirt and shorts stuck to my body like a second skin, cooling my overheated flesh.

It felt wonderful.

Ryder ran for the cover of the trees also, stopping next to me. Rain ran down his arms and over the brim of his hat. His wet shirt was glued to his abdomen, outlining the muscles and the black inky patterns of his tattoos.

Heat crawl up my neck.

"You're wet. Come here," he said, reaching out to pull me toward him. Wrapping an arm around me, he gathered me close to his chest, providing perfect shelter from the rain. As his hands spread over my back, wrapping me in his arms, our bodies pressed together. I sucked in a breath when his erection nudged my abdomen.

"Sorry," he said, huskily.

I looked up into his eyes. Rain ran down his cheeks and lips, catching on his unshaven jaw. I swallowed hard. Butterflies took flight in my stomach.

I wanted those lips on me again.

As the rain poured down, he tried to keep me covered but there was no escaping the storm. Rain pelted us from all sides. Ryder held me tightly as the wind threatened to tear us apart.

"Put your injured hand between us," he said, taking my hand from his back and laying it on his chest, right over his heart. As his hard body pressed against mine, his warmth seeped through my clothes, heating my skin.

Absently, I ran the tip of my tongue along my lower lip, catching a raindrop. His eyes followed the movement, watching my mouth. One of his hands moved to the top of my bottom and brought me closer against him, pushing me against his pelvis.

I sucked in a breath. *Oh, my!* He wanted me again. He may deny his feelings all he wanted but his body screamed to possess mine again. His hardness made me want him with a need, a craving, that I'd never felt before. *What was he doing to me?*

His fingers squeezed my bottom gently, kneading me through my wet shorts. His other hand brushed raindrops from my cheek as I dropped my eyes to his chest, hiding my desire from him.

"Water," Brody said, interrupting the moment by holding out two water bottles to us.

Taking one, I took a long drink while Ryder's arm stayed around me. The cool rainwater felt good going down my parched throat. I couldn't get enough.

I watched Ryder's strong throat work as he drank from his bottle. I never knew watching a man drink could be so erotic.

After we were done, Ryder returned the bottles to the rocks to refill again. The rain continued to pour down, turning the ground under our feet to mud. We stayed huddled under the trees, soaking wet and chilled.

Ryder stayed near me but didn't touch me again. I silently reprimanded myself for wanting him. A girl needed a man that loved her, not just lusted after her. By the time my overheated blood had cooled and I told myself that I was a fool for loving him, the rain had tapered off to a soft mist.

Ryder gathered our water bottles and recapped them. I felt a huge amount of relief as he handed my bottle back to me. It was full. We had just been thrown a life vest in the form of water. We could survive days without food but not without hydration.

I wasn't the only one happy with our luck. A huge smile spread across Ryder's face, revealing perfect white teeth. The smile transformed his face from sullen and dangerous to lighthearted. I missed the laid back, playful Ryder. Somewhere along the way, he had become lost to me.

"I say we start walking while it's cooler," Brody said, trying to squeeze rainwater out of the bottom of his shirt.

"There's nothing up ahead for a few miles. I say we walk until we find some shelter then bed down for the night," Ryder said, stuffing the water bottles in our backpacks.

"Should we change clothes?" Eva asked. She was soaking wet like the rest of us.

"No, our clothes will dry quick in this heat," I answered, pulling my wet shorts away from my skin.

I felt eyes on me. Glancing up, I found Ryder staring intensely down at my t-shirt. I realized my lacy bra was clearly outlined, leaving nothing to the imagination.

I started to tug the fabric away from my body but then stopped. Let Ryder suffer, my inner bad girl whispered. *Let him see what he can't have again. Tease him on what he's missing.* But I didn't anticipate that the yearning in his eyes would leave me speechless.

Reaching down, I picked up my backpack, needing to break away from the craving I saw in his eyes.

"I'll carry it," he said, stopping me.

"No, I can get it."

His eyes burned into mine, challenging me. Ever so slowly, they ran down my wet shirt then back up to stare into my eyes.

I looked away, knowing I could never win this contest. "Fine!" I handed the backpack over, unhappy to give into him.

He smiled triumphantly as he slung it on his broad shoulder.

We started walking down the empty road again. My wet shoes squished with each step. It was going to be a very uncomfortable walk until they dried.

We had only walked a couple of feet when Ryder grabbed my hand and held me back. "Hold on a sec, Maddie."

When Eva and Brody were a few yards ahead, Ryder started walking slowly, dropping his hand away from mine.

"I'm sorry for acting like an ass earlier."

The baseball cap was back on his head, hiding his eyes from me and causing his wet hair to stick out around the edges.

He stared off into the distance. "I was out of line."

"It's okay."

"Like hell it is." He sighed deeply. "I was scared shitless that those men were going to hurt you but it was a low blow for me to say what I did."

Yeah, referring to sex with me as screwing did hurt.

He stopped and turned to look at me. My breath hitched when his shaded eyes moved down my body again. "When that slime ball touched you, I saw red. I could have pulled him apart with my bare hands."

"Ryder...."

"I was terrified," he said, stopping me. Scrubbing a hand across his whiskered jawline, he looked around at the empty farmland.

"There was one other time that I felt that way, Maddie." He paused then swung his eyes over to me again. "Remember when you wrecked your daddy's truck?"

I thought back to that night. I had been seventeen and driving home from a high school football game. It was late and the old dirt road I was on was empty. The moon had been shrouded behind thick clouds, making the truck's headlights work harder to pierce the night's darkness.

Out of nowhere, a large deer had jumped in front of the truck and froze in fear. I immediately stomped on the brakes but it was too late. With a sickening thud, the truck hit the deer. Its body crashed into the truck's grill, rolled over the hood, and smashed into the windshield before flying off. In the end, my dad's truck was totaled and I was taken to the local hospital to be checked out.

"What about that night?" I asked.

"My mom called and said an ambulance brought you into the ER from a car accident. She didn't know anything about your condition." He looked away and pulled the brim on his hat down lower. He clenched and unclenched his back teeth, his jaw tense.

"I left the ranch right away. Next thing I know, I'm passing your dad's truck sitting on the side of the road. The whole front end was smashed together like an accordion. Hell, the front end was almost gone. When I saw that, I was terrified you were dead. I think my old

Bronco hit a hundred miles an hour getting to the hospital." He grimaced. "I felt sick to my stomach on that drive to the ER."

I remembered that night vividly. My dad was beside himself with worry when I called him from the hospital. I also called Ryder but only got his voice mail. I remembered wishing he was with me but figured since it was a Friday night, he was probably either on a date or drunk. Apparently, I was wrong about both.

"When I got to the ER, you were sitting there, looking perfect and unharmed," he said.

I remembered what happened next. "You were furious with me. Your mom finally made you leave." I had been waiting for my dad to pick me up when Ryder stormed into the ER waiting area with a frantic look on his face. One minute he had looked panic-stricken and the next he was furious.

"I wasn't mad at you. I was pissed with myself for caring so much. I shouldn't have taken it out on you. Then or now," he admitted.

"So what you're saying is when you yell and cuss at me, you care about me?" I asked, not able to resist teasing him.

"Something like that," he said, smiling down at me.

"That's screwed up, Ryder."

"Yeah, well, I never said I wasn't screwed up." He studied me a second before continuing. "What you don't know is that I got stinking drunk after leaving the ER."

He pulled up the side of his t-shirt, showing me the tribal tattoos running along his side and curving around his back. "I got this that night."

I couldn't tear my eyes away from his bare, tanned abdomen and the intricate black tattoos wrapped around his muscles. My heart raced. All I could think about was wanting that body against me again, inside me, doing things that made me scream in ecstasy.

"I also woke up in some girl's bed the next morning." He looked off into the far distance, wincing as if the words hurt him. "She had long dark hair and brown eyes. Very short too. I picked her because...well, she reminded me of someone I wanted and couldn't have."

My heart pounded. It felt as if it would jump out of my chest, run over to him, and jump into the palm of his hand. Right where he had me.

He glanced over at me, waiting for me to say something. I wanted to tell him that some random bar-fly girl didn't deserve him. I did. But he wanted the one-night stands, I wanted more.

He sighed and ran a hand over his face before facing me again. Taking a step closer, his voice dropped. "I fuck up all the time, Maddie. I don't want to drag you down with me."

"Too late," I whispered, breathlessly.

"Hell," he muttered under his breath.

We were both in trouble.

Chapter Seventeen

We walked in silence.

I had no idea what to say to him. We both wanted each other but the love was only one-sided. It made me ache deep inside, knowing he didn't love me, but I knew that no matter what, he would care for me in his own way.

When we finally caught up with Eva and Brody, she gave me a questioning look. "What were you two discussing?"

"None of your business, Eva," Ryder answered with annoyance as he stopped to pull out his water bottle. "You know she doesn't have to tell you everything."

"Oh course she does, I'm her best friend. What are you?" she asked with a smirk.

I grimaced at the implied meaning.

"Don't mess with me, Eva," Ryder warned. "You'll regret it."

"Hey, man, cool it," Brody said, stepping between her and Ryder.

"This is between Maddie and me. She needs to mind her own damn business," Ryder said, pointing at Eva.

"She is my business, dick-wad," Eva hissed from around Brody's back.

"I'm standing right here!" I said with frustration, tired of being fought over.

Ryder sighed in resignation. "Listen, Eva, I'm glad she can rely on you but damn it, you need to back off," he said, facing her and placing his hands on his hips.

"Just understand that if you hurt her, I'll cut you in that very special place all the girls around town love."

Ryder clenched his jaw in aggravation while Eva looked ready to kill him.

This had gone on too long.

"That's enough! I don't want to listen to the two of you fight all the way home. Both of you kiss and make up," I demanded. I gave each of them a warning look before walking away, not waiting for anyone to follow.

After a few minutes, Eva caught up to me. She didn't speak and neither did I. My mind was on home and my dad. I just wanted to be with him. Safe and secure. I didn't want to think about the future, I couldn't think about the past. I just needed to survive.

If Ryder and Eva wanted to fight, they could fight. If Ryder and I were nothing but friends, I would learn to deal with it. But I wanted to deal with it later, after I saw my dad, after I was in my own house, after I dealt with life changing around me.

The cool weather had disappeared and heat descended on us again. I wondered what time it was. Maybe close to dinner? My stomach growled, the peas from earlier already forgotten. I didn't see any meal in my future but I tried not to dwell on it too much.

We still had not seen a home, a car, or another person. Only acres of farmland surrounded us, making me feel lost and alone.

Hours passed. Occasionally, Brody would pull out the map to see where we were. I didn't want to know how many miles were left. I just wanted to walk until we arrived home. If I thought about it too much, depression would press down on me.

My rib and broken finger still hurt with each step I took. The gash on my head had stopped throbbing miles back. I tried not to think about the lingering pain or the amount of time it was going to take for my bones to heal. I just had to take it one day at a time, one step at a time.

The sun went down and we walked. The moonlight was bright enough to see the road in front of us. It was an eerie feeling, walking down a deserted road at night. It felt as if we were the only four people left in the world.

Ryder walked beside me in the dark, ready to reach for me if need be. His baseball cap now swung from his backpack, leaving his hair at the mercy of the wind and his eyes for me to see.

I took off my baseball cap and ran my fingers through my hair, loosening the ponytail. At the same time, a pack of coyotes howled somewhere in the distance. The sound sent a shiver up my back.

"It's just coyotes, Maddie," Ryder chuckled when I took a frightened step closer to him.

"I know. I just can't stand the noise. It sounds so…bloodcurdling."

"You weren't afraid of them when we snuck out at night."

"That was different. We were kids and we were always near the house. This is the middle of nowhere," I said, remembering those nights. Sometimes, I would wake up to Ryder throwing pebbles at my bedroom window. After I snuck out, we would sit in the barn or lay on the ground, watching for falling stars and talking. It had been one of my favorite things to do with him.

"There was one particular night…I was sixteen, you were thirteen. We were in the barn, hanging out at one o'clock in the morning when the coyotes started howling," he said, one corner of his mouth turning up in a smile.

I blushed. I remember that night vividly.

"You asked me what it was like to kiss," he said, his eyes cutting my way.

"I remember," I said, quietly. My cheeks burned with embarrassment.

"I was so freaking happy to know you hadn't kissed anyone yet," he said, smiling in the dark. "And then you asked me to practice with you."

"What was I thinking? I was only thirteen," I muttered, feeling mortified. Nothing had changed. I was a fool for him then just like I was now.

"I'm glad that I was the first to kiss you," he said, looking over at me with eyes so blue under the moonlight, "and take you to bed," he finished with a low voice.

"I'm glad it was you too," I said, throaty.

He smirked with a flirty, don't-trust-me grin. "I'm always willing to help a friend out."

"Ryder..." I began, cringing at the word 'friend.' I wanted to tell him that he was more than a friend and I wanted more from him than just sex but I didn't get a chance to say anything.

Car lights beamed behind us from down the road, illuminating the area brightly.

At first, I was excited. *We would see other people!* Maybe we could catch a ride. Or maybe they would have food to spare. But then I saw the look on Ryder's face.

He grabbed my upper arm and hauled me quickly over to the ditch. Eva and Brody followed with Brody pulling Eva behind him.

When our feet hit the dirt, Ryder pushed me down on my stomach and laid his arm over my back. Mud oozed around me, soaking into my shirt and coating my arms. My rib screamed with pain from the fast drop to the ground but I was more afraid of what was happening than I was the damage to my side.

Ryder put a finger to his lips, signally for me stay quiet. Brody and Eva laid beside me silently, watching as the headlights drew closer and closer. I felt panic bubble up as Ryder's arm pressed down on me. If he was nervous, I knew we were in trouble.

The lights were now even with us. I watched as an old mustang raced by, packed with young men, laughing and yelling at the top of their lungs. Someone threw a beer bottle out of the window, narrowly missing us. As the car flew down the road, voices lingered behind in the nighttime silence.

After their lights disappeared, we crawled out of the ditch, covered in mud.

"Why didn't we flag them down?" Eva asked with exasperation as she tried to pick mud off of her pink shirt. "We could have caught a ride."

"Because I wanted to see who we were dealing with," Ryder answered.

"Yeah, a car load of drunks isn't exactly a good thing when we have two girls with us," Brody said. "We have no weapons and neither of us wants a repeat of what those convict bitches threatened to do to you two if we didn't cooperate."

I saw Ryder clench his jaw hard. "That won't happen again. Heads will roll if anyone touches them," he snarled.

"Well, hell!" Eva muttered. "Can we not catch a break here?"

I felt the same way. I was tired and my stomach was rumbling painfully. Help would have been nice.

We started walking again. This time we stayed close together, spooked by the darkness and the threat of danger.

"So Ryder, I heard you are an avid hunter," Brody said, breaking the heavy silence.

"Yeah, I hunt. What about it?" Ryder asked, still obviously upset with Brody from earlier.

"I was just thinking that if the power doesn't come back on, we'll have to hunt for fresh meat. That takes guns and ammo. You got them?"

"Yeah," Ryder answered, not giving details.

"I don't eat venison," Eva said, stubbornly.

"If you want meat, you will," Brody said.

"You'll be doing a lot that you usually don't do, Eva," Ryder mumbled as he looked around us. "Better get used to it."

I knew what he said was true. If the power didn't come back on in the next few weeks, the simple day-to-day living was going to be more complicated and a whole lot harder. We had to be stronger, more willing to do what needed to be done, to survive.

"My dad and I will have to hunt. We don't have enough food to last us longer than a week," I said worried, wondering how long we could maintain that kind of life. We didn't know how to sterilizing water or live off the land. How we would survive, I didn't know.

"You don't have to worry, Maddie, I'm not going to let you starve," Ryder said grimly, watching the distance. "What's mine is yours."

I felt my heart quicken at those four words, so full of meaning. I wanted to read so much more into them but knew that was just my heart talking. *Friends took care of friends. That's all there was to it. Stop overanalyzing everything he said.*

I shot Eva a don't-you-dare-say-a-word look when she raised her perfectly arched eyebrows at me. It was time to steer the conversation in a different direction before Eva got it in her head to prod Ryder to elaborate.

"Do you think your brother is okay?" I asked Ryder.

The moon chose that moment to pass behind a large cloud, momentarily shrouding us in complete darkness. Completely blind now, I was thankful when Ryder's hand wrapped around my wrist, keeping me close to him.

"I figured Gavin hauled ass out of Dallas and headed home right away," Ryder said, his fingers holding onto me.

I cleared my throat, trying to ignore the tingle his touch caused.

"I hope he's safe."

"I'm sure he's fine," he said, with a surprising amount of tension in his voice. "Don't worry about him. Gavin is too much of a badass to be brought down by this."

I wish I could be that positive about my dad. Concern for his safety was constantly on my mind.

"Do you think my dad's okay, Ryder? He's home alone and with his heart…"

Ryder looked down at me, just an outline against the dark sky now. "My parents know he has health problems. They'll make sure he's okay. And you know my mom; she's a ballbuster. She probably insisted that he stay with them so she could keep an eye on him."

"I hope," I whispered, sadly. "He can be stubborn."

"Must run in the family," Ryder said, the corner of his mouth lifting up in a grin.

I smiled tentatively at him. "Well, it's rubbed off on you."

"I'm not complaining if anything of yours rubs on me," he said, huskily as his thumb lightly brushed over the sensitive skin of my inner wrist.

"Does that line work on all the girls, Ryder?" I asked with a nervous laugh, blushing.

"No, but it got you to smile, didn't it? That was my goal." Stopping suddenly, he cupped my jaw and turned my face up toward him. "I've missed your laugh, Maddie."

I felt those darn butterflies take flight in my stomach again.

Abruptly, he dropped his hands away as if he suddenly realized he was touching me. As his blue eyes looked deep into mine, I felt the invisible wall go up between us again, cutting him off from me once more.

"I know you're going to worry about your dad. You wouldn't be the Maddie that I know if you didn't. But try to relax. I'll get you home. I promise," he said, all playfulness gone.

And if there was one thing Ryder always did, it was keep his promises.

Chapter Eighteen

I was so exhausted that I was having trouble staying awake as we walked. I prayed silently for shelter, help, a reprieve from this awful situation. Something. Anything. I just prayed.

When Brody and Eva stopped unexpectedly, I didn't realize it until Ryder came to a standstill directly in front of me.

I felt the air fill with tension. Looking around Ryder's tall body, I saw a minivan parked in the middle of the road with all its doors thrown wide open.

I watched with panic as Ryder pulled the hunting knife from the back of his waistband. He held it in a strong grip, ready for any threat.

I felt terror, knowing he was going to check out the car. *What if it was a trap?* I glanced around but my view was obscured by the blackness of the night. If there were people waiting to attack us, we would never see them coming in the darkness.

"Stay here, Maddie," Ryder said, leaning over and whispering in my ear. I nodded in understanding as his hand lingered on my arm. With one more glance at me, he started creeping toward the abandoned car.

Brody, Eva and I stood together, watching as he slowly approached the vehicle with his knife ready. Without a noise, he peeked into through the open passenger door. I saw him stand up and glance around, looking for any danger. Not seeing any, he motioned us over before he started rifling through the minivan's contents.

When we walked up to the car, Ryder pulled his head out.

"Nothing. No water or food," he said.

"Shit!" Brody exclaimed loudly, the sound echoing through the empty night. He threw his backpack on the ground in frustration and started pacing back and forth in front of the car.

"I say we stop here for the night," Ryder said, sounding more like he was giving an order than making a suggestion.

We stood in indecision. No food, little water, exhaustion, and extreme heat made thinking rationally difficult. Being on the verge of collapsing didn't help either. But there was nothing around us except trees and empty pastures. The only form of shelter was the car unless we wanted to sleep out in the open.

"Hell, I'm not going to stand here all night," Eva muttered. She climbed into the back of the minivan and looked up at me, patting the seat next to her.

I slowly climbed in, my ribs and fingers protesting in pain. I didn't care that I was covered in dried mud. I just had to sit down. Leaning my head back against the worn seat, I closed my eyes, thankful for our newfound luxury.

I was drifting off to sleep when Eva whispered, "I'm sorry I jumped on Ryder, Maddie. I just don't want him to use you like he does every girl he meets."

I glanced out the open door at Ryder, standing beside the car and talking softly to Brody.

"I don't want the two of you to fight, Eva. Just let it go," I said around a wide yawn.

"I can't let it go, Maddie. He's a man whore. Sure, around you he's…different but I'm worried he'll hurt you."

I sighed. "I've realized that if he hurts me then he hurts me but I can't say no to him. I never have been able to."

Eva didn't say anything. I thought she had fallen asleep when she spoke again. "And I don't think he can say no to you, Maddie."

That wasn't true but I was too tired to argue. I snuggled closer to her, unable to keep my eyes open a moment longer.

Sometime during the night, I woke up to Ryder covering me with a jacket. I felt him slide in next to me on the bench seat, surrounding me with his body heat. He pulled me to his side and placed my bandaged hand on his abdomen. I laid my head on his chest, feeling it rise and fall with each breath he took. Strands of my hair caught on his whiskers as his lips rested against my head, whispering something low that I couldn't hear.

With nothing except darkness and nature pressing down on us, I should have been afraid but with Ryder beside me, I was content. Feeling safe and secure, I closed my eyes and sleep claimed me.

~~~~

I woke up the next morning to the sound of talking outside of the minivan. Stretching, my ribs objected to the movement.

Eva moved beside me. I wondered if I looked as bad as she did. Besides the circles under her eyes, her hair and clothes were caked with dried mud. I looked down to discover that I was just as dirty.

"I need coffee," Eva grumbled.

"I need more than coffee. A bed, hot shower, and maybe some air conditioning would be nice," I mumbled, stretching my cramped legs.

Feeling sore, I slowly crawled out of the minivan. The sun was rising on the horizon, bringing with it the early morning heat. Now that we had light, I glanced around. Nothing particular stood out to me. Only pastures and cows.

Ryder and Brody stood a few feet away, studying the map and talking quietly. When they realized we were awake, Ryder glanced at me with a grumpy expression. *Apparently, not everyone got a good night's sleep.*

"Turn your back, boys, I'm changing," Eva said. When Ryder and Brody turned around, she hurried to yank her shirt over her head.

I needed to get out of my dirty clothes also. Digging in my bag, I pulled out clean shorts and a t-shirt but I found that changing clothes with one injured hand was difficult. When Eva saw my dilemma, she stepped over to help me.

"Oh, shit, Maddie! I'm sorry!" Brody said when he turned too soon and saw me halfway naked.

Ryder whipped around, a furious scowl on his face. It disappeared when he saw me standing in only my bra and shorts. His eyes were intent on my ribcage as he closed the distance between us. Stopping inches in front of me, he ran his finger along my side lightly, causing a tingle to race around my abdomen.

"You're covered in bruises, Maddie. Does it hurt?" he asked, looking into my eyes.

"Not as much as earlier," I answered, feeling my heart quicken at his touch.

He gazed down at me with hunger as I slipped my shirt on.

"What's the holdup?" Brody asked, sounding impatient as he stood with his back to us.

Eva walked past me, picking up her backpack and rolling her eyes. "Get a room, you two."

Ryder stepped away and I could tell he was struggling to fight the same desire I was feeling. *Would sex with him be as good the second time as it was the first? Oh, Lord, where had that thought come from? And why would I ask myself that anyway?* This was Ryder. He oozed sex. It would be epic the second time just as it had been the first.

I stuffed my dirty clothes in my backpack, telling myself it didn't matter because there wasn't going to be a second time. Ever.

Within seconds, we were leaving the minivan behind and walking again.

"Sorry 'bout that, Maddie," Brody said, walking beside me. "If it's any consideration, you have a hot body," he said with a wide grin.

I smiled back, knowing that he was teasing, but then I caught Ryder glaring at Brody. He looked ready to pounce and start throwing punches.

Brody chuckled. "Don't worry, Ryder, it was just an observation."

"Don't observe," Ryder growled.

"Damn, you have it bad!" Brody scoffed, shaking his head in disbelief.

I snuck a peek at Ryder. He pulled the baseball cap out of his backpack and smacked it down on his head, pulling the brim down low and hiding his upper face. I could see his jaw clenching and unclenching in anger.

He didn't deny Brody's words. My mind went crazy thinking about that.

Chapter Nineteen

I wasn't sure how many miles we covered or how much time passed but when the sun reached its highest point, I couldn't walk any further. The heat was overwhelming. Our water was gone, we hadn't eaten for close to twelve hours now, and we were all suffering from heat exhaustion.

We passed a few houses but decided not to approach strangers in their own homes. A person's very existence was now being challenged and most would be willing to do anything to protect their family and property. With only a hunting knife between the four of us, we didn't want to take a chance on confronting someone who shot first and asked questions later. We needed an empty home, safe from all threats.

I tugged the brim of Ryder's hat further down on my head, trying to hide my already sunburned face from the sun. The heat caused my body to throb with each heartbeat. My head was pounding and my legs were cramping.

I suddenly realized that I was no longer sweating. Looking over at Eva, I saw that she didn't appear to be sweating either.

"I think Eva and I have heat exhaustion," I said, weaving on my feet. "We need to stop before we get worse."

Brody ran over to Eva, suddenly frantic. He held her face in his hands tenderly, turning her toward him. "Worse?"

"Heat stroke. It will cause nausea, vomiting what little water we have in our system, fainting, and eventually death," I said. "The ER sees it all the time when temperatures get this high."

"We had a woman die last year in the ER from heat stroke," Eva muttered, weakly.

Ryder thrust his water bottle out toward me. "Here, have the rest of my water."

I squinted at him under the brim of my hat. I couldn't take his water. *What would I do if he suffered from heat stroke?* We all needed to stay hydrated, even him.

"Don't argue with me, Maddie," he said with a low, cold voice.

"You drink it. I'll be fine. I just need a place to sit, preferably under some shade," I said, the heat zapping the last of my energy.

"I'm not asking you, I'm telling you to drink it." His ball cap was able to shade his red face from the sun but it couldn't hide the frown on his lips. I knew that when Ryder wanted something, he usually got it.

Taking the water bottle, I gave him a go-to-hell look as I drank the rest of his lukewarm water. He watched me closely, his eyes never leaving my face until the last drop of water was gone. It wasn't much, but at least it wet my mouth and dry throat.

Satisfied, he led me to a small group of trees. It didn't offer much in the way of shade but I didn't care.

"I'm going to scout ahead, see if I can find an empty home or some kind of shelter," Ryder said. He handed the knife to Brody and started walking away, his stride full of purpose.

Squinting against the sun, I watched him. His muscular back was outlined under the mud-encrusted t-shirt and his bottom looked perfect under his shorts. He looked rugged and wild with his whiskered jaw and tanned skin. The heat must have been affecting my mind because all I could think about was grabbing him as he moved on top of me. Whimpering and crying out as he took me to a place I had never been before. *Oh, hell! I was becoming delusional.* Heat stroke was now imminent.

I watched until he went around a curve in the road. For what felt like hours, I worried. He had no weapon, no way to defend himself. I couldn't think of anything else until he rounded that corner. At last, I saw him in the distance.

"Let's hope he found something," Eva said.

"If he didn't, we're in trouble," I warned, standing up on wobbly legs.

Soon he was stopping beside me, his tall frame blocking the sun. "There's an empty house around the corner. Looks locked up tight but I think we can get in."

"Don't have to tell me twice. Let's go, girls," Brody said, picking up his and Eva's backpacks. Ryder slung ours on his shoulder and waited for me to follow.

When we walked around the curve in the road, I saw the old ranch house. It sat in the middle of an overgrown yard. White paint peeled from the siding and a few shingles were missing. Not far from the house set a large barn that had seen better days and behind it, acres of farmland.

Eva and I followed Ryder and Brody down the gravel driveway. Fear made me jumpy. *What if Ryder was wrong and there were people still here? We had already fallen for one trap, were we walking into another?* I remembered Greasy's smirk and his revolting breath. My step faltered as the memory made a shiver wash over me.

"I'm going to check out the barn. You two stay here with Brody," Ryder said, giving me a stern look before walking away.

A few feet from us, he stopped. I watched as he rubbed the back of his neck and looked at the ground. With something akin to frustration, he swung around and stalked back to me.

"Run like hell, Maddie, if there is trouble," he said.

I swallowed nervously and nodded my head in understanding. There was no way I was leaving him behind but he didn't need to know that.

I watched him walk away with an uneasy feeling. If there were people in the barn, Ryder could be walking into an ambush. With all his tattoos and bad attitude, he could easily scare a person into doing something rash and stupid.

I held my breath as I waited. Time seemed to move slowly. Every sound had me jumping. Every noise, a reminder of how vulnerable we were.

When Ryder reappeared, relief washed through me.

"I think it's safe. Looks like no one has been here recently. Whoever lived here is long gone," he said, picking up our backpacks.

"So we're staying here?" Eva asked.

"Yeah, but we need to get in through the back door so no one sees us from the road," Ryder said. He started walking to the house, followed by Eva and Brody.

His words soaked in. "Hold on. We're going to break in?" I asked with disbelief.

Ryder kept on walking, his back to me as he answered. "Yeah, what did you think we were going to do? Have a tea party?"

"We can't break in! People live here!" I said, outraged.

Ryder stopped and turned around to look at me with exasperation. "We're doing this, Maddie. It's not your decision."

"I don't want to be a part of breaking and entering! We're not criminals!"

He separated the distance between us quickly, his strides matching his sudden ill temper.

"You need water and shelter. I'm breaking and entering for you."

I crossed my arms over my chest and stood my ground, refusing to budge or look away from his heated eyes.

"I refuse to do this!"

"Maddie, don't make me mad. I'll carry you into that house if I have to."

"You wouldn't!" I said, backing up slowly.

Ryder took a step toward me, dropping the backpacks on the dusty ground. Fury glowed from his eyes. If I was a small animal and he was the predator, I was about to be his dinner.

"Ryder! Don't you dare touch me!" My voice quavered as he came closer. I knew he wouldn't hurt me but, dammit, I was tired of giving into him.

"Or what?" He walked slower, tracking me. "What are you going to do to me if I touch you?" His words said one thing but his voice said another.

I turned to run. He lunged forward, wrapping his arms around my middle and hauling me back to him. I tried to escape but he swung me up on his shoulder like I weighed nothing. The air was knocked out of my lungs when I landed hard on him. Shooting pain raced along my ribcage from the impact. My face bumped into his strong back, reminding me of what was underneath his t-shirt.

"Ryder! Put me down!" I yelled as he started walking.

SMACK! His palm connected with my backside, lingering on it longer than was necessary.

"OUCH!" I shrieked.

"Shut up, Maddie! I'm not in the mood for your games," he said with force.

"I'm not playing games! I just don't want to break into an innocent person's house!"

Ryder ignored me and continued around the house. Hanging upside down, the blood started to rush into my head. The slowly healing gash on my forehead started to pulsate with each step he took.

"I'M NOT DOING THIS!" I shrieked.

As we reached the back, I looked up to see Eva and Brody standing on an old wooden porch, staring at us in astonishment.

"I don't want you to starve to death or die of heat stroke so shut the hell up!" Ryder said sharply as he walked up the steps with me bouncing on his shoulder.

He was willing to break in for me? That was so wrong but I had to admit, also romantic. He had officially turned my mind to mush, I decided with despair. I was now one of those girls. The lovesick, out-of-my mind bimbos he always hooked up with. *Great!*

I looked up at Eva. Her green eyes were round with shock. I mouthed 'help' to her and she had the nerve to smile sweetly at me. *What happened to the girl who threatened to beat up Ryder earlier? Where had she gone?*

"Now are you going to behave?" Ryder asked.

I fumed. *I wasn't a child! How dare he treat me like one!*

I was about to retaliate when an idea hit me. Letting myself go limp, I weakly said, "Put me down, Ryder. You're hurting me."

It worked. He instantly set me on my feet, keeping his arms around my waist. Worry replaced the aggravation on his face.

"So should we break a window or try the door?" Brody asked, growing impatient.

"Let me try the door," Ryder said, letting go of my waist. The door was old and hanging on its hinges. He jiggled the door handle, rammed his shoulder against it, then bent down to look at the lock.

"You got that knife?" he asked, sticking out his hand to Brody.

Brody handed the knife over and watched as Ryder stuck the tip between the door and lock. Using all his strength, he tried to wedge the door open.

"No use. We'll have to break the window."

There was only one window that we would be able to reach. It was near the door and looked small, barely big enough for a person to fit through.

I watched in wonder and amazement as Ryder tugged his t-shirt over his head and started to wrap it around his hand. Each movement caused his muscles to flex, the tattoos to move, and his biceps to bulge.

"Close your mouth, Maddie," Eva whispered beside me.

Ryder's eyes caught mine and his lips twitched in amusement. Blushing, I looked away. *Darn!* I thought I was in control again and then he pulls the taking-off-shirt move.

Turning his attention back to the window, he pulled back his fist and let it fly, smashing the window. Glass shattered. If it wasn't for that t-shirt, he would have torn up his knuckles, reminding me of all the nights he had shown up at my house with bloody hands after bar fights. I would tape them up and sent him on his way, hiding the blood from his parents.

"Is Maddie going in?" Brody asked, motioning to the broken window.

Ryder put his shirt back on before glaring at Brody. "No, I'm not sending her in there alone."

"But she's tiny."

Eva started to fume beside me. "And what am I? An amazon?"

Brody grimaced. "I didn't mean it like that, Eva."

"Whatever, Brody," she said, walking closer to the broken window. "Lift me up, Ryder."

With his help, Eva slowly eased through the window, avoiding the small shards of glass on the window sill. A second later, she disappeared on the other side. We waited patiently as she unlocked the door.

Entering the house, my eyes adjusted to the darkness. We stood in a very small living room. It contained a couch, an old recliner, and an older TV. It was stifling hot inside but at least the room was dark and we were out of the blazing sun.

"You two stay here. Brody and I will check out the rest of the house," Ryder said before moving away.

As we waited, I wondered about the people who lived here. Where were they? Were they alive? Safe? The thoughts wouldn't stop bombarding me. I didn't feel right being in someone else's home but I guess if we wanted to make it home, we needed supplies. This house was the answer.

"It's clear."

Before the words were out of Brody's mouth, Eva grabbed my hand. "Let's check the kitchen for food."

In the kitchen, we found dirty dishes in the sink and an empty coffee cup on the small kitchen table. One chair had been knocked over and a few cabinet doors were left opened. Apparently, whoever had been here had left in a big hurry.

Eva didn't waste any time. Dropping my hand, she rushed over to the sink and turned the faucet on. No water flowed from it. Next she opened the refrigerator door but quickly closed it when the smell of rotten food filled the room. I started checking the cabinets for anything we could use. Finally, I hit the jackpot.

"Eva!"

She ran over to me and looked with awe in the open cabinet. There was bread, peanut butter, two bags of potato chips, cans of soups, and canned chili. Enough food for three or four days.

"Thank God!" she squealed, throwing her arms around me.

I had never been so happy to see canned food before in my life. I pulled some out and sat them on the counter. We couldn't eat it all and I refused to take everything. *What if the homeowners made it back home only to find there was no food left?* I couldn't live with myself if someone went hungry because of us. Ryder could just be mad at me. I wasn't taking all the food.

"We have to find water," Eva said, letting go of me to start searching. She opened the remaining cabinets then a tiny pantry.

"Damn, nothing," she said in a despondent whisper when the kitchen came up empty for the one thing we desperately needed.

Ryder walked into the kitchen, his eyes cutting over to me. "Anything?"

"Food but no water," I answered, rubbing a hand over my eyes.

"Hey, you okay?" he asked, his footsteps loud on the old linoleum floor as he crossed the room to me.

I reluctantly raised my eyes to meet his. Nodding, I leaned against the counter.

"I'm fine," I lied. The truth was I was tired and hungry. Thirsty and covered in dried mud. I wasn't fine but none of us were.

He reached out to lift my chin up. "You're not fine, Maddie. Sit down."

"I said I was fine, Ryder," I snapped, pulling my chin away. I hated that his touch made me burn, that his nearness made me aware of the control he had over me. But more than anything, I hated that we could only be just friends.

He clenched his jaw in frustration, an angry scowl replacing the soft look on his face.

"I'll take care of her, Ryder. You go find some water," Eva said, grabbing my hand and tugging me to follow her.

I gladly left the room, the anger still burning in me. One of these days, Ryder would learn not to push me around. And one of these days, maybe I wouldn't need him so much.

Chapter Twenty

The people that lived in the tiny house were older, retired. There were pictures of them around but it was the colorful drawing of a horse, taped to the bedroom mirror, that gave it away. Someone had written in bright red crayon "for gramps and gram." My heart ached as I looked at the drawing. Someone's grandmother and grandfather were gone, for today or for always, I didn't know. But I did know that if we were having trouble surviving, the chances that this couple would make it home were slim to none.

Not wanting to think about it any longer, I gathered what I could from the bathroom. Toilet paper, Band-Aids, aspirin, bandages. It was all like gold now.

In the kitchen, Brody and Ryder had emptied the fridge of all the unspoiled food. Pickles, jelly, two soda drinks, a few plastic bottles of water, and a bottle of wine were now sitting on the counter along with what we had found in the cabinets. *We would eat like kings tonight.*

Ryder handed me a bottle of water when I walked into the kitchen. I hesitated to drink it because we hadn't found more water yet but I was too thirsty to argue.

I took a long drink. The water felt wonderful going down my parched throat.

"Small sips, Maddie," Ryder reminded me.

Knowing he was right, I slowed down, not wanting it to come back up when it hit my empty stomach. With half the bottle left, I handed it to Eva, knowing she needed it just as badly as I did.

Brody pushed away from the counter. "I'm going to check out the garage. Maybe they have water stored somewhere else."

I knew water was essential but I couldn't wait to tear into the food. I was opening a package of bread when Ryder stopped me.

"You two sit. I'll make sandwiches," he said, pushing me into a nearby chair. It felt wonderful to sit in a real chair again. It was amazing how the simplest things could be missed when they were gone.

I watched as Ryder spread peanut butter on a slice of bread. Handing me the sandwich, his eyes moved over my face. I felt the intensity from his stare all the way down to my toes.

Trying not to squirm under his scrutiny, I took a small bite of the sandwich. It tasted wonderful. I didn't know peanut butter and jelly could be so heavenly. *Must be starvation talking.*

Eva opened up the chips and we dug in, so hungry that I had to remind myself to slow down or I would be sick.

Brody walked in and I just about jumped up and hugged him. He carried a huge case of bottled water. "They kept it in the garage," he said, setting it on the counter. I never thought I would cry over water but I wanted to at that moment.

Ryder got up and grabbed a few bottles. He placed one in front of Eva and then one in front of me.

"Drink, Maddie," he said, giving me another stern look.

I knew I should call him out on his bossiness but I was still so thirsty. The water was hot from sitting in the garage but it was wet. Never again would I complain about drinking lukewarm water.

We ate as much as we could, appreciating every little bite. Afterwards, we opened every window in the house, allowing the slight breeze to cool the place off. The house had plenty of rooms but we all stayed together. Safety in numbers and all that.

Until the house cooled off, we decided to sit on the porch. Eva and I shared the old porch swing, gently pushing it with our feet. Ryder took a seat on the porch stairs, looking out over the pasture, while Brody leaned a chair back and propped his feet up on the railing. We were all full and content and for the moment, safe.

Nature lured us into silence. Branches swayed in the breeze, birds chirped, and cicadas made noises somewhere in the trees.

I leaned my head back, closing my eyes. I immediately thought of my dad and wondered if he was okay. I imagined the moment when I finally walked through the front door. He would wrap me in his arms and hug me fiercely. I would be home. I would be safe. My mind replayed the scene over and over until I became drowsy.

I was almost asleep when Brody spoke, "I'm going to check the house for weapons. We need something better than a hunting knife if we want to make it home in one piece."

As Brody left, I opened my eyes and found Ryder watching me under the brim of his hat. I looked away, a blush reddening my cheeks. That's when something caught my attention. Cattle were slowly moving toward a line of trees fifty yards behind the barn. It was hot and if I knew cattle, they were heading toward water.

"Ryder, do you think there's a creek down there?" I asked, pointing to the trees.

He stood up so he could get a better look. "Might be. Why? What are you thinking?"

"If those cows are heading toward water that means a creek and a creek means a bath."

"Don't tease me, Maddie," Eva muttered, standing up to look.

I jumped up and ran down the porch steps, now more than ever wanting to get clean. "Let's go check it out."

"Hold up. I'll go grab some stuff and get Brody," Eva said, turning back toward the house.

Ryder and I waited for her. Standing two steps above me, he towered over me easily, making me feel small and at his mercy.

"So, you still pissed at me for breaking in?" Ryder asked, putting his hands on his waist and looking down at me.

"Maybe."

"You are so bullheaded, Maddie." He took off his hat, running his fingers through his flattened hair. "I've never met a woman that drove me as goddamn crazy as you do."

I shifted to my other foot nervously as his words sunk in. *Was I really that bad?*

Replacing his hat, he walked down the stairs, passing me.

"Don't worry! When we get home, you'll be free of me!" I called after him as he started across the yard.

He turned around and walked backwards, one side of his mouth quirking up.

"Who said I wanted to be free of you?"

My heart thumped like a rabbit as I watched him turn back around and cross the yard in long strides. *Damn him!* One minute he was saying we were only friends and the next he was making comments like that. He was such a contradiction and it was driving me crazy. But I didn't have time to dwell on it. Eva and Brody came barreling out of the house carrying our backpacks and towels, both of them excited.

Ryder waited for us at the barbed wire fence. I ignored his wide stance and crossed arms as his stare bore down into me.

Without waiting for help, I crawled through the fence just as I've done a million times growing up. My broken rib ached but I was determined to do things without his help. He needed to know that I was perfectly capable of surviving without him.

The sun beat down with a vengeance as we cross the pasture. The heat felt like fire against my skin. Now that I had a full stomach, I just wanted a cool bath.

Knee-high grass brushed softly against my bare legs as we walked. Any other day, I would have enjoyed the time outside but right now, I was very conscious of Ryder walking closely behind me.

Arriving at the top of the ravine, we stood in awe at the sight of water running below us. It was around thirty feet wide and slow moving. Large boulders were deposited here and there, causing the water to ripple and swirl. The trees provided abundant shade, which meant the water might be cool.

I couldn't tell how deep it was but I didn't care. I was covered in dirt, sweat, and grime. I had never been smeller in my life and I desperately needed to get clean.

"I get to take a BATH!" Eva squealed, jumping into Brody's arms and giving him a loud kiss on the lips. Brody seemed to enjoy her enthusiasm as he held her, not letting her go until she wrestled out of his arms.

We left our shoes and socks at the top of the ravine and slowly made our way to the creek edge. Standing on the shore, we looked down into the brown, mucky water.

Eva started to pull her shirt off. "It looks disgusting but I don't care."

"Damn straight!" Brody agreed, stripping his clothes off in a frenzy.

I looked away in embarrassment but found a bigger problem. Ryder was pulling off his shirt. Muscles and tattoos taunted me to reach out and touch them.

The corner of his mouth lifted when he caught me staring. Keeping his eyes on me, he tugged his shorts down slowly. Very slowly. He left his boxers to hang low on his hips, causing another blush to race over my face.

Brody snagged my attention, yelling as he jumped off of one of the boulders into the creek, acting like a little kid in the neighborhood swimming pool. I watched as his head popped up above the water, flinging water everywhere as he grinned with happiness. Ryder followed suit, running and jumping feet first into the watery depths.

"Come on, Eva!" Brody yelled, treading water.

"Can I take my clothes off first?" Eva yelled back, laughing.

"Oh, I'll wait for that!" he said with a grin. Lifting his arm, he threw something on the ground at our feet. I looked down and found a wadded up pair of underwear.

"He's naked, Eva!"

Eva laughed at my surprise. "As soon as I'm in the water, I will be too!"

"You're going skinny dipping?"

"Yeah, I have to get out of all these clothes." She paused and gave me an inquisitive look. "Don't tell me you're embarrassed? You can't see squat under that nasty water."

Eva was right. No one could see below the surface but I wasn't so sure being naked around Ryder was such a good idea.

"Wait. Have you ever been skinny-dipping?" she asked.

"Well, no, Eva. I just don't do that kind of thing."

She looked at me with astonishment. "All the times you and Ryder went swimming as kids and you never went butt-naked?"

I blushed. "No. If we had, I wouldn't have been a twenty-one year old virgin."

"Wow! That says a lot about how you feel about him," Eva said, pulling off her shorts.

"Yeah, I know. He never tried anything with me so I thought I never had a chance with him. He was always dating these beautiful blondes with perfect bodies and here I was; short, average, and lacking in all the right places."

"You're gorgeous, Maddie. Women would kill to look like you."

"But how do I know Ryder isn't just using me because I'm convenient? Or maybe I was just a challenge for him and now he can mark it off his to-do list. Sleep with Maddie. Check! " I sighed with despair. "I don't know what to think anymore."

"Do you love him?"

I could only tell her the truth.

"Yeah, I do. But if he doesn't want a relationship and doesn't believe in love, where does that leave me? I can't just be his plaything."

"Would you sleep with him again?"

I thought about that night with him. How it felt, how I wanted to repeat it over and over despite the 'only friends' clause hanging over our heads.

"In a heartbeat. I just can't resist him."

"And therein lies the problem. No one can resist him and he knows it," Eva said knowingly, giving me a look of pity before wading into the water.

I knew she was right. Women, both young and old, flocked to him like bees to honey. He ate it up too; flirting, teasing, and seeing just how far he could take it. Most of the time, it was all the way. Not many women said no to Ryder Delaney.

I wanted to think I was special, that I wasn't just another one of those weak-willed women, but my inner voice called me stupid. I wasn't any different than the other women who came and went through his life.

"Hey, Maddie!" Eva flicked water my way, trying to get my attention. "Get in here!"

A bra and panties went flying through the air, landing near me. She laughed then yelped playfully when Brody grabbed her from beneath the water.

I smiled, their exhilaration rubbing off of me. Then I looked at Ryder.

His eyes were on me, scorching me. My smile faltered. My breath caught. He slowly started walking out of the water, looking like one of those models you only saw on TV commercials. The water dripped off of his ripped abdomen to run down into boxer shorts that stuck to him like a second skin. I couldn't look away. I had to remind myself to blink. To swallow. To breathe.

"You coming in, Maddie?" he asked, stopping inches from me. His eyes held a challenge, one that I instantly resented.

"Yes," I answered, refusing to let him see the effect he had on me. Feeling nervous and out of my comfort zone, I attempted to lift my shirt over my head. My bandaged hand caught on the material, snagging the bandage and making me wince.

"Turn your back, Brody!" Ryder shouted over his shoulder, not breaking eye contact with me. His blue eyes gleamed, uncontrollable desire burning in them. Taking the edge of my shirt, he started to lift the thin cotton upward.

I smacked his hand away. "What are you doing, Ryder?"

"Helping."

He paused a second, waiting for me to give permission. When I didn't, he pulled the t-shirt over my head anyway.

Brazenly, his gaze lowered to my bra. "I'm not going to pass up the chance to get you naked."

"Ryder…"

"Let me take the bandage off your ribs."

My heart skipped as his fingers brushed against my ribcage, unwrapping the bandage carefully.

"Shorts too," he said, sliding his fingers under my waistband.

"This isn't a good idea, Ryder." My voice sounded breathless, sultry, not at all like myself.

He slowly pushed my shorts down.

"Why?"

"Because friends don't do this."

"It's all in innocence, Maddie," he said in a raspy voice, pulling my hair out of the ponytail holder and letting it fall down my back. "Don't you like my hands on you?"

I couldn't answer as his hand moved from the nape of my neck down my arm. Taking my injured hand, he ran his thumb over the bruises. His jaw flexed at the sight of my broken finger, still splinted and wrapped. His eyes blazed at me, the fire in them from anger instead of need.

"You can't bathe with this broken finger."

"I'll manage."

"No, I'll help."

I wasn't sure what he meant but I followed him deep into the water anyway. Holding my bandaged hand above the surface, I stopped when the water reached my chest. My eyes grew round as Ryder pulled off his boxer shorts and tossed them on the bank. *Oh. My. Goodness. He was naked and only a foot in front of me.*

I started to step back when his hand lashed out to grab me.

"Come here."

As he pulled me closer, his hands moved to the small of my back. With one little twist of his fingers, he had unclasped my bra. I gasped and sank lower into the water as he slid it from my arms and flung it back to the creek shore.

His fingers ran down my ribcage, stopping at the top my panties. When his thumb hooked onto the waistband and started to tug downward, I used my good hand to push his hand away.

"I can manage, Ryder."

Using my uninjured hand, I pushed my panties down. Gathering the tiny bit of lace, I raised my hand to throw it to shore.

"I'll do it. You always threw like a girl," he said with a grin. His large hand enveloped mine, taking the lace from me. Effortlessly, he threw my panties dead center in our pile of other discarded clothing.

I frowned as he gave me a teasing smile. *He was up to something.*

"Brody toss me the soap."

I watched with nervous anticipation as Brody threw the bar of soap and Ryder caught it midair. *What was he planning?* I was afraid to find out from the look on his face. It was never a good thing when Ryder looked mischievous.

"Come closer," he said, his deep voice sounding like pure silk.

I took a step, calling myself a fool the entire time. This close I could see his black spiky eyelashes and the blue specks in his eyes. His nose was perfect, just the right size for his face, but it turned slightly from being broken in a bar fight many years ago. There was a small scar above his right eyebrow, thanks to a beer bottle to the face. I remembered each injury, each fight. I was always there, picking up the pieces and patching him up. Taking care of him like he took care of me. That would never change.

Taking my injured hand, Ryder placed it on his broad shoulder. "Keep it here so the bandage won't get wet."

With one hand resting on his shoulder, I watched as he created a soapy lather in his palms. The anticipation was killing me. *What exactly did he plan on...Oh!* I jumped when he ran his soapy hands down my arms to my fingertips and back up again.

"Relax, Maddie, it's just soap. You're acting as if we've never swam together before."

Having spent most of our summers swimming in the river that cut through our properties, I knew he was right but skinny dipping put a whole new spin on things.

"Things are different between us now," I said, sounding husky.

"No, not really. I wanted you then and I want you now. The difference is now I know what it feels like to be with you. Before I could only use my imagination and my imagination was nothing compared to being with you."

Words escaped me.

I pulled my lower lip between my teeth as he lathered his hands again and ran them over my shoulders then down to disappear beneath the water. Fingers skimmed lightly over my breasts, sending sensations throughout me. Pulling me closer, his hands traveled down over my stomach. I could feel his leg nudging between my thighs, silently asking me to let him in.

I wanted to obey, to let him touch me, but I came to my senses. Reaching down, I grabbed his wrist before his hand dipped any lower.

"Ryder, stop," I pleaded, hoping he didn't hear the yearning in my voice.

The corner of his mouth shot up in a crooked smile. "I'll leave that to you but I wouldn't mind helping if you need me to."

For a second, I was tempted to let him do whatever he wanted.

"Turn around. I'll wash your hair."

I turned, conscious of him so close behind me. Placing his hands on my shoulders, he leaned me back, letting my hair disappear beneath the water. Once my hair was wet, he started massaging soap into the strands. His large fingers moved in my hair, rubbing my scalp with just the right amount of pressure. I closed my eyes, feeling the heat from the sun on my cheeks and his body behind mine.

His fingers moved down to the nape of my neck, pushing my long hair over my shoulder and out of the way. He started rubbing the stiff muscles at the base of my neck, almost making me moan with pleasure. From there, his hands slowly traveled to my shoulders again, leaning me back and washing the soap away.

I didn't want it to end.

"What the hell are we doing, Maddie?" he whispered in my ear as his hands lingered on my waist.

"You're washing my hair, Ryder, nothing else," I answered, turning around.

His gaze dropped down to my lips. "I think it is something else."

"Purely innocent," I said, breathlessly.

"No, there's nothing innocent about this," he rasped, pulling me toward him.

My body slammed into his, knocking the air from my lungs. Staring at me with unbridled hunger, he wrapped my legs around his hips. I felt his hardness nudge between my thighs, begging for entry. I gasped and met his heated eyes.

"We need to find some privacy," he murmured, clenching his jaw hard.

"We can't do this Ryder, not again."

He squeezed his eyes closed, the internal struggle written all over his face. When he let go of my waist, I slid my legs off of him but remained close. I couldn't back away even though I should.

As Eva and Brody headed back to the creek bank, Ryder tugged me close again.

"You make me weak," he whispered near my ear. "So damn weak."

I let out a soft moan as his warm breath tickled my ear. If he only knew how weak he made me, we might never leave this creek.

"We're heading back to the house," Brody said, plunging me back to reality. He took Eva's hand and helped her out of the water, giving Ryder and I privacy.

When they were gone, nervousness had me pulling away from him. We were alone. There was nothing stopping us now. He could take what he wanted. But instead, he took my uninjured hand and led me toward the creek bank. When the water almost dipped below my breasts, I stopped, too embarrassed to go further.

"Ryder, hold on," I said. Slowly, I began unwrapping the dirty bandage from around my broken finger, wincing when it hurt.

"What are you doing?"

"I want to wash my finger."

"Here, let me," he said, taking my hand and slowly unwinding the bandage.

He sucked in a breath when he unwound the last bit of cloth. My finger was still black and blue but the swelling had gone down significantly.

"Shit, Maddie, that has to hurt," Ryder said, looking at me with concern.

I shrugged. "I can deal with a little broken finger. I'm just happy I made it out of the club alive."

He took my face in his hands and stared deeply into my eyes. Time stood still. I could hear the birds above and a dragonfly buzzing around the water. I waited, knowing he was going to kiss me, hoping he would.

Abruptly, he dropped his hands. "Let's get you dried off," he said, starting for the shore.

"I can get out on my own," I said, reluctant for him to see me naked. "Turn around and give me a minute."

"You can't climb out with one good hand. That finger is going to hurt like a sonofabitch if you hit it," he said, giving me a frustrated look. "I promise I'll be good."

I didn't believe him.

"I won't touch you except to help you out."

"No looking or touching?" I asked, raising an eyebrow.

He laughed. "No looking? That's impossible! You're too beautiful not to look at."

"Fine. I'll do this on my own," I said stubbornly, taking a few steps closer to the shore.

"Okay, you win!" he said as his hand shot out and grabbed my arm.

With one hand on me, he led me carefully to the creek bank. I kept my eyes trained on his back, refusing to look any lower. He was the perfect combination of muscles and leanness, his body toned and oozing sexiness. Without clothing, the effect of him was ten times greater on me.

When our feet hit dry ground, he grabbed a towel and wrapped me in it. As I squeezed water from my hair, I watched as he wound a towel around his waist, leaving it hanging on his hips.

He began rummaging in our backpacks for clothes.

"That was the best bath I've ever had," he said.

"I prefer a real bath in a real tub," I said, holding onto my towel tightly.

He looked up, giving me a seductive grin. "I'm not complaining. I could bathe in a creek with you forever."

I blushed. *Forever?* Ryder didn't do forever. I told myself that it was just an innocent statement, nothing more. I couldn't read more into it like some lovesick schoolgirl crushing over her first love.

With his help, I quickly shimmied into shorts and a shirt without dropping the towel from around me. The grin on Ryder's face grew wider as he watched me wiggle underneath the towel. I didn't care. I was determined to maintain what little amount of modesty I had left.

Once my clothes were on, he backed away. I felt relief but it was short-lived. Without warning, he dropped his towel, letting it fall to the ground. My face grew hot as I looked away, embarrassed.

"Every time you blush, I fight the urge to take you right then," he said, with laughter in his voice.

The sound of him pulling on his shorts had me hot and bothered. His words just made it worse.

I couldn't help but ask, "Is that why you are always embarrassing me?"

"Hmmm. Maybe."

My gaze shot to him. I tried not to stare at what I saw. His white t-shirt fit him like a glove and his dark brown shorts clung to his hipbones. His face was sunburned and his sun-kissed hair was wet, begging to be touched.

As he took my hand and led me up the incline, I wondered how we would resist this attraction. I wasn't sure it was possible anymore.

Chapter Twenty-One

The sun was setting quickly by the time we arrived back at the old house. Eva immediately rewrapped my finger in the bathroom, chastising me the whole time for walking around without a bandage or splint.

She was just finishing when a car engine rumbled loudly outside. We looked at each other with round, alarmed eyes. The first thought that ran through my mind was - where was Ryder? Fear had me hurrying out of the bathroom and into the hallway. If the convicts followed us here to finish what they started, Ryder would be right there, ready to fight and willing to die.

Eva and I were halfway down the hallway when Ryder stepped in front of us. He held a finger to his lips, telling us to be quiet. Grabbing my hand, he dragged me toward the nearest bedroom. Brody passed us, holding a handgun pointed at the floor. I wondered briefly where he had found it.

Ryder led me to a corner of the bedroom with Eva following close behind.

"Stay here and stay quiet," he instructed in a no-nonsense voice. I nodded and watched as he swiftly left, on to fight an unseen enemy.

Eva huddled close beside me, gripping my arm tightly. We could hear people talking outside but their words were muffled. *Was it the homeowners returning?* I felt sick knowing that Ryder was going to confront them, possibly putting himself in danger.

I suddenly needed to be next to him. With our world in shambles, I was afraid to let him out of my sight. *What if something happened and I was in here hiding like a coward?* I would never forgive myself.

I shrugged off Eva's hand when she tried to stop me from leaving. *I have to be with him!* I had only made it a few steps when she grabbed a handful of my shirt and without speaking, started to follow me out of the room.

We made our way into the growing darkness of the hallway. I could hear voices in the living room. One angry, another pleading. Moving quicker, Eva and I rounded the corner and stopped.

Ryder stood with his feet apart, a shotgun propped on his shoulder. There was only one person who had his attention right then - the stranger standing outside the old screen door.

I faltered, feeling the tension in the room. The wooden floor beneath my feet creaked loudly, announcing our presence. Brody's head whipped around at the sound. He motioned for us to leave but I ignored him.

"We're looking for food and water," the stranger said. He was middle-aged, balding, and a little pudgy in the middle. Behind him, I could see a haggard-looking woman and four small children.

The man glanced over at me. Ryder's back stiffened as he took a step in front of the stranger, blocking his view.

"Eva, go get this guy some supplies," Ryder said, his voice low and deadly.

Eva let go of my shirt to hurry into the kitchen. The air was thick with tension as we waited for her to return.

"You live here?" the man asked, his voice cracking.

"No questions," Ryder warned.

I could hear one of the children start to cry and the woman quickly hushing her.

"It's dangerous traveling," Ryder said. I saw his eyes glance over to the crying little girl. "We ran into some trouble on the road earlier."

"Thanks for the warning," the man said.

Eva rushed back, her arms loaded with some food and water. Stuffing the gun into the back of his waistband, Brody met her halfway across the room and took the supplies from her. Ryder eased the screen door open as Brody handed the food over.

"Thank you! We haven't eaten in a day."

"You have a weapon?" Ryder asked, his voice calm now.

"No. We were driving home when it hit."

"Go get him a gun and some ammo, Brody," Ryder said, keeping his eyes locked on the stranger.

"What? Are you crazy?" Brody exclaimed with disbelief.

"He has kids, Brody," Ryder said, flatly.

Brody stalked past me, the anger on his face evident of what he thought of Ryder's decision. A few minutes later, Ryder was handing over a pistol and a handful of ammo to the man despite the pissed off attitude Brody was giving him.

"Thank you!" the man said, his voice shaking.

Ryder shut the screen door, sending a clear message. "You can leave now," he said, his voice hard again.

The man nodded and turned to walk down the porch steps. My heart leaped in panic when Ryder swung open the screen door and followed the stranger out. His shotgun was pointed at the ground but ready to pull up and shoot if necessary.

In a few minutes, we heard car doors slamming shut then a vehicle roar to life. The tension was leaving my body when Ryder yanked open the screen door and stalked in, his eyes finding mine.

Within seconds, he was standing in front of me, livid.

"What the hell were you thinking, Maddie? When I say stay in the room, I mean stay in the room!"

"And I didn't want to cower in some corner when you were out here in danger!" *No way was I going to bow down to his every demand!*

I could tell he was itching to strangle my neck but instead he took a deep breath and walked around me, heading down the hallway.

Leaving Eva and Brody behind, I hurried to follow him. He walked quickly but I was only a few feet behind him when he entered the master bedroom. The shades were pulled in the room, casting shadows in the corners and leaving the room dim.

Without thinking twice, I closed the distance between us. I just needed to be near him. I needed his touch.

He looked stunned as I reached up and pulled his head down. My lips met his with hunger. As his hands glided down to my hips, I opened my mouth slightly, inviting him to enter. His tongue slipped inside to stroke against mine. One of his hands cupped my bottom and drew me closer.

"What's this?" he asked against my lips.

"Me taking charge."

His lips took over, hungry for more. I threaded my fingers through his hair as he held me against him.

"What happened to 'we can't do this again'?" he murmured against my mouth.

I managed to get an answer out despite his hands slowly trailing up my back.

"It's just a kiss, Ryder."

"It's never just a kiss with you, Maddie. It's so much more."

His kiss deepened, a groan escaping from deep in his throat. His hands ran beneath my hair, cupping my head, as his lips turned gentle on me. With one last kiss, he gently set me away from him. Staring at me with forced restraint, he took a deep breath. I saw him slowly bring himself back under control. We stared at each other, both of us wanting the other. We were fighting it, this hunger between us. And we were losing.

Without a word, he turned away and walked into the closet. I let out the breath I had been holding and ignored my body screaming to be touched.

"So Brody found a shit load of guns and ammo hidden in here," his voice said, sounding muffled in the closet. A minute later, he walked out and laid a pistol on the bed. "I need to know you will be safe before I go."

"Where are you going?" I asked, my desire replaced with concern.

"I'm going to make sure that man left." He picked up the pistol and started to load it. "I want you to keep this gun on you at all times." After it was loaded, he held the pistol out to me. "Remember what I taught you - don't hesitate and shoot to kill."

I looked at it with distrust. Ryder and my dad insisted I learn to use a gun from a young age. Ryder had spent many Saturday afternoons shooting targets with me. As a little girl, I went hunting with my dad often but targets and deer were not the same as a human.

"I won't shoot a person, Ryder."

His eyes became hard as he waited for me to take the gun. "You can and will if someone is hurting you, Maddie. Hesitate a second and it will be too late. All it takes is one shot to the chest and you'll be safe."

I took the gun reluctantly, studying it as it lay in my hand.

"Maddie," he paused, waiting for me to look up, "promise me you'll protect yourself."

I nodded numbly, feeling the weight of the pistol in my hand.

"I'll be back soon."

He left, leaving me alone.

I stood in a stranger's bedroom holding a loaded gun, worried about my best friend that I was in love with. I wondered what had happened to my life.

~~~~

Dusk descended quickly. Our dinner consisted of cold canned chili and stale potato chips. Brody wouldn't let us build a fire to warm the chili because it might attract unwanted attention. We didn't care that we had to eat it cold. We were just thankful for the food. Deciding the living room was the safest place in the house, we sat everything on a small coffee table.

The room was slowly becoming darker with the setting sun, making the house eerie. I worried about Ryder every second. Taking a seat on the couch, I stared at the congealed chili, wondering when he would return.

"I want to go home. I miss my parents," Eva said, sitting in a chair across the room. "I was so happy to leave a few days ago. Now I would give anything to see them again."

"I miss my dad also," I said.

"Ryder's parents will take care of him," Eva said, reassuringly. "You don't have to worry."

"So are you and Ryder really just friends because it seems like there's more between you two," Brody asked, picking up a stale chip and popping it into his mouth.

"She's in love with him. He doesn't do relationships," Eva answered before I could. "He doesn't want anything from her except sex."

I blushed at her frankness.

"That's bullshit," Brody declared.

Before I could respond, Ryder walked through the door. Glancing at the three of us, he rested the shotgun against the wall.

"Speak of the devil," Eva mumbled.

Ryder ignored her. "There's no sign of them."

"Still can't believe you gave them one of our fucking guns," Brody said, tossing a water bottle to Ryder.

Ryder caught it easily with one hand.

"If I hadn't, I would be signing a death sentence for those kids."

"Awww, he actually has a heart!" Eva said, sweetly.

Ryder shot her a look of warning before taking a seat beside me. The small couch didn't allow that much room for the two of us. His leg and arm continually brushed against mine, causing tingles to rush over my skin. I didn't mind. I was just happy he was safe and back in the house.

After eating, we sat quietly and watched the candle that Eva found, flicker and burn in the darkness of the room. Somewhere in the house, a clock chimed softly, announcing the late hour. The open windows let in a cool night breeze and with it the sounds of the night.

Everyone shared a bottle of cheap wine except me. My hangover was still too fresh in my mind, making me shudder when I remembered how sick I had been. Never again.

"So how did the two of you meet?" Brody asked, motioning to Ryder and me with his half empty glass of wine.

"He was nine, I was six. He showed up on my doorstep, wanting to play, after my dad and I moved in," I said, looking over at Ryder. He took a drink of his wine, watching me closely. "We played together every day that summer and every day he threatened to beat me up."

"Nice, Ryder! A real lady's man!" Brody laughed.

"I was nine and she was an annoying little girl," Ryder reasoned.

"I was not annoying! I was just better than you at some things. I could run faster, hide better, and climb higher," I said, stubbornly. "I always won any competition we had."

Ryder scoffed. "You won because you were as small as a pixie and I let you win."

"I don't think so! I always won, fair and square!"

He raised an eyebrow. "You sure about that?" Taking another long drink of wine, he looked over at Brody. "Did I mention she was annoying AND stubborn?"

Eva laughed. "Nothing's changed. She's still just as annoying and stubborn as she was back then."

I didn't think it was very funny. Okay, so I was stubborn but I wasn't annoying.

Seeing my hurt look, Eva jumped up from her chair and rushed over to me. Plopping herself in my lap, she hugged me fiercely.

"We love you anyway, Maddie!" she said, squeezing me tightly.

"I love you too," I said, easing out of her arms. "Now get off me, Amazon."

Disgruntled, she pouted her perfect lips at me and climbed off of my lap.

Ryder sat forward and leaned his elbows on his knees. The candlelight flickered over him, enhancing the sharp angles of his face and the stubble on his jaw. The tender expression on his face left me speechless and confused. I pulled my lower lip between my teeth, suddenly nervous.

"Maddie, stop," he whispered huskily, leaning toward me. Reaching out, he pushed my long hair behind my ear, his gaze lowering to my lips. I wasn't sure what I was doing to him but I knew what he was doing to me. I wanted him again, no matter what the consequences.

As if he realized what he was doing, his hand dropped away from me. Coolness replaced the desire in his eyes. Sitting his empty glass on the coffee table, he shot to his feet. Restlessly, he started pacing back and forth in the tiny living room like a caged animal.

"So what the hell are we going to do?" Brody asked, all playfulness gone. We didn't have to ask what he was referring to.

"Survive. It's the only option," Ryder answered, stopping to look out the window into the dark night, his mind elsewhere.

"We're all fucked," Brody said, slurring his words. "How are we supposed to fight off a goddamn enemy without communication? We're talking about Revolutionary War shit now."

"Yeah, well, we won that one, remember?" Ryder said, still staring outside.

"Hell, dude, that was different. We're pussies now. We don't know how to live like this. No electricity, no communication, no transportation? And what about food? No one knows how to survive without a Walmart around the corner. Might as well bend over and kiss our ass goodbye."

"You're drunk, Brody," I said. "Lay off the wine."

"No, he's right." Eva said, upset. "That man's kids looked like refugees. Imagine all the people that will die without food and water. Children. The elderly. One little infection and you could be dead."

I thought of my dad, alone with a heart condition. I thought of how vulnerable we were, walking home in this new wasteland.

"How do we know it won't be one of us that dies or starves to death? I can't live like that, wondering if I will be next or one of you," I said, not being able to keep the morbid thought to myself.

Ryder looked over at me, his blue eyes drilling into mine. "Nothing is going to happen to you, Maddie."

"You can't promise that, Ryder. Nobody can."

"I might die trying but nothing will happen to you," he said, roughly.

Somewhere in the distance, a coyote howled, sending shivers along my spine. The sound was lonely and dejected, reflecting how we all felt.

"Let's just promise to take care of each other," Eva said around a yawn.

"Always," I whispered quietly, knowing I would do anything for the three of them.

Eva stood up and grabbed Brody's hand, pulling him out of the chair.

"We're going to bed."

I was speechless as I watched her drag Brody out of the room. *She was staying with Brody tonight and leaving me with Ryder?* I narrowed my eyes at her as she passed but she only gave me a mischievous grin.

"Where do you want to sleep?"

I looked up at Ryder, momentarily confused by his question. *Did he mean where did I want to sleep or where should we sleep? And why was I so nervous all of a sudden?*

"We're sleeping together, Maddie. I'm not letting you out of my sight."

Butterflies took flight in my stomach. I swallowed hard. "Can we just sleep here?" I asked, indicating the living room. "I would rather not sleep in some stranger's bed."

"Okay. I'll go grab some sheets and pillows."

I waited for him, watching the candlelight flicker and shadows bounce around the room. The tiny flame became smaller and smaller as the candle fought to stay lit. Darkness was no longer an option. It was now a constant, a reminder of the world that was gone. Just like resisting Ryder was no longer an option.

He walked back into the room, his arms loaded with pillows, sheets, and a quilt. After pushing the coffee table out of the way, he spread the quilt on the floor. I felt jittery, knowing we were going to share a bed again.

I swallowed nervously as he pulled his shirt over his head and tugged his shorts off. His boxer briefs remained, hanging low on his hips. My heart started to race as he turned a heated gaze toward me.

"Relax, Maddie," he said, walking slowly toward me. "I'm not going to bite."

"Listen, Ryder…I…." *What did I want to say again?* My mind went completely blank. I held up a hand to stop him. I knew that if he touched me, I was a goner.

When the back of my knees hit the couch, he still moved closer, stopping only when my palm was flat on his chest.

A tense moment passed as we stood toe to toe, our eyes saying what we didn't dare. My hand looked small resting on the black tattoos covering his chest. I wanted to run my hand further down to the top of his boxer shorts, explore him like he had explored me. Instead, I pulled my hand away.

"Why are you so nervous?" he asked.

"Because I don't know what to think about us anymore." The words spilled out, unrehearsed. "I mean, where do we stand? You said you don't want a relationship and you could never love me but…"

His lips crashed onto mine, cutting off my words, as his hands moved to hold my head in place. He frantically deepened the kiss, wanting more, taking more. His wet, teasing tongue pushed past my lips, demanding entrance.

Oh, the man could kiss! My hands did what they wanted to do earlier. They ran over his solid lower stomach. He sucked in a breath when my fingertips grazed the top of his boxer shorts.

"I want you, Maddie," he rasped as his lips moved to my neck, leaving wet kisses in its path. His hands ran down my ribcage to the edge of my t-shirt. "Just one more night."

His lips slammed down on mine again, all gentleness gone. He tugged my bottom lip with his teeth as his hands moved beneath my shirt. I couldn't hold back the moan when his fingers pushed my shorts down over my hips.

Within seconds, he had me stretched out on the floor, careful not to hurt my ribs. His hand slipped down to my inner thigh, skimming lightly over my panties.

"I can't get enough of you," he said before taking my mouth again, demanding more this time. As his hand moved against me, his tongue thrust into my mouth, taking what he wanted.

I was on fire.

He pulled my panties down quickly. I was frantic to have his fingers on me, inside me. I gasped as he fulfilled my wish. His mouth moved to kiss the sensitive skin right behind my earlobe as his fingers tormented me.

"I want you on top of me," he said, pulling away suddenly and taking me with him. As he sat up and leaned back against the couch, I straddled him, feeling delirious with need.

Grabbing my head, he sealed his mouth to mine. His tongue raged inside with lush, firm strokes. Both of his hands moved over my t-shirt, teasing my breasts through the thin material.

"Please, Ryder…"

"Hmmm, begging. I like it," he said, leaning over and nipping at my breasts through my shirt.

I gasped at the sensation, my hips moving against him of their own accord. He moaned at the movement as his hands dropped to hold onto my waist.

His hardness got my attention as it nudged me through his boxer shorts. I reached down between us and wrapped my fingers around him. His fingers tightened on my hips as my hand teased him.

"Maddie, you don't know what you're doing to me."

"Show me," I said, breathlessly.

"Shit!" he said under his breath, kicking the boxers off quickly.

When he was free, I wrapped my hand around his hard length. Grabbing me behind the neck roughly, his lips slashed across mine.

"I don't have a damn condom," he said before his tongue dipped into my mouth again.

My hand continued to torment him, causing an animalistic groan to move up his throat. Without breaking our kiss, he pushed my hand away swiftly before grabbing my hips and lifting me up. Slowly, he entered me, his hands guiding my hips. As his tongue lashed out against mine, he slammed into me, filling me completely.

I came instantly, every inch of my skin pulsating.

He held me still as waves of ecstasy rushed over me. His mouth silenced my moans as his tongue met mine.

I broke the kiss off as the need to move overtook me. I sat up, placing my hands on his chest. The sensation of being on top was overwhelming. I felt in control. Powerful. I started moving, feeling him deep inside of me.

"Damn, Maddie," he moaned, his grip tightening on my hips each time he thrust deeper.

I threw my head back and arched my body, the sensations racing through me.

"You look so good riding me," he said, watching me move. His hands disappeared under my shirt, seeking my breasts.

I grabbed his shoulders, holding on for dear life as the rough texture of his fingertips caressed my nipples. My hips moved up and down, having a mind of their own. I felt an orgasm coming again.

Without withdrawing, he flipped me onto my back. His lips found my earlobe as he pulled my legs up to wrap around his waist. Holding his weight off of me on his elbows, he started moving faster.

I couldn't stop the sounds that came from my throat as the ripples of another orgasm hit me. His hands tangled in my hair as he kissed me deeply, taking my loud moans into his mouth.

"Christ, Maddie!" he said against my mouth as his hips jerked into me hard. "I've never…oh, God…fuck, you feel too good to stop."

He groaned, driving into me powerfully. His body tightened, thrusting into me once more. Filling me, completing me.

~~~~

Our bodies were still connected, his hands entangled in my hair, when his kiss turned tender.

Breaking away, his blue eyes raked over my face with worry.

"Shit, I came inside of you," he said, hoarsely. "I was going to pull out but...you felt so damn good, I couldn't stop."

Until that moment, safe sex hadn't been on my mind. I was fearless with him, consumed by him. I wasn't sure either of us could have stopped.

"I wanted to feel you. Just you wrapped around me, nothing else." He kissed my lips lightly as one of his hands reached down to caress my bottom. My body started to respond again at his touch.

Pulling away, he looked down into my eyes. "I want you to know that I've never had sex without a condom."

"Never?"

"Not even once. You were my first."

On hearing those words, I pulled his head down to meet my lips again. Moving slowly, his palm glided lightly over my side, to the edge of my breast, and then to cup my jaw gently.

He ended the kiss, his lips pulling away from mine reluctantly as he pulled out of me. Rolling onto his side, he tucked me next to him. I rested my head on his firm shoulder as his arms gathered me close.

He threw a blanket over us, cocooning me next to his warmth. My body still tingled all over, each nerve ending feeling alive and awake. I knew I would never be the same again.

Chapter Twenty-Two

We left before the sun rose the next morning. Our backpacks were loaded down with food and water and both Brody and Ryder had guns and ammo.

We covered countless miles during the morning but by afternoon it was blistering hot and we had to stop. The heat was relentless, reflecting off of the pavement and baking us.

So we stopped and rested, alone in the middle of nowhere. Around dusk, we continued on, determined to get home that night. Ryder stayed beside me, matching his stride to mine, asking often if I was okay. I didn't tell him that the pain in my ribs was excruciating or that my finger throbbed. Even the gash on my head ached as my sunburn started to pull the scab apart. I wanted to see my father so I dealt with the pain.

Ryder and I only exchanged a few words as we walked. Despite last night, I still didn't know where I stood with him and now I worried about what would happen when we got home. *Would we act as if nothing happened or would we continue this non-relationship, physical thing we had going on?* I had questions but no answers.

The sun went down in a blaze of pinks and purples. It was beautiful and awe-inspiring but I couldn't enjoy it. It seemed unfair to enjoy something so beautiful when millions would start dying soon from dehydration or hunger. I just wanted to go back in time to when the only thing I had to worry about was studying and completing my hospital rotations. Now I had to worry about surviving.

Night fell quickly, leaving only moonlight to light our way. I had no idea where we were until Brody stopped to check the map.

"Eagle Pass is up ahead," he said. "If we go around, it'll add hours to our time. If we go straight through town, we'll cut our time in half." He looked over at us in the dark. "What do you want to do?"

Ryder took off his hat and ran fingers through his sweat-drenched hair. He glanced over at me with concern, looking exhausted with the weight of both our backpacks wearing him down.

"I think we better go through town. Maddie looks terrible," he said.

Yeah, I was exhausted and pain raked my body but really – terrible?

"I'm willing to fight any crazies to get home," Eva said, readjusting her backpack on her shoulders. "I'm just that desperate."

"Then let's do this," Brody said, the decision made.

An hour later, we arrived on the outskirts of Eagle Pass. The town was completely in the dark. No streetlights shined down at us and no bright lights glared from storefront windows. The silence was oppressive, a physical being that enclosed us in its clutches.

"This is something out of a horror movie," Eva whispered as we passed a grocery store that was completely destroyed. All the windows were shattered and the doors were hanging from their hinges. Empty boxes and trash littered the parking lot along with a couple of abandoned cars. Somewhere in the distance, a woman screamed. The sound sent a cold shiver up my spine.

As we drew closer to the center of town we saw hundreds of men, women, and children lingering around the large stone courthouse. Voices reached out to us. Talking, shouting, and crying. Some held candles and others were lucky enough to have flashlights. There were so many people that they blocked our path. We would have to walk through the cluster of bodies.

Ryder grabbed my hand and laced his fingers through mine.

"Stay right beside me, Maddie."

My fingers tightened around his. There was no way I was letting go of him.

We pushed through the edge of the crowd. I glanced around at the mass of men and women. Everyone looked dirty and exhausted. Some had such a faraway, lost look in their eyes that they reminded me of the lifeless zombies portrayed in movies.

We passed a vendor trying to bargain with a woman for a bottle of vodka. A man yelled for help. I jumped when someone started screaming a few feet from me.

My heart beat faster with fright when the crowd closed in around us, bringing us into its fold. Someone pushed into me and terror flooded my mind. The memories of being trampled in the club came back to me. My blood ran cold, afraid history would repeat itself.

The crowd thickened. Ryder's hand accidentally let go of mine when a man fell into him. A gut-wrenching panic filled me when people rushed between us, separating Ryder and I.

He glanced back at me as the crowd surged around us. "Maddie! Grab onto my backpack!"

I shoved my way through, trying to wrap my fingers around the nylon strap of his backpack but someone grasped my arm, yanking me away.

"Please, you have to help me! Please!" the man begged, tugging my arm.

I looked frantically back at Ryder. He was shoving people out of the way, charging forward to get to me. All it took was one look from him and the man let me go.

Shielding me with his body, he took my hand and wrapped it tightly around the strap of the backpack.

"You've got to hold onto me tight. I'm not losing you, Maddie. Not again."

I nodded, hell bent on not letting go.

We started pushing our way through the crowd again. He reached back, grabbing my waist and pulling me closer to him. I was now wedged into the backpack, holding on for dear life. Glancing around him, I saw that one of his fists was wrapped around Eva's backpack, keeping us all together.

Next to us, a man preached about the end of the world. A small child stood a few feet away, crying softly as she clung to her mother's leg. Someone begged desperately for water.

This was what the end of the world looked like, I thought. Days after the electromagnetic pulse hit, people were suffering and dying. Within a matter of minutes, the United States had turned into a third world country. This was our reality now.

We were almost to the edge of the crowd when suddenly a man tried to yank Brody's backpack off his shoulder. Brody turned to fight the guy off but the man refused to let go. Eva screamed as she was pushed to the ground in the scuffle. My hold was torn away from Ryder's backpack as he charged forward.

I helped Eva to her feet just as Ryder pulled his pistol on the man.

"Let go, mister," Ryder's deep voice boomed out.

The stranger instantly took off running through the crowd, empty-handed.

Ryder stuffed the gun in his waistband and grabbed my hand again. We hurried through the crowd, the skirmish spooking us to move faster.

A few minutes later, we finally broke free of the mob. I could now breathe easier without the press of so many bodies around me.

"Holy SHIT!" Brody exclaimed angrily as we hurried away. "What the HELL was that?"

I glanced back at the suffering, pleading horde. "That's desperation," I said, simply.

Ryder's free hand snapped to his gun again when a man appeared in front of us.

"You kids need a ride?"

The man looked like someone's grandfather. He had grey hair and a thick white beard covered his wrinkled face. His eyes shined brightly as he glanced down at Ryder's gun. "I got an old truck that still runs. I'll trade you a ride for supplies."

"How far will you go?" Ryder asked, his eyes assessing the guy.

"Depends on what you have to trade," the man said, glancing over at me.

Ryder took a protective step in front of me. "We have nothing to trade," he said, menacingly.

"Listen, kid, I've got a girl off at college. Ain't heard from her since the lights went out. I ain't going to hurt nobody, no how."

A minute passed as we all stood in silence, debating his trustworthiness.

"We've got over two hours drive time to get there," Brody warned.

The guy looked away as he scratched his beard. "Gonna take something awful nice to git there."

"Cut the bullshit," Ryder said, impatient. "What do you want?"

The guy looked down at the pistol sticking out of Ryder's waistband. "That there gun and any ammo you got."

"Hell, no!" Brody blurted out in outrage. He looked over at Ryder with disbelief. "You can't be serious, Ryder! We're not given up our goddamn gun for a ride!"

"Shut up, Brody," Ryder said, his eyes still on the man.

"Hell, no, I'm not going to shut up! We're not doing this!"

Ryder's cold blue eyes swung around to pierce Brody. "We are going to do this! You want to walk another ten days, go right ahead dumbass."

"This is about Maddie, isn't it?" Brody asked, glaring at me.

Ryder ignored the question. "You can have the gun and ammo when we get there unharmed."

"Deal," the man said, sticking his hand out. Ryder shook his hand, possibly sealing our death.

We followed the old man over to a dark blue 1960s Ford truck, complete with white-walled tires.

"Two in front, two in back," the man said, climbing into the driver's seat.

Brody and Eva climbed in the truck bed while Ryder and I got into the cab. The man obviously had spent many hours rebuilding the truck. The white leather interior was brand new and the dash looked fresh from the factory. The motor turned over smoothly with a roar of the engine.

Within seconds, we were leaving the town behind. Ryder and the man started talking about the EMP attack and how the townspeople were frantic to find supplies. He said there was no law left. Anywhere.

As the wind whipped through the windows, I tried to listen to their conversation but the exhaustion that I had been fighting all day finally won out. My eyes closed and sleep pushed at the edge of my consciousness.

"Lean against me, Maddie."

Ryder's deep voice had me opening my eyes again, suddenly awake and aware of him pressed against my side. As his arm reached around me, I laid my head against his shoulder. Within seconds, I was asleep.

Chapter Twenty-Three

I jerked awake as the truck slammed to a stop, throwing me forward slightly. Ryder's arm was the only thing keeping me from falling into the floorboard. I sat back up and looked at Ryder beside me. The dashboard lights cast a bluish glow over his unshaven jaw and cool blue eyes.

"We're at Eva's," he said, quietly.

With disbelief, I glanced out into the night. Despite the darkness, I recognized the street that led straight to Eva's house. I felt the truck bounce as Eva and Brody jumped out of the truck bed. Panic squeezed my heart. *I couldn't leave her! We had to stay together!*

Holding back a sob, I followed Ryder out of the truck and watched as Eva and Brody swung the backpacks onto their shoulders. Eva's blonde hair shined brightly under the moonlight as she walked toward me. I could see sorrow in her eyes but it was also mixed with excitement. She was home.

"We made it, Maddie," she said, tears falling down her face.

I threw my arms around her as my own tears fell. Loud sobs escaped from my chest as her arms wrapped around me. I didn't want to see her go.

"I love you, Maddie."

"I love you too, Eva. Stay safe."

Eva swiped at her face, brushing away the tears. "You're a bitch for making me cry."

I had to laugh despite the misery twisting my heart.

Eva reached over and poked Ryder in the chest. "You better take care of her, Ryder, or I will hunt you down."

One corner of Ryder's mouth quirked up in a half smile. "Take care of yourself, Eva. Maddie will be fine."

He looked over at Brody. "If you need anything, come out to the house."

"Yeah, same goes for you. You need anything, look me up," Brody replied, sticking out his hand for Ryder to shake. Ryder took Brody's hand, shaking it strongly.

Before they walked away, Brody gave the old man his hunting knife in exchange for the ride. With a final, tearful goodbye we went our separate ways. I was reluctant to leave Eva but desperate to see my dad. Knowing he was close was killing me.

The tears continued to fall as we drove away. I realized that just a few days ago, I was riding down this road in Eva's truck. The tears fell harder as I remembered how carefree we were then.

"It's going to be okay," Ryder said. His hand moved to rest on my leg. The rough pad of his thumb brushed over my skin, reminding me that I still had him and he wasn't going anywhere.

I wiped the tears away quickly. "I'll miss her."

"You'll see her again."

We left the town behind and headed for the country. I watched with anticipation for the deserted road that would lead me home. Finally, the old man stopped the truck on a familiar dirt road.

"This is as far as I go," he said.

Ryder handed the pistol and ammo to the man. "Thanks for the ride."

"You kids stay safe."

Ryder and I stood in complete darkness as the truck's taillights disappeared down the road. Gravel crunched under our shoes as we walked, breaking the silence of the night.

My broken rib protested at more walking but I didn't care. I was close to my dad. Nothing was going to stop me from seeing him.

I almost ran the rest of the way when the house came into view. No lights welcomed me. Only moonlight led the way, letting me see the old ranch house sitting quietly among trees and small scrub brush.

I wondered how late it was. *Midnight? One?* My dad was probably asleep. I hoped we wouldn't scare him by showing up in the middle of the night but I guess that was better than not showing up at all.

Ryder's steps faltered as we drew closer to the house. I looked around, wondering what had made him suddenly tense.

"Something's not right, Maddie," he said quietly, glancing around the overgrown yard.

"Why do you say that?" I asked, trying to hold down the panic that something might have happened to my dad.

"In this heat, the windows should be opened but they're all closed. Something's off."

I searched the dark porch for the potted cactus that held a spare key. When I found it, I dug in the dirt, finally pulling out the key. My hands shook as I unlocked the front door. *Please, please be here, Dad!*

I took a step inside but Ryder stopped me with a hand on my arm. He pulled me behind him protectively, guarding me with his body. I followed him into the house, letting him lead the way. The hardwood floor creaked under our feet as the heat inside hit us like a brick.

We slowly made our way down the hallway. I stayed close behind Ryder, afraid to be separated in the pitch darkness. He was right. Something wasn't right.

Knowing the layout of my house as well as I did, Ryder led the way to my dad's bedroom. What greeted us in his room made my heart stop.

His bed was empty.

Ryder walked further into the room but I froze in the doorway, stunned that my dad was not here. I felt sick to my stomach. *Could he be lost? Sick? Injured?*

Ryder opened a drawer in the bedside table, no longer trying to be quiet. He rummaged around until he pulled out a flashlight. Flicking it on, he shined it around the room. The beam bounced off the empty bed and untouched surroundings. Everything was in its place, looking exactly as it had when I left.

"He's with my parents," Ryder reassured me.

"I hope so," I whispered, not knowing what I would do if he wasn't.

Within thirty minutes, we were walking into his parent's front yard. The house was dark but we could see that windows were opened to let in the night breeze.

"Maddie, if your dad's not here, I'll find him, I promise."

My heart melted knowing that Ryder would do that for me. Just another reason why I loved him.

The wooden porch creaked loudly as we approached the front door. Ryder was reaching out to open the screen door when the business end of a shotgun appeared in the dark doorway, pointing straight at his chest.

Alarmed, I grabbed a handful of Ryder's shirt and tugged. My knuckles turned white from the tight hold I had on him.

Ryder held his ground, unafraid of the shotgun barrel inches away from him.

"It's me, Dad. Ryder."

The shotgun lowered immediately and somewhere in the house, a candle flickered to life.

"RYDER!"

Roger Delaney appeared in the doorway, grabbing Ryder by the arms and hauling him close. I heard Roger sniff loudly as they hugged. His watery eyes glanced at me, widening in surprise. "Maddie! Thank God!"

His huge arms wrapped around me, enclosing me in his warmth. My throat swelled with emotion. Roger wasn't a touchy-feely kind of guy so to see him like this was moving.

Someone cried Ryder's name with a mixture of disbelief and happiness. I heard running feet before Janice rushed from the house, throwing her arms around Ryder and almost knocking him over.

"Thank goodness! We were so worried!" she cried with tears running down her face. Reaching over, she pulled me to her. My face was smashed against Ryder's chest as she hugged both of us fiercely.

After another moment of tight hugs and surprised exclamations, Janice finally let go and held us out at arm's length.

"I prayed so hard that you two would make it home. Are you okay?"

Before we could answer, Roger motioned us inside. "Let them get in the house, Janice."

She wiped her tears away and pulled us into the candlelit room. I was happy and thankful to see them but I still wondered where my dad was.

Janice reached up and ran her hand over the rough stubble on Ryder's chin. "Now I've got both my babies at home."

"Gavin's home?" Ryder asked with hope.

"Got here yesterday. He's at your place. We didn't want to leave it empty," Roger said, stepping into the circle of candlelight. "There's been some vandalism around here."

I hated to break up their homecoming but I had to ask, "My dad wasn't at home. Do you know where he is?"

When I saw the look Janice and Roger exchanged, my heart sank. She took my hands in hers and gave me such a sad look that my lip started quivering. I fought the hysteria rising up in me. *Oh God! Was he still alive?*

Before Janice could answer, she noticed my splinted finger.

"What happened, Maddie?"

"She broke her finger and cracked a rib. Can you take a look at her later?" Ryder asked, still standing close to me.

Janice looked up at Ryder, obviously wanting to know more but not asking.

"Sure."

"What about her dad?" Ryder asked.

She hesitated. A silent message seemed to travel between the two of them. My heart beat faster as I waited for the terrible news that I knew was coming.

"He's in Gavin's old room," she said with a resigned sigh.

I grabbed the flashlight out of her hand and started down the dark hallway, ignoring her attempt to stop me. I heard her plead with Ryder to help but my heart was pumping too loudly in my ears to hear what else was said.

"Wait, Maddie," Ryder said, close behind me. He tugged on my arm but I shrugged him off as I practically ran down the hallway.

Coming to an abrupt stop, I threw open the closed bedroom door. Shining the flashlight at the bed, I sucked in a shocked breath. My dad was in bed, lying so still under the blankets that for a moment I wondered if he was alive. I instantly wanted to break down and cry but instead I swallowed hard and slowly crept forward.

At the edge of the bed, a sob escaped me. He looked so pale and frail beneath the dark blue blanket that I almost didn't recognize him.

"Dad?"

He slowly opened his eyes. It took a full minute for his gaze to focus on me. With tears in my eyes, I looked over at Ryder. He was standing just inside the doorway, looking pale as he stared at my dad.

"Maddie?" my dad asked hoarsely, weakly struggling to sit up. I hurried to help him then threw my arms around his thin shoulders. I cried as one of his arms wrapped around me.

"You're here," he said, shaking with emotion.

I couldn't speak as I sat on the edge of the bed with my arms still around him. Pulling away, I saw him struggling to speak. I knew immediately that something was wrong. His mouth drooped on one side and his left arm lay limply beside him.

"Dad?" I whispered with alarm. "What happened?"

His eyes were full of sadness. With panic, I looked over as Janice forced her way around Ryder in the doorway.

"Maddie, I wanted to tell you before you saw him. We think he had a stroke."

I looked back down into his brown eyes as my tears fell unchecked. "Oh, Dad!" I cried, giving him another hug.

"Maddie, so happy." His words sounded forced and pieced together with difficulty.

I felt Ryder move to stand behind me, giving me the strength I needed to face this nightmare.

"He has some muscle weakness in his mouth and left eye that comes and goes. His left arm is completely numb and he has some trouble walking so he's been using a cane. Also, his speech is deteriorating," Janice said, quietly. "With his medical history, I'm almost certain it was a stroke. How severe, we won't know without tests."

My dad reached up with his good hand and smoothed the hair away from my face. "So happy," he said with a crooked smile. I forced a smile on my face, knowing he would want to see it.

Janice walked to the opposite side of the bed and helped him lie back down. It hurt to see her covering up my larger-than-life dad as if he was a child.

His hand reached out shakily toward Ryder. "Thank you. Bring her home."

Ryder reached around me to grasp my dad's outstretched hand. "You know I would do anything to keep her safe."

My dad's eyes twinkled at Ryder. Looking at me again, he whispered, "Love you. Remember."

The tears fell harder. He was talking to me like he was dying. I shook my head in denial, refusing to listen.

"Let him get some sleep," Janice said.

I leaned over and kissed his forehead. "Love you, Daddy."

We were heading out of the bedroom when his weak voice stopped us. "Ryder. Stay."

As Ryder turned to go back into the bedroom, Janice took my arm and led me away. Before she pulled me around the corner, I turned to see my dad's hand reaching for Ryder's. *What did my dad have to say to Ryder that he couldn't say in front of me?*

In the living room, Roger had lit a lantern that cast a soft glow around the spacious room. The large stone fireplace and the brown leather furniture gave the room a warm comforting feeling that I needed right now.

"Are you hungry?" Janice asked, pushing me gently to sit the couch.

"No, thank you," I answered, numbly.

Taking a seat beside me, she took my hand in hers and studied my face.

"Roger found him like that two days ago when he went over to check on him. I've done everything I could." She paused a second before continuing. "From one nurse to another, you need to know that without medication or medical help, there isn't much we can do for him. And since the hospital doesn't have electricity..." She took a deep breath and let it out slowly. "I'm not sure how much time he has left, Maddie."

I nodded, the tears falling harder. I lost one parent long ago. I couldn't lose the other. *How could I live without my dad?* He was my foundation. We depended on each other. I would have no family left in the world, a world falling apart a little each day.

"Let me get you some water, dear."

After Janice left, I sat alone, gripping my fingers tightly to stop them from trembling. Studying my dirty shoes, I told myself over and over that this wasn't real. None of it was real. I would wake up in the morning, back in my apartment. My dad would call and tell me about his day. I would go to school and see my friends. My old life would be back.

"Your dad is strong. He'll pull through this," Roger said from across the room.

I nodded, tears making my eyesight blurry. As much as I wanted that to be the truth, as a nursing student I knew that recovering from a stroke without medical help would be next to impossible. Janice and I would do what we could but the rest was up to Fate or God or whoever was controlling this crazy world we lived in.

I looked up as Ryder walked into the room, his long legs covering the space between us within seconds. When he sat next to me and took me into his arms, I felt comfort that only he could give me.

"He's alive and safe, Maddie, be thankful for that," he whispered against my hair.

I knew Ryder was right. I think it would have been worse not knowing where he was, lost to me forever.

Roger cleared his throat. "When did you two leave?" he asked.

Ryder pulled away, suddenly aware we weren't alone. Leaning forward, he put his elbows on his knees and looked at his dad.

"Right away. It took us three days of driving and walking to get here," he answered, running a hand over his face.

"Here, hon," Janice said, returning with a small cup of water.

My shaky fingers took the cool plastic cup. I took a sip, not really thirsty but knowing I was still dehydrated.

"I'm glad you're home, son. Really glad," Roger said with a catch in his voice.

"You heard anything?" Ryder asked.

"There's been some talk on the short wave radio. Terrorists detonated the EMP in a declaration of war and most of the U.S. is in the black. Stuff like that. I've heard that the military is crippled pretty badly right now. Y'all see anything?"

Ryder was about to answer when his mom interrupted. "It's late, Roger and they look exhausted. Let them go to bed. You can ask the questions tomorrow."

"Sorry, kids. She's right. The two of you look exhausted."

"Since it's late, you can stay here, Ryder. I'll make you a bed on the couch and Maddie can have your old room," Janice said, heading for the doorway. "I'll get some blankets."

While she was gone, Roger asked Ryder a few more questions about what we saw. Ryder told him about the hospital and the plane crashing but didn't talk about the convicts or the club. There would be time for that later. For now, we needed sleep.

When Janice returned with sheets and pillows for Ryder, the memory of our makeshift bed and what we did in it raced through my mind. I looked at Ryder, wondering if he was remembering the same thing but his cool eyes gave nothing away.

"Let's get you settled in, Maddie," Janice said.

I said goodnight to Roger and stood up to follow her. Ryder kept his eyes downcast, not looking at me. I stood in indecision. *What did I say to him? Now that we were home, would things be different?*

His blue eyes looked distant as they finally met mine and his voice was flat, void of emotion.

"See you in the morning, Maddie."

"Night, Ryder."

I was sleeping in Ryder's old room, somewhere I hadn't been since he moved out. Under the flashlight beam, it didn't look the same. Gone were the posters that lined the wall. There weren't any dirty clothes lying around or smelly shoes in the closet. Now an antique iron bed sat in the middle of the room, covered with a light blue quilt. Lace curtains blew gently in the nighttime breeze. It was a guest room now, not the teenage boy's room I remembered.

"You keep that flashlight in here with you," Janice said, pulling the covers back for me. "You need anything during the night, don't hesitate to wake us."

I felt like crying all over again as I stood in a room I used to know so well. *How many times had I sat in here with Ryder, talking about school or other silly adolescent stuff?* When we were little, we spent hours in here building tent forts or making big plans for the future. Now the room had changed. We had changed. The world had changed.

I just wanted to escape it all.

Janice rounded the bed quickly to wrap her arms around me, just like my mother would have done if she were still alive.

"You're home, Maddie. You're safe with us. It will be okay," she whispered, patting my back reassuringly.

"Thank you for taking care of my dad."

"Of course, hon, you know we wouldn't let anything happen to the two of you." She pulled away and rubbed my arm in a loving gesture. "I knew that Ryder would take care of you and get you home."

"There were times that I didn't think we would make it."

"But you did." She pushed my hair out of my eyes. "Now, get some sleep. We'll see you in the morning."

As she left, I stood wearily in the middle of the room, staring at the bed. Too tired to care what I slept in, I pulled off my dirt-encrusted shorts and climbed under the cool sheets. With my last bit of strength, I turned off the flashlight and placed it next to me in bed.

Even though I was exhausted and sore, sleep would not come. I thought it was because I was in a room that didn't look familiar anymore but the truth was I hadn't slept alone for almost a week now.

I missed him and I needed him.

Ryder was sleeping only a few rooms away. I could easily go to him, let him pull me close, give me comfort and fall asleep next to him. He wouldn't push me away. He would probably welcome me. Only Ryder could provide the reassurance I needed that everything would be okay. That my dad would be okay. That the world would be okay.

That we would be okay.

Chapter Twenty-Four

I rolled over, feeling warmth on my face. Opening my eyes slowly, I squinted against the bright light streaming from the window. Somewhere outside, a baby calf bawled loudly for its mother. The sound reminded me of where I was. Home.

The crisp sheets felt wonderful against my skin as I stretched carefully. My ribs felt tight and achy this morning and my broken finger felt blissfully numb. Feeling along my hairline, I was happy to discover that the gash was healing nicely.

I slowly climbed out of bed. Pulling my shorts back on, my eyes fell on my backpack sitting in the corner of the room. I couldn't remember bringing it into the bedroom with me. *Someone must have brought it in this morning.* I grew warm. Ryder. He was here, watching me sleep, standing over me.

Feeling embarrassed at the thought, I dug clean clothes out of the bag and changed quickly. Finding a toothbrush, I dry brushed my teeth then ran fingers through my long, straight hair. I needed a bath but first, I needed to check on my dad.

I found everyone sitting around the large kitchen table, including Gavin and my dad. Despite seeing the cane resting against his leg, I was happy to see my dad looking more like himself than the weak man from last night.

"Look who decided to join us! Good afternoon, squirt!" Gavin said, embracing me in a bone-crunching hug.

"I'm so happy you're okay, Gavin!" My words were muffled against his chest as he squeezed me tightly.

Gavin was tall and handsome like Ryder. He had the same bright blue eyes but the similarities ended there. Gavin had short black hair where Ryder's was light brown and always needing a haircut. Both were tough as nails and stubborn as hell but Ryder was more of a loose cannon than Gavin ever was. Both were fiercely protective of each other but were known to get into drag-out fights as well.

"Take it easy, Gavin, she's hurt," Ryder said as he glared at Gavin with controlled hostility.

Ryder still managed to look good despite the exhaustion lining his face. His hair was curling slightly at the edges and the stubble on his jaw was growing more each day, making him appear even more dangerous and unapproachable. The white shirt he wore emphasized the darkness of his skin after days in the sun and highlighted the tattoos racing up and down his arm. I had missed him so much last night that the sight of him this morning was like a cool drink of water on a hot day.

"Crap, Maddie, you're hurt?" Gavin asked.

"I'm fine. Ryder is just being overprotective."

"Yeah, a broken rib and finger are 'just fine,'" Ryder said, sarcastically.

"Shit! Want me to take a look at it?" Gavin asked me.

"Hell, no! Mom can look at it." Ryder answered, fuming.

"I'm an EMT, Ryder. I do this for a living," Gavin tried to reason with him.

I ignored the argument that seemed to be brewing between the two of them and took a seat beside my dad.

"You okay this morning, Dad?"

He smiled at me and gave me a thumbs-up. Tears threatened again but I reminded myself that we were together and we were both safe. The rest we would take day by day.

Janice sat a plate of food in front of me that contained bread spread with jelly and something that looked suspiciously like bacon but she said it was deer meat.

"You're not going to see her without a shirt on, Gavin, so back off," Ryder said angrily as he glared at Gavin.

Gavin threw his hands up in frustration. "She's like our baby sister, Ryder! What's the big deal?"

"Okay, you two, that's enough. Take it outside," Janice warned in an authoritative voice.

Ryder stared at Gavin another second before pushing back from the table and walking out the back door, letting it slam loudly behind him.

"What got into him?" Gavin asked with a smirk.

I wondered the same thing. Ryder hadn't looked at me once since I walked in the kitchen. *Was he already trying to distance himself from me?*

"Sleep good?" My dad asked, patting my hand. Worry about Ryder vanished as I looked at my father. He was still pale and seemed so weak that I suddenly lost my appetite.

"I slept fine, Dad. How about you?"

"Good. Tell…getting here."

I tried not to cry when I heard the sluggish and broken words he had trouble speaking. The energy it took for him to say the words broke my heart more.

"Ryder's been weirdly closed-mouthed about it," Gavin chimed in. "What happened?"

I told them everything about the club, the plane going down, and the men stealing Eva's truck. My dad looked stunned as I explained how we walked for hours without food or water and how we broke into someone's home.

By the time I was finished, both he and Janice were in tears.

After everyone ate, Gavin and Roger headed outside, discussing something about a water filtration system. My dad wanted to return to his room so I helped him down the hallway slowly, talking the whole time about the EMP and loss of power.

When I returned, I helped Janice clean the kitchen. She filled me in on life without electricity. There were plenty of candles and lanterns so light wasn't an issue. Roger had rigged up a shower outside that was just an enclosure large enough for one person. A water tank was attached on top that would catch rainwater or could be filled with water from the creek. They were in the process of building an outhouse but until it was finished, we would have to make due with the woods near the house. Their cellar held canned fruits, vegetables, and meat. She said they had enough stored water to drink but they were also sanitizing creek water to use for bathing and cooking.

In the bathroom, Janice continued to talk as she examined my ribs and finger. Deciding both were healing nicely, she started to bandage them.

"You and your dad can stay here as long as you want, Maddie."

"Thank you, Janice, but we don't want to be a burden."

"Nonsense. You two are family," she said, giving me a warm smile. "You always have been."

~~~~

Later that night, I was helping my father to his room when Ryder walked past me in the hallway.

"I'm heading home, Maddie," he said, not bothering to look at me as he continued walking. "I'll see you later."

It was then that I knew; I was back to being just a friend, something I had been all along. I closed my eyes against the pain in my chest. I knew this moment was coming. I just didn't expect it to hurt so much.

Chapter Twenty-Five

For the next three days, I went through the motions of living. I helped my dad brush his teeth and shave. When he needed help walking or even eating, I was there. I stayed by his side constantly, worried to let him out of my sight for too long.

To pass the day, we would sit on the front porch and watch the horses and cattle in the pasture. At night, I lay in bed and listened to the night sounds outside the open window but my mind was always on Ryder.

He was always near during the day, working around the ranch. His meals were spent with us but after dinner, he said goodbye and went home, leaving me alone once again.

~~~~

"What's up, shorty?"

I looked over as Gavin walked up. The old straw cowboy hat he wore hid his face from the sun but couldn't hide the sparkle in his eyes.

"Not much, Gavin. What's up with you?" I asked, turning my attention back to the horse I had been petting. My dad was taking a nap and Janice was busy so I had walked down to the fence line, needing some time alone. Ryder had hardly spoken to me since we arrived home but I was determined to let it go. It was time to move on.

"Oh, just taking a break from working on that dang outhouse. I swear digging a hole with a shovel isn't the easiest job around here but this shitter is going to be the best shitter around."

I laughed lightly. "But it will be so much better than using a bush," I said, smiling. The silly look on his face reminded me again of his easy-going personality. He was so different from Ryder that sometimes I had to remind myself that they were brothers.

He rested his elbows on the barbwire fence near me and looked out at the land. I watched the horse walk away, finding a tasty patch of grass nearby. A few moments passed in silence. The only sounds were grasshoppers somewhere in the tall grass, chirping their mating call.

"You know, Maddie, I'm happy you made it home. I was worried about you."

"I'm happy you made it home too, Gavin. Dallas is a big city and couldn't have been easy to get out of."

"No, it wasn't, but I only had myself to worry about." Gavin paused, peeking at me from under the brim of his hat. I blushed, knowing this conversation was going somewhere that I didn't want it to go.

"It's not any of my business but what happened out there?"

I knew he was referring to Ryder but I couldn't bring myself to say anything. Playing dumb seemed the safest thing to do.

"I told you what happened," I answered. "We were at a club, we had our truck stolen, and we walked home."

"There's more to that story than you're telling. Something happened between you two."

I started to protest but he held up a hand, stopping me. "I know Ryder's reputation with women and I know how he is with you. I can only guess what happened and it pisses me off. I just want you to know that I'm here for you. Ryder might be my brother but he can be a jackass too."

At his sincere words, I felt tears start behind my eyes. *Since when had I become such a crybaby?* I sniffed loudly and wiped a stray tear away as I looked out at the pasture.

"Oh, hell! I hit the nail on the head didn't I? Shit, Maddie, I'm sorry my brother is a jerk!"

He reached out and pulled me toward him. I went willingly, needing a shoulder to cry on.

I sniffed loudly into his shirt as he patted my back awkwardly. "If I was him, I would never hurt you," he mumbled in a whisper.

My back stiffened but then I relaxed. This was Gavin. He was harmless.

"Oh, shit! I'm in trouble now," Gavin said, staring over my shoulder. He slowly unwound his arms from around me, keeping his eyes locked ahead.

I wiped my eyes free of tears before glancing behind me. Ryder was stalking toward us, the anger on his face speaking volumes.

"What the hell are you doing, Gavin?" he asked, callously.

I took a few steps away from Gavin, knowing that Ryder had a short temper and I seemed to be the cause of it most of the time.

"Just talking, Ryder, you need something?" Gavin asked, innocently.

Ryder's jaw clenched and unclenched several times as his cold eyes glared at us. I hoped he couldn't see the remains of my tears. The last thing I wanted was for him to know how hurt I was.

"Dad needs you," Ryder said. "Now!"

"Okay." Gavin reached over and rubbed my arm affectionately. "Remember what I said, Maddie. You need me, you know where to find me." With a smirk at Ryder, he walked away.

Ryder looked at me, his eyes frosty. "What was that about?"

I folded my arms over my chest, protecting myself. "Nothing. We were just talking."

I started to walk by him, afraid I would either burst into tears or start screaming at any moment.

His hand snapped out, grabbing my upper arm to stop me.

"Maddie?"

"Yes?"

He swallowed hard, taking his baseball cap off and running his hand through his sweat-soaked hair.

"Gavin's a good guy."

Oh, no, he's not going to suggest…

"And any woman would be lucky to have him…"

I tried to interrupt him. I couldn't listen to this.

"But I'm still here," he looked at me deeply, "and I don't plan on leaving."

I stood still, frozen by his words. He slapped his hat back on his head and pulled the brim low. Without looking at me again, he walked away, leaving me with those words ringing in my ears.

Maybe there was hope.

~~~~

I was still dreaming of that hope days later when a stranger approached the house from the road. I was sitting with my dad on the porch, enjoying the warm sun, when I saw him. He looked dirty and thin. He appeared unarmed but looks could be deceiving. We had learned that the hard way.

A safe distance from the house, Ryder's dad stopped him with a loaded shotgun. I saw them exchange a few heated words but they were too far away for me to hear.

"You two, get in here!" Janice hissed from the doorway, yanking my attention away from the stranger.

I quickly helped my dad to his feet. As I was helping him toward the door, a movement out of the corner of my eye caught my attention. Ryder and Gavin were striding purposefully toward the stranger. Both had shotguns in their hands, looking ready to go to war.

Ryder's hard eyes flickered over to me, rapidly moving down my body before glancing away. He stopped feet away from the stranger, his stance wide. I could see the tautness in his shoulders and the rigid muscles of his back. The threat was real and he was ready.

Inside, my hands shook as I lowered my dad into a kitchen chair. Hurrying over to the window, I peeked outside.

"Get away from the window, Maddie!" Janice whispered frantically.

I ignored her, Ryder's safety the only thing on my mind. The men were tense, ready to strike at a moment's notice. I could see Ryder's hand tighten around the shotgun he carried at his side.

Abruptly, the man turned and walked away. I let out a sigh of relief but the fright didn't go away. Maybe we weren't as safe here as I thought.

Chapter Twenty-Six

One day rolled into another. I tried not to worry about Eva and Brody, all my friends at school, or the health of my father. Janice reminded me many times to take one day at a time and not to worry about the future. I wish it were that simple but my future looked bleak.

One afternoon, I was helping Janice lay out food for lunch when Ryder walked into the kitchen. My body immediately started humming, alive and awake as if it had been in a deep sleep until now.

"Mom, can you pack two lunches for me?" he asked, reaching around me to pluck an apple from a basket. According to Janice, this was the last batch of apples from her garden. After this, there would be no fresh fruit until next year.

"Sure, hon, are y'all still working?" Janice asked.

"No, I want to take Maddie home with me for a while."

He wanted to be alone with me?

Janice's eyes swung from Ryder to me, surprised. "Give me a second and I'll fix you two something."

From under my lashes, I peeked up at Ryder. He towered over me, making me feel small and vulnerable. This close, I could see the heat in his eyes, reminding me that we hadn't been alone together in days.

"That okay?" he asked when he caught me staring at him.

"Yes," I answered. *Like I would say no?*

After Janice gathered some food for us, we headed toward the barn. The sun beat down merciless, making heat waves ripple around us. As we walked, grasshoppers jumped out of our path, making noises as they leaped away.

"Are we riding horses?" I asked, matching my stride to his.

"Nope," Ryder answered, giving me a smile that could melt a girl's heart.

"So what are we…?"

He pulled a set of keys out of his pocket. "Bronco."

"What? It still runs?" I asked, surprised.

When he smiled and nodded, I automatically threw my arms around him. I was happy, knowing how much he loved that Bronco. From the time he was sixteen, he had spent hours working on it, pouring every dime he earned into rebuilding it. I was glad it survived the EMP, it meant that much to him.

My happiness only increased when Ryder slowly wrapped his arms around me. The innocent hug turned into so much more as his hands slowly moved lower to rest on my hips. His fingers spread wide to grasp me tightly, drawing me closer. I breathed in deeply, loving the smell of him. Three simple days had me missing him so damn much that it hurt.

When he let go of me, my body protested. I took a deep breath and tried to slow my pounding heart as he walked away.

When I finally got ahold of myself, I followed him into the huge barn. It held two tractors, a horse trailer, Ryder's old Bronco, and his dad's 1950s Ford truck. Various farm equipment and feed were placed haphazardly around also.

In one area of the barn was a room, locked up tight against intruders. I knew that behind that door was an arsenal of survival supplies. From packages of toilet paper to boxes of nonperishable food, the room was packed. Bags of wheat, rice, and beans were stored among cases of bottled water. I also knew that beneath the floor was a safe room complete with enough supplies to last a couple of days. When someone said Roger and Janice were survivalists, they had no idea to what degree.

I climbed into the smooth leather seat of the Bronco at the same time Ryder took a seat behind the wheel. I held my breath as he turned the key in the ignition. The roar of the motor was a wonderful sound to hear. After backing out of the barn, we were on our way.

Ryder lived further back on the property. It was about a mile from his parent's home, connected by a dirt driveway. They couldn't see his house, he couldn't see theirs. He had built it with that in mind. Years ago, he told me that he didn't want them knowing about his late night visitors. I cringed, remembering that now.

The house looked the same as the last time I saw it; a one-story ranch house made of rugged Texas stone. A barn sat a short distance away, full of various farm equipment.

Ryder unlocked the door and let me walk in first. All the windows were open so it was hot but not stifling. Natural sunlight streamed in, lighting up the home brightly.

It wasn't a big house but just the right size for him. It had two bedrooms, a living room, one bathroom, and a small kitchen. The place was a typical bachelor pad. His living room contained a leather couch and matching chair. Over the stone fireplace hung a large flat-screen TV. No pictures were on the walls and the place was empty of knickknacks. Last time I was here, there were empty beer bottles everywhere. At least, someone had cleaned the place up.

"Let's eat on the back porch. It'll be cooler," Ryder said, leading the way through the kitchen to the backdoor.

What I loved about his home was right outside that door. Large mature trees surrounded a huge wooden deck and a narrow flowing creek. The water could be heard running along the creek bed while the tree limbs above blew gently in the wind. It was so secluded and quiet that it was easy to imagine we were the only two people left in the world.

We sat down on the steps leading to the edge of the water. His outer thigh brushed against mine intimately as we sat side by side.

"What am I doing here, Ryder?" I asked, squinting my eyes against the sun to look at him.

His old ball cap was pulled low so I couldn't see his eyes, just his freshly shaven jaw. I watched as he clenched his teeth then swung his eyes around to look at me. Heat was still there, lingering around the blue irises.

"Eat your sandwich, Maddie. You've lost weight," he said gruffly, looking back at the creek. His shoulders flexed as he leaned forward to place his elbows on his knees. The memory of grabbing those shoulders as we made love made me hot and bothered. I quickly looked away, forcing myself to take a bite of sandwich. After my last bite, he stood up.

"Let's go."

"What are we doing?" I asked.

"Target practice," he answered, walking toward the door. "After that stranger showed up, I decided you need it."

I was here for target practice? Really? Was I naïve to think he just wanted to be alone with me?

"I don't need to practice, Ryder. I'm a perfect shot, you know that," I complained, really wanting to practice on something else with him.

He glanced back at me as he walked down his hallway. "You haven't practiced in four years. It's about time you did."

I tried not to look in his bedroom when we passed it. Continuing down the hallway, we entered the spare bedroom where he kept a safe and a small desk.

He started to unlock the safe but stopped and looked over at me. "If something happens, the combination is 11-19-54."

I hated when he said stuff like that. If I needed the combination that meant he wasn't around and if he wasn't around...well, I just didn't want to think about it.

"You can use this one," he said, pulling out a 9mm pistol and a box of bullets.

"A handgun? Really? Why not a shotgun like I always practice with?"

He started loading the gun, answering my question at the same time. "A shotgun is fine but a pistol...a pistol can be concealed and it's better in close quarters."

The thought of killing or injuring someone sent a chill down my spine.

"You know I don't like them," I argued, following him back through the house to the porch.

He sat some empty cans down near the creek and hopped back on the porch to hand me the gun.

"You need to feel comfortable with it."

I took the thing with disgust, as if it were a dead animal he was trying to hand me.

Giving me a frustrated look, his voice dropped low, "Maddie, humor me and do this,"

I sighed and carefully aimed at a can. He moved behind me, spreading his legs on each side of me so that I was cocooned against him. Wrapping his arms around me, he placed his hands on top of mine and lifted the gun slightly higher. My body flared to life. I tried to focus on the target and ignore the rapid beating of my heart.

He dropped his hands away and took a step back. "Remember to take a breath and let it out slowly before you take the shot, just like I taught you."

I nodded and filled my lungs with air. Holding it a second, I let out my breath slowly then squeezed the trigger. The recoil threw me back but Ryder's palm was instantly there, on the small of my back, preventing me from falling further. His hand moved lower, resting at the top of my bottom, familiar and warm.

"You hit it dead on," he said, looking at the fallen can and dropping his hand away. "Five more rounds and then you're done. We need to conserve our bullets."

By the time I finished, he was satisfied that I knew what I was doing. Handing the gun over to him, I watched as his large hands expertly handled the gun, carefully checking the chamber and slipping the safety on. When he went inside to return the gun to the safe, I took a seat on the porch steps and waited.

The heat was bearing down with vengefulness as the sun rose higher in the cloudless sky. Sweat was making my hair stick to my scalp and my clothes damp with perspiration. I eyed the creek with longing. The last time I had a bath was two days ago. I really needed to get in that water.

I glanced back at the house. Ryder was still inside somewhere. *Should I?* It wouldn't be the first time I bathed around him and it probably wouldn't be the last. Modesty seemed to be a thing of the past since our bathroom now meant the bushes and a shower now meant an outdoor spray down of water. Plus, I would rather bathe here, when it was just the two of us rather than outside his parent's home where anyone could walk in on me.

Jumping up before I changed my mind, I hurried inside. I wasn't sure where Ryder was so I went into the bathroom and gathered his shampoo and soap. Before I left, I grabbed the towel hanging on a hook behind the door.

"I'm taking a bath!" I yelled over my shoulder before walking out the back door.

At the edge of the porch, I quickly took my clothes off and folded them neatly into a pile. I hurried into the water. It was cool against my overheated skin. I quickly began to soap my body and hair as best as I could with a broken finger. The memory of Ryder doing that for me had my skin overheating all over again.

As I was washing the soap out of my hair, I heard the back door slam shut. I swung around, my breath catching.

Ryder halted mid-stride. He held two red plastic cups in his hands and looked ready to drop them in surprise.

I couldn't hold back a grin when I saw the shocked look on his face. There wasn't much I could do to blow Ryder's mind and render him speechless but I guess I just did.

"I couldn't resist a bath," I said at the same time that he said, "I was searching for vodka," in a hoarse voice as he stared at me in awe.

"You had to search for liquor?" I teased with a smile. "I thought the almighty Ryder was always prepared for a party."

"Looks like I'm missing out on one now."

It was my turn to be shocked when he sat the cups down and took off his hat. His eyes held mine as his shirt and shorts followed. My mouth formed a little 'O' as his boxer shorts disappeared next.

Never taking his eyes off of me, he stalked toward the creek, his stride slow and purposeful. I swallowed hard at the sight before me. He had the body of a Greek God and the ink of a perfect badass.

Within seconds, he was beside me, causing the water to ripple around us. Clasping my waist, he yanked me against him, knocking the breath out of my lungs. My eyes rounded at the feeling of his erection against my stomach, hard and ready. He stared down into my eyes a second before his mouth descended on mine with hunger.

My arms had a mind of their own as they wrapped around his neck, lightly running over the hair laying on his nape. His hands traveled slowly up my ribcage, stopping beneath my breasts to caress me. His mouth became frantic, forcing my lips open. I couldn't resist biting him playfully as his tongue darted between my teeth. A deep growl vibrated from his throat as I took his tongue into my mouth, sucking on it gently.

I gasped when one of his hands moved to cup my breast, flicking a thumb across my nipple. Frantically breaking off the kiss, he lifted me up so that my breasts were even with his mouth. Taking a nipple, he wrapped his lips around it, gently at first but then harder, with more urgency. I gasped and grabbed his hair, my fingers threading through the silky strands. His lips moved to my other breast and gave it just as much attention, licking and biting to the point I thought I would scream with the intensity.

He lowered me, his lips going back to take my mouth again. As his tongue invaded my mouth roughly, he wrapped my legs around his waist. Fingers pushed against my bottom, bringing me closer to his hardness.

"I've missed you beside me at night," he said, his lips moving to my ear, nipping at my earlobe. "I lay awake wanting you. I go to sleep dreaming of you."

I grabbed his hair and pulled his lips back to mine, kissing him deeply with a need that could never be fulfilled.

As his lips conquered mine, he lifted me up effortlessly. Excruciating slow, he lowered me onto him, inch by inch under the water. I gasped as he stretched me, filling me completely.

His mouth left mine to look deep into my eyes. In those blue depths, I saw desire so strong, I wanted to start moving on him. His hands held my hips still as he moved in for another kiss. His lips smashed against mine, taking what he wanted. I threw my head back as the sensation of him deep inside of me ran from my head to the tips of my toes. His lips grazed my neck, biting me gently, making the torture, oh, that much more blissful.

He clasped my hips hard, still refusing to let me move as he pulsated deep inside of me.

"Ryder…" I pleaded, begging to end the exquisite torture.

He moaned low against my throat, the sound vibrating through my body. "You feel so right, Maddie," he whispered in a husky voice.

When I started to whimper in frustration, he started moving, his hips pulling away before thrusting hard. I grabbed his shoulders, holding on tight as the waves of ecstasy washed over me. As my hips moved up and down on him, his hands reached for my breasts again.

The fever his fingers caused pushed me over the edge. I moaned loudly as the orgasm hit me full force. This time, he didn't try to stifle my cries with his mouth.

I opened my eyes to find him watching me. Biting my lower lip, I blushed. That seemed to cause a frenzy in him. He started pumping into me harder, watching as my tongue licked the spot on my lower lip where a second ago my teeth had been. His fingers knotted in my hair, yanking my face closer. His mouth slashed across mine, his tongue thrusting into my mouth to taste me.

"I'm going to come inside of you again, Maddie," he whispered against my lips as his body pumped in and out of me. "Because you're mine. Only mine."

I nodded, willing to agree to anything he wanted as his body ravaged mine. One hand grasped my hip firmly as his other hand stayed tangled in my hair. When he threw his head back and groaned, I couldn't resist kissing his neck, letting my tongue lightly touch his hot skin.

"Shit!" he moaned low in his throat, panting.

When he thrust faster, I instantly came again, letting out a cry when everything in me shattered. He shouted as his body bucked beneath me, reaching for his own release.

His lips moved to my ear. "I love you, Maddie," he whispered in a strained voice as he pounded hard into me one last time before filling me.

My body instantly went still. *He loved me?*

His lips softly kissed mine as his fingers stayed threaded through my wet hair. The kiss was so gentle, so unlike all his frantic, sexual charged kisses that I felt tears threaten at the tenderness.

Pulling away, he ducked his head under the water. A second later, he popped above the surface, slinging his wet hair back and causing water to fly in all directions. I swallowed hard at the sight of his muscular chest above the water. I wanted to run my hand over those tattoos, following them around his shoulder, down his chest, and lower.

"Let me take a bath then I'll take you back," he said, matter-of-factly.

What? That's all he had to say after telling me he loved me?

I stood, dumbfounded, as he started to soap his body down. My mind couldn't quite wrap around the fact that he loved me. My heart was still pounding and his words just made it beat faster.

When had he changed his mind? And why was he acting like it wasn't a big deal? We needed to talk about this, but first, I needed some clothes. Talking while in the nude wasn't a smart thing to do around Ryder.

I was pushing my way through the water to get out when his fingers wrapped around my upper arm. He didn't say anything but his eyes searched my face, looking for something.

"I'm going to get out. I'll wait for you inside," I said, trying to keep my mouth shut and not blurt out all the questions I had.

He nodded but his eyes were penetrating, trying to look deep inside of me. Finally, he let go of my arm, releasing me from his scrutiny. I turned my back and walked to shore, not really caring if he saw me naked or not.

I quickly gathered my clothes and ran inside to get dressed. My broken finger needed a new splint but I wasn't worried about it right now. I threw my clothes on and braided my long hair. Taking a seat at the kitchen table, I absently ran my hand over the wooden tabletop as I waited for him.

So how would I start this conversation? I needed to hear him say that we were much, much more than friends now. I wanted him to say that for the first time in his life, he was in love.

The back door opened and butterflies took flight in my stomach. He was wearing only shorts, leaving his tanned chest bare, glistening with water. His eyes burned into mine as he walked past me. I watched him leave the kitchen silently. Standing up, I smoothed down my shirt in a nervous gesture.

I found him in his bedroom, pulling on a new pair of boxer shorts. My face reddened at the sight.

He looked up at me, not at all surprised to see me standing in his doorway.

"You okay? You look worried." Without waiting for my response, he turned to his closet and started rummaging around for something.

I couldn't believe his lackluster attitude! Minutes ago he said he loved me. Did he forget? Did he not realize how huge this was? I assumed that if he ever felt this way about me, he would be more...I don't know...affectionate after declaring his love. Apparently, I was wrong.

He started to pull on clean shorts, watching me carefully as I took another step into the room. His blue eyes held nothing. No tenderness or love lurked there.

"Ryder, you said you loved me."

Staring at the floor, he ran a hand through his hair, causing the ends to stick up all over. Taking a deep breath, he looked at me.

"Maddie...hell," he muttered under his breath.

He sat down on the edge of his bed, his stomach muscles rippling with the movement. His tattoos twisted and flexed as he put his head in his hands and rested his elbows on his knees.

I suddenly had a bad feeling.

"It was just something I said. I was coming. You felt good on top of me. It just came out. Guys do that shit. Blurt things out because the sex feels so good. Half the time, they don't mean it," he said, looking up at me with bleak eyes.

A feeling of despair squeezed my heart and wouldn't let go. *Oh, Jesus! How could I be such a fool?* For the third time, I had slept with him knowing I was still nothing to him except a friend. Used and stupid, that was me. The thought filled me with outrage.

"So what you're saying is you DON'T love me. You were just enjoying yourself and it just, I don't know, slipped out on accident?"

Ryder ran a hand through his hair again. Standing up, he started pacing around his bedroom only to stop and yank a shirt off of a hanger, pulling it on quickly, his movements angry.

Stalking over to me, he stopped feet away and placed both hands on his hips.

"I told you that I don't do relationships and I don't fall in love."

I flinched, the words cutting like knives. Feeling delirious with hurt and anger, I turned on my heels and hurried out of the room. I couldn't be in the same house with him anymore.

Chapter Twenty-Seven

I was almost to the front door when he grabbed my arm, swinging me around to face him. I looked up into those blue eyes and my heart broke in two. He might deny it all he wanted but I was just another notch in his bedpost. I died a little at the thought.

"Don't touch me, Ryder."

The blood drained from his face.

"Don't leave," he said, his throat working hard to swallow.

I yanked my arm away from him, the hurt and anger ripping at my insides. "Why can't I leave? You got what you wanted, right?"

"Maddie…"

"You don't want a relationship? Fine! I'll make it easy on you. Don't come near me again!" I threw over my shoulder as I flew out the door and down the steps.

Ryder followed one step behind me, barefoot. I shifted away from him when his hand snaked out to grab my arm again.

"You can't just walk away! Damn it, I never wanted to hurt you!"

"TOO LATE!" I shouted.

Grasshoppers jumped out of my way as I ran down the dirt road. The heat was oppressive, pushing down on me like a blanket and making it hard to breath. Or maybe it was just the hurt shredding my heart into a million pieces that made it hard to breath.

"STOP!" he bellowed.

I stopped, keeping my back to him. My breathing was rapid and my hands were shaking. A burning sensation rushed into my face, either from the sun or from my boiling blood, I didn't know.

I kept my eyes focused on his chest when he moved to stand in front of me. I couldn't look into his face and see regret or pity. That would be the death of me.

"I'm sorry," he said in a rugged voice. "God, I'm sorry, Maddie! Don't push me away."

The tears fell. My heart now lay shattered.

"I should have known that I was just a plaything for you! Something to fill your time! Or maybe I was simply a challenge. Is that it, Ryder? Whatever it was, I hope you had a good time because it isn't happening again!" I cried, tears blurring my vision and running down my cheeks.

"You're not..." His voice broke but I couldn't listen to him, not anymore.

"I can't do this anymore! I'm going home. To MY home!" I moved around him and started down the road again. I was going to pack my dad's things and we were going home. We would figure out how to survive on our own and be just fine. I couldn't be near Ryder anymore. It was impossible to resist him so I had to leave. Maybe then my heart could heal.

"You're not going home!" he shouted, following me. "You want to see me pissed, just try to leave! If I have to, I'll tie your ass down!"

"You have no right to tell me what to do!" I shouted back, wiping the tears away as I walked quicker.

"Really? I have no right to tell you what to do? How about all the fucking times I've saved your butt?"

He was fuming mad but I continued walking.

"And how about the fact that I came inside of you two times?" he shouted.

I turned around to stare at him in astonishment.

"What?" I asked in shock. *Where was he going with this?*

He walked over to me, stopping an inch away. "What if you are pregnant? If you're carrying my baby, I think I have a right to be concerned about you."

I saw red. A hazy, madness infused, lost-my-mind kind of red. A lock-me-up-and-throw-away-the-key kind of red. Without thinking twice, I pulled back my fist and let it fly.

When my hand connected with his jaw, pain radiated up my arm from the impact on my broken finger. I saw stars and blackness pushed around my vision. Pulling my hand close to my chest in agony, I wavered on my feet.

"Shit!" Ryder exclaimed, reaching out to grab one of my arms and keep me on my feet. "Are you okay?"

The punch I landed on him was forgotten as he pulled my hand away from my chest to inspect it for damage. I cringed with excruciating pain when his fingers lightly touched the uncovered digit.

"Damn, Maddie, do you hate me that much?" he muttered under his breath, his hurt eyes flickering up to mine before examining my hand again.

I opened my mouth to tell him that I didn't hate him; I hated what he was doing to me but loud cussing cut me off.

Gavin was jogging toward us, looking shocked. "What the hell is going on?" he asked, out of breath.

"Maddie just nailed me," Ryder said, letting go of my hand to rub his jaw. His blue eyes blazed down at me but not with anger or frustration. Just sadness and regret.

"You probably deserved it," Gavin said, turning to me. "You okay, Maddie?"

"Can you just take me home, Gavin? To my home?" I asked shakily, avoiding Ryder's eyes.

Gavin glanced over at Ryder, looking for approval. Ryder shook his head no, frustrating me all over again. I was tired of Ryder always getting what he wanted, bossing me around like he was my keeper. *He already had my heart, what more did he need?*

"I'll walk you back to the house, how about that?" Gavin said.

"I won't bother you there, Maddie, I swear. But you have to promise me that you won't go home. It's not safe," Ryder said, not hiding the threat behind his words.

I glared up at him. He was so scrumptious and irresistible that part of me wanted to promise him whatever he wanted but I stiffened my backbone. He already had gotten enough from me. I wouldn't promise anything. My dad and I needed Janice and Roger but I was determined to do it on my own terms.

"I'll stay with your parents but I don't want to see you. Don't touch me, don't come near me, don't talk to me. Just stay the hell away from me, Ryder."

He studied me with pain-filled eyes, his mouth set in a grim line. Finally, he nodded once.

The tears fell faster down my face as I walked away. I just lost my best friend. The only man I ever loved. What was left of my heart was with him. I felt empty already.

Gavin kept a few feet behind me, not talking, just giving me space. I was glad. I just needed to be alone. My chest ached more and more with each step I took. I flicked a stray tear away. The hurting and utter destruction left by Ryder was killing me. *This must be what it felt like to have your heart broken by someone.*

Finally, the house came into view. I needed to compose myself. I couldn't let my dad see me this way. The last thing he needed was to worry.

Gavin broke the silence, his voice soft. "He's an ass, Maddie. He doesn't deserve you."

I wanted to argue. Ryder deserved me, someone who knew every secret he had and still loved him. I accepted him. Tattoos, bad attitude and all. But no matter how much I loved him, it wasn't enough. I wasn't what he wanted. *Why couldn't I fall in love with someone like Gavin?* Always a gentleman, Gavin offered a girl a future. He was not irritating, frustrating, and incapable of loving someone. But he was not Ryder.

"You want me to beat him up for you?" Gavin asked with a twinkle in his eye.

I couldn't help but smile weakly. "Not today, Gavin, but I'll let you know."

"And there's the Maddie that I know. I missed her," he said, walking around me into the house.

I took a deep breath and followed him inside, ready to face my future without Ryder.

Chapter Twenty-Eight

For two weeks, Ryder and I avoided each other. Often, I would hear him outside, working with his dad and Gavin but he never stepped foot inside the house. He ate all his meals at home and spent any free time there as well.

Every time I heard his voice through the open windows, pain would shoot through me. Not once did he attempt to see or talk to me. I wanted to ask Gavin if Ryder ever asked about me but I was terrified of what his answer might be.

No one questioned what happened between us. I'm positive that they knew but I was thankful not to have to talk about it. I couldn't.

I lost plenty of sleep during those two weeks. Each night, instead of sleeping, I replayed the words he said and the passion we shared. I cursed myself for being such a fool. I cursed Ryder for being cold.

I cursed life.

During the day, Janice kept me busy. She taught me how to make bread from their stock of flour. We canned the last of the vegetables from her garden, getting what we could before winter hit. Wanting to conserve food, the men shot squirrels or deer for fresh meat. Occasionally, someone would go fishing. Our meals were cooked outside in a fire pit set into the ground. Showers were lukewarm, but at least I was clean. And the outhouse was finished so no more trips to the bushes, thank goodness.

Because of the Delaney's, my father and I had food, water, supplies, and enough candles and lanterns to last a long time. Without them, I'm not sure my dad and I would still be alive.

My dad's health declined rapidly in those two weeks. He had more trouble walking around and was losing weight quickly. To my horror, I watched his appetite slowly disappear over a matter of days. I refused to face the realization that he was dwindling away before my eyes and there was nothing I could do.

The only communication we had with the outside world came from the shortwave radio that Roger would listen to at night. The news was always the same – the government couldn't get supplies to people, the military was spread thin, and millions were dying. Information about the war was nonexistent. We were in the dark, literally and figuratively.

~~~~

One sunny afternoon, I was walking out of the barn when Ryder's Bronco pulled into the driveway. He jumped out and strolled purposely toward the house without seeing me in the barn doorway.

I froze. My heart raced and my nerve endings came alive for the first time in weeks. He looked wonderful in a white t-shirt, jeans, and scuffed cowboy boots. The ever-present baseball cap was pulled low, hiding his eyes from the glare of the sun. His smooth, freshly shaved jaw was clenched tight with tension. Something was on his mind.

After he went inside, I stood indecisive. *Should I go inside or wait until he was gone?* I hadn't been in the same room with him in fourteen days. I wasn't sure if I could hold up under the torment it would cause.

I chastised myself. I was a grown woman. No man (no matter how good looking and irresistible) was going to stop me from doing what I wanted.

Taking a deep breath, I strolled to the back door, giving myself a pep talk. *I'm strong. I can resist him. I'll just act as if nothing is wrong.*

Opening the door, I stepped into the large kitchen. The darkness of the room momentarily blinded me after being in the sunlight for so long.

When my eyes adjusted, I could see that everyone was there. In the far corner of the room stood Ryder, his arms crossed over his chest in a defensive manner. His blue eyes flicked over to me. I felt heat run through my body, unrelenting and powerful. His eyes slowly traveled down my body and back up to meet my eyes. After a second, he looked away, dismissing me without a second thought.

Against my better judgment, my body wanted him again with a passion and need that scared me. I tried to ignore him but my heart kicked into overdrive and I felt an uncontrollable yearning to be near him again.

"Well, let's do this then," Roger said on a sigh. "I'll gather a few supplies and we can head out."

They were leaving? I frantically looked around for someone to tell me what was going on.

Janice answered my unspoken question. "The boys are going into town. There are some rumors that things have gotten bad there."

"I'm going!" I said with urgency.

"NO!" Gavin and Roger responded at the same time.

"I have to make sure Eva is okay."

"It's not safe, Maddie. You're staying here," Gavin snapped with frustration.

My eyes moved to Ryder who was staring at the floor, clenching his strong jaw. He refused to look at me and that stung. A lot. I knew he was fuming right now but I didn't care. My friends were out there, possibly starving. I wasn't going to sit here and do nothing.

"I'm going. Don't try to stop me."

"Mom, talk some sense into your little protégé," Gavin said with exasperation.

I bristled at his new pet name for me. He had decided it was funny because I was always following his mom around, trying to learn everything I could from her.

"I'm going," I stated stubbornly, practically stomping my feet.

"No."

Ryder's voice was like a gunshot going off in the room, causing me to jump in fright. No one messed with Ryder when he sounded like that, including me.

Without looking at me, he walked over to the table and pulled a 9mm pistol from his waistband. He laid it on the wooden table in front of his mom.

"For Maddie," he said, his voice hard.

He started to walk away when he stopped and looked back at his mother. "And make sure she stays in the house while we're gone." With that, he walked out the door without a backward glance.

Gavin and Roger followed him out but I didn't notice. I sat heavily in the nearest chair as the tears choked my throat. Ryder was having no trouble staying away from me. *This is what I wanted, wasn't it?* I had told him to leave me alone and he was doing a damn good job of it. Too good.

"I'm sorry, honey. You know how overprotective they can be," Janice said, taking a seat at the table and reaching over to pat my hand.

I nodded, fighting the tears. I had cried so much in the last few weeks that I was surprised I had anymore tears left.

"It's okay," my dad said, taking my other hand. He attempted to smile but the side of his mouth drooped, more pronounced than it had been a few days ago.

I forced a smile for him. He was all I had left. My dad had been strong for me my whole life. Now it was my turn to be strong for him. I took a deep cleansing breath and squeezed his hand reassuringly.

The three of us sat for a while and talked about what might be happening in town. Each night, we heard on the handheld radio horrible stories of people dying of thirst and hunger. Robberies were now a common occurrence and people were being shot for basic supplies. It was now a dog-eat-dog world that we lived in.

I worried. The men could be walking into a dangerous situation. They were armed to the hilt with rifles and pistols but that didn't make me feel better. *What if something happened to Ryder?* No matter what he thought of me, I still loved him and living without him wasn't a possibility.

Not wanting to upset my dad with my unhappiness, I told them I was going to take a nap. I was exhausted. At night, sleep wouldn't come and during the day I felt like a zombie.

Sitting in Ryder's old room that I now occupied, I looked around slowly. There was nothing in here that was mine except a small backpack and a few clothes hanging in the closet. I lay back on the bed and stared out the open window.

I suddenly wished I could go home. Some more clothes and maybe some books would be nice to have. Gavin and Roger had gone over there last week to make sure everything was okay but I hadn't known or I would have insisted on tagging along also.

I wanted to see my home again. I needed to be surrounded by my own stuff. Maybe it would make me feel better.

From my window, I could see Roger's truck sitting in the barn. I knew where the keys were and I knew it still had gas. Janice would try to stop me but I decided it was time I went home.

Chapter Twenty-Nine

"Absolutely not, missy!" Janice said when I told her what I was going to do.

I checked the pistol to make sure it was loaded and the safety was on. Stuffing it into the back of my shorts, I met her terrified eyes.

"I'm not asking permission, Janice. I'm a grown woman and I make my own decisions," I said, grabbing a bottle of water and putting it in my backpack.

"It's too dangerous. There might be people traveling the roads and looking for supplies," she pleaded, wringing her hands as she followed me around the kitchen.

"Yeah, well, I'm a good shot. Just ask your son. He taught me all I know," I told her, grabbing the keys off of the key holder in the kitchen.

"Ryder will kill me for letting you go!"

I almost told her he had no control over me but I didn't say anything. It wasn't exactly true anyway. He did still have control over me – my heart and body responded to him just by hearing his name.

"I'll go."

Janice and I both turned around to see my dad leaning heavily on his cane inside the kitchen doorway.

"Dad…" I began. He was so weak that I wasn't sure it was a good idea.

"Get mom's things," he said, quietly.

My heart softened at those words. He wanted to have my mother's things. I realized that, like me, he just needed to go home.

"Okay, Dad, let me pull the truck to the porch and I'll help you."

"No, Maddie! You can't go!" Janice cried, trying to step in front of the door.

I looked down, hiding my frustration from her and noticed that my cheap tennis shoes were barely hanging on my feet. I needed shoes and home had them.

Looking up, I recognized the scared expression on her face. *How many times had I looked like that when I thought of Ryder in danger?* The wrinkles on her face only emphasized her worry. I briefly thought of how much we had aged in the last few weeks. I might have been a silly college student when I left, but a woman had returned home.

"Janice, I need to go. Please?" I pleaded. My eyes shifted over to my dad, leaning heavily on his cane. "I don't know how much time we have left."

Her blue eyes, so much like Ryder's, glanced at my dad. When she looked back at me, I saw her resolution.

"Okay, but be careful and remember to take the gun," she said, pulling me close for a hug. As she tightened her arms around me, she whispered against my hair, "They are going to kill me, but I like your spunk."

After helping my dad to the truck, I placed the backpack and the pistol between us on the old, worn-out seat. Within minutes, I was driving down the dirt road that would lead to our house. Tall weeds were starting to grow in the middle of the road, having free rein to travel wherever they pleased with the absence of cars. Within months, the road would be gone, just a thing of the past, at the mercy of nature and time.

"Maddie."

I glanced over at my dad, trying not to cry at the weakness I saw in him.

"Ryder love you," he said, watching me closely.

I shifted nervously in my seat. "No, Dad, he doesn't love me," I said, watching the road carefully.

"He told me."

I looked over at him in shock, almost running off the road. I yanked the wheel to the left, righting the truck, and glanced at my dad again. He had a small smile on his face.

My mind went wild. *Why would Ryder tell my dad that he loved me when he didn't?* I thought back to the day Ryder and I had fought, the day we stopped talking. I realized with sudden awareness that he had never denied loving me, he just said he didn't fall in love. Such a tiny difference in words. *How could I have missed that?*

I shook my head in denial. It was a misunderstanding, it had to be. Ryder probably told my dad he loved me as a friend and my dad took it as something more. That was it. Just an innocent statement. I couldn't let it get to me.

I pushed it out of my mind as I pulled into the driveway. Our small house sat closer to the road than Janice and Roger's home. While their house was hidden, ours was right on the long, dirt road. I suddenly felt too exposed being here but by the time I parked by the back door, I had brushed off the uneasy feeling.

After helping my dad out of the truck, I grabbed my backpack and the pistol. Holding onto my dad's elbow, we slowly climbed the porch steps.

The smothering heat from inside hit us as soon as the door was opened. I immediately started opening windows to let in a breeze.

"Okay, Dad, I'm going to start gathering stuff. I'll pull out Mom's box and you can go through it."

"Miss her," my dad whispered as I helped him down the hallway.

"Me too, Dad," I said, letting him lean on me for support.

"My soul mate."

I choked back a sob at his words. After all this time, he still loved her and missed her every day. I believed he never got over her death. How could someone when they loved that deeply?

"Ryder…you…belong together," he forced the words out past his slack mouth. I shook my head, denying his words.

At the entrance to his bedroom, he stopped and turned to look at me. "When I'm gone, he'll take care…you. He'll love you like…I loved your mom. Soul mates."

I blinked at the clearness of his words. For the moment, he sounded like my dad, not a man racked with sickness.

"Daddy, don't talk that way."

"No, I'll see her again. Soon."

I sniffled and helped him into the room. From the back of his closet, I pulled out a large box while he watched me from the edge of the bed. As a little girl, I had loved to go through her keepsakes. It contained all kinds of things of my mom's. Awards, pictures, a diary, her favorite perfume, and the love letters she and my dad wrote each other. I sat the box on the bed and watched as my dad gently lifted the top off. His eyes watered as he lightly touched each item.

I left him in his room and headed to mine. There was so much that I desperately wanted to take back with me - pictures, knickknacks, trophies, my favorite childhood stuffed animal. But I knew that I only needed what was necessary to survive.

I stared at the clothes hanging in my closet, thankful that I had not taken everything to college with me. I pulled out shorts, t-shirts, tennis shoes, and jeans. We still had a month before it turned cold but I grabbed a lightweight jacket anyway. Going to my dresser, I pulled out bras and panties. After grabbing socks, I was finished packing.

What else did I need? My eyes landed on my cluttered desk, covered with pictures and books. I picked up a photo of Eva and me on prom night. The silly expressions on our faces made me smile. Without thinking twice, I pulled the picture out of the frame and placed it on my pile of clothes.

I was placing the picture frame back on the desk when the one behind it caught my attention. It was a close-up of Ryder and me at my high school graduation. I wore the traditional graduation cap and gown. He had on a blue starched shirt that matched his eyes perfectly. We had our arms thrown around each other's necks, smiling great big smiles for the camera. I immediately took it out of the frame, sitting it gently on top of the other.

In my dad's room, I gathered more clothes for him and he picked out a few things to take with us.

When we were done, I helped my dad down the porch steps to the truck. While he waited for me, I made numerous trips to load everything into the truck bed.

Pausing as a cool breeze blew over my heated face, I glanced around at the overgrown yard. The grass was so high that it almost reached my knees in some places. The two horses my dad had were now at the Delaney's, making our pasture quiet and empty.

A slight chill raced up my spine as I turned to go back inside. I squinted against the sun, looking into the distance. My eyes swept over the area, not seeing anything unusual but feeling as if we weren't alone. Someone was watching us, I just knew it.

I rushed up the porch steps and practically ran into the house, the feeling of being watched still chasing me. I wanted to go through the house one more time before we left and some silly feeling wasn't going to stop me.

Ryder's parents had already emptied the kitchen of all food so I continued on through the house. In the bathroom, I grabbed all the toilet paper, shampoo, soap, and tampons that I could carry in a bag.

The eerie feeling was still tugging at me when I hurried out of the bathroom. I had just turned the corner into the hallway when the sound of an engine echoed through the house. My first thought was that the guys were already back and had decided to stop here first. I knew that there would be hell to pay if Ryder found me here.

The sound of shouting stopped me halfway down the hallway. It didn't sound like anyone I knew. Panic filled me. If it wasn't one of the men, that meant it was a stranger.

We weren't alone.

Chapter Thirty

I felt sick with fear as I raced down the hallway, dropping the bag along the way. *Oh, God! My dad!* My heart pumped wildly in my chest when I thought of him outside, alone. *Please, God, let him be okay!*

I felt along my back, feeling the comforting steel of the gun wedged into my waistband. *I could do this, I had a gun. I had to protect my dad.*

When I rounded the corner into the kitchen, my feet refused to move another inch. My mind went blank. I became immobile.

A large man was walking through the backdoor. He was big and unkempt, taking up most of the doorway. His shaved head showed every ridge and valley in his skull, including the teardrops tattooed beneath his right eye.

I didn't wait around to find out what he wanted. I had to get to my dad and the front door was now my only option for escape. Turning, I ran back down the hallway as fast as my legs would take me.

"Git her!"

I raced down the hallway, moving faster than ever before. The roaring in my ears couldn't hide the sound of heavy booted feet running after me.

I was close to the door, so close, when I was grabbed roughly from behind. NOOOO!

Two large, beefy arms clamped around my waist, completely lifting me off the ground. I let out a pain-filled scream as an arm smashed my cracked rib. Dirty fingers immediately covered my mouth, stifling all sounds coming from me.

I fought. With everything I had, I fought. My legs kicked with strength and my arms flailed wildly, trying desperately to escape.

The man didn't care how much I struggled. He held me tightly and effortlessly. "We found her, Robbie!" he said in a deep baritone voice.

When I saw the second man, all the blood drained from my face. For a second, I was confused. *This couldn't be possible!*

The convict, Greasy, was in my kitchen. He stood feet away, looking skinnier and dirtier than last time I saw him. Those evil eyes and the sinister grin smeared across his face were forever seared into my brain, reminding me of that terrible day. *But what the hell was he doing here?*

"I been thinking of you a good long time now, sweetheart," he said, ambling closer. His bad breath and body odor hit me, filling my nostrils and making my stomach roll with nausea.

When his dirt-encrusted hand reached out, panic overwhelmed me, flooding my head and body with the deathly need to get away.

I squirmed frantically in the man's firm hold, desperate to get away. My fists connected with his head a few times and my legs kicked as hard and fast as possible but when my heels hit his shins painfully, he didn't budge an inch. The man was strong, his massive body holding me tightly.

My struggling became even more frenzied when Greasy's hand grabbed a handful of my hair.

"I like this hair, all dark and silky. I want to wrap myself in it."

A shudder raced down my spine when his warm, repugnant breath washed over my face. I tried to scream but the other man still had his hand over my mouth, keeping my head secure and my body immobile. I opted to kick out with my feet, aiming for anyplace on Greasy that would keep him away from me.

Avoiding my legs, he yanked hard on my hair, stinging my scalp with pain as he giggled playfully. The sound was unnerving.

Greasy's fingers let go of my hair and reached out to run along the top of my t-shirt. I whimpered in utter terror as they skimmed lightly along my collarbone.

The sounds coming from my mouth were muffled as the man behind me tightened his hold on my mouth and ribs, causing agony to unfold throughout my body. Stars appeared at the edge of my vision and tears pooled in my eyes.

"Put her down! You're hurting the poor girl," Greasy said with creepy concern.

Following orders like a henchman, the man dropped his arms from around me. I took a deep, gulping breath, finally filling my lungs with badly needed oxygen. My body shook violently. I felt weak with fright and unable to move.

Oh, God! Oh, God! I wasn't going to survive this! My instincts screamed that these men would kill my dad and me without thinking twice. If I wanted to live, it was up to me to get us out of here.

Reaching behind me, I quickly grabbed for the gun hidden in my waistband. My hand came away empty.

The man behind me chuckled. "You looking for this, sweetheart?"

I whipped around to see him dangling the pistol between his thumb and forefinger.

Seeing his sinister grin, I felt hopeless. With no way to defend myself, I was at their mercy. There was no one to help and no one would come looking for us until much later. By then, it would be too late. My dad and I would not be alive.

No, I refused to think that.

"You ain't very smart, girlie. I done saw that gun as soon as you turned tail and ran. Snatched it right up, real quick," the man said in a thick Texas drawl.

Greasy snickered and took the pistol from his partner. "You want this, baby doll?" he asked, in a slimy voice that sounded like evil reincarnated. "It's a nice piece. Well taken care of. Clean. Your boyfriend's?"

I kept quiet. These men were scum and didn't deserve any kind of answer.

Greasy shoved the gun in the front of his pants. I prayed it accidentally went off.

"Where's your boyfriend?"

I ignored his question as my eyes swept the room for any kind of weapon. A knife, a glass jar, anything would do. I just needed to get to my dad and a weapon was the only way to do that. Fear for his well-being overwhelmed me, making me frantic and not thinking clearly. *I have to get out of here!*

The adrenaline rushed through my body, giving me strength. I took off, making a wide circle around Greasy and heading to the hallway.

I didn't get very far.

Greasy grabbed me, jerking me off my feet. I screamed as I hit the floor hard. The impact on my tailbone was excruciating.

"Why you have to be that way, girlie? I'm just trying to be nice and friendly like! This ain't no way to greet an old friend," Greasy said darkly as he dragged me down the hallway with a strong grip on my arm.

I smacked into a chair as I was dragged away. With my free hand, I reached up and desperately started scratching

Greasy's hand with my short fingernails. He didn't notice as he continued to pull me along.

"I traveled all this way to see ya and ya ain't even happy I'm here," Greasy whined as he dragged me into the living room. The big guy followed close behind us with a huge smile plastered on his face.

I cried out with pain as Greasy threw me into a chair and stood over me threateningly. The look on his face was a cross between a lunatic and pure evil.

He gripped my jaw with strong, bruising fingers. "You ain't talking no more?" he asked, looking me up and down slowly. Shrugging his thin shoulders, he hissed, "That's okay, we don't need no talking for what I have in mind."

His thumb ran over my bottom lip cruelly.

I saw red. *No way would I let this scum touch me. He would have to kill me first.*

As his thumb made another track over my lower lip, I knew what I had to do. I bit down hard on his thumb and kicked my leg up as hard as possible at the same time, nailing him in the balls.

With a painful cry, he clutched himself and fell to the floor. Indiscernible words spewed from him as he withered into a fetal position and held his manhood.

I saw my chance. Jumping over him, I ran as fast as I could to the front door. *If I could only make it outside, I would be free.*

"CATCH HER!" Greasy screamed as he struggled painfully to his feet.

My heart pounded as I reached for the door handle.

"NOOOO! NOOOO!" I was grabbed from behind and hauled back against a hard body again. Frustrated tears ran down my face as the big guy pulled me away from the door. He flung me violently across the room like a rag doll. I landed against the wall hard, the impact vibrating through my head and body.

Get up! Get up! Ignoring my protesting body, I got to my feet and ran down the hallway, tripping a few times in my haste.

My heart was pounding so hard that I didn't hear the footsteps behind me. The heat was sucking all my energy but I moved fast around the corner, determined to get away from this nightmare.

Then it ended.

I screamed as I was tackled from behind by Greasy. I went down hard, landing on my stomach. When he crawled up my body like an insect, I screamed wildly. Grabbing my long hair, he wrapped it around and around his fist until I cried out from the tearing in my scalp. I fought as he pulled me to my feet by my hair.

"You shouldn't have kicked me like that, bitch! Now I can't be nice," he growled as he shook me hard. He started walking down the hallway, yanking me by my hair.

I tried to drag my feet but the pain in my scalp was excruciating. Tears ran down my face as I reached up to tug at the hand pulling my hair. *Oh, God! I couldn't fight him! This was it. My time was running out.*

Greasy threw me into the nearest bedroom. I hit the floor, smacking my elbow. Ignoring the pain, my eyes frantically raced around the room, looking for anything that I might use as a weapon.

There was nothing.

He didn't take his eyes off of me as he slammed the door and started to advance on me. I crab-crawled backward until the bed blocked my path.

"I've been thinking 'bout you since that day. Took me forever to find you," he said, looking me up and down.

"How did you find me?"

They were the first words that I had spoken to him. I wished they sounded more kickass but instead they came out as a whimper.

He smiled, reminding me of a snake. Reaching into his back pocket, he pulled something out.

"You left this behind." *My driver's license.* "Maddie Jackson. 21 years old," he said, reading the information.

I swallowed past my dry throat. When they stole the truck, my purse was on the seat. My license still listed my father's address. I had never changed it and now it would get me killed.

"I asked around town and some really nice folks told me where to find you." He laughed sinisterly. "They were so gullible. For food and water, people will talk."

Greasy kneeled down by me and reached out to touch my hair again. I looked away as the skin on my arms crawled at his disgusting touch.

I was trying to figure out how to escape when suddenly he was on top of me, covering my body with his. I screamed as loudly as I could.

His hands were everywhere as his weight held me down. I fought, kicking and scratching with a renewed fury. My fingernails came away bloody as I took long claw marks out of his cheek. Ignoring me, he tore at my shirt. *Please, no!* I didn't want Ryder or my dad to find me raped or dead.

Reaching up, I drilled my finger into his right eye as hard as possible. He howled with pain but didn't roll off me. Instead, he backhanded me hard. Once then twice. Blackness threatened to pull me under but I fought it, refusing to give in to the peace it offered.

With a curse, he grabbed both of my wrists cruelly and held them above my head. I cried out when he buried his face in my neck to nuzzle my skin. Bucking and fighting against him, I used all my energy to fight.

He ignored my struggling as if it were nothing. Using his free hand, he reached into his back pocket. A second later, he pulled out a switchblade knife. Flipping it open, he smiled down at me with a crazed look on his face.

I looked at the blade with terror. *Oh, shit! What was he going to do?*

With a spine-chilling giggle, he started cutting my shirt down the middle. I cried out as the blade pricked my skin several times as he sawed through the cotton. He continued to giggle as more and more of my abdomen was revealed.

I froze as the blood started to trickle slowly down my stomach. I wasn't sure how badly I was cut but knew that if I struggled the knife would slice me more.

When my shirt was completely cut in two, he used the knife tip to push the edges back, leaving only my bra. Hysteria bubbled up in me as he licked his lips in anticipation.

The tears were now racing down my face as I tried to hold onto what little sanity I had left. I prayed for help from somewhere, from someone. Terror was making me feel dead inside, numb to what was about to happen.

Finished with the knife, he placed it on the floor. His hand went to my abdomen as his other hand continued to crush my wrists painfully.

"NOOO!"

I turned my head away in disgust when he pushed his face into my neck again. Through my tears, the glint of the knife caught my eye. It lay inches away. Suddenly, I knew what I had to do.

I had one shot at this. It may be the only opportunity I had left. I forced my muscles to relax. He had to trust me.

He had to believe I wasn't a threat. My body went limp beneath his.

"That's more like it, sugar," Greasy said against my skin as he slowly released my wrists. The blood flowed quickly back to my fingers. I flexed them slowly, needing the strength.

As his hands moved to my waist, I slowly reached for the knife. Moving in a split second, I grabbed the hilt and held it tightly in my fist.

Greasy smirked unknowingly as he pulled back to look down at my bra.

I ignored his nightmarish grin as my mind raced back to Anatomy class. The location of all the major arteries and organs filled my mind like a picture out of a textbook. If I was going to do this, I had to make sure it counted.

When his hand reached up to grab my bra, I saw my target. With hate and fear rolling through me, I quickly sliced him underneath his left arm, putting as much strength as I could behind the cut. He screamed as blood started splurging immediately from the wound.

I had hit the brachial artery.

Blood flowed down his arm in rivers to land on top of me. The floor beneath us quickly became red with his blood.

I started to crawl out from under him when he gripped me hard by the ribcage, unknowingly grabbing my still-healing cracked rib. I screeched at the pain that coursed through me.

"You cut me!" he screamed, glancing down at the blood pouring out of him. He held a hand over the cut but it didn't stop him. I watched in horror as he unbuckled his belt and took it off. Roughly, he grabbed my wrists and yanked them above my head.

"NO!" I screamed as he tightly wrapped the belt around my wrists, again and again, then tied it to the bed frame. The blood was instantly cut off from my fingers, leaving them numb and useless.

"Now, let's finish this," he said, wavering above me unsteadily. His eyes rolled back in his head and he turned ghostly white.

I watched with a combination of horror and relief as he looked at me one last time before falling on top of me, passed out from the blood loss.

I twisted my hands, trying to get out of the belt. It held tight, rubbing against my tender wrists and tearing at my flesh. I tried to use my body to push Greasy off of me but he was too heavy. Then, to my horror, I felt him take his last breath.

Oh, God! Oh, God! I now had a dead body on top of me. Starting to feel hysterical, I struggled to escape. The blood continued to gush from him, making everything slick and wet. I felt bile rise in my throat at the metallic smell in the air.

I couldn't push him off. *Oh shit, I couldn't get him off!* My mind went a little crazy. *I had to get him off me!* As the warm blood drenched me, I went berserk. I screamed and screamed until my throat was raw.

Over my screams I heard a gunshot ricocheted through the house. I instantly thought of my dad. I had to get to him! I pulled at my wrists until they were raw but the belt refuse to loosen.

When I heard footsteps running down the hallway, I started shaking. *That couldn't be my dad. He couldn't run. I had to hide!* If the other man found me, I knew that he would kill me without blinking.

The door flung open, slamming violently against the inner wall. My sobs turned into cries of relief.

I was safe.

Chapter Thirty-One

Ryder was standing in the doorway.

His face was pale but his hand was steady on the shotgun propped on his shoulder. Gavin appeared beside him, his rifle aimed and pointed into the room.

"RYDER! Get him off me!" I screamed, squirming under the body. "Get him off! Get him off!"

I saw his lips move and his gun lower but I couldn't hear any of his words. The roaring in my ears drowned out everything.

Before I knew it, Ryder and Gavin were beside me. Ryder started loosening the belt around my wrists as Gavin rolled Greasy off of me.

When my wrists were free, Ryder lifted me up and carried me a few feet away from the pool of blood. Setting me down, he frantically started running his hands over my body.

"Are you hurt, Maddie? God, are you hurt? ANSWER ME!" he roared, his face full of fear when I didn't respond.

Hands on me! No more hands on me! I pulled away in fright, terrified of being touched again.

Seeing my scared expression, he tried for a gentler tone. "Are you hurt, Maddie?"

I flinched as he reached out to touch me.

"What did the bastard do to you?" he hissed in shock as he looked down at my cut shirt.

"He's dead, Ryder," Gavin said, gravely.

"Good or I would kill him myself for touching her."

Ryder glanced at me again, his eyes running down my body. I saw him swallow hard. "Shit, Gavin, there's blood everywhere." He looked over at his brother with agony. "I don't know if she's hurt. She won't let me touch her."

That's when the shaking started. From the top of my head to the tips of my toes, I shook. Big, violent tremors that racked my body. I couldn't control it. My mind was still in a dark place.

Gavin crouched down and reached out to touch me. I started crying and cringing away from his hands.

"She's in shock, Ryder," Gavin whispered. "We need to get her calmed down before she hyperventilates. Put her head between her knees to get the blood flowing again. You do it. She'll trust you."

I wanted to yell that I wasn't scared of them. No, I was scared of the memories flooding my mind. Memories of that man's hands all over me and the feeling of hopelessness. But the words stuck in my throat as I huddled into a ball.

"Maddie, it's okay. I'm going to put my hand on you," Ryder said, gently. He helped me sit up and gently pressed the back of my head down between my bent knees.

"Breath normally, Maddie. Don't hold your breath," Gavin instructed.

I tried to focus on my breathing and the feeling of Ryder's hand on the back of my head but my eyes moved down to my chest. I saw blood everywhere. Dark, red, and sticky. I was covered with it.

"Get it off!" I started to scream, trying to wipe the blood away as I backed up against the bed frame. "Ryder, please get it off!" I cried, wiping my abdomen frantically.

Gavin jumped up and pulled the cover off of the bed. Grabbing the blanket from Gavin, Ryder started to wipe the blood off my skin.

"Maddie, you're safe. No one's going to hurt you again," he said soothingly as he concentrated on getting the blood off of me.

I started to calm down as the blood started to disappear. His warm voice soothed my nerves. My mind cleared, the fog lifting.

"Where's my dad?" I asked, hoarsely.

"Outside," Gavin said, flatly.

"Son of a bitch!" Ryder hissed. His hands shook badly as he wiped away the blood from the small cuts on my stomach. "Gavin, he cut her."

Gavin quickly kneeled back down next to me. Out of the corner of my eye, I noticed that he had covered the body with a blanket.

"Maddie, I'm not going to hurt you," Gavin said in a calming voice. "I just need to make sure you're okay."

"Nicks. Just nicks. I'm okay." My words were choppy and broken as Gavin started poking around on my stomach. I couldn't stop my body from trembling from shock.

"Maddie, this is my fault. I shouldn't have left…" Ryder said, his voice breaking.

I looked over at him and saw his anguish. Pulling away from Gavin, I crawled into Ryder's lap, needing to be as close to him as possible.

His arms went around me, holding me tightly as I knew he would. I felt his large hands span across my rib cage, pulling my shaking body closer.

"The cuts are minor and should stop bleeding soon," Gavin said quietly behind us.

I felt Ryder nod in understanding as his hands slowly moved up my back. Fresh tears filled my eyes as he held me against him. I had been so afraid that I wouldn't see him again and now here I was, in his arms. Suddenly, I had to tell him the truth.

"I love you, Ryder."

He pulled away to look deep into my eyes. "God, Maddie…I…"

Yelling from somewhere in the house interrupted him. A thread of panic had me clenching Ryder frantically before Janice rushed into the room, breathless.

She took one look at me and all the blood drained from her face. "Maddie?"

"She's okay, Mom," Gavin said.

Her mournful eyes moved over to Ryder and she shook her head no as a silent message traveled between them. I wanted to ask her what was wrong but she rushed away.

"I'll be outside, Ryder," Gavin said solemnly before grabbing the guns and leaving.

"What's going on?" I asked Ryder.

"Let's get you a shirt," he said, avoiding my eyes and my question. He helped me to my feet and kept a hand under my elbow as I walked shakily out of the room.

A few seconds later, we were in the middle of my bedroom. I stood silently, my arms wrapped protectively around my abdomen, as Ryder rummaged in my closet. I tried to keep my mind blank. If I thought about what happened, I might lose the thin hold I had on my sanity.

Ryder finally pulled out a long-sleeved flannel shirt that was shoved forgotten in the back of the closet. His blue eyes held me captive as he walked toward me with purpose.

The shirt in his hand was forgotten as he gently ran his fingers along my jawline.

"Fucker hit you?" he asked, enraged.

My eyes filled with tears but I brushed them away.

"I don't want to talk about it. I just need to get these clothes off."

He nodded in understanding as he struggled to bring his rage back under control. With his help, I quickly took off what was left of my bloody t-shirt and bra. I refused to let my eyes linger on the half dozen nicks that covered me. There was no time to break into tears again. I needed to check on my dad.

I cursed my shaking fingers when the buttons would not go through the tiny buttonholes. Ryder brushed my hands away and finished buttoning up my shirt. His large fingers easily slipped each button into place, providing me with a sense of security I desperately needed.

From somewhere in the house, a door banged shut, causing me to jump in fright.

"It's okay, Maddie," Ryder said.

My heart raced as memories rushed me. "Where's the other one?" I asked, taking a protective step closer to him, my arms wrapping around my body, suddenly cold.

"I shot him point blank." His eyes bore into mine, looking so lost that I wanted to cry all over again. I saw him swallow hard. "We need to go see your dad."

He took my hand and led me through the house. Outside birds still chirped and the sun still beat down without mercy.

Life went on.

I saw Gavin standing at the back of the pickup truck. His arms were resting on the top of the tailgate and his head was hanging down in despair. When he looked at me, I saw anguish in his eyes.

"Maddie, I'm not leaving you. I'll be right beside you," Ryder said, giving my hand a reassuring squeeze. I didn't have time to wonder what he was talking about.

My heart stopped and all the air left my lungs in a whoosh as we rounded the end of the truck.

My dad lay flat on the ground, pale and still. Janice and Roger knelt on either side of him, both upset as they looked up at me.

"Dad?"

When he didn't respond, I rushed over, dropping to my knees beside him and ignoring the gravel digging into my bare skin.

"DADDY!" I cried as tears ran down my cheeks, unchecked. "OPEN YOUR EYES!" I wailed, shaking him. When he didn't respond, I looked to Janice for help.

"He's fading, Maddie," she said.

No, no, no! My dad couldn't be dying! I fell on his chest, huge racks of sobbing erupting from my throat.

Janice touched the back of my head gently, trying to give me comfort. I listened as his breathing became shallower and shallower, each rise and fall of his chest coming less and less frequently.

He couldn't die on me! He was all I had left! My throat closed up, suffocating me. I grabbed his hand and squeezed tightly. I prayed he would come back to me. I just wanted him to open his eyes and look at me again. *Please! Please!*

"Maddie," Janice said, quietly, "he's gone."

"NO! NO!" I cried, hugging him fiercely.

Time passed but I still stayed by his side. Janice tried to move me away but I shrugged her off.

"I have to stay with him," I said, absently.

Janice backed away and didn't try to touch me again. I wasn't sure how long I sat there. The heat was unbearable but I didn't care. Roger and Gavin came and went but Janice and Ryder stayed with me.

"Maddie, it's getting dark. We need to bury him," Ryder said, only inches away from me.

"No."

"Maddie, you know we have to do this," he said, softly. "Dad and Gavin dug a spot by the old oak tree."

The tears fell down my face harder as his words broke through my sorrow. My dad loved that old oak tree. He had said that it looked so proud all alone in a field of grass. At one time, there was an old rope swing that hung from one of its branches. He had spent many hours pushing me. I could still feel his hands on my back, pushing me higher into the sky. Closing my eyes, I would lean back and let the sun warm my face. He would laugh and say that I looked like his little angel flying through the air. He would want to be buried under that tree, on the land that he loved.

"That's the perfect place, Ryder," I whispered around my tears.

"He once told me that he hoped to hang another swing in that tree for his grandchildren and push them, just like he did you," he said, his voice catching.

My tears fell silently now. My dad once told me that he hoped Ryder and I gave him plenty of grandchildren to spoil. I was eighteen at the time and thought he was crazy for believing that Ryder and I would marry. When I said exactly that to my dad, he smiled and said that God worked in mysterious ways.

Ryder reached over and brushed a tear away from my cheek. His eyes ran from the top of my forehead to my chin, studying each of my features. I saw his jaw clench in anger as he gazed at my bruised face. Taking a deep breath, he slowly rose to his feet and reached down to help me up.

I glanced around, noticing my surroundings for the first time. A shiver raced down my spine. Apparently, the men had drove Eva's truck to get here. It sat just a few yards away. Ryder's Bronco sat at a weird angle in the driveway, looking as if he had left it in a hurry. The truck that I had driven was still loaded down with supplies, waiting to leave. Everything had happened so quickly that I was still trying to make sense of it all.

Ryder took a step back when his mom walked over to hug me.

"I'm so sorry, Maddie."

"Did they hurt him?" I asked, needing to know the truth. When she pulled away to look at me, I saw that her eyes were swollen from crying.

"No, he wasn't hurt. I think he had another stroke. When I got here with the boys, he was lying down where he's at now."

"I tried to get to him!" I cried around new tears.

She wrapped her arms around me again and cradled the back of my head like she would a baby's.

"I know, honey, I know," she said, holding me while I cried.

~~~~

We buried him right before sunset. By the time the sun went down, Gavin was shoveling the last bit of dirt on his grave. I numbly stood by Ryder. He held his baseball cap, fidgeting with the brim the entire time while Janice quoted scriptures from the Bible.

I couldn't have asked for a better funeral for him. The birds chirped in the tree overhead and insects buzzed around us. A summer breeze rushed through the branches and leaves above us. The sounds of nature were his funeral music and I thought it was beautiful.

Ryder promised me that the other two men were not buried on our land. I didn't ask what they did with them. I didn't care.

I didn't want to leave my dad here alone, but knew I couldn't stay by myself. He wouldn't want me to.

Janice and Roger each drove a truck back. I didn't ask who I should ride with; I wanted to be with Ryder. I needed my best friend right now.

I never heard him walk up as I waited by his Bronco. When he lightly touched my elbow, I jumped away in fright.

"Let's go, Maddie," he said, clenching his jaw hard as he coolly stared down at me.

I wanted to tell him that he didn't scare me. That I knew he would never hurt me. It was the memory of Greasy's hands - touching, jerking, grasping - that still sent terror through me. But I couldn't speak. The words just wouldn't push past the lump in my throat.

Ryder radiated coldness as he helped me into the passenger seat and slammed the door shut. Getting in the driver's side, he started the Bronco without a word or glance at me.

As we drove out of the yard, I kept my eyes on the grave until it could no longer be seen. My tears turned into sobs as I left my dad behind.

~~~~

Back at Janice and Roger's house, the men were unloading my supplies while Janice tried to get me to eat something.

"You need to eat, Maddie. You've already lost too much weight," she pleaded. Like any good southern woman, Janice thought that food would heal any sadness or tragedy.

I shook my head no to her prodding as I watched blackness descend outside the window.

I hadn't spoken since we left my house. I was still trying to come to terms with the fact that my dad was no longer alive. At any moment, I expected him to stroll into the kitchen and smile at me. He would tell me that everything would be okay and not to cry.

I swiped a lone tear away as Ryder walked into the kitchen, interrupting my thoughts. He had on that damn ball cap again with the brim pulled down low but I could still see his eyes quickly flash my way before moving to look at his mom.

"We've got everything unloaded, Mom," he said, his voice sounding scratchy.

"Okay, hon. Come in and eat some dinner before you run off," Janice said, going around the kitchen to light a few candles. She didn't mention the fact that it had been two weeks since he had eaten with us. I felt guilty that I was the guest here and I had kicked her own son out.

Ryder took a seat at the table, looking everywhere but at me. He seemed unapproachable and cold, his back rigid against the chair. As his mom gathered food, Ryder and I sat in silence. I knew I should get up and help her but I couldn't gather the energy. I just wanted to sit here and not think.

A few moments later, Gavin and Roger sauntered into the kitchen and sat down around the table. The tension was so thick, you could cut it with a knife. No one spoke as Janice placed canned vegetables and canned chili in the middle of the candlelit table. Everyone started loading their plates. Everyone but me. I just kept my gaze outside the window, the total darkness now obstructing my view.

"You eating?" Gavin asked, pausing before putting a spoonful of chili in his mouth.

I shook my head, my eyes never leaving the window.

"I can't get her to eat anything. She'll end up sick by the time winter gets here," Janice complained.

I didn't respond. I couldn't. *Would I ever eat again?* Food held no appeal for me. My stomach revolted at the thought of eating. From the corner of my eye, I saw Ryder watching me. I could literally feel those icy blue eyes drilling into me sharply.

Trying to ignore the heat from his stare, I looked down at my hands. Startled, I noticed that there was dried blood underneath my short fingernails. My heart rate kicked up, making me woozy. *Oh, shit! Oh, shit!* My mind started running wild. *It was still on me! The blood was still on me!* I frantically looked down, expecting to see blood all over my shirt.

Feeling the hysteria rise up again, I jumped up, causing my chair to fly backwards. Everyone stared at me with stunned expressions but I didn't care.

"I've got to take a shower!" I said, rushing from the room. No one followed me as I hurried down the long hallway.

Blood! There was blood everywhere! I could feel it! I could smell it! I had to hurry before it soaked into my skin!

After grabbing some clothes and a lantern, I ran out of the house, stripping clothes off along the way.

The shower stall was a few feet from the house; close enough to be safe but far enough away to provide some privacy. Since the sun heated the water and it was now dark, the water was probably lukewarm. For now, all I needed was water no matter what the temperature.

I scrubbed my fingers and chest as hard as I could under the trickle of water. With only lantern light to see by, I wasn't sure all the blood was washing off but I scrubbed until there was no water left. The small nicks on my abdomen started bleeding again but I didn't pay attention to them. If I looked too long, I might just sit down and cry myself to death.

My broken finger was still splinted but I had learned to use my hand despite the bandage. I rubbed myself dry quickly and pulled on clean clothes under the yellow glow of the lantern. As I was walking up the porch steps, I heard arguing coming from the house.

"She's going with me!"

It was Ryder, sounding angry and fighting mad.

"Hell, no! She's hurting right now and doesn't need you messing with her!" Gavin yelled.

"You don't think I know she's hurting?" Ryder shouted. "I know her better than anyone!"

"She's scared to death of anyone touching her and you can't keep your goddamn hands off of her!" I heard Gavin spit in fury.

"Boys..." Roger said, threateningly.

"I stayed away from her for two freakin' weeks!" Ryder snapped coldly.

"Maybe she should stay here, Ryder, after everything she's been through," Janice interjected, her voice calm among all the anger.

"No. I'm not letting her out of my sight again. She's going home with me," Ryder said, determined.

I swallowed hard.

"Why? Two weeks too long for you to go, Ryder?" Gavin asked, sarcastically. "Gotta have it all the time and Maddie's convenient?"

I flinched.

Suddenly, I heard a chair fall and someone shouting. The sounds of a scuffle erupted from the house.

I darted up the steps and flung open the door, afraid of what I would find.

Ryder had his brother pinned on the floor. His fist punched Gavin again and again, frustration and anger behind every hit. But Gavin fought back, plowing his fists into Ryder's ribs, hard and quick.

Roger jumped into the mix, trying to pull the two apart. He only succeeded in getting himself thrown off balance and pushed away. Janice watched the fighting with panic, wringing her hands helplessly.

I felt ill when I saw the blood gushing from Gavin's nose when Ryder continued to hammer his face.

This had to stop.

Suddenly, Gavin was back on his feet and had Ryder pinned up against the wall. One hand held Ryder immobile while the other pulverized Ryder's face. The sound of flesh hitting flesh rang in my ears, making me flinch every time Gavin's fist connected with Ryder's jaw or cheekbone. Roger and Janice were shouting at Gavin to stop but he didn't hear them. Instead, his punches landed quicker and harder.

Between hits, Ryder's eyes meet mine from across the room. His arms dropped to his side and I saw him go limp, no longer fighting. He was giving up.

Gavin didn't notice but continued to slam his fists into Ryder without mercy.

With one powerful blow, blood gushed out of Ryder's nose, covering his face and shirt. As Janice cried out, my stomach rolled at the sight of blood. *Please, no more!*

I realized that Gavin was beating Ryder to a pulp and Ryder was not going to fight back. Another minute of this and Ryder wouldn't be standing.

Roger and Janice couldn't separate them. I probably couldn't either but I was determined to end it. We had all had enough violence for one day. *No more.*

I was next to Ryder in seconds. Wedging myself between him and Gavin, I planted myself between them. Gavin ignored me and grabbed a handful of Ryder's shirt, yanking him closer. I was thrown back against Ryder's steel body as Gavin drew back his arm for another strike.

I was right in the line of fire.

Ryder flew into action, breaking Gavin's hold on him before grabbing my arm and pushing me out of the way.

"You gonna fucking hit her?" he roared, shoving Gavin away.

Gavin stumbled back against the table, glaring at Ryder.

"You know I wouldn't!"

"Hell, right you wouldn't or you would be dead!"

"STOP IT, BOYS!" Janice shouted, stepping between them. "I'll not have fights or threats made in my house!"

Ryder wiped his bloody nose on his shirtsleeve, his eyes never leaving Gavin's. I wanted to feel brave and strong but when I saw the blood, my stomach revolted.

I turned and ran out the back door as fast as possible. I barely made it to the grass before my stomach emptied what little it had in it. Crouching on my knees in the damp grass, I didn't hear Janice and Ryder behind me until they were both at my side. Cringing, I pushed Ryder away when he touched me. If I smelled blood or even looked at it, I was afraid I would throw up repeatedly until my throat was raw.

Ryder moved away, giving me space. But I could still smell the blood on him.

Janice gently rubbed my back as I started to dry heave. "It's okay, Maddie," she whispered as wretched sounds escaped me.

I shook my head in denial as I fought off another wave of nausea. *It wasn't okay!* This whole thing was so screwed up that I couldn't think straight anymore. The world was falling apart around me and I was going down with it.

My heart ached when Ryder rose quietly and walked away. I wanted him beside me. I needed him with me but I was afraid. *Would I ever forget what happened?*

"You don't have to go with him," Janice said as she brushed strands of hair away from my face.

"No, I want to go with him," I said. I only felt safe with Ryder. It was that simple.

She smiled. "I believe for the first time in his life, Ryder is in love."

I wanted to tell her that I wished that were true, that I loved her son with my whole being but heavy footsteps interrupted us.

"Let's go," Ryder said in a cold voice, standing above me stiffly.

I looked up at him under the moonlight and cringed at the sight of his face. His right eye was bloodshot and the skin around it was bruised and already swelling. There was crusted blood under his nose and his full bottom lip was split and swollen. He kept his eyes locked on the far distance, refusing to meet my eyes.

I rose unsteadily to my feet, wobbling some when the world spun around me. Without waiting, Ryder started walking toward the Bronco. It was then that I saw he had my backpack slung over his wide shoulder.

What was I doing? He didn't want a relationship and here I was going home with him. In a normal world, moving in together was a huge step. Of course, we were no longer living in a normal world.

Chapter Thirty-Two

We drove down the dirt road with only the Bronco's headlights and the bright moon lighting our way. Only the sounds of crickets and the wind whipping through the open windows could be heard. It was a lonely silence, filled with misery and sorrow.

Ryder kept his eyes locked straight ahead. Not once did he glance at me or acknowledge my presence.

Leaning against the door, I turned my face away and let the tears fall. My dad was gone. Life would never be the same. I would never be the same.

Soon we were pulling up next to Ryder's house. I wiped the tears off of my cheeks and climbed out of the Bronco on shaky legs. Ryder yanked my backpack and a shotgun out of the backseat, the tension still rolling off his body in waves. He turned his cold eyes on me briefly before trudging toward the front door.

Without speaking, we entered the empty house. Without lighting a candle or using a flashlight, Ryder disappeared down the dark hallway. I followed, moving slower as I felt my way through the darkness.

His bedroom was pitch black but my eyes adjusted quickly. Standing in the doorway, I watched him throw my backpack on his bed. Without a word, he passed me in the doorway, making sure not to touch me. I was left standing in the room, feeling more alone than I ever had before.

When the front door slammed shut, I jumped, the sound reminding me of gunshots. Terror had my heart pounding, remembering the horror of earlier.

My legs suddenly felt shaky and unable to support me. Sitting on the edge of the bed, I looked around the room.

Would Ryder and I ever be the same again or would we just live here without talking to each other? Two people tolerating each other? But no matter what, I would rather be here than anywhere else.

Ryder returned carrying the bag of my clothes. After putting it in the closet, he turned, his eyes on me.

"You can have the bedroom. I'll sleep on the couch," he said. "I know you don't want to have anything to do with me and I can't blame you but I want you here. I have to know you're safe."

I nodded, my throat closing with unshed tears. I should have told him he was wrong - I wanted to be here and I needed him right now but instead, I stood quietly and averted my eyes from his blood-covered shirt.

Walking over to the closet, he yanked a shirt and a pair of shorts out, his motions angry.

"I'm heading to the creek for a bath. Yell if you need me." The sharpness in his voice matched his stride as he walked out of the room.

I stood in the dark, suddenly exhausted. I just wanted to go to sleep and forget everything. Forget the men attacking me, forget my dad dying, forget all the blood and terror around me.

Feeling lethargic, I exchanged my clothes for a t-shirt that hit me mid-thigh. Knowing Ryder wasn't in the house, I crept along the hallway to the bathroom. In the dark, I brushed my teeth without water and avoided looking at myself in the mirror. By the time I crawled into Ryder's bed, all my energy was gone.

When I pulled the covers over me, the smell of him surrounded me, cocooning me in comfort and reminding me of all that was lost.

Turning onto my side, the tears started to fall, one after the other. *I may never stop crying.* I squeezed my eyes shut, needing to block everything out. If sleep would just come, I could escape it all.

~~~~

He was squeezing my wrists, breaking the bones under his hand. "You're going to like thissssss," his voice hissed, sounding more like a snake's than a human's. "That boyfriend of yoursssss issssss dead. He bled ssssso much when I cut him."

I struggled but the fight was draining from my body. In horror, I watched as redness started oozing out of his eyes and mouth. He laughed evilly as blood trickled down on me, warm and sticky. At first, it was just drops but then it started gushing out of him, covering me completely, entering my eyes and mouth. Holding me down, he started carving designs into my stomach with his knife. I screamed again and again.

"MADDIE! WAKE UP!"

I jerked awake, fighting the hands that held me down. He was back! Not again! Please, not again! I started to kick at him, struggling to get away.

"Maddie! It's me!"

I stopped fighting when I heard the familiar voice.

"Ryder! He was here!" I cried, sitting up and throwing myself at him. My arms went around his neck and held on for dear life. "He was holding me down and there was blood everywhere! It was in my mouth and soaking into my skin!"

He pulled me into his lap, shushing me the entire time. His arms wrapped around me, tugging me close. I was surrounded by warmth immediately. It seeped into my body and chased away the chill.

"He wasn't here, Maddie. It was just a dream," Ryder reassured me, his voice low in the stillness of the night. "It's just the two of us. No one else is here. You're safe."

I squeezed my eyes shut, the awful images still there. Awake or asleep, the last twenty-four hours haunted me.

"Hell, Maddie, you scared the shit out of me screaming like that," Ryder said softly as his hands moved up and down my back. With each stroke of his hands, my heartbeat slowed down and my breathing returned to normal. The shaking left my body, little by little, leaving me exhausted. Pulling back, Ryder looked at me, concerned. The darkness of the room couldn't hide his black, swollen eye or cut lip. I cringed to think that I was the cause of it.

He smoothed my hair away from my face before dropping his hands to my waist. The soft cotton of his shorts rubbed against my inner thighs, making me feel that familiar flare of desire. His naked chest and the tattoos wrapped around his arms and torso only added to the feeling. I saw him swallow hard when his erection nudged me through his shorts.

"Crap, I'm sorry," he said, looking away in disgust. He moved me off of his lap, putting distance between us. "Go back to sleep, Maddie. I'll be right down the hall if you need me."

When he started to leave, I grew frightened. I didn't want to be alone. With him beside me, I wasn't scared. I was safe.

Desperate, I clambered over to the edge of the bed and grabbed his arm.

"Don't go."

"I can't stay. I can't be near you without wanting you. Trying to resist you is close to impossible and you don't need that right now."

"Please? Stay."

I saw the indecision on his face for only a second. When he started crawling into bed next to me, I felt relief.

His muscular arm went around me, pulling me close as the other hand flung the covers on top of us.

"I don't know if this is smart, Maddie," he said, resting his hand on my hip. "It kills me every time you push me away but I'm scared to be near you because I can't keep my damn hands off of you." He laughed but it held no humor. "Pretty fucked up but hell, everything's pretty fucked up right now."

His thumb made slow circles on top of my hip. With each movement, my t-shirt inched up a little more but I didn't care. I was safe and starting to feel relaxed. Nothing could replace the feeling of Ryder next to me. I was starting to drift off to sleep when his deep voice rumbled beneath my ear.

"I was so scared," he said, his voice breaking. "We parked a mile outside of town and walked in. It was a hell-hole. People were begging, sick, and starving. It looked like a war zone." He took a deep breath and continued. "When we ran into the sheriff, he told us some guys were sniffing around, asking about you. As soon as he described them, we hauled ass back."

I studied his hand, resting innocently on his abdominal muscles. It was capable of bringing me to my knees in passion, holding me upright when I needed it, or taking someone out with violence. He had more power in that one hand than I had in my whole body. *Yeah, I was safe here with him.*

"When I walked in and Mom said you were gone, I lost it. I was out of my mind. When we got to your house, your dad was lying on the ground and weakly pointing toward the house. Then you started screaming." He yanked the covers off of his legs in frustration. "God! Your screams went on and on! I thought I would go berserk, listening to you. Gavin yelled at me to stop – not to go in the house and get ambushed - but I went anyway. There was no way anyone could have stopped me. That big guy met me as soon as I opened the door and I didn't hesitate to put a bullet in him. But when I saw you lying under that weasel, screaming…" He laid his arm across his forehead and stared up at the ceiling. "I've never been so fucking scared."

Shadows danced across his face. The anguish in his eyes caused me to hurt. Most people would think that Ryder was hard and incapable of caring but I knew differently. This was a side of Ryder that he didn't let many people see.

"I'm sorry your dad died, Maddie. He was a good man."

Hearing his words, tears made trails down my face. I wiped them away, wondering how I had anymore tears left. *Did they ever end?*

We lay in silence as night sounds echoed through the open window. When his hand went lax against my hip, I thought he had fallen asleep. His rough voice proved otherwise.

"Go to sleep, Maddie. I'll stay next to you for tonight."

I closed my eyes and wished it would be for more than just one night.

Chapter Thirty-Three

Time passed slowly. For weeks, Ryder and I were roommates only, barely speaking and trying to avoid each other at all costs.

At night, we slept separately – me in his bed and him on the couch. Many nights, I had nightmares of men and blood. When I cried out in my sleep, Ryder would check on me but he never crawled into bed with me again nor did he touch me again after that first night.

Our days were filled with surviving, doing what was necessary to make it one day at a time. Ryder worked outside most days but he was never far from me, never leaving me alone. For that I was thankful. His parents came by often, as did Gavin. The fight between Ryder and Gavin was a thing of the past, chalked up to the grief and horror of that day.

We continued to live as best as we could despite the lack of electricity and the threat of war. News of what was happening was sporadic and not very reliable. Roger listened to the shortwave radio and sometimes a lone traveler would stop but it didn't happen very often. From what we learned, conditions had not changed. In fact, things had become worse. Millions of people were dying from starvation, dehydration, diseases, or the war. Thousands were vacating the cities. Not only was the United States under attack but Americans were also fighting Americans. There was no societal structure left, no police, and no government. There were reports that the terrorists had landed on our soil and were scouring the countryside in droves. We didn't know how safe we were but Ryder made me keep a gun on me at all times.

I thought of my dad and cried for him often. Ryder took me back to his grave every few days. Each time, I didn't dare go into the house. One day, I would return but for now the horrific memories were still too fresh in my mind to venture inside. My house was no longer my home. It was a place of death and sadness, somewhere I didn't want to go.

Most of our days were spent in silence. The only time Ryder and I talked was during meals and even then our conversations centered on simple things such as the weather or surviving. Ryder insisted on teaching me how to make fire using only sticks and the best way to purify creek water. He taught me how to tie a knot that would hold anything and how to set a small trap.

But we never talked about us.

~~~~

It was early one morning that things begin to change. Ryder announced he was going hunting and insisted I go too. I refused.

"I'm not leaving you alone. You're coming," he said, growing angry.

We were standing in the kitchen, glaring at each other, neither of us willing to bend. He wanted me to go hunting with him. I just wanted to stay home.

It was the end of September and still hot. My threadbare shorts were now hanging off of my body and my t-shirt had seen better days. I had lost weight over the past few weeks but what did a person expect when we lived off of canned goods, wild game, and the occasional vegetable from the garden?

I wasn't feeling too well that morning so I was determined to stay behind. I thought that I was getting a cold because the nights had turned chilly despite the warm daytime temperatures.

"I don't want to go," I whined. I know I sounded childish but my stomach was churning and I didn't want to go traipsing through the woods. I refused to tell Ryder that I was sick. If he could become so cold and distant toward me, I could keep a simple thing such as a little stomachache from him.

"You're going. We're getting low on meat and you need to know how to kill and skin an animal," he insisted as he loaded a rifle with bullets. He laid it down on the kitchen table and started loading a second rifle.

I watched his long fingers work effortlessly for a second before my gaze traveled up his trim body. He had also lost weight over the last couple of weeks, becoming leaner and harder. My mouth watered as his muscles flexed beneath his tan shirt and worn jeans. The ever-present baseball cap shielded his eyes and left his unshaven jaw bare, begging to be caressed.

"I'm not killing anything," I said stubbornly, ignoring the heat rushing through my body.

"If something ever happened to me, you need to know how to survive," he said, finally looking at me. "That means killing something."

I squirmed under his gaze. "Don't say that, Ryder. Nothing will ever happen to you."

He stayed quiet, refusing to argue further with me. Crossing his arms over his chest, his icy stare drilled into me, breaking my resistance to mere pieces.

~~~~

The woods were shaded and silent as we crept through them. I followed Ryder closely, my stomach churning the whole time. I tried to focus on the hunt but it was impossible to do with the way I felt.

After about half an hour, I tried to shoot a squirrel but missed (which I was secretly thankful for). An hour after that, Ryder shot a good-sized buck, sending it to the ground with only one shot. The wind blew dead leaves around the animal's body while sunlight peeked through the canopy of branches above us, spotlighting his kill. As my eyes ran over the deer, my stomach churned in protest.

Ryder pulled a large hunting knife from his jean's pocket and kneeled down next to the deer.

"I've got to gut it before we take it back."

I averted my eyes when he placed the tip of the knife near the deer's lower abdomen.

"Maddie?"

I turned away, wrapping my arms around my middle in comfort.

"I can't, Ryder," I said, barely able to get the words out.

"Okay. We'll work up to the field dressing later. Just don't look."

I soon realized that having my back turned didn't help. First, I heard a cutting sound and then an awful smell hit me. I covered my mouth, fighting the nausea but it was too powerful to ignore.

"Oh, no!" I cried, running over to a fallen log and losing my breakfast in the dirt and leaves.

"Maddie? Are you okay?"

I shook my head as another wave of nausea hit me.

"Shit!" Ryder said, distressed. Within a second, he was kneeling beside me in the dirt.

For the first time in weeks, he touched me. His warm hand rested on my back for a second before disappearing.

"Take a drink."

I felt weak and shaky as I took the water he offered. Taking a long drink didn't help much but it did make my raw throat feel better.

"I'm sorry I made you do this, Maddie. Let's just head back," he said, helping me to my feet.

"No, you stay. I'll go."

He shook his head, staring down at me coolly.

"I have a gun and it's a short walk. I'll be fine," I said. When he opened his mouth to argue, I added, "We need that meat, Ryder." No longer did I have an appetite but I knew that he was getting tired of eating meals that came from a can. Right now food was more important than my queasy stomach.

"Three shots in a row and I'll come running, understand?" That was our signal for trouble – three gunshots, one right after the other.

I nodded. Leaning closer, he gathered my long hair in one hand. Taking off his baseball cap, he placed it on my head, tucking my hair underneath. I knew what he was doing. If any strangers wandered onto our land, they might see a woman alone as an easy target. With my long hair hidden beneath a hat, I appeared as only a boy from a distance, keeping me safe.

Ryder was standing so close that I could smell him. Something woodsy, sexy. Something that spoke to my insides, making them come alive. Glancing down at my lips, his hands lingered on the back of my nape. His fingers lightly brushed across my skin, burning me. My heart jumped when his eyes met mine again. Gone was the coldness. Now hunger blazed from his eyes, leaving me spellbound.

A split second later, I watched as a blanket came down, hiding his emotions. His whiskered jaw clenched before he turned away.

"I'll be there shortly," he said over his shoulder, returning to the deer.

As I walked home, I tried to pay attention to my surroundings but my mind was on Ryder. I ached for him still.

We were living in the same house, we were together twenty-four hours a day, seven days a week but I missed him with all my being.

~~~~

By the time I made it home, I was feeling sick again. Pulling out some homemade bread that Janice made, I took a few small bites, hoping it would help settle my stomach. Instead, the nausea became worse. Suddenly feeling weak and sick, I plopped down in a kitchen chair. Closing my eyes and resting my head in my hands, I tried to push the queasiness away.

Knowing I couldn't hold it down any longer, I ran outside. In what had to be an all-time fastest record, I crossed the porch and made it to the edge of the grass before my stomach emptied its contents for the third time that morning.

My body shook violently, sending chills through me. *Did I have a stomach bug? The flu?* I hadn't felt good for a couple of weeks but the nausea had just started.

Suddenly, all the blood drained from my face. Pushing myself to my feet, I feebly made my way back into the house. Going through the kitchen, I hurried into the extra bedroom where a small desk stood against a stark white wall.

Pulling open the top drawer, I yanked out the Sports Illustrated calendar that Ryder always kept there. Ignoring the blonde smiling back at me from the month of August, I ran a shaky finger over the dates. My heart started pumping wildly in my chest.

I was over a month late.

I was pregnant.

Chapter Thirty-Four

"Maddie?" Ryder yelled.

The back door slam shut, echoing throughout the house. I lay in bed, curled on my side, trying to come to terms with the fact that I was pregnant.

Fright flowed through me, making the nausea return. *What was he going to say?* He didn't want a relationship and I didn't want to push him into having one because of a baby. Without question, I wanted this child but how could I tell him when he didn't love me? And how would we bring a baby into this Godforsaken world?

"Shit, you scared me!" he said, stopping in the bedroom doorway to glare my direction.

I pushed myself into a sitting position and met his stare. He looked rugged in his worn jeans and the cotton shirt that hugged his body perfectly. His light brown hair was in desperate need of a haircut but looked sexy as hell, curling around his ears and neck.

"You didn't answer me," he snapped, walking over to the edge of the bed and frowning down at me. His cutting blue eyes were cold as they traveled over my body. "You look like hell. Still feeling bad?"

"I'm just tired."

I swung my legs over the side of the bed near him, determined to pretend as if nothing was wrong. It was time to change the subject. Quick.

"Did you finish with the deer?"

"Yeah, the meat's in the smokehouse now." He scrutinized me closely. "You sure you're okay?"

Oh, hell! He knew me too well to know when I was lying but I wasn't ready to tell him the truth yet.

"I'm fine, Ryder."

I know he didn't believe me but he accepted my answer and left without another word.

Heaviness settled over me. I couldn't bring myself to tell him yet. By my guess, I wouldn't show for a few months yet. By then, maybe I could come to terms with the fact that I might be having his baby but I didn't have his love.

~~~~

While the sun slowly set outside, we were inside, eating a dinner consisting of deer meat and canned vegetables. Neither of us spoke, the tension stretching between us like a tightly pulled string ready to break at any moment. Ryder seemed distant and withdrawn, more than usual tonight.

I pushed food around my plate, anger replacing any hunger I had. I needed him now more than ever. I was pregnant and I was scared. But I was also tired of playing his games. Ryder either wanted me or he didn't. The mixed messages he was sending me were annoying. And I was tired of living in this house with him as if we were two complete strangers.

"Eat, Maddie."

I jumped as Ryder's deep voice boomed from across the table. Glancing up, I caught him staring hard at me, waiting for me to take a bite.

"No," I said, glaring back at him in defiance.

His lips thinned. "You can't survive if you won't eat and I'll be damned if you die on me."

"I'm not hungry."

He sat his fork down quietly despite the anger ready to explode from him.

"I don't give a damn if you are hungry or not. I said to eat!"

I cocked an eyebrow at him.

"And I said, no."

Suddenly, he was beside me, yanking me out of my chair. His hands were hard on me. His eyes were full of heat, either from anger or need, I do not know. My breath caught in my throat when his hands started traveling slowly up my sides.

"I can count every rib on your body, Maddie," he whispered huskily as his fingers slowly spread wide, caressing me. I felt my body come alive from his touch.

Leaning down, his lips brushed against my ear. "Now eat, Maddie."

The deep vibration of his voice was still moving through me when he stepped away, sitting down again and giving me a challenging look. It was then that I knew he won.

"You're an ass, Ryder," I said, flopping down in my seat with irritation. Picking up my fork, I took a bite of green beans, not really tasting them.

A look of satisfaction spread across his face as he picked up his fork.

Damn him! One touch and I became putty in his hands. But maybe, just maybe, I was the one who won.

~~~~

By the time we were finished eating, the wind had picked up, rattling the windows throughout the house. Large, black clouds were gathering off to the West, moving quickly in the darkening sky.

Ryder was cleaning his rifle at the table silently, acting detached and unapproachable. The moment of closeness we had earlier was gone, as if it never happened.

My heart ached. Despite the late hour, I decided a bath was just what I needed. I needed to clear my head and be alone. Maybe then, I would feel better afterward. Without speaking, I left to get a towel and soap from the bathroom.

Walking back through the kitchen, I was almost out the door when his voice stopped me.

"Where are you going?"

"I'm going to take a bath before it gets dark," I answered, watching him clean the stock of his gun.

"A storm's coming," he said without looking at me.

I didn't respond. *What was I supposed to say? Yes, Ryder, I know a storm's coming but I have to get away from you?*

As I stepped out into the cool evening air, I wondered why I was here. He wanted me with him but he was annoyed by my presence. *Why keep me around?*

The water was cold so I took a quick bath. By the time I got out, the sun had disappeared on the horizon, leaving the land dark. The storm was still rumbling overhead, promising to be a powerful one.

I was dripping wet and cold when the strong wind hit me. Clutching the towel around my body, I ran for the house. The wind pushed me inside forcefully. Candlelight illuminated the kitchen, casting a soft glow over the entire room.

Ryder was lounging in a kitchen chair with a shot glass in his hand. He threw back the whiskey before setting it next to a half-empty bottle of the same stuff. *This was the first time I had seen him drink in weeks.*

I took a deep breath and skirted the table without acknowledging him. As I walked past, I felt his eyes on me, leaving heat behind in their trail.

In his room, I let out a breath of relief and dried off quickly. Hurrying to pull on one of his large shirts, I tried not to think of sleeping alone again tonight.

"Maddie," a low, hoarse voice said from behind me.

I turned quickly, wondering how long he had been there. Standing in the bedroom doorway, his eyes raked down my bare legs. From there, his focus moved up my body to my lips, lingering there a moment before meeting my eyes. I felt hot and bothered as the temperature in the room shot up a notch with that one look.

Without breaking eye contact, he tossed back another drink. Like a big cat on the prowl, he slowly stalked into the room, keeping me in his sights. As he passed the dresser, he set the shot-glass down, never taking his eyes off me.

"Get in bed."

My heart pounded as he towered over me. There was something raw and uncontrollable about him tonight that I had never seen. I knew I couldn't resist this Ryder.

"Get in bed," he repeated.

"Ryder, what you are doing?" I asked, standing my ground. "Are you drunk?"

"And what if I am?"

He took a step closer and my heart threatened to jump out of my chest.

"Then you need to back off," I said with a hint of uncertainty. *Did I really want him to?*

"You going to make me?" he asked with a smirk, taking another step closer.

"I'll scream if you touch me," my voice quivered.

"I'll make sure you do," he said huskily, desire dripping with every word.

My mouth went dry. Heat filled my insides.

"Ryder..."

His hands snapped out, grabbing my upper arms. I cried out at his fierceness. Yanking me toward him, his mouth covered mine, taking what he wanted, giving so much back in return. Large, work roughened hands moved to grasp my wet hair as his lips claimed me as his own.

I had missed his touch so much that I couldn't get enough. My hands wrapped around his neck, pulling him closer. The persistent I-need-Ryder ache screamed to be fulfilled. Deepening the kiss, his tongue slipped inside - pushing, punishing, crushing me.

I moaned as his hands slid underneath my shirt, grabbing my bottom roughly. He squeezed once before gathering a fistful of my panties, feverishly tearing them off with one jerk. I gasped as his hand moved back to my bare bottom.

"I want you like this. Bare for me."

Warm lips moved down to my ear, kissing the sensitive spot right below the lobe. His teeth nipped at my skin and his fingers caressed my bottom. I couldn't hold back a shudder as his hands roamed higher up my back, pushing my shirt up along the way. In one motion, he pulled the shirt off and flung it across the room, leaving me naked in front of him.

"Perfect," he growled.

His lips moved to my collarbone as his hands grasped my hips. I sucked in a breath as one large hand moved across my stomach possessively.

Leaning down, he placed his mouth on my breast, causing a wave of sensation to shoot through me. A soft moan escaped before I grabbed hold of his hair and tugged.

"I love when you pull my hair." His warm breath brushed across my nipple, teasing me.

Dropping to his knees, he kissed his way from my breasts to my stomach. Warm hands played along my waist as his tongue darted out to lick my hipbone lightly.

"I'm here, Maddie, on my knees. For you. Only you," he rasped, looking up at me.

I almost came undone when his hand moved lower until it was between my legs. His fingers started to caress me, lightly at first but then with more urgency. I cried out when the first stirrings of an orgasm hit my body hard. His eyes burned up at me, watching me, as his hands continued their torture.

Wanting more, I yanked his shirt over his head and threw it across the room. My hands went back to his bare shoulders, holding onto him as his touch made me weak in the knees. Abruptly, he stood up, his fingers leaving me. Cupping my bottom, his mouth returned to mine, demanding and hard. He hauled me flush against him, the hardness in his jeans pushing into me, begging to be free. My fingers moved frantically down to release him.

"No. Not yet," he whispered against my mouth, moving my hands away.

I sighed in disappointment only to feel elation again when a hand cupped my breast. His thumb ran over my nipple, oh so slowly. My hand skimmed along the muscles lining his abdomen. A hiss escaped from him when my fingers moved down to trace along the top of his jeans. Without warning, he shoved me back on the bed.

I watched anxiously as he slowly crawled up the mattress, stalking me with a fiery look in his eyes. A basic carnal need rushed through me as he got closer.

Without taking his eyes off of mine, he leaned down and kissed my stomach tenderly. From there his lips brushed against my ribcage then under each breast. Without breaking eye contact with me, he took a nipple in his mouth. His tongue darted out to tease me, driving me crazy with pleasure. I arched my back beneath him, my hands tangling in his hair.

His lips left my breast to move to my collarbone then to the hollow in my neck. His hot tongue licked the sensitive spot before moving to the side of my neck. As his body slowly made its way up mine, the roughness of his jeans rubbed against my naked body, making the already sensitive nerve endings come alive. I let him nudge my legs apart gently as his mouth sucked at my earlobe.

"I've missed you," he said in my ear. "God, I've missed you so much."

One of his hands traveled down my side as the other wove through my hair.

"I can't get enough of you," his voice rumbled as his lips left a wet path along my jawline. "I've been in misery without you."

His fingers moved down between my legs. I sucked in a breath as he teased me without mercy.

"I want you, Maddie. Forever."

I didn't hesitate.

"I'm yours, Ryder. Forever."

His lips hungrily covered mine, never getting enough. As he ravished my mouth, he reached down to unzip his jeans, pushing them down just enough to free himself. My legs wrapped around his jean-covered hips quickly. With one thrust, he was inside me. I let out a cry at the same time he let out an animalistic growl.

His hands knotted in my hair, holding me tight as he started moving, withdrawing slowly only to plunge back into me, burying himself deeply.

I opened my eyes to find him watching me. My teeth bit into my lip when he rocked into me. Lowering his head, he nibbled on my lower lip and ran his tongue over the place my teeth left a mark.

I moaned and reached out to grab the tangled sheets underneath me, needing to hold onto something. His hand answered the call by entwining his fingers with mine as his hips drove into me.

"Maddie!" he moaned against my arched neck. "God, baby. You feel amazing."

I tugged his head down so that my lips could find his ear. He thrust into me faster as I sucked at his earlobe. With one hand, he grabbed both of my wrists and held them above my head, leaving me at his mercy. Leaning down, he took my nipple into his mouth.

"Mine," he growled against my skin, plunging in and out of me.

The orgasm hit me without warning. I arched my back and cried out, the sensations too much to handle.

The waves were still crashing over me when his hips slammed into me hard. He threw his head back and roared as the orgasm rocked his body. Thrusting into me one last time, his body went rigid.

We were both breathing hard as the aftermath pulsed through our bodies. Holding himself off of me on his elbows, he looked down at me, still buried deep inside.

"You okay?" he asked with concern. "Did I hurt you?"
"No. Not at all."
"Are you sure? Holding you down like that..."
"Ryder, I'm fine. You would never hurt me."

"I would rather die," he said, hoarsely. "You need to know that. I would die for you, Maddie."

Tears gathered behind my eyes. "Ryder, I don't want you to die for me. I just want you to kiss me."

He complied, kissing me tenderly, leaving me breathless all over again. He kissed me first on one shoulder and then along my collarbone, taking his time. I ran my fingers through his hair, loving the feel of his lips on me.

When he rolled away and gathered me close, I knew that he would never let me go again.

~~~~

Loud thunder woke me during the night. Lightening flashed, illuminating the room and chasing away the darkness. The rain pounded hard against the house and the wind blew violently beyond the window.

I was alone in bed. The other side was empty and cold. Ryder was gone.

Uncertainty rushed through me. *Tonight had felt different somehow but was I reading more into it again? Had he got what he wanted and escaped to his own bed, leaving me alone once more?*

I hurried out of bed and shut the window against the rain. Picking my shirt up from the floor, I pulled it on quickly, blushing at the memory of Ryder yanking it off of me. Just the thought had my insides heating all over again.

Running a hand over my flat stomach, I imaged his baby resting there, protected. *Maybe I should tell him now.*

A loud crack of thunder made me jump in fright. I was still haunted by the memories of Greasy's attack. That day would live in my mind forever no matter how much I tried to forget it. Trying to control my fear, I went in search of Ryder. I didn't want to be alone anymore.

The hallway was pitch black but the occasional flashes of lightening lit the way. I found Ryder sitting in the darkness, wearing only his worn jeans. A shot-glass hung loosely in his hand, the drink forgotten as he watched the rain through the windows.

"Ryder?"

"What are you doing awake?" he asked quietly before tossing back his drink.

"The storm woke me up."

Setting the glass on the coffee table, he took my hand and gently pulled me to stand between his long legs.

"Why are you in here?" I asked.

"I couldn't sleep," he said, watching me with a wary expression. "I'm scared shitless."

"Of what?" I asked, surprised. The Ryder that I knew wasn't afraid of anything.

His eyes raked over my body slowly.

"You."

I swallowed past the sudden lump in my throat. I didn't want to have another knockout fight with him about love or relationships. Not after what we shared tonight.

"Ryder, I don't want to do this." I pulled my hand out of his and turned to leave as tears threatened. I couldn't listen to this again with his baby nestled innocently in me.

He reached out and grabbed my hand quickly before I could get very far. "Come here," he said, softly.

I hesitated a second before crawling into his lap. Holding my head with both hands, he looked into my eyes. I saw worry and uncertainty reflected back at me. Pulling me closer, he brushed his lips against mine. My fingers automatically laced through his hair as his hands moved possessively over my hips.

"You are my everything, Maddie," he whispered against my mouth. "God only knows why you want me but I'm glad you do."

Pulling back, I saw apprehension in his eyes. "Ryder, I need you. This..." I motioned between the two of us, "This is what I want. You and me. It's that simple."

He glanced away nervously. "I don't deserve you, Maddie."

I opened my mouth to argue but my eyes glanced down at his naked chest instead. Suddenly, I wanted to touch the ink that ran beneath his skin. With feather-light touches, my fingertips brushed over the tattoo at his shoulder. I traced it down his side, over the hard muscles of his stomach and around to where it disappeared on his hip. With my touch, he became wild and untamed. The tender moment was gone.

His lips savagely captured mine as he pulled me to straddle his lap. When his tongue pushed into my mouth, I gasped with desire. Warm hands tightened on my bottom, pulling me closer. I felt him under me, hard and powerful, proving how much he wanted me again.

He slowed the kiss down, becoming gentler as one of his hands moved up to tangle in my hair. Breaking the kiss away, his eyes looked at me with intensity.

"I love you, Maddie."

My heart stopped.

I could no longer hear the thunder outside or the hurricane-like force of the rain against the house. All I heard were those three words.

"I've loved you since I was a snot-nosed kid chasing you around the farm. I've just been too much of a chicken to tell you."

"But you said you didn't love me," I whispered in disbelief.

"I've never said I didn't love you. Not once," he said, surprise crossing his face. "I've always loved you, Maddie."

"But all the times you told me that you don't fall in love..."

"I lied. I fell in love with you."

His warm fingers reached beneath the hem of my shirt to caress my hip.

"Maddie, you have to understand that I've never said I love you to anyone. I was scared that if I admitted it, I would screw everything up between us and lose you forever." His voice dropped. "I was an asshole for hurting you."

Leaning over, he kissed the corner of my mouth. "You're all I need and want. Just you. Now and always."

His lips moved hungrily over mine. I kissed him back with more love and passion than I thought was possible.

"I want to sleep next to you forever," he whispered. "I want to have babies with you and grow old next to you." Taking my face in his hands, he looked deep into my eyes. "I'm yours, Maddie and I'll love you for the rest of my life."

Tears of happiness fell down my cheeks. I couldn't have stopped them if I tried.

"I love you, Ryder. I always have."

"Don't cry, Maddie. I hate to see you cry," he said, wiping my tears away with his fingertips.

"I'm sorry, it's just that...I've wanted to hear you say those words for so long."

"I should have told you sooner. I was a damn stubborn fool."

He started placing soft kisses on my jawline, moving down to my neck. The tears disappeared. My body was on fire. I closed my eyes as his lips explored every inch of my neck and his hands moved underneath my shirt. I gasped when his thumb grazed over my breast, slow and leisurely. Moving back to my lips, he kissed me with a renewed passion, full of need. His hand continued to torment my breasts as his tongue ravaged my mouth. The storm raged outside but we didn't care. Our only awareness was of each other.

I considered telling him about the baby but decided against it. I wanted to be absolutely sure I was pregnant. With everything that had happened, maybe I was just late. I had heard that could happen to women. Until I knew, I would enjoy this moment. It wasn't every day that Ryder Delaney admitted he loved me.

~~~~

Morning sickness woke me up sometime later. Lying in bed, I breathed deeply, trying to control the sickness. When the nausea became too much, my eyes flew open. Within a second, I was out of bed and running for the back door. The early morning chill hit my bare legs as I raced down the porch steps. When I reached the dew-covered grass, my stomach emptied. The wet grass squished under my bare feet but it didn't matter. My body shook violently as the nausea hit me again with more force.

I prayed that Ryder wouldn't wake up to find me like this. He would become crazy with worry if he saw me this sick.

After there was nothing left in my system, I brushed my teeth quickly and crept back to the bedroom. Ryder was still asleep, taking up most of the bed. The sheet barely covered him as it lay low on his waist. Sprawled on his stomach, the tattooed muscles of his back appeared as sharp angles and defined shapes. Even in sleep, he looked dangerous and unapproachable.

But he loved me.

I was shivering uncontrollably when I crawled into bed next to him. Without opening his eyes, he reached out and pulled me closer.

"You okay?" he mumbled, sleepily.

"I'm fine. Go back to sleep." *A little white lie never hurt anyone.* I drew in a quick breath when his hand moved down to rest on my stomach.

"You would tell me, right?" he asked, opening one eye to look at me.

I nodded yes. *Okay, two white lies might be pushing it.* But a second later, only one thought was on my mind.

Lips against my neck and warm hands on my body caused a fire within me.

"I don't want to sleep. I want you," his deep voice rumbled in my ear.

I moaned as his lips kissed my earlobe gently. When he rose over me, I saw love and passion reflected in his eyes. I saw hope and a bright future despite the darkness around us. I saw life and happiness.

Chapter Thirty-Five

If I only knew that later my happiness would turn to sorrow, I might have stayed in bed longer.

"Boys, we got a problem," Roger said as we sat around the kitchen table later that night.

Gavin and Ryder stopped eating to look at their dad. The glow of the candlelight reflected off of Roger's large frame, highlighting the worry on his face.

He waited until he had their undivided attention before continuing. "We got enough food for ten more months. We can hunt and grow vegetables but with winter coming on, things could get lean. Might be tough times ahead." He pointed his fork at Ryder. "You need some more wood for this winter. Don't want Maddie to freeze to death."

"Done," Ryder said, simply.

"And you," He pointed the fork at Gavin. "We got to start butchering cattle for the winter. You up for the job?"

Gavin nodded before taking another bite of food.

"Heard on the shortwave that the terrorists are moving further inland. Damn government is fighting with all they got but they still can't hold the bitches back," Roger said, looking at each of us. "Now I ain't sure they'll head this way but we need to be prepared to bunker down and defend ourselves. You remember the drill?"

Gavin and Ryder both said 'yes, sir' at the same time.

"Good. Be prepared to do it within minutes," Roger said.

"I figure I can get Maddie to the barn in five minutes tops," Ryder said, popping a piece of cornbread in his mouth.

Listening to them made me wonder how a baby would survive in this world. No diapers, no baby food, no doctor. Just terrorists and fright, hunger and death. This was no way to raise a child. *How would I do this?*

My hands shook as I pushed beans around my plate. I hated the little things. They were one of our major staples and I had come to loath them with a passion. If it was up to me, I would never eat another one.

"Maddie, you need to eat more. You've lost too much weight," Janice said in that nurturing way she had.

I felt everyone's eyes on me, an object under a microscope waiting to be dissected. I forced myself to take another bite of beans. They felt like sharp little rocks going down my throat.

"You feeling okay, Maddie?" Gavin asked. "You're looking a little green."

Oh, hell!

"Are you sick?" Ryder asked, narrowing his eyes at me when I didn't answer Gavin.

I took a long drink of water, hoping to stall for time and push down my nausea. Ryder was having none of it.

"Maddie, answer me," his deep voice demanded.

"I'm fine," I said, meeting his penetrating stare and ignoring the tingles that raced down my body. His voice could do that to me.

He gave me a warning look but didn't question me further. One more demand from him and I might explode in anger. Or haul him to bed with need.

For a few minutes, the only sounds were the small clinks of silverware on plates and the sound of the wind whipping around the house. Candlelight flickered and danced around the room, fighting the darkness and winning for an instance before the shadows fought back. Suddenly, the quiet of the night was interrupted by a noise outside. Footsteps. Without warning, everyone flew into action.

Ryder jumped out of his chair, hauling me with him. Pulling the pistol from his holster, he flicked the safety off before turning frigid eyes on me.

"Something happens, you hide. Understand?"

I nodded, resisting the urge to put my hand over my stomach in protection.

Brutality lined his face. The tension in his body made his muscles bunch under his shirt, ready to strike. Somebody showing up here after dark meant only one thing. Danger.

Janice blew out the candle, plunging the kitchen into darkness, obscuring everything. The sound of heavy boots on the wooden porch echoed through the kitchen, sending a thread of fear through me.

Ryder grabbed my upper arm, his fingers biting into my tender flesh. Non-too-gentle, he pushed me toward his mother. She led me to the corner of the kitchen, away from the back door and all the windows. The two solid walls would protect us from whoever was outside. It wasn't much in the way of security but it would have to do.

Above the loud pounding of my heart, I heard Janice flip the safety on the gun she held at her side.

All of a sudden, the footsteps stopped. We held our breath, waiting on a knock, a shout, anything. Fear raced through me along with a terrible foreboding. People were suffering without electricity. Certain death waited for most if the power grid wasn't restored soon. People would become desperate when faced with dying. That meant the chances of someone trying to steal our supplies increased. Strangers could prove to be deadly, willing to kill to get what they wanted. I prayed that wasn't the case now.

Another moment passed with not a sound from outside. I was beginning to think that the person had left when a loud rapping on the door that made me jump in fright.

"Who's there?" Roger asked in a booming voice that spoke of power.

"My name's Cash..." a voice answered.

Cash? I knew a Cash from high school! He was...

"MADDIE!" another voice yelled.

Wait! I knew that voice!

Breaking away from Janice's grasp, I darted across the kitchen, only one purpose in mind.

"Maddie, NO!" Ryder bellowed, reaching out to stop me.

I managed to avoid his hands as I ran past him. Ignoring another shout from Ryder, I flung open the door. And froze as I looked down the barrel of a shotgun.

Before I could open my mouth to scream, Ryder was in front of me, putting himself in the line of fire. He snapped his pistol up and aimed it at the stranger's head. At the same time, strong hands reached around my waist and jerked me back, taking me away from the danger.

As Gavin hauled me back, I watched with terror as Ryder and the stranger trained their guns on each other with lethal accuracy. Animosity rose between them as they stared at each other.

"Drop the fucking gun," Ryder growled, pulling back the hammer.

"Not gonna happen," the stranger said. "You pull that trigger, I'll still have time to fill you full of buckshot."

"I don't think so, boy," Roger said, stepping next to Ryder with a loaded shotgun. "If you know what's good for you, you'll lower that weapon."

Time slowed down to a crawl as the three men faced off. Suddenly, the sound of my name echoed through the night, calling me.

"MADDIE!"

"Let me go!" I screeched, squirming in Gavin's tight hold. I landed a hard punch to his midsection, desperate to get away. His arms loosened just enough that I could wiggle out from beneath them.

I took off. Past Ryder. Past the stranger. Past the cocked guns, ready to shot anything that moved. I ran.

"GODDAMN IT!" Ryder roared behind me.

Ignoring him, I flew down the porch steps and across the rain soaked yard. *There he was!* When I reached Brody, I flung myself into his arms with relief. *He was alive!*

He pulled me tight against him. "Maddie, I'm so glad to see you."

I untangled myself from his arms to peer at him under the moonlight. Utter exhaustion lined his thin face. There were dark smudges under his eyes and his cheeks were hollowed from hunger. His clothes were ragged and his once perfect hair was now long and unkempt.

"Where's Eva?" I asked, glancing into the darkness. Any minute now I expected her to come bounding out of the shadows with her take-no-prisoners attitude, trying to tell me what to do.

"They have her! The bastards have her!" Brody cried loud enough to wake the dead.

He pulled me forcefully to his chest, cutting off my air and taking my mind back to a dark place. Greasy, hands holding me down, the feeling of suffocating. It all came back. The panic became a living, breathing monster that I couldn't control. I closed my eyes and concentrated on taking deep breaths, trying to chase the nightmare away. But when Brody dropped to his knees and took me with him, hysteria threatened to push me over the edge. *It's only Brody. He won't hurt you. You're safe.* When the panic faded, I felt the sting of his words. Eva was taken.

"Who took her?" I asked in a shaky voice.

Brody didn't answer. He was lost somewhere in his own personal hell. His arms tightened around me, holding me like I was keeping him afloat.

"Let her go, Brody."

At the sound of the deadly voice, my eyes snapped up to find Ryder pointing a pistol at Brody.

I never even heard him walk up.

Ryder's cold eyes shot my way before swinging back to Brody. "Don't make me pull this trigger because I sure as hell will if you hurt her."

Oh, shit! I had to calm Brody down. Ryder could become downright dangerous if something of his was threatened.

"Brody, it's okay. We'll help," I said in a calming voice.

I must have gotten through to him because his arms dropped away, falling to his sides like heavy weights.

Ryder hauled me to my feet and put himself in front of me, blocking me from the perceived threat. His gun stayed trained ahead, not quite trusting Brody completely.

I placed a hand on Ryder's back, trying to calm him down. The muscles beneath his shirt tensed at my touch, reminding me that this man was a force to be reckoned with when he was mad.

Shouting came from the house, loud and angry. A cloud obscured the moonlight for a moment but I could still see Gavin and Roger holding the stranger at gunpoint. Just one wrong move and shots would fly. This might be a shoot-first-and-ask-questions-later way of life now but I'd be damned that I would become a part of it.

Stepping around Ryder, I placed myself between him and Brody. No one was getting hurt tonight if I could help it.

I saw the exasperation on Ryder's face as he swung his gun away. *There would be hell to pay for doing this but he could just be pissed at me.* No one was hurting Brody.

I ignored Ryder as best as a girl could and focused on Brody. "Who has her?" I asked.

"The damn terrorists! The bastards are rounding people up and throwing them into concentration camps!"

They had Eva? All the blood drained from my face as what he said hit me. I swayed on my feet, suddenly feeling dizzy and weak. The world tilted at an odd angle before Ryder grabbed my arm, steadying me.

"You okay?"

I nodded numbly, shaken.

Brody suddenly closed the distance between us, getting right in my face. This close, I saw his desperation and fear. It scared me because it reminded me of how much danger Eva was in.

Ryder stepped in front of me again, pushing me behind him.

"Back the fuck off, Brody," he growled.

Brody held up both hands to show he was no threat. "I'm not going to hurt her, Ryder. I came out here…" He stopped and rubbed the back of his head with agitation before starting over. "You got to help me, man. We've got to go get Eva."

Ryder studied him a full minute before pointing to the stranger on the porch. "Who's that?"

"Cash Marshall, an old high school friend. He was with us when they grabbed Eva."

Ryder's frosty eyes shot my way. "Cash Marshall? You've got to be joking!" he said with disgust.

My eyes rounded with surprise. Cash had been my lab partner our senior year of high school. He had also been my prom date. And Ryder had been crazy jealous. From the look on his face now, I guess time had not changed his feelings.

"Look Ryder, I need your help. I gotta get Eva back," Brody pleaded, drawing our attention back to him.

"Let's talk inside," Ryder said.

I followed the two of them toward the house as the gentle night breeze blew around us. The noises of the night followed. The nighttime sounds that I had once feared, I now had come to love. They lured me to sleep at night and gave me peace. They were my lullaby. But tonight there was no peace. My best friend was in enemy hands. There was only terror.

As we ascended the porch steps, I felt Cash's eyes on me. This man was nothing like the nerdy, gangly boy I remembered from high school. He was now tall and lithe looking with a face cut from stone.

"Maddie," his deep voice said in acknowledgment.

I barely got in a hello before Ryder stepped in front of me, blocking Cash's view. His don't-even-think-about-it stare spoke volumes as he glared at Cash.

"Remember me?" Ryder asked. His voice was quiet but I could hear the animosity underneath.

"Yeah, you threatened me years ago," Cash answered with coldness, not intimated by Ryder. "Something about kicking my ass if I hurt her."

"This time I'll just kill you." Ryder's words dripped with venom.

Cash nodded, curtly. "Understood but I'm here for Eva, not Maddie."

"Then let's do this."

Chapter Thirty-Six

Brody's story unfolded with grimness and hopelessness. His words made me question our own chances of surviving.

According to him, the hostiles were slowly making their way across the country, capturing people or simply killing them along the way. The military and locally formed militias were trying to fight them but without communications, electricity, or supplies, we were crippled and the enemy knew it.

If people were not being killed, they were starving to death or dying from diseases. Brody said the most dangerous place to be right now was in the middle of a city. Supplies were nonexistent and starvation was prominent.

So at the insistence of Eva's parents, Brody and Cash took Eva and left town, heading for Maddie's house and safety. Along a deserted road, the terrorists ambushed them, three versus twenty. The shotguns Brody and Cash had were no match to the military-grade weaponry the hostiles carried. Within moments, they were outnumbered, outgunned, and Eva was captured.

That was four days ago.

Worry for Eva had tears filling my eyes and my throat closing up tight. The thought of her in danger, possibly hurt, had me squeezing my eyes shut tightly and saying a quick prayer that she was safe.

I slowly opened my eyes to see Brody rubbing his hands together nervously. He was beside himself with panic. The fatigue lining his face proved that it had been days since he last slept.

"So you were there when they overran the town?" Ryder asked Cash.

"Yeah, I was there. It happened in the middle of the day. Worse day of my life."

In the lantern light, I could see Cash swallow hard and shift in his seat uneasy. "At first they shot everyone in their path. Men, women, children, didn't matter to them, they were killed. After a while, they stopped shooting and started rounding people up like cattle. Next thing I know, the place is a concentration camp. Don't know what is worse, being dead or being starved and beaten."

Brody jumped up from his chair and started pacing around the room liked a caged animal.

Cash had the same coldness in his eyes that Ryder and Gavin had in theirs. This world had made them harder, meaner, and more than ever, deadlier.

"The town is on lockdown but I know a way in. There will be guards everywhere, heavily armed and itching to kill," Cash said. "It could be a bloodbath." The silence stretched as his words sunk in.

"How much ammo y'all have?" he asked.

"Enough," Ryder answered, leaning forward in his chair and resting his elbows on his knees. "We've got what we need to get her out and then some."

Brody stopped pacing long enough to throw his hands up in aggravation. "So are we gonna do this or just talk about it?"

Gavin spun the cylinder on his gun, his gaze locked on the movement. "I say we go kick some foreign ass."

Roger pushed away from the wall he had been leaning on. "Y'all do this, gotta do it right. Ride all day. Stake out the place. Watch all the comings and goings. Who is in charge, what is their weakness, and what they have for firepower. Then hit them at night when they least expect it," he said, fiercely. "Take hell to them, boys."

My body trembled as the reality of what they were going to do sunk in. I suddenly had a bad feeling. Something was going to go wrong. They were walking into a death trap.

Janice must have thought the same thing because she began to argue with them. "No," she said, her voice shaking with tears. "It's too risky. I want my boys here safe."

"We have to go, Mom," Ryder said, the gentleness he reserved only for his mom overriding his frigid tone. "We're not losing any more people. We've lost enough."

I studied the fraying edge of my shorts, afraid if I looked at him, I might start bawling like a baby. Every day I grieved for my dad and wished Eva was here to lean on. Ryder was right. I couldn't lose her too.

As much as I hated to think about him in danger, Ryder was an expert fighter and skilled hunter. He could be cold and calculating. If anyone could get her out, he could.

"We'll leave the day after tomorrow," he said.

"That's too long! She could be dead by then!" Brody's voice rose with panic.

"We need to get our shit together, Brody!" Gavin scowled.

"How long will you be gone?" My voice wobbled with fear, sounding meek among the angry voices.

"I figure a week will get us there and back," Cash answered as his eyes moved slowly down my body.

I felt a thread of unease. Not from his scrutiny but from the idea of them being gone for one week. That unease doubled when I saw the murderous rage on Ryder's face.

He stood up suddenly, towering over me like a great, powerful tree that provided protection. The muscles of his arms pulled his shirt taut as he picked up his pistol and stuck it in the holster slung low on his hips.

"Maddie and I are heading home," he said in a clipped tone, his full lips pulled tight in annoyance. His body was rigid and his eyes were throwing hate Cash's direction. Angry and barely holding it in check, Ryder was at the boiling point. The sooner we left, the better. I didn't want Cash beaten to a bloody pulp.

I followed Ryder out of the house quickly, one step behind him. The moon was hidden behind the clouds, making it hard to see where we were walking. He stayed close, his solid presence my only beacon in the darkness. We were halfway to his house when he finally spoke.

"Spit it out, Maddie," he said roughly without breaking stride. "I know you want to say something."

Yeah, I did want to say something.

"It's too dangerous." The words tumbled out of me. "Going after Eva is a death sentence, Ryder."

"Everything is dangerous nowadays, Maddie," his deep voice said, coldly. "Hell, I can wake up tomorrow and get killed by someone stealing our food."

"But I need you here." I stopped in the middle of the road, waiting for him to say something. An owl hooted nearby, sending a shiver up my spine. *Or was it from the fear of Ryder leaving?*

He sighed and rubbed a hand over his face, staring off into the dark distance. I studied his profile. The longer hair and scruffy jawline gave him a look of uncontrollable wildness. The hardness in his eyes belied the danger lurking in him. He looked nothing like the boy I had known but I loved him more now than ever before.

Finally, he turned to face me. Taking a step closer, he pushed my long hair behind my shoulder. His touch sent the familiar tug of desire through me, burning me like nothing else could. It was frightening how much power he had over my body.

"I keep thinking that if you were taken, I would give my life to save you. Nothing would stop me from finding you. Nothing." He lifted my chin up gently with one finger. "I have to go. For Brody. For you."

His words should have made me feel better but instead I grew irritated and irrational. *Why did he have to be so damn brave? And double damn him for always playing the hero!*

"Fine, you want to go? GO! You've been trying to leave me forever!" I said, putting my hands on my hips in anger.

"What?" he asked, dumbfounded.

"You wanted to enlist in the Army," I said, crazy mad now. "If it wasn't for me, you would be out there fighting right now. Playing the hero! Saving the day! Well, here's your chance! Go!"

"The only reason I wanted to enlist was to get away from you!" he said, hardness lacing his words.

Hurt cut through me like a knife.

"I hated seeing you with someone else, Maddie. Knowing I could only have you as a friend drove me ape shit crazy." He looked into the distance and scoffed, shaking his head in disbelief. "I was desperate to end my suffering but I didn't know what to do. Other girls didn't help and drinking didn't take away the pain. My only choice was to leave. I wanted you too much to stay."

"So, you were just going to pick up and leave me without a second thought?" My voice grew louder with each word.

"I was fucking MISERABLE!" he exploded, taking another step closer.

"And now?"

His eyes drilled into mine. I saw the coldness disappear, replaced by the desire I recognized all so well.

"Now?" He reached out to lightly touch my bottom lip with the pad of his thumb. "Now, I'm complete."

He took my hand, his large one holding my small one. "You see me for who I am, Maddie. Not my ghosts. Not my bad habits. Not my past. Just me. You've always seen just me."

Stepping closer, he brushed against me as his hand curved around to the back of my neck.

"You're my light in the darkness. I belong to you, Maddie. Without any doubt, I belong with you and I love you. I love you more than all the stars in the sky."

Bending down, he kissed me gently on the lips. "I love you here, on the land we used to play on."

Another feather light kiss to my lips.

"And here." He put my hand over his heart. "You're my heart."

Tears filled my eyes.

"I don't want to fight, Maddie. I just want to take you home and forget about the world around us."

"Then do it."

His lips covered mine urgently. I closed my eyes and leaned my head back as his hand moved to caress the base of my throat.

"I love you, Ryder," I whispered against his lips.

He pulled away to look deeply into my eyes. I saw him swallow hard. I saw the sudden nervousness in his eyes. Even his hands seemed to be shaking.

"Marry me. When I get back, marry me, Maddie."

My breath hitched. Only in my dreams did I expect to hear those two little words from him.

"I want eternity with you. I can't imagine my life any other way," he said.

His words wrapped around me, cocooning me in their warmth. Standing next to him in the darkness, nothing else mattered. The war, the despair around us; they were small compared to the love between us.

"Maddie?" he asked, his back growing rigid at my silence.

"Yes," I whispered. "I'll marry you."

His lips claimed mine with an urgency like no other. I felt all the love and passion he had for me in that one kiss.

"We won't have a church or a preacher. I don't even have a damn ring," he said huskily, drawing back to look at me.

"I don't care. I just need you." I threaded my fingers through his hair and brought his lips back to mine. "Don't leave me, Ryder. I couldn't handle life if something happened to you," I said beneath his lips.

"Nothing will keep me away from you, Maddie. I promise, I'll return. I'll always return to you."

Always.

Darkness had replaced the light in my world. I thought my life was over when Ryder rode away but it was only just beginning.

~~~~

Read the rest of Maddie and Ryder's story in "Promise Me Light."

ACKNOWLEDGMENTS

To my husband, John - who never gave up on me and continued to tell me I could even when I thought I couldn't. Thank you for helping me and believing in me before you had even read the story. I can never repay you.

To my two children - you never complained when I spent hours in front of a computer, headphones in and music blaring, lost in a different world. Thank you for listening to my crazy ramblings about EMPs and loss of electricity. If there is one thing I want you to remember from my time writing, it is to always follow your dreams. Make them a reality.

To my grandma - thank you for putting "Shanna" by Kathleen E. Woodiwiss in my hands when I was younger. One of my favorite memories is spending hours discussing books with you. My love of romance and reading is due to you.

To my late father - you were always my biggest supporter no matter what I wanted to do. Thank you. This one is for you.

ABOUT THE AUTHOR

Paige Weaver lives in Texas with her husband and two children. *Promise Me Darkness* is her first published book but she has enjoyed writing since childhood. When she's not busy imagining other worlds you can find her chasing her kids around and living her very own happily ever-after story.

She loves hearing from readers. Connect with her online or via email to learn about upcoming books and other information.

Email - paige@authorpaigeweaver.com

Web - authorpaigeweaver.com

Twitter - @AuthorPWeaver

Facebook - AuthorPaigeWeaver

Made in United States
North Haven, CT
24 February 2022

16467927R00224